INTENT TO KILL

AMY BARNETT

Intent to Kill

Editing and Proofreading by Elaine York, Allusion Publishing
http://www.allusionpublishing.com/

CHAPTER 1

PARTNERS IN CRIME

Their stolen red convertible was the only thing standing between them and certain death. It housed them as they ripped through city streets, took bullets meant for their bodies, and cradled them in the white leather seats when it locked in a spin.

Adam Vandemilio sat in the passenger seat, shades on, muscled bicep resting along the windowsill, his body jolting violently from side to side as the car swerved at the hands of its driver, his girlfriend Mercedes Preston. She was the best driver in Ridge City. And she was his everything.

She was the only person he'd ever met who was more callous, more vicious, and more fiery than he was. Together they would burn the world down, or at the very least, they would die trying. They lived hard and fast, knowing *one day* they'd slip up and die, but at least they'd go out big.

Unfortunately, Adam suspected *today* was that day.

Whipping his head around to check the approaching threat, Adam grimaced. "Baby, they're still right on our fucking tail." It came out as a yell, to be heard over the buzz of the traffic swirling past as they sprinted up the highway.

"I know," Mercedes replied calmly. Her fingers gripped the wheel even tighter, locking her eyes on the rearview mirror as she blew the blonde waves from her face, flipping her long hair over her shoulder.

The light blazed down through a clear sky, the asphalt shimmering to sun-like levels with palm trees etching shadows overhead as they bolted down the wide highway dodging traffic. Reckless and on the run, with several cars on their tail, the only thing hotter than the sun was the chase.

"He's really sent his whole fucking arsenal after us this time," Mercedes said, swerving to overtake a road train.

"After *me*, baby. After me," Adam corrected.

"Anyone who's after you is after me."

Adam smiled. He couldn't argue. He felt the same way. They were in this together. Forever and always.

"Well, regardless of who they're chasing, they're not giving up easily." Adam narrowed his eyes as he spotted several black sedans gaining on them, darting through traffic just as carelessly as they were, but without the skill to back it up.

Bullets pierced the front windshield, narrowly missing his head. Mercedes shifted off-road, bouncing along the uneven terrain of grass just long enough to slip out of sight before gunning it back onto the highway again.

"You gonna start shooting back yet?" Mercedes asked.

"Not yet," Adam said. "I think you've got one more bold move in you."

Adam inclined his head to the sight in front before turning over his shoulder and smirking. The road was coming to an end, culminating in solid concrete pillars.

"Dammit, alright," Mercedes said, leaning across Adam's body to click his seatbelt into place, shooting him a disapproving look for forgetting it in the first place. What? He wanted to be limber. It wouldn't be the first time he'd jumped mid-drive from her car onto the windshield of another.

Mercedes shifted gear, planted her foot on the gas, and jerked to the left, narrowly avoiding the concrete blocks and making the wheels spin.

She soared onto uneven grass, bouncing upwards as the car hit an incline and beelining for the bridge. Oh, he saw where she was going with this, and fuck, it *was* bold. Gulping, he gripped the center console.

Mercedes shot him a taunting glare, not even watching the road, as she tugged the wheel. They smashed through the guardrail at full speed and sailed off the bridge, flying weightlessly as if the car *would* somehow sprout wings and take flight.

His heart thumped and stole his breath, the drop leaving his organs behind. Goddamn, he loved that feeling. He was having far too much fun. This situation was serious, he had better start acting like it. But teetering on the edge of life and death was where he'd happily set up a home.

They landed in a crash against the concrete ground, braced in an aura of smoke and fumes. With a crack, his head banged hard on the dash at the miracle landing, leaving only a gash on his brow and, upon inspection, a cut on his girlfriend's lip.

"Jesus," Adam said.

"You wanted bold," Mercedes shrugged.

"I did," Adam said, feeling a warm, thick droplet crowd out his vision. Wiping the blood from his eye, he swiped a thumb over his mouth—cut lip there, too.

A smashing sound at the rear had him turning. Four cars had followed them over the railing. Scratch that—four *obviously suicidal* cars had followed them over the railing. There was only one driver skilled enough to pull off a trick jump like that.

Yeah, that was what he thought. Behind them was a mass of crumpled sedans, standing upright by the trunks and practically saluting.

But that wasn't all, much to his surprise, countless more pursuit vehicles had found a much more sensible route down, engines coughing as they accelerated.

"How the fuck did they get down here so fast?" Mercedes said.

"They really won't quit, will they?" Adam said.

Mercedes took off again, pinning them both to the backs of their seats.

Lucky the chase was boosting him with adrenaline that he sucked up like a junkie because his body was ready to give out.

It had been a long stretch of denial that had led him to this chase. He had believed himself and his team were invincible, unstoppable, and that nothing in Ridge City could ever take them down, no matter how antagonizing they were.

Now, though, he had nowhere left to go. On the run for days and surviving on fumes. Where Adam was once sure that nothing could ever stop him, he was now sure that it would, and soon. Shortly the running would have to end. At some point Dorian Blake would catch him.

Now off road, they raced through the loading docks of industrial warehouses at the edge of the city, surrounded by enemy vehicles.

"Time to enter the game, player," Mercedes said.

Finally in agreement, Adam opened the glove box to pull out two Colt .45 pistols, shoving ammo inside as he loaded them quickly.

He undid his seatbelt and stood in the front seat, resting his hands on the windshield as he fired multiple shots in succession. As he ran out of ammo, Mercedes threw more up to him. It was if they'd done this a thousand times. Because they had.

He found his way into the backseat, kneeling upright and firing from there, too.

Adam's headshot to the nearest car's driver swerved it off the road, rolling and exploding in a haze of fire. Two more and others were down, too, sending more smoke, more flames, and more charring smells into the air. Plopping down into the backseat, Adam smirked when he caught Mercedes grinning wickedly, almost lustfully, at the explosions behind them.

"You like that?"

"Do it again."

"You're sick, baby, that's why I love you," Adam said, joining her in the front seat again.

Adam's face hit the side window as they were nudged to the side, a car approaching from the left to push them off the road.

"Motherfuckers!" Mercedes said. She hit the brakes suddenly, dropping her speed so she could slip in behind her opponent. Once there she snaked to the right, and jarred the wheel to the left, hitting the tail of the opposing vehicle and sending it flying off in a crumpled heap. She had always given much better than she got.

"Let's finish this off, only a few to go," Adam said.

"Oh, you're done now, are you?"

"Just about," Adam said.

Mercedes gripped the wheel with her knees, freeing her hands to load her gun and shoot at the drivers alongside them.

Adam followed suit and grabbed his backpack from behind the seat—grenades. He pulled the pins and threw them strategically into the open windows of nearby enemy vehicles, and in the direct paths of the ones farther away.

The ground shook beneath them like a thundering earthquake as the explosives shattered and cars flipped at all angles.

Maybe they would have to stop running, maybe they would be caught, but they would always fight until the end.

They were just starting to make a dent in the opposition, starting to wrap it up and relax, when in the distance Adam eyed even more cars approaching to replace the ones they had taken out. A quick glance at Mercedes confirmed that she had seen it, too. Dorian Blake's army was never-ending and malicious. His gang of soldiers a bottomless pit of faceless, unimportant henchmen built to die. If they cut off the head of one, two more grew back in its place.

Adam reloaded his weapon and climbed into the backseat to shoot again. Raising his gun to his eye line, he only fired a few shots before the sound of tires screeching ahead demanded his attention.

Out of nowhere, a Blake Family truck appeared to block their path. It was too late to stop. Too late to do anything but smash directly into the side of the truck. Head on.

The force crumpled the hood, sending Adam flying out of the car in a parade of glass and metal.

He heard pounding.

Was that his heart, or the sound of his limbs hitting the concrete? Didn't matter—his heartbeat was all he could feel—at least it was still there.

The noise around him became just a distant echo. Every muscle in his body screamed when he peeled himself from the ground and squinted to see the onslaught of black sedans still heading their way.

Favoring his left leg, Adam hobbled to the driver's door of the shattered red convertible, where Mercedes laid groaning, her head resting gently against the seat.

"Come on, baby, come on! We gotta run." They were no strangers to a chase, but Blake's men were closing in.

Mercedes cursed and pushed the door open, missing her footing and falling.

Adam couldn't afford to give her time to recover, he plucked her from the ground, carrying her bridal style as he bolted from the open loading docks into an alleyway to continue their escape on foot.

The bright Ridge City sunlight was lost as they pushed farther into the maze, covering them in a cloud of cold darkness that was completely at odds with the tropical climate of the city. Adam put Mercedes down when she was fully coherent, and hand in hand, they ran.

They ran past dumpsters, over broken bottles smashing under their feet, and through piles of trash that nearly tripped them.

Passing exit after exit, they found themselves confined, scurrying around in an aimless panic like rats trapped in a cage. Some exits blocked by vehicles, others blocked by burly men with guns and all-too-happy trigger fingers, but the message was clear. It was a trap. And they had been caught.

Adam embraced Mercedes again, and they ran as fast as they could toward the last available light source they could see. That exit *was* blocked, but only by two haphazard-looking rookies, and Adam easily got the jump on them.

Running out the only way they could, into an open, brown grass clearing along the tracks in the train yard, Adam didn't dare let himself slow. They jumped and ducked their way across the yard, underneath trains and over the tracks, breath laboring and agility showing its head because they didn't once trip. They were too well practiced.

They stopped in a fierce panic when they hit yet another dead end, stranded at the edge of the rail yard, standing atop a large concrete overlook. It was a steep drop down onto the train tracks below, an un-survivable jump. Cursing his luck, Adam swore, finding his was running out.

"We can make it," Mercedes said. "We can do it."

But the steep concrete edge looked a lot like the end of the road.

Adam looked back at where they had come from to see loads of Blake's men in the distance, rushing at them, guns in hand, to end it once and for all.

"You can make it," he said. He bent forward and put his hands on his knees to take a breath.

"What?"

His heart bottomed out, as if it were telling him he knew what he had to do, even as it skipped a beat in denial. "You gotta go, baby. You gotta leave me here."

"No way!" she said. "In for life, remember?"

"I know," he said. But there wasn't time for protests, only action.

Hadn't he spent enough time already denying his fate? Hadn't he caused enough damage as it was? Realization settled unpleasantly into his stomach like an undercooked, bloody piece of meat. He could no longer save himself. But maybe he could still save her. He was the only one whom Dorian Blake was really chasing after all.

"Blake will never be ab-"

"Baby! This is bigger than us. Blake already has Paul," Adam sighed. "And Carlos. And Dan. Three of us already down. He will never stop hunting me. I'm the one he really wants."

"Exactly!" Mercedes said. "He won't kill them, but he will kill you. For what you've done? You think he forgives that kind of shit? If he catches you, you're a dead man. End of story."

"He doesn't know you had anything to do with this, I can still save you," Adam said.

"Don't you dare. Fight your way out of this with me, and then we will go together and save Paul, Dan, and Carlos."

"We've been running for two weeks, baby," Adam said.

"There's what? Twenty guys heading our way? We've taken down more than that before. Get your gun up and let's fight." She frowned and reached into her pocket to grab her weapon, blowing more blonde hair from her face as she gripped her gun with both hands.

Adam looked again at the hordes of men rounding up toward them. A few more minutes and her secret would no longer be protected. He couldn't let them see her face.

Sighing, he said, "Okay. But first, kiss me."

He grabbed her by the neck and pulled her in deeply, kissing her hard as the outside world melted away lazily. As always, it felt like they were the only two left in the world. Like it was only ever meant to be the two of them. Their lips parted slowly, letting the hot breeze run between them as they broke away.

He drank her in one last time, knowing that for him she would always be the only sun that could clear the storm.

"I love you," Adam said, and he knew he was saying it for the very last time.

As he let go, he placed his hand roughly on her sternum. With all his force, he pushed her backward, over the ledge, just at the time that a train was passing below.

She gasped as she stumbled and started to fall from him, her face etched in an unforgettable hue that looked a lot like disappointment. And heartbreak.

She fell almost in slow motion, her legs dangling out in front of her, her hand outstretched above to reach him. Her body getting farther and farther from his with each passing second. She landed with a bang onto the passing train below.

Adam looked on as she slammed into the train car, the echoes of her angry protests whistling back at him as he watched the train grow smaller in the distance, until she was just a speck on the horizon, until he was satisfied that her identity would remain a secret.

Adam lifted his hands to surrender, hearing the click of guns surrounding him and an angry cold barrel pressing into his head. It was finally over. Months of pursuits, struggles for power and wrests for control, all finished. But they hadn't seen her. *She* was still safe. *She* was going to live. But him? Dorian Blake was going to kill him.

He was right after all, it turned out. Adam Vandemilio died that day.

***

FEBRUARY 1991

(Five Years Later)

They were reckless when they were younger. Adam knew that now. There was a time when they would've ripped their lives apart and burned the city to the ground just to take what they wanted. There was nothing they wouldn't have done for each other.

But they were also stupid. When they started a war with Dorian Blake five years earlier, they were doomed to fail from the start. Ridge City was built on a system of crime, it was its lifeblood, and nobody was more powerful than Dorian Blake—head of the Blake Family crime empire. Nobody fucked with Dorian Blake. Nobody challenged Dorian Blake. Nobody looked at Dorian Blake with even a funny kind of side eye and lived to tell the tale.

Adam had known that, but with much more passion than sense, purposefully pushing against every status quo that had been set, he put together his own crew. Himself, sharpshooter Paul, lawyer Dan, drug runner Carlos, and driver Mercedes.

Yes, nobody fucked with Dorian Blake. Nobody could take him down. That's why it was so surprising when Adam's team of five came so close to doing just that.

It'd been five years since Adam had set foot in Ridge City. Five years since he'd left behind his city and his friends, swearing that he would never return. Now, there he was, breaking another promise that he swore he'd always keep. He'd always been bad at keeping his word, but he'd been worse at following the rules, even the ones he set for himself.

It was an insignificant Tuesday when Adam drove his car over state lines and back to the place where his heart had always felt it belonged.

Doing a happy little flip in his chest, it beat harder, before almost stilling completely when he remembered what he'd come back to do.

The impossible.

Even under a cover of darkness, the city looked the same as it ever did: wet, dirty, and hot, but with a promise of adventure.

Classic Florida.

Strong sandy beaches wrapped around the eastern coast, smoke polluted skies while garbage polluted the nose, and there was a labyrinth of miniature waterways that ran all the way to the west. The southern mansions were still sitting pretentiously high on the hill, surrounded by a moat of pristine ocean.

There were two sides to Ridge City. Tropically paradisiacal yet devastatingly derelict. But the most interesting things never happened in plain sight. The beauty of the city was in what it was hiding.

Adam arrived at the Tropics Hotel at eight fifteen. Exiting his car, he stopped to inhale the smell of the sea and listen to the chorus of waves crashing upon the sand. It was one of the cheaper hotels in town, only two stories and positioned directly opposite the beach with the glow of pink neon lights bouncing up off the pavement. It was nothing fancy. But it would do.

Adam pushed through the glass doors into the lobby and was pleased to find it smelled better inside than it did outside.

"Reservation?"

"No, but I'll be staying a while, so book me out an apartment. Something long term."

The clerk placed a key on the counter without even looking up. In response, Adam thumped down a thicker than necessary roll of cash. "I'll need you to hand over every key you have for this room. I don't like being surprised."

That certainly got the guy's attention. Arching one brow, the clerk finally looked up and took Adam in, almost needing to stretch his neck to see it all.

Adam knew he was intimidating, that's why the clerk should've known better than to look at him for too long. Adam gritted his teeth and the clerk snapped into action faster than if he'd been caught with his hand down his pants.

He returned with two more keys and placed them on the counter for Adam to take.

Even the manager's key.

The point of coming to the Tropics Hotel was that it was on the bad side of town, one of the only hotels that wasn't owned by Dorian Blake and his empire. Blake Family associates wouldn't be caught dead on this side of the city. Which gave Adam the greatest chance of not being seen or found until it was absolutely in his best interests to be.

"What's your affiliation?" Adam asked as he shoved the extra keys in his pocket. He carried only one suitcase and a heavy duffle bag that he flung over his shoulder, making it look like it weighed nothing more than a child's backpack.

"We're not run by the gang bangers if that's what you're asking," the clerk replied. "Used to be Cortez Cartel, but now we're independently owned."

Adam nodded and repositioned the duffle on his shoulder. Now the idiot behind the counter was openly staring at the tattoos up and down Adam's right arm, a colorful array of bright hues, saturated against his olive skin.

"Nice tats," the clerk said.

Adam ignored the dick with the death wish and signed a false name on the guest registry. He handed over the check-in slip to the clerk, who looked down at the paper with raised brows and finally—fucking finally— started to look a little bit afraid.

"You never saw me," Adam said.

"I never saw you," the clerk stuttered, pocketing the bribe.

Nobody saw him, nobody knew him. And that was exactly the way he needed it to be if he was going to make sure that everyone still believed he had died five years ago.

On the second floor, he opened the door and stepped inside his room. Directly in front of him was a small kitchenette and dining table with giant plantation windows running along the back wall. To the left, a studio bed sat upon a stacked wooden platform, and down a corridor to the right was an open living area, laundry, and bathroom.

Looking at his room, his heart thundered again—it could've won the fucking Olympic gold in gymnastics for all the flips it was doing—and the wave of fear that he now always had bubbling below the surface threatened to worm its way up.

It hadn't been there five years ago…this was a fear that had taken his mind and body hostage ever since he faced death. Ever since he was callously murdered (almost) by Dorian Blake. It was paralyzing and gripped him as if it, too, were holding on for dear life, taking everything he had to wrestle from its sharp bleeding claws.

Adam slammed the door and ripped through his suitcase pulling out file after file, furiously pinning notes to the walls. The ramblings of a mad man, and he certainly fit the bill.

Truthfully, he wasn't ready to come back. Emotionally, nor otherwise. His plan was half-gunned, under baked, and probably life-risking. Five years might have seemed generous enough for plotting revenge. But when it was Dorian Blake he'd be up against, it was barely enough. But he no longer had a choice. He had to stop Blake now, and he had to stop him *right now*, or he would never get the chance again.

He pulled the last note from his suitcase, a newspaper, the most important piece of evidence collected. It was page four, a picture of the soon-to-be Ridge City Mayor and his bride. The caption read: "Mayoral Candidate Dorian Blake tips ahead in the polls after announcing engagement to marry long-term girlfriend Mercedes Preston."

***

Mercedes sat on the edge of her bed, crossing her legs at the ankles and clutching the newspaper in her manicured fingers. With a wrinkled frown she stared at page four, the announcement of her engagement, and wiggled her finger to sparkle the diamond on her ring underneath the light from the chandelier.

She was going to marry Dorian Blake. *Willingly* marry Dorian Blake.

There was a time when she had wanted to stop him. End his reign of terror. Now, though, Dorian was about to become the Mayor of Ridge City, and once he did, he would be too powerful to ever take down. Not only was she not planning to do a thing about it, she was riding all the way to the top alongside him, however ill-advised she knew that would be.

She lived alongside her husband-to-be in his ridiculously large and ostentatious riverside mansion. A far cry from her trailer home roots. Even the bedroom they shared was at least three times the size of the home she had grown up in. It had a four-post canopy bed, a full-suite sofa, and two large, old mahogany wooden doors for the entry.

When she found her betrothed standing over her, she smiled full and bright, her heart fluttering like it was a bird trapped in her ribcage. Some would've confused the feeling. But she knew what her heart was begging of her.

"Do you like the picture, darling?" Dorian asked.

"It's perfect." She rose, and Dorian pressed a gentle kiss to her cheek. "Very mayoral."

"I think so too." He snatched the newspaper and marched over to the large bay windows to hold it up to the sunlight. "It's a great shot of me, isn't it?"

Her delicate white sundress glided with each light step she took toward him in her strappy heels. "You always look handsome," she replied as she rested her hand in the crook of his upheld arm.

Somewhere in the background, a single gunshot rang in the breeze. Gunfire, ambushes, and explosions were no stranger to the mansion. It was, after all, Dorian's favorite place to torture people. When she looked up at her fiancé, she found him less concerned and more irritated by the unexpected sound, as if he hadn't planned to schedule murder into his day. Not today, anyway.

Like a curious child, Dorian shrank away and casually strode toward the sound. Following after his lazy, unhurried steps, Mercedes passed through the mahogany double doors and into the crimson and gold painted halls, for once ignoring the exquisite ornaments nailed there that fascinated her.

Exiting onto the second-floor rear balcony, Mercedes found Dorian with his hands rested against the white stone railing, scowling down into the gardens below.

Dorian's mansion was coveted and beautiful for a reason. The house was five stories, and the gardens were three. Roman-style pool, Athenian water feature, stunning sun beds, *fucking hedge maze*, and a sweeping view over the airy river waters that ran parallel to the back of the house—you name it, Dorian's house had it. Hell, the mansion even had its own private boat dock on the last level, which either held a powerboat or a yacht in its perimeter depending on Dorian's mood that day. That day it was a yacht, which said in no uncertain terms: I'm not in the mood for murder.

Next to Dorian, his favorite Second, T.B., smirked over a shoulder when Mercedes approached. Smiling wickedly like he had a secret, he tilted his head toward the gardens, taunting her to look.

Mercedes's heart did a startled flip when she slid along the railing to see Dan, Carlos, and Paul standing next to the pool, with a fresh dead body leaking blood onto the pavement. Grimacing, she watched Paul subtly kick the body over. An unimportant, nameless man. Now faceless, too, and unrecognizable. Paul's handiwork then. It'd been five years since she'd raced, but this now-dead idiot somehow figured her out and was about to spill it all. That's why he needed to die.

Even after five years, Dorian had never given up searching for Adam's driver.

"What the fuck are the three of you doing together?" Dorian barked. "I thought I split you up."

T.B. smiled deviously. Everyone knew she was close to Paul, a punishment for him was a punishment for her. And T.B. had never liked her.

Mercedes's eyes flicked back to her friends. Dan and Carlos raised their brows at her, too, a silent conversation passing between them. Her secret was safe for now.

"Terrible coincidence," Paul said, stepping up. "Wrong place, wrong time. Apologies, boss."

Dan stepped ahead, too. "I was only stopping by to drop off some paperw-"

"Don't explain," Dorian said sternly. One snap of his finger was enough to end a life. It was Dorian's game, and everyone else was just playing 'try not to die' on any given day. "Just disperse."

"Yes, boss." Dan, Carlos, and Paul all nodded and went their separate ways, making sure to exit in different directions. It was not lost on Mercedes that they'd simply left the dead body lying by the edge of the pool. The afternoon cleaning crew would probably find it just as it looked now. Oh well, they'd cleaned up worse.

"Fucking idiots." Dorian pushed off the railing, stopping in the archway of the door to the house to vent to T.B. "You'd think after all the mercy I'd shown them, they wouldn't group up to disrespect me like that."

Dorian folded his arms across his chest, the sleeves of his suit crinkling as they pushed upward to reveal the thick hair crawling down his over-muscled forearms.

"You're right, boss," T.B. said.

"I let them live with the sole intention of finding out who the fifth guy was," Dorian sighed. "And we never fucking did that, and they're still walking around living."

Like she thought to herself, it was Dorian's obsession five years ago, and it still was now. He'd known that Adam Vandemilio had a driver, one whose identity he'd never been able to discover, and he drove himself mad thinking there was someone out there in Adam's corner that he couldn't pin down or control. Oh, if only he knew that he had done just that.

"Maybe there were only four guys, like they said," T.B. said, but Mercedes knew he'd only said it to provoke a reaction.

"Don't be ridiculous," Dorian spat. "There was always a fifth. Not like it matters now anyway. Adam Vandemilio is dead."

"Of course," T.B. said.

"There was always a fucking fifth," Dorian repeated as he stomped up the halls, T.B. on his heels like a good little suck up.

There certainly was a fifth, and if Dorian ever found out it was her— that she was the fifth member of Adam Vandemilio's crew—he'd kill her, too. And, she surmised, with her he'd actually make it stick.

CHAPTER 2
IN FOR LIFE

I f Adam knew one thing, it was that he was useless on his own. Blake held all the cards and all the power. If he stood any chance of going up against the Goliath, then he needed his old crew at his side.

Unfortunately, Blake held them, too.

His first few days back in Ridge City he laid low, reminding himself, against his natural instinct, that this mission was a marathon, not a sprint. There was no point in charging across the finish line guns blazing...announcing his arrival...sweeping the girl off her feet...

No! Dammit, this wasn't about her.

Yes, it was.

No! No, it wasn't.

She wasn't the only one who had moved on without him, his city and his friends had as well. No one seemed to neither know, nor care, who Adam Vandemilio was, and he could count on one hand the number of people who would ever recognize him if they came face to face. For now, he was a ghost.

Inside the local post office, a small storefront nestled along the beach strip, he settled into a private writing bay along the window.

Catching a glimpse of his reflection, he looked up. He couldn't understand how the city had forgotten him so easily—he looked the same as he did five years ago. Thick bushy eyebrows hanging over his dark eyes. A rough face with square jaw. Bronzed caramel hair in a choppy cut with more length over the front of his face. Though, where his eyes used to be ambitious, they now looked angsty. Hollowed.

He longed to feel alive again.

Shaking the view, he focused on the task at hand. The snippets from the yellow pages had crumpled slightly when he ripped them from his wall and shoved them in the pocket of his jeans, but they were still legible.

None of his friends were all that difficult to track down. He swore it was as if they were Hansel and Gretel, dropping bread crumbs for him to assure a speedy discovery.

Dan had been the easiest to track down. His law firm had tacky, infomercial-style ads all throughout the book. Going full time for the Blake Family had obviously agreed with him. He had one of the largest offices in the county, with a personal assistant to boot.

Paul was next. He was working at one of the Blake Family's shooting ranges. A marksman and former hitman by trade, working at a shooting range was a waste of his skills. Instead of making incredulous shots across canyons, he was stuck behind a desk.

Carlos was a little harder to find. It was his job to stay hidden. But that didn't mean the man didn't have an address. Carlos was a cooker by trade, but Blake had him funneling supplies of cocaine to low-level drug runners.

Again, a waste of his talents. There was much more to Carlos than just managing drug supplies to dealers. He could have been creating the next big hit.

It certainly wasn't difficult to find Mercedes. It wasn't as if she was trying to hide, wrapping her arms around Dorian Blake's neck on page four of the gossip column. Easy to find, sure, but she was the one he dreaded to see most of all.

Exiting the post office with his envelopes in hand, Adam stepped onto the street, the humidity hitting him so forcefully, it was as if he'd stuck his face into an oven.

On the good side of town, he was well underdressed in his black muscle tee. The lusher side of the city was filled with greenery, sparse gardens and glistening turquoise rivers. Classic southern east coast. An enviable place to live for those who could handle the heat, but didn't mind a city run by criminals. Most couldn't stomach staying longer than a week. At best. That's why tourism was a massive industry for Ridge City.

Before jumping into the driver's seat of his car, Adam slipped three of his yellow envelopes into the mail, holding onto the fourth. He was about to shove into first and pull out when a truck displaying the Blake Family logo turned into his path, freezing him on the spot. With a quick honk it was on its way, slowly pottering out of sight. But Adam clenched his jaw and shallowed his breathing, a familiar bubble of anxiety threatening to rip his guts out.

Just a truck. Breathe.

He would not let his fear get the better of him, but there was a voice in his head asking how long he could push it down without being swallowed whole. Hell, it was already chomping on his side.

***

"Carlos! My man, have a seat." Blake's calm choice of words was at odds with the venomous tone he paired them with. Carlos assumed that he did it on purpose to give people a feeling of unease.

Carlos stood at attention in front of Blake's private booth. Nobody would ever guess it was only nine in the morning from the atmosphere inside the Neptune Club. Blacked-out windows and strobing green neon lights hid the time of day. The place was a myriad of unfiltered noise— slot machines spilling in the gaming lounge, bottles slamming at the bar, high-heels traipsing across the stage.

"Scoot over, Shaundi," Blake said, he and the stripper both sliding up the red leather bench as Carlos reluctantly slipped in beside them.

"You look somber. Why don't you have a drink?" Again, a nice gesture laced in venom.

"Not this morning. I'm just here to check in," Carlos said.

Without taking his eyes off his sidepiece, Blake managed a nod. Luckily, he didn't seem to notice the heaving sigh that escaped from Carlos as he placed his duffle bag on the table and zipped it open.

Inside, six bags of cocaine and a roll of fifty thousand in hundred-dollar bills.

Carlos was happy to admit he was a drug dealer, proud of it even. He didn't think of himself as a bad person—after all, he was a dedicated member of the Hispanic Catholic community and his mom always said he was a sweet boy. Maybe he did bad things, but God would have to forgive him. God had never lived in Ridge City.

"We couldn't move these?" Blake said. "I'm disappointed."

"I don't know what to tell you," Carlos shrugged. But he did know, really. Blake's cocaine supply was weak compared to what was being cooked up interstate. People were trudging all the way up to Darton just to get a hit. "I can try to move it down to some lower players tonight."

"Or we could have our own fun," Shaundi said, sticking her acrylic fingers into the white powder and dragging it to her nostrils. Before she could take the hit, Blake snatched her wrist in mid-air and slammed it down onto the table.

"Just because I fuck you doesn't mean you have the right to touch anything that's mine," Blake barked. "Get out of here. Now."

Whimpering like a wounded animal, Shaundi shook herself out of Blake's grip and took off.

"You can leave now, too," Blake said, not sparing Carlos another glance.

Carlos didn't need to be asked twice, he left the money but took his duffle with him out the back of the club.

Walking past the bar, through the kitchen, and into the back alleyway, Carlos lit a cigarette and leaned against the railing, which, with him being shorter than most, came up to him at chest height.

Carlos longed for the old days. When he didn't have to make his living slinging drugs for somebody else's fortune. But the rich were the rich and the poor were the poor. There was no changing your station. Carlos knew that better than anyone. He'd tried once to take down Dorian Blake.

It couldn't be done. Instead, it had cost him everything.

He blew the long strands of black hair out of his eyes as he flicked his cigarette off the edge into the pristine turquoise river that ran directly behind the club.

Resting his duffle on the railing, he fumbled through it for his mail, twisting another cigarette between his teeth.

Promotional coupon. Bill. Pizza menu. Promotional coupon.

He puffed on his cigarette and curiously grabbed the next yellow envelope. No return address on the back and weird, nearly illegible, handwriting on the front. It was like a four-year-old had addressed it. With their toe.

Thumbing his cigarette, Carlos coughed as he slid the envelope open and pulled the paper from the sleeve.

He was mid-puff by the time his brain caught up to what he was seeing on the crisp white paper. Coughing, he spat the cigarette into the water below and furiously turned the paper, and the envelope it had come in, over and over in his hand.

There was only one person who could've possibly sent it.

It said: *In for life?*

***

"Paul..." a nervous voice stuttered. "Could you come over here please?"

He'd only just sat down in the back office of the gun range. Groaning, Paul shot upright and made his way to the front counter where a trainee was trying to help a customer.

"Yes?" Paul's tone was light. He was too indifferent with life to be bothered to be either angry or pleasant.

"They say they want to purchase a Carbine-edition M4, but I don't see it in the system?" The kid fumbled with the buttons on the cash register, hitting as many wrong notes as a top one-hundred pop songs chart.

The thugs standing opposite the counter were dressed in all white, with dark skin like Paul's, and over six-foot tall like him, too. He supposed they would've been intimidating had he not had at least an extra six inches on them.

"Make yourself scarce, kid," Paul said, running his hand over his bald head.

Nodding wordlessly at the thugs to follow him, Paul began to lead them through the range. He didn't need to look back to know they were keeping up as expected.

They pushed through the strip paneling doors onto a concrete loading dock where large pallets of illegal gun shipments were littered around the floor. Again, without a need for words, Paul pointed them in the direction of the M4 shipments at the far back.

"Don't you want to know what we're going to do with all these?" one of the thugs asked. God, the last thing he needed was for them to be chatty.

"I don't need to know anymore than I need to," Paul said.

"Nice tattoo, what does it mean?" the other thug said.

Paul looked down at his arm where he had a stripe tattoo with the words 'in for life' nestled in cursive along it. He was almost caught smiling and stroking his thumb along it before he thought better and straightened, storming away before they could ask him any more questions he didn't want to answer.

He didn't need any more reasons to be in trouble.

Paul never thought he'd be comfortable sitting behind a desk, but the back office at the shooting range had become just that. Comfortable. He often wondered how productive it was to be comfortable. He was of the thought that a great life was one filled with uncomfortable situations and fortunate misfortunes.

Spread out before him, Paul sorted through his mail, flipping through the colorful assortments of paper.

He cataloged a few letters before he got to one he didn't recognize. Yellow envelope, scribbled handwriting, no return address. Slipping it open, he pulled the note from within.

That made two times today that Paul had felt more than emptiness. First when he nearly smiled, and now when his face froze over with an icy drip that he couldn't determine the reason for. Was it fear? Or was it anger?

Without missing a beat, he stood up and placed the note in the shredder, watching as the same words he'd had inscribed on his body dissolved.

In for life?

***

"No! No. Don't do anything else. Tell her to shut her mouth and not say another word to the police until I get down there," Dan screamed into the landline.

Lawyer Daniel, Dan to his close friends, had never had his own practice before he started working for Dorian Blake. Now, he had one of the largest offices in the county, with all the latest trims and furnishings. He had the big black leather chair and the glass-top desk. He had the glass windows, the trophy cabinet, the personal assistant. The fucking drawer stocked full of free cocaine.

On the outside it looked like a sweet ride with a lot of perks, but Dan's heart wasn't as superficial as he'd led his enemies to believe. All the fancy trims, all the incentives, each and every one had cost him all the things he'd ever cared about.

Once a fully fledged gangster, Dan now spent his days perched behind a desk using his second-rate law degree to make sure the right people went down for the crimes Blake wanted them to go down for.

His landline rang again, and his assistant answered eagerly.

"Sir, you have a call on line four," she said.

Dan fell into a rage. "I've fucking told you don't answer anything that comes through on line four!" Dan had always been poorly tempered. There was only one person he'd ever known who was more reckless than he was.

The call waiting on line four came flashing onto his phone. Before answering, he hit the encrypt button and pressed the large handset to his ear.

"Hello."

"Dan, I was told to call you, I'm in jail." A random Blake Family criminal was on the line.

"Alright, what digit did they give you?" Dan asked.

"Fourteen."

Dan held the phone to his ear with his shoulder and flipped open a large binder on his desktop. His lanky fingers searched through the list of codes until they settled on the one in question. Fourteen was to bribe the police for release. Lucky day for this random idiot.

"And what did you do?"

"I shouldn't say..."

"The line is encrypted, go ahead."

"It's what?"

Sighing and rolling his eyes to the sky, Dan held the phone to his chest while he took a deep breath. He'd once been told that his superior intelligence was a curse as it would only make everyone else look undeniably stupid.

"For fuck's sake, it's secure. It can't be tapped. Out with it."

"Oh, okay. I rammed my car into the police station. But I fucked up, I think I really hurt someone."

"Case number?"

"I don't know."

"Fuck, fine. I'll sort it out." Dan slammed the phone down in the cradle. Then smashed it down again several times for good measure. No reason, really. Just giving an outlet for his rage.

His assistant pushed open his door with her hip and avoided eye contact as she traced the length of the room to place coffee and a danish on his desk. Right next to the new mail.

Not even bothering to wait for his assistant to be gone, Dan sat at his desk and straightened a line of coke before sniffing it into his nose, and throwing his head back to relish it as the tight brown curls bounced on his head. He stretched his legs out on the desk and picked up his mail. He could hardly read it through his bloodshot eyes.

One by one, he threw away piece by piece of mail until he came to an envelope he didn't recognize.

Interesting.

Removing his legs from the desk, he wiped the leftover coke from his nose and flipped the letter in his hands. No return address.

Like a kid tearing into a candy wrapper, he unwrapped it impatiently, shredding the envelope to pieces to get to the treat inside.

His frown turned to a manic smile as his red eyes poured over the note. He couldn't contain his elation, the grin burned his cheeks. Things were about to get interesting. Things hadn't been interesting in such a long time.

In for life?

***

The best thing about the mansion on Burke Street, in Mercedes's opinion anyway, was the pool. Before she'd come to live there, she'd only ever swam in the ocean. Pools were something only rich people could afford. And though she was many things, rich wasn't one of them.

"Fuuuuuuuck!"

Floating on an inflatable bed in the midst of the pristine water, Mercedes lifted her head at the obscenity. She heard Dorian slamming doors and bashing through the house, generally sounding like he was ripping the interior to shreds, before she saw him strut directly out onto the pool deck.

"Hello, darling," Mercedes smiled as she saw him. "Look how nicely they've cleaned up the deck."

Up to that point, he hadn't seemed to notice that she was there. Shooting a nervous glance over his shoulder, his face raw and straining, he ignored her comment and clipped his words. "Honey, didn't realize you'd be home."

Not one second after he turned his back on her again, Dorian was joined by his three upper-level associates. His Seconds-in-charge. His right-hand men. His very important people.

"Business?" Mercedes asked.

Dorian nodded without looking over his shoulder.

"Want me to leave?"

He hesitated.

"It's not like I'll understand what you're talking about anyway."

Of course she fucking would. But he didn't need to know that.

His underestimation of her was one of many shortcomings she enjoyed playing on. Dorian was incredibly stupid for such a smart man. Overly

30

educated, charming, handsome, law and business degrees to boot, and he *still* thought women were better for nothing more than fucking, looking pretty, and making good wives. If he only knew.

He agreed without acknowledging her. "Give your updates."

"Business as usual. Gun shipment off today, no issues," Antonio answered. Also known as the least favorite, always desperately, pathetically, and embarrassingly trying to prove himself.

Yani shouldered past him. "Small hiccup with the girls. Wanted a bigger cut, so we slapped them around a bit and took the whole payment. Don't think we'll be getting noise from them anymore." He was always brutal and apathetic. He had nothing to prove to anyone. If he cared, he would've been the favorite, had Dorian not had an unhealthy obsession with how off the nuts, bat-shit crazy T.B. was.

"The drive went off without a hitch, caught up to the transport and took what we needed," T.B. said.

"And the code?" Dorian asked.

"Updated," T.B. said.

"To?"

Oh God, yes.

Delicately swatting her hands in the water, Mercedes attempted to turn on the float, hoping to hear just that little bit better.

"Victory day," T.B. said.

Not quite what she was after, but it'd do. She smiled to herself and placed her sunglasses over her eyes before dipping into the water to exit the pool.

"I'm going inside," she said. She wrapped a towel over her bikini-clad body, kissing Dorian's cheek as his eyes got stuck on her long, tan legs, glistening with pool water. "T.B., Yani, Antonio, always good to see you."

She made a point to list them in order of favoritism. Antonio's nostrils always flared when she did.

Victory day? What was victory day? Never mind—she'd figure it out later.

Repeating the secret in her head for good measure, she sprinted up the stairs to her bedroom, heading straight for the third drawer in her dresser.

It had been a habit she'd picked up when she was younger, always hiding her secrets and cash in the dresser. Banks had been out of the question when she'd made all her money via illegal street racing. Since she'd had Dorian's money, she no longer needed to stash cash, but she still needed to stash secrets, so to the third drawer they went. In a notebook wrapped up in a green plaid shirt she never wore.

Adam's green plaid shirt.

She watched the entry as she pulled the notebook from its hiding place, her eyes fixed like lasers to the double mahogany doors.

When she slid open the notebook, something crumpled to her feet, disarming her focus on the door.

A yellow envelope sat on her bare, peach-painted toes.

Someone had slipped an envelope into her secret notebook?! How did anyone know it was there? She'd never told anyone about it.

Okay, she'd told one person about it. But what did that matter? That person was dead. To her, at least.

She nervously picked it up off the floor. Messy handwriting. No return address. Tearing it open, she peered at the note inside.

Her heart reacted immediately—like it had spent the day visiting a theme park and riding a string of nonsensical, ridiculous, why-did-anyone-ever-go-on-these thrill rides—somehow both dropping to her butt and climbing straight out of her stomach through her throat simultaneously.

She clutched the note to her chest and inhaled, closing her eyes like it wouldn't still be there when she opened them again.

It couldn't be. It wasn't what she thought it was.

Returning the letter to the wrongful place she'd found it, she slammed the drawer shut and held her hands at her heart, the words from the note replaying in her head.

In for life?

CHAPTER 3
THE BIG FIVE

Four men, one woman. The Big Five. The crew that nearly tore down an empire before they themselves were torn apart. Once you were in, you were in for life.

Or so it was supposed to be.

It'd been five years since Adam had seen anyone from his old crew. Enough time that maybe those old alliances were off the table. That maybe *in for life* was just a saying and no longer a promise. After all, every one of them had since pledged loyalty to Dorian Blake.

Adam stood outside the shooting range, planted there for half an hour contemplating his decision. It'd been risky sending out his message, but taking a chance on someone, betting they'd still be on his side...that was riskier.

When he finally got the courage to walk across the road and push at the door, his hand felt like a loaded gun. Once he opened that door, once he stepped through and took his shot, there was no going back.

He only hoped he'd made the right decision.

Adam charged through the doors like he owned the place, because he once did. He'd picked out the blue, fluorescent lights, the metallic shooting bays, the brown paint peeling from the wall.

Scanning the room, he looked past the tired faces, patrons fumbling guns and missing shots, hitting only the plaster board at the range wall.

He spotted Paul from across the room.

They locked eyes, and Paul's face dropped. The shock there only a second before Paul schooled his features, sneaking a double-take at Adam. Like he couldn't believe what he was seeing. After all, the last time Paul had seen him Adam, he'd promised he'd never come back to Ridge City.

His body still hadn't moved, which made Adam all the more tense. Did he choose the wrong person to trust? Or would Paul come around just like he suspected he would? He had to start somewhere, after all.

Smiling tightly, Paul shooed away his client, snapping glances around the room as he stepped toward Adam. He approached slow at first, picking up the pace the nearer he drew.

"You shouldn't be here." Paul grabbed Adam's shoulder and guided him into the shadows. "Everybody thinks you're dead. You have to leave."

"Good," Adam said, exhaling in relief. He'd chosen right, for once. "You got my note."

"Yes, I got your note. You should not have sent that. Paper evidence? Come on, Adam."

"You tore it up. That's how I knew you were the one I could trust."

"What?" Paul hid his face under his palm, checking over his own shoulder like he was barely even listening.

"You tore it up. You read it for yourself, and you weren't going to show anyone. You made sure no one but you would see it."

"How do you know—you know what, never mind. You've got to get out of here. Now. Before you're seen."

"I appreciate the concern, but I'm here for a reason."

"You don't understand–" Paul shouted, halting as he drew the attention of the room. Chuckling darkly, Adam stumbled when Paul shoved him into the back office, drew the blinds, and locked the door.

"Blake owns this place now. You can't come storming in!"

Adam opened his arms wide, trying not to smile menacingly, but probably failing. That smile always showed up when he knew he was misbehaving. Which was often. "Paul…I haven't seen you in five years, can't you pretend to be happy to see me?"

"Of course, I'm happy," Paul said, almost seeming surprised with how forceful his voice was. Uncertainty crossed his face before he sighed, wiping his forehead. "Of course, I'm happy to see you."

Gesturing again, Adam opened his arms and Paul finally gave in, placing thunderous slaps on his back.

"You look good," Adam said. "Bulkier, though."

Paul laughed. "It's all muscle, mate."

"You don't wanna say how good I'm looking?"

"You scrub up alright," Paul said. "Aged, though."

"I haven't aged a day." Adam brushed away the friendly insult, running his hands over his hair, nearly catching his skull rings in his locks.

"You really do have to leave though. If Blake sees you, he'll kill you properly this time."

36

"I'm not going anywhere," Adam said. "I need your help."

"I was afraid you were going to say that," Paul sighed. "You're not taking Blake down now. Haven't you seen the news? He's about to be the mayor."

Fuck, he didn't need to be reminded. Of course, he'd seen the shit show that had been going on in his absence. Why else would he be back?

Arching his brow, Adam said, "Yeah, I've seen the news. I know exactly what Blake has been up to, and exactly who's sleeping in his bed."

"Right, yeah," Paul said, studying the floor. "That doesn't change the fact that you being here is a fucking terrible idea."

"I was never going to let him get away with what he did to me."

"God, that may be the stupidest thing you've ever said. You *know* what Blake would do to you, to all of us, if he found out you're not really dead."

"He took everything from me. Now I have to take it back. This is non-negotiable, and I can't do it without you."

Paul clenched his jaw. "You have to get out of here before you get yourself killed, again, and take all of us with you this time."

"Look," Adam said. "I wouldn't come back here without a plan. We're getting Carlos, Dan, and Mercedes back. We're getting back the cars, the bars, the fucking mansion. AND—we're gonna kill Dorian Blake."

Pausing for dramatic effect, always a showman, Adam took a deep breath. "Are you in?"

Paul looked at Adam like he'd just sprouted a third arm out of his forehead and waved. "Jesus Christ, Adam. No, I'm not fucking *in*."

"Oh, come on, you never used to be afraid of a fight."

"This isn't a fight! It's a suicide mission."

"That's a bit dramatic." Adam rolled his eyes.

"There's nothing here *to* fight. This is Blake's world now, we just live in it."

"Wow, you're more beaten down than I thought..." He searched his friend's eyes, but only found answers he didn't want to see.

He'd seen their new lives firsthand, how far they were living below their potential. But he never thought they would start to believe they weren't capable of more. Blake could break their bodies, but never could he break their spirits. Or so Adam had thought.

"The fight isn't over, it's barely even begun. Come on. Let's kill this son-of-a-bitch," Adam said.

"For fuck's sake."

"Come on," Adam prodded. As if Paul would finally break from sheer annoyance if he asked enough times in a row.

Paul rubbed at his eyes. "Is there anything I can say to make you go away?"

Adam shook his head. "It's now or never, man. Just say you'll think about it."

He'd settle for that, for now. Because they'd all come around eventually. *All of them.*

"Dammit," Paul said, clenching his fists. "Fine. I'll think about it."

"Alright," Adam smiled. "Well, I am actually gonna get the fuck out of here before someone sees me. Come by the old lot after your shift."

***

JULY 1985

"This is it?" Dan scoffed.

Paul opened the door to his trailer at the Ridge City trailer lot, Adam, Dan, and Carlos shuffling inside behind him.

Adam cringed as Paul pushed dirty clothes down the back of the couch. Seeing Dan and Carlos's disgusted faces, he elbowed his friends in the ribs. Could they just behave and play nice for one goddamn day?

"It's better than nothing. Paul's offering a place for us to work from," Adam reminded them.

"A dingy, dodgy place," Carlos said.

He wasn't wrong, the whole trailer took on an orange hue through the closed blinds, and the appliances were falling apart at the joints. At the front of the trailer was a small dining table and couch, while at the back were curtains that hid Paul's bed. Barely big enough to fit his six-foot frame.

"Well, none of you are exactly rolling in the dough, are you?" Paul hit back.

"Fucking Blake Family errand boy," Dan hissed.

"Second-rate Cortez pusher," Paul said, pushing into Dan's face.

"Enough!" Adam said, jumping to break them apart. "If we want to be a team, we can't keep yelling at each other. We've done well so far, going out on our own. Let's try to trust each other."

"For all we know this one is pushing facts back up to the Blakes," Dan said.

"Or you're pushing facts back to the Cortez's," Paul said.

Adam pinched his nose. It had been too much trouble trying to integrate Dan and Carlos, lifelong Cortez Cartel members, with Paul, a Blake Family associate. A lot harder than he thought it would be. Divide and distrust were second nature. Stiff as a rock, harder to break.

"It's not Blake's versus Cortez's anymore... not for us, at least, let's cool that attitude," Adam said.

"Look, I like the money that we make on our own, but I don't know if I can ever trust a Blake bag-boy," Carlos said.

Paul folded his arms and stretched to make himself as large as possible. Wisely, Dan and Carlos took a hesitant step back.

"If we're going to go it alone, we have to start acting like a team, and at some point, like family," Adam said.

"This isn't my fucking family," Dan said.

Adam threw his hands in the air in defeat. "Can I get a word?" Adam said to Paul. "Dan, Carlos, why don't you divide up the cash from today's job."

Snickering, Dan and Carlos squeezed around the tiny table.

Outside the trailer, Adam held the door open, ushering his arms until Paul joined him.

The lot was nothing pretty, that was for sure. It was a dirt-only park, not a shred of greenery in sight, and frequent dust storms blew through the area. Every trailer around the semi-circle in that corner, including Paul's, had a cheap green-and-white awning with plastic deck chairs sitting underneath.

"Dan and Carlos, they really are good guys, I swear," Adam said, shutting the door as calmly as he could, considering.

"I know," Paul admitted. "They don't want to trust me because I'm aligned with the Blake's and they're aligned with the Cortez's, I get it."

Dan and Carlos had saved Adam's ass more times throughout their lives than he could count. And Paul was a good guy, like so many others, pushed into working for the Blake Family based solely on what side of the city he lived on. "I wanted us to go out on our own so we didn't have to do this Blake versus Cortez thing anymore, it's just not coming together."

"It's not all bad. We're making a lot of profit," Paul said.

"Yeah, I know," Adam sighed, sitting down on a plastic chair and cradling his face.

"Money isn't nothing. Fuck knows I need it. Putting my little sis through med school was not fucking cheap."

Paul's sister was the first black doctor to graduate in Ridge City. It was a big deal.

"I *need* this to work," Paul said.

"I know. So do I. I just need to get everyone to stop snapping at each other."

"I shouldn't snap back at them, it's just—"

"I don't blame you. I just feel like there's something missing. We need something to bring the team together."

Paul nodded, but didn't reply. It seemed Paul didn't have any more answers than Adam did himself.

"Doesn't it just feel like something is missing?" Adam asked.

"It definitely feels that way," Paul said.

"We need something that's going to turn the four of us into something great, you know?" Adam said. "Three Cortez exiles and one Blake deserter don't really glue together."

Adam was about to cut his losses and call it a problem for another day when he looked up at Paul. The man was grinning ear to ear, looking like he'd discovered his birthday and Christmas presents had all arrived on the same day.

"Then we'll need glue," Paul said. "Maybe four people isn't enough."

"What do you mean?"

"Four people. It doesn't work. It's not enough."

"You think?" Adam said, standing up to face him.

"We need five, an odd number. One more person. The Big Five," Paul smiled. "You want someone to bring this team together. Say, someone who's never been able to make their own choices. Someone like you. Whether they're forced into this life, or whether they're forced *out* of it?"

Adam narrowed his eyes, forced out of it? Where the hell was Paul going with this?

"We need a driver for our next job, right?" Paul said. Adam nodded. "Then we can kill two birds with one stone. We need a driver and we need a fifth player on our team. Hear me out—I know this girl."

***

FEBRUARY 1991

Adam arrived at the old trailer park lot just before four. He'd left his car and sat down across the road on a park bench. Out of sight, where he could see the old dirt park but could not easily be seen himself. It had been difficult to find a comfortable place to spy from, considering the lot was all but deserted.

The place had been prime territory before it was burned in late 1986. It used to be his home. It was the place that he and his friends went from being five idiots, to a coherent team capable of taking over a whole city. It seemed a fitting spot for a reunion.

At four exactly, Adam watched as Paul entered the ruins and stopped where his old trailer used to stand. Now nothing left, the only structures remaining were crumbling, half-fallen brick walls and rusted tin.

Paul looked nervous, like a gazelle sensing a lion, bouncing from foot to foot, eyes darting left and right. Producing a radio from his back pocket, Paul spoke quietly into it.

That sneaky little shit...

Luckily Adam had come prepared, planting a receiver in the nearby ruins before Paul's arrival. He tuned the radio and listened in.

"He's not here yet. I know the deal. I'll give you the signal when he gets here," said Paul.

Goddammit.

Adam had doubted it, hoped his old friend wouldn't betray him, but he needed to make sure.

Adam sighed, holding the radio to speak a direct line to Paul. "So it seems you're not the loyal companion I remember you to be."

Startled, Paul looked upward, speaking to the sky as if Adam were the voice of God. "Adam? You caught that, did you?"

"I told you I had a plan. I'm not doing it the stupid way this time round."

"Well, it's not what you think, okay?" Paul replied, still searching around the park, but Adam was too well hidden.

"Why don't you stop me if I'm wrong. To me it looks like every one of our old crew is aligned with Dorian Blake. I followed Carlos to the club, found you at the range, Mercedes is living in his house, and Dan has a very nice new office."

"I can't argue with you so far," Paul said.

Adam stretched his arm across the back of the green wooden bench and held the radio close, eyeing Paul in the distance. "So, what's the deal then? What have you spilled to Blake so far?"

"It's not like that," said Paul. "We did our part to help you disappear. After that... well, you know what we had to do. You really think anyone would go anywhere near Dorian *by choice*? After... what we did."

"The others?" Adam narrowed his eyes.

"We're still a team, the four of us."

"Five," Adam said.

"Four," a female voice said.

That voice sent shivers crawling down his spine.

It was soft like velvet, just as seductive, and sent his head straight into the clouds.

Adam felt her shadow before he dared a look. When he turned, there she was, everything he imagined every night before he closed his eyes.

Mercedes slid next to him on the wooden bench.

Her hair, shorter now but still almost at her waist, blew gently in the wind. The waves that she'd had in the eighties were swapped for dead straight locks that brushed up against her sculpted cheekbones and framed her perfect, peach-pink lips.

Mercedes was just as beautiful as the day he first saw her. Now, though, there were no bruises scattering her face as a symbol of their adventures. There was no smudged eyeliner or wind-whipped mascara running down her cheeks. This woman was poised and elegant. She wore leather pants and shit-kicking high-heeled boots, but everything about her oozed classy confidence.

"It's good to see you, baby," Adam said.

"Can't say I agree," she smiled, though she avoided looking at him, instead staring out across the dirt field.

"You got my note." Adam ran his fingers through his dark hair.

"Oh, I did," she said. "Taunting us after all this time. That was fucking stupid, Adam. But then again, you've always had cobwebs in your brain."

He smiled at the comment. She was icier than he remembered, but still as sharply witted. Her dirty mouth and sick mind were the parts of her he first fell in love with.

"So what're you doing here, baby? Far cry from your mansion," he said.

She laughed at the low shot and crossed her legs. "I like my mansion. It has fine, expensive, silk sheets, perfect to get wrapped up in."

The air seemed to sizzle. He had to look away before he pounced on her right there. "I love it when you talk dirty."

"Just... take your bullshit and leave, Adam. As you can see, we're doing fine on our own."

He gave her a disbelieving look.

She scoffed and faced him finally. "Everyone thinks you're dead. I'd rather it stayed that way."

"So would I, for now, at least." Adam wiggled his brows. "Just admit you need some help getting the band back together."

Her expression grew irritated, her mouth turning into a thin line as she leaned across Adam's body, her lips inches from his, her breath close enough to feel it on his mouth.

He stretched along the bench, waiting to see what move she would make. His breath stilled when she reached toward his pants. To his utter disappointment she simply pulled the radio from his pocket.

Leaving him sighing at her teasing, she smiled when she pulled away. "Paul, on your left."

Adam watched as Paul finally made the connection. He waved with a flick of his wrist as Paul jogged over and Mercedes stood to greet him.

"You sneaky motherfucker!!" Was that Dan's voice he'd just heard? Adam *oofed* when he was tackled to the ground. In a tangle of limbs, Dan hung onto him like a needy squid. "I knew that note was from you, you dramatic fuck."

Adam laughed as Dan let him go and stood up. Brushing the dirt from his pants, Adam looked up to find a solemn Carlos staring down at him.

He wasn't sure what to make of it, until Carlos extended him a hand, helping him from the ground and pulling him into a bear hug, too.

"You are one stupid dickhead," Carlos said as they pulled away. Dan and Carlos joined Paul at Mercedes' side.

Well, that was one thing that he didn't count on.

He thought he was rushing back to pull together the leftover pieces of his crew, slapping Band-Aids over bullet wounds and gluing them together haphazardly. But no, there they stood before him, not broken but together.

"Alright, I'll play," Adam said. "I want in."

Mercedes crossed her arms. "No way. You're out. You've been out for five years."

"She's right, man," Carlos said. "It's far too dangerous for you now."

"So get in your fucking car and drive away now before I make you," Mercedes ordered.

"Hey, that's not the doting girlfriend I left behind here."

"Left behind being the key word there," Carlos said, his voice a warning.

Interesting. Adam hadn't anticipated that anyone other than Mercedes would be bitter at his absence. It seemed he had hurt more feelings than just hers when he fled Ridge City five years ago. He'd *barely* escaped with his life, to be fair. They should've known that, they were the ones who dragged him to safety and helped him fake his death.

"I think we should give him a chance," Paul said.

Mercedes, who had been death glaring Adam, turned on her childhood best friend. "Paul?"

"He's come back with a plan, so he says. We're in all the right places with no idea how to pull the trigger," Paul said.

"What the fuck?!" Dan shoved at Paul.

"We have no intention of pulling triggers," Carlos agreed.

"There's no triggers," Mercedes said. "We've got everything we need. Life is perfectly fine just the way it is."

"But it's not great, is it?" said Paul.

"I don't know about you, but I never sought out to be mediocre." Adam shrugged, but his opinion was about as welcome as a surprise finger to the ass.

"If you're in, you're in for life," Paul reminded them.

That seemed to do it—Dan, Carlos, and Paul all turned to Mercedes and winced.

Adam was surprised to find they'd stuck together all these years, but he shouldn't have been. Not with her at the helm. She made them a team and she kept them a team. She built this family from the ground up. She had single-handedly molded every one of them together for life. And, to Adam's advantage in that moment, the phrase *in for life* was still a promise.

Mercedes unfolded her arms and kicked the dirt. "You don't even know what he wants."

"I just want back in," Adam lied, to which Paul replied with a raised brow.

"No," Mercedes said.

"M..." Paul clasped her shoulder. "We don't leave each other high and dry. That's not what family does."

"He's not my family," she spat, acting like Paul was the only person listening. Adam rolled his eyes, but inside his heart bled.

"Yeah... yeah, he is. We all are." Paul rubbed her back. It was clear that her mind had been made up for her.

"Fine," Mercedes gritted out, turning her death glare back on Adam. "But we're not stupid kids anymore, Adam. We plan what we do, we do it carefully and get it right. You follow my rules."

"Wouldn't *dream* of breaking them," he said. He was trying to flirt, why did it come out like a taunt? Fuck.

Adam could practically see her counting to ten, forcing herself to not kick his teeth in. "First, Dorian still thinks you're dead, so keep your face hidden. Second, keep your fucking hands off me. And—*and*—this last one is very important." Adam wasn't sure what she was searching for in his eyes, but she must have found it because she continued. "Your coming back will not save me. I *do not* need to be saved. So don't try." She pointed her fingers toward him in accusation.

In his periphery, Adam looked over to Dan, Carlos, and Paul, who were staring at the dirt, looking like they'd literally rather get a blowjob from a shark than participate in this conversation. So much for support.

Adam always knew she would be the hardest to bring back around, but the intensity of her hate was surprising.

"You know I only live to please you, baby," Adam laughed.

"You're still such an ass," Mercedes said.

"Fine," Adam said. "I'll be careful and I won't touch you."

"*And?*"

Adam sighed. "And…fine, I won't try to *save* you." Looking out for her was second nature for him, this would be the hardest promise to keep. But little did she know he'd come back hoping *she* would save *him*.

"Good," she said, keeping his eye contact until she turned and began walking away. He couldn't help but notice her spinning her engagement ring on her finger once her back was turned. Like it was a nervous tic. He'd deal with that later.

"Ahhh, the Big Five!" Adam shouted.

She didn't look back as she flipped him off.

CHAPTER 4
BURNING UP

Mercedes pushed through the front doors of her mansion home. She'd felt more emotion in the past hour than she had in the past five years. The encounter at the old lot left her simmering with a deadly cocktail of rage…and something else that she wasn't willing to look too closely at. Either way, it was something she had to keep to herself now that she was back inside the discomfort of her home.

When the door slammed shut behind her, she saw Dorian's Seconds, T.B., Yani, and Antonio, all gathered in the adjacent living area. Luckily, Dorian wasn't with them to witness her late arrival.

"You're home late," T.B. smirked.

Observant little prick, he was.

She smiled and pulled a bottle of fine scotch from behind her back. "I couldn't show up empty-handed."

Walking into the crimson-walled lounge, she handed the bottle to T.B., who was leaning over the fireplace. A grand and elegant addition to the home, serving as a focal point which was only for show. Nobody needed artificial heating in Ridge City.

Passing the bottle down the line like it was a representation of their chain of command, Antonio finally popped it and poured a glass for everyone. Everyone except Mercedes. She'd already worked up quite the attitude over the afternoon's events, so she had to hold herself in extra tight to keep from lashing at him for that.

"This is a very nice bottle," T.B. said, savoring the taste as he sipped from a custom-made crystal glass with the letters D.B. initialed on the side. He didn't need to know that she'd actually bought the bottle for herself, planning to drown her emotions in solitude under layers of alcohol. Smother her feelings until they couldn't come up for air.

"And where is my future husband?" Mercedes said.

T.B., Yani, and Antonio shared a condescending laugh between them. She often had to pretend she wasn't aware of Dorian's extra-curricular activities. And pretend hard she did, because these geniuses weren't actually very good at hiding anything. Dorian had many girlfriends, she had somehow become his favorite one seeing as none of the others shared the same address, just the same man.

Yani finally spoke up. "Just finishing some things up at the Club."

Mercedes just raised her eyebrows. She should have been offended by how little they thought of her, but it worked in her favor so often that it wouldn't be smart to speak up. With nobody watching her, she could be busy watching them.

"And why are you still standing around here?" T.B. said. The others paid her very little attention, but T.B. had taken a special disliking to her.

She gathered that T.B. himself had no idea why he hated her so much. They were both drivers, even if T.B. didn't know it, they'd gone head-to-head on the roads many times before. He thought he was the best driver in the city. He was wrong.

"Going to bed," she said, teeth grinding.

The mansion was a decadent prison. The staircase was made of marble and gold stretching all the way up to the fifth floor. There were fine Italian sculptures of small men with tiny dicks littered throughout.

Fitting, she thought.

She was always gifted the most expensive jewels, always invited to the high-class parties. Lucky she was a good actor, because like an automatic transmission in a Corvette ZR-1, she didn't belong.

She slid under her silk sheets, still reeling from the day's events. Adam had come back to Ridge City. And that changed everything. Things that she didn't want changed.

She would pretend that Adam had no effect over her. That she didn't think of him. Because she conceded that while she knew he wasn't dead, the man she had loved all those years ago certainly was.

When they'd first fallen in love, Adam was wild and crazy. He never thought once about his actions. He acted selfishly and insanely. She used to love the way his mouth moved when he shouted every word he said with a passion, and how his eyes would bulge with an unpredictable insanity. His untamed brown hair would bounce whenever he threw a punch or took one. He was the brilliant kind of bulky, and incredibly broad shouldered. His body was built up by muscle, but was wide enough that it would take up just as much space even if it weren't. He had a strong grip that felt soft when he latched onto her hips.

Dorian was dangerous, too. Just not in the way that ordered her thighs to clench. While he did the kinds of bad things that she loved with a sickness, it just wasn't the same.

Snapping her from her thoughts, Dorian entered the bedroom, his suit messy and tie half undone.

"You're still up. Hello, darling," Dorian said. He finished removing his tie and stripped down, rushing into the bathroom to shower. When he returned and slid into bed beside her, she concluded the shower hadn't been long enough. He still smelled of so many different women that it was like a perfume store had thrown up on him.

"The boys said you bought them scotch." The silk sheets moved in between them as he placed his palm on her thigh. Her brain was stuck in comparison mode, and she struggled not to cringe. Dorian's hands on her thighs were like fluffy pillows, where Adam's used to be rough and calloused, so much so that they could cut her skin.

"Mmm, I hope they enjoyed it." She wiped the remaining night cream from her hands and returned her six-carat diamond engagement ring to her finger.

"They did. Too much. They're all tanked. Don't do that again."

"Sure." She wasn't fucking planning to, but damn if his disapproval didn't make her want to do it again.

Mercedes turned over in bed, hopeful that, as usual, he wouldn't stay long.

She also wished Adam wouldn't stay long. That he'd stayed away. She'd fought so hard to keep everyone together after he'd left. She gave everything she had to make sure she didn't lose the others the way she lost him, and him being back jeopardized every bit of hard work she had put into keeping them safe.

Dorian wasn't the love of her life. He wasn't a thrill. But being with him kept them safe. Only sometimes did she allow herself to miss the great love that she had when she was younger. Back in the day, she and Adam would have given up the world just for one last kiss. They would've killed, murdered, beaten their way through anything to find their way back to each other. It was a fire of love so strong she was sure she'd never have another in her lifetime. And after what it cost her the first time, she never wanted one like it again.

***

JULY 1985

Behind the bar at the Neptune Club, Mercedes spun the vodka in her hands, spilling droplets on the floor as it tipped upright, and she expertly poured the drink into six shot glasses.

Mercedes lived a double life. By night, she worked full time bartending at the Neptune Club. By day, she'd street race under an alias, sporting a black helmet to hide her face and her blonde hair. Dangerous, because she had to keep hidden. Worth it, because she was the best.

Sometime just before midnight, Paul appeared through the front doors of the club. He sat down at the bar stool in front of her, resting his hands on the sticky countertop, and shoveling peanuts into his mouth with the same tact as a circus elephant.

"Envelope for you, my dear." Paul slid a pay packet over the bar. She couldn't collect her own race winnings, not without giving away her cover. She'd either get Paul to pick them up on her behalf, or pretend to be her own girlfriend, picking up money for a racer boyfriend.

"So how much did you win on the track today?" Paul asked.

"A hot five hundred," Mercedes beamed. She served Paul a scotch on the rocks in a short glass…on the house, of course. "And you, my friend?"

Looking a little too smug for her liking, Paul smirked, rubbing his hands over his bald head and puffing up his chest. He was a brute of a man. Thin but still insanely muscular. His dark skin perfectly complemented his golden eyes, and contrasted magically against the gray shirts he insisted were his color. He was right. "You'd never believe me."

"Go on," Mercedes said. Tipping a mix into a shaker, she raised the drink above her head and shook.

"Two thousand."

"Fuck off," she said, slamming the shaker back onto the bar.

"And that was just my cut."

"It's those three guys you're hanging around with now, isn't it?" Mercedes sighed. Paul was her first and longest friend. Like a brother. His business was her business. Especially when he made it his business to be an idiot.

"They're good guys, M."

"I don't believe it," Mercedes said, pouring the contents of the shaker into a cocktail glass garnished with a lemon. "They're making dangerous work more dangerous than it has to be. Are you even picking up legitimate jobs? Who do they work for? The Blake's or the Cortez Cartel?"

Paul's mouth tightened, but Mercedes knew she had made her point. She nodded and went back to flipping liquor into shot glasses. "If you're not working for the Blake's or the Cortez Cartel, then you're asking to die."

"Mercedes." Paul lured her in with his finger. "Look me in the eye."

She wasn't overtly interested in listening, but for Paul she'd do him the courtesy of pretending to hear him out. Resting her hands on the bar, she leaned in.

"You are the best driver in this town. You drive circles around the fuckwits that these guys have working for them. Aren't you sick of being overlooked just because they can't see anything other than a pair of tits on you?"

Paul was right. Mercedes was the best driver in the city. By a mile. If she were a man, the money she would make would set her up for life.

"Fuck this system, fuck these guys, and fuck working for the Blake Family in this useless joint. Look," he said. "We need a driver for our next job."

"Of course." Mercedes broke away. That was plenty. She'd heard him out. "I knew you wanted something."

"I'm serious," Paul said. "If you've got skills, they won't give a shit what's in your shirt."

Mercedes glanced over Paul's shoulder where someone she'd never met before was making a direct approach toward her, his smile just as beaming as the insane look in his eyes. He was oozing confidence, and looked more alive than anyone should've felt in Ridge City. Every eye in the strip club turned to him, seeming to sense his aura. Threat? Unclear. But likely.

The mystery man pushed in between Paul and the adjacent bar stool, leaning across the counter and eyeing her up and down. "Well, hello."

"Mercedes Preston, this is Adam Vandemilio," Paul introduced.

"I don't care," she said. She really didn't. Turning her back, she began mixing cocktails behind the bar. But still, she watched them both from the mirrored wall in front of her where alcohol bottles sat on a perch. Paul was shrugging at Adam, but the arrogant-as-ever mystery man didn't look deterred. He looked sold.

She didn't react as she watched Adam jump the bar, inappropriately entering the area reserved for employees, and pressed his face over her shoulder. It was a challenge for her to ignore how close he was to the back of her body. It would only take one misstep for him to be pressing into her.

"Hey, I saw you race today," he said, his lips smacking together as he chewed on a toothpick.

Mercedes said nothing, trying to brush him off with the least amount of effort required.

"You left them all in your dust. It wasn't even a competition," he said.

"You caught that, huh?" she said, not for a second dropping her disinterested tone. She was certain Paul's new friends were bad news. Dodging the advance, she set five cocktails on a tray and moved onto the club floor.

Arrogant Adam followed her, jogging to keep up so he could whisper in her ear. "Yet you don't drive for either of the major gangs."

Well, that wasn't deserving of a response. A ridiculous observation, really. She placed some cocktails in the midst of a bachelor party and continued circulating the club floor.

"From what I can tell, you've got the skill."

Mercedes rolled her eyes, but continued to ignore him, pushing through the crowded room. As if she didn't already know how skilled she was.

"So, my questions is–" Adam started to say before a group of drunk customers pushed their way through, finally separating her from Adam's impending approach.

She took the opportunity to retreat deeper into the club, letting the patrons block his way. Checking over her shoulder, she watched as her over-confident suitor pushed around the swarming guests. Not wanting to be swayed, he jumped up and began stepping directly onto tables (stepping directly onto tables!) as he hopped over the booths, narrowly missing crushing fingers and drinks, and jump landed in front of her.

"Why?" he finished.

"Why what?" She slammed more cocktails down at a private booth.

"Why don't you drive for them?"

Mercedes scoffed. "Seriously. You know why."

"Enlighten me," Adam said.

Mercedes faced him, holding her empty tray in folded arms. "According to them, the only job women should be doing is one that's done on their knees or flat on their back."

He should've already known that, but when she looked at him, she noted he was genuinely confused, cocking his head from left to right like a cute little puppy that didn't understand human words.

"That makes no sense."

She shrugged. "The way they see it, with their small dicks and even smaller minds, it's hard to believe I'm capable of anything else."

"They underestimate you?" Adam asked. He squinted in confusion, and then a devilish smile spread across his face. The wickedness of his grin caught Mercedes's attention, drawing her in like she was prey, already stuck in a trap and waiting to be devoured by the very lips that smirked at her.

"That's good." He crossed his arms, eyes scanning the sky as if he were witnessing a thousand dirty dreams in his head. "That means they'll never see you coming."

"What's your game here?" Mercedes asked, giving him a skeptical look.

"There's no game. Not with you, at least. I just want you on my team."

"You want me to drive for you?"

He looked into her eyes like he really saw her. Not the girl slinging drinks behind a bar, not the trailer-raised, penniless kid. But a cunning mind. A vicious driver. He saw *her*.

"No, baby," he said, moving close to her face again. "I want you to drive *with* me. We go hard and we live to die. There is no in between, if you're in, you're in for life. It's dangerous, and maybe one day we'll fuck this up but, damn, we'll go out big."

***

FEBRUARY 1991

"Get into the fucking water, it's beautiful!" Dan screamed as he ran, fully clothed, into the open ocean.

After Mercedes had left them to return to her husband-to-be, Adam had spent the afternoon at the old lot making up for lost time with his three best friends in the world. They reminisced on the harebrained schemes they cooked up back in the day, drank hard liquor, and shot their empty bottles off the hood of his car.

When night fell, they ventured down to the beach across from Adam's hotel, the safe part of the city, where Dorian Blake would never find them.

With Dan's excitement, it was clear he was still coming down off the coke he insisted on having. "Did you hear me? The water!" Dan dipped his head fully under, shaking off his curls and dancing freely into the ocean.

Adam, Paul, and Carlos laughed from their spot on the beach, beer bottles in their hands.

"We're alright here, bud," Paul called back to him.

Ignoring his free-spirited friend dancing off into the ocean, Carlos smiled to Adam. "You know what I miss?" He pushed a cigarette into his mouth and flicked it alight before offering the pack to Paul. "Doing bad shit just for the fun of it."

"I feel like my life used to be so much bigger than it is now." Paul lit a cigarette over his own mouth and blew out a large puff of smoke.

"Back in the day, you know, whenever we would carry out a hit or finish a run it was just fucking fun. It used to give me this rush," Carlos said. "Fuck, man. I felt so high after any of those jobs."

Adam remembered the feeling fondly, hoping it was one he would find again someday. "Higher than I could ever get from drugs."

Adam and Carlos clinked their bottles.

"I don't get it," Carlos said. "It's exactly the same shit I used to do but it just... isn't the same. There's no conflict. No fire."

"That's our fault." Paul extinguished his cigarette in the sand.

"Yeah? How?" Adam asked, leaning his elbows back into the sand.

"You know about the Cortez Cartel?" Paul said. Adam nodded. He knew it well, just after he'd skipped town, the Cortez Cartel had all but disappeared. The gang that was once a bitter rival to the Blake Family...gone. Where there used to be a choice between Cortez or Blake, each empire as terrifying as the other, there was now only one. So just like the Cortez Cartel, the thrill was gone.

"None left anymore. On the surface, at least," said Carlos.

"Exactly. After you left, after we'd lost it all, the Cortez's basically had nothing left, either. We'd stolen it all," Paul said.

"We hit the Cortez's just as hard as we hit the Blake's, maybe harder, accidentally." Carlos made little rings in the air with his exhaled smoke.

"So it was all there for Blake to take," Adam sighed as he realized. "Fuck. We put the Blake Family in prime position to wipe out their last remaining rival in town."

A yelp from the ocean caught Adam's attention. A large wave had surprised Dan, and he bowled over, going under for long enough that Adam frowned in concern. Thankfully, he was quickly back up, shaking the water from his curls. "Fuck you, waves!"

The bastard was lucky he didn't drown.

"Alright," said Carlos, wiping the sand from his shorts. "I'm gonna go get this dickhead before he drowns himself." Carlos put out his cigarette in the sand and headed for the water.

Adam turned back to Paul and the topic at hand. "So Blake rounded up everyone in the Cortez Cartel, and what? Fucking killed them all?"

"Most of them. The big wigs all got executed. Some surely are in hiding. Others were converted to work for Blake. Same as us," said Paul.

Adam brushed his chin. "He's not worried about having all these angry people working for him?"

"Oh, he's not afraid of us," Paul laughed. "Carlos, Dan, me, we're all walking reminders of what happens when you try to fuck over Dorian Blake."

"But you stuck together."

"Of course, we fucking did. In for life, remember?" Paul clutched at the tattoo on his arm, cursive writing with the words written on it, and Adam wondered if Paul had meant to do that consciously. "Truthfully, we wouldn't have stuck together if Mercedes didn't make us. She made us stick together even when we wanted to run."

"Like I did?" Adam recoiled at the cheap shot, audibly gulping. He knew he fucked up by leaving them. He knew he shouldn't have waited as long as he had to come back. He also knew friends like his, who welcomed him back like family, were rarer than money or gems.

"I never blamed you for running."

"I had to. He thinks he killed me."

"Damn right. That's why I don't get it." Paul turned to face him. "You're the luckiest son-of-a-bitch that you got away the first time. I wanna help you, man, I really do. But why do you wanna come back here and face him again?"

Did he really not know the answer to that?

Carlos arrived back at their side, carting Dan over his shoulder. He deposited the giggling fool onto the sand, sitting down next to him as Dan began making sand angels.

"Nothing is the way it should be," Adam said. "I cannot let him win. I want my fucking life back."

Adam took a few calming breaths and gazed toward the water. "I want to *feel* something, goddammit. I miss you guys... and I will *never* be able to really feel alive again without–"

He glossed over the memories, stopping short of pouring his heart out onto the sand. Taking a sip of his bottle, he paused.

"Without?" Dan asked, red eyes crossing as he sat upright.

Adam hesitated. "Just without the life we made before. I want it back. And I want to keep it this time."

Adam returned his gaze to the ocean. He couldn't help but notice his friends share a look between them. Everyone knew the truth about what he really needed to feel alive again. And hopefully they were smart enough to recognize he'd deny it vehemently if they ever asked.

CHAPTER 5
KILL DORIAN BLAKE

FEBRUARY 1991

"Hey, baby," Adam smiled, jump landing through the open window into Mercedes's bedroom.

"What the fuck?!" Mercedes startled, clutching her heart. "What are you doing here? Trying to get yourself killed? I thought you were smarter than this now." She secured the mahogany double doors with a bolted lock.

Following suit, Adam closed the elegant box window behind him and helped himself onto on her sofa, running his fingers along the suede material. "Settle down, I knew you were alone."

"How did you even get up here? This is the third floor," she said, standing between his open legs and crossing her arms.

Adam flashed his teeth but didn't answer. Blake's historic mansion was heavily guarded, the only property on the street, and encircled by an abundance of lush gardens and all wrapped up and secured within high stone walls. But there was a low spot along the western edge that could be scaled, landing directly in the middle of the hedge maze. It was a short climb up the pool slide onto the trellis and into Mercedes's third-floor bedroom.

He pushed past her, pacing the room's spread of trinkets. "Living very large, I see." He snatched an elephant sculpture to juggle with.

"What do you want?"

"Straight to the point." He glanced at her over his shoulder, depositing the sculpture back in its place, though her salty tone secretly broke his heart. He missed the sparkle in her eyes that she had when she thought the world of him.

"The guys are coming by for a little heist planning. Come," he said. "They said I'd have to come get you."

"I always hated your heists."

"Don't flirt with me so openly," he begged, hand on his heart, but she didn't argue. Instead, she sat on the edge of her bed to pull on high-heeled boots. In front of her mirror she brushed her hair into a high ponytail and grabbed her pager from the nightstand. But Adam's eye had gotten stuck on the heeled boots, which made her long legs even longer, and had him drawing an eye up her entire body.

The years had been kind to her, indeed. He averted from looking at her ass as she bent down to pick up a jacket—for her privacy and for the sake of keeping his lap still. When his thoughts returned, she was staring at him. Sighing, she flicked her hand toward the window.

Right, yes, the window. They had places to be.

Clearing his throat, Adam did as instructed.

They followed his path down the trellis, along the pool slide and into the hedge maze. When they reached the stone wall, he pulled ahead, holding out his hands to boost her over.

"Fuck off, I can get over a wall." She proceeded to show him how. From a running start, she jumped to grab the wall with her fingertips, using her upper-body strength to hoist herself to the top.

Legs spread over the wall, she glared down at him, giving him a knowing look. She flipped to the other side, and Adam followed in the same, but much less graceful, movement.

His car was hidden behind a row of trees across the road, and when they reached the hood, she branched off to the passenger side—the wrong side, in his opinion—tugging at the locked door.

"Open the doors, Adam," she sighed as she ran a frustrated hand over her face before death-glaring him.

"You can't be serious." He frowned, resting his hands on the hood of the car.

"What?" She flicked the words off her tongue.

"Get in the fucking driver's seat." He tossed the keys across to her and she caught them with a hesitant frown.

It took her longer to get into the car than it did him, but once inside she stroked the steering wheel like it was the first time she'd touched it. She obviously hadn't been behind the wheel in a long time.

They had barely driven five minutes before Adam picked up the conversation, itching to get inside her head.

"So, Dorian Blake," Adam began. "Is he packing? Seems to me like he'd have a *tiny* dick."

"For fuck's sake." The car cruised cautiously through the back streets of the city, like any normal, law-abiding citizens, as Adam directed her toward his hotel along the beach.

"The dude gives off serious small dick energy, is all I'm saying." He smiled at her. "You don't really fuck this guy, do you?"

"We're engaged, so what do you think."

Ouch. Why did he ask? The idea of anyone else's arms holding her made him want to tear down concrete walls with his bare hands, and he definitely had the fiery anger to do so.

Adam rolled his hair in hands, looking over at her like a nervous kid with a crush. Which, he supposed, he was.

"A guy like that? No way he could satisfy you."

Her voice raised. "Oh really, what do you know?"

"I know you don't love him."

That shut both of them up. Adam paused to gauge her reaction. It could have gone either way. Why after all that had happened would she willingly climb into bed next to Dorian Blake?

There were only two options that he could possibly conceive. Either Blake had swept her off her feet and she was maddeningly in love with him, or, she had no choice.

She kept her stare toward the road, the clicking of the turn signal amplifying the silence.

Adam could guess exactly which one it was when she chose not to answer. "I know what love looks like on you. You're not wearing it right now."

After a few seconds of silence, she spoke up. "You're my past, Adam. Dorian Blake is my future. I don't think you know me well enough anymore to have any idea what I'm feeling."

He turned to her with wide eyes. Sure, she shared a bed with Dorian Blake (for now), but she shared all her secrets with him. He knew her heart better than he knew his own.

But what if he *was* wrong?

He flicked his tongue against the back of his teeth as they drove in silence. If she was right, if he really didn't know her anymore, and if she really did think that Dorian Blake was her future, she would *not* be happy with what he was about to say.

***

Adam opened the door to his room at the Tropics Hotel. Dan, Carlos, Paul, and Mercedes all stepped inside, their eyes catching on the walls strewn with newspaper clippings and mad ramblings.

"It looks like a serial killer hideout in here, man. You might need psychiatric help," said Dan.

"I can recommend someone good." Carlos clapped Adam on the back.

"You weren't kidding about the five-year revenge plan," Paul said.

Adam shrugged, not bothered by the mess he had already created. Though he did have to admit, it didn't make him look sane.

Carlos went to the window and lit up a cigarette, while Dan and Paul examined the papers along the walls, running their fingers along the texts.

"Well," Mercedes said, throwing dirty clothes off a stained polyester chair and sitting down. "You're looking certifiable. What did you bring us here for?"

"He said he had a plan," Paul said absent-mindedly, still raking over the walls.

"Oh, you have a plan?" she teased, lying back in the chair. Her hair flicked over the back and rippled like a wave in the water, testing all his self-control.

"I do, and the plan is simple."

"Go on, then," Mercedes smiled.

"Kill Dorian Blake."

The room went still and silent.

Even the background noise from the street seemed to disappear, as if the whole world stopped to catch its breath when those three fatal words were uttered. As if anyone would ever be stupid enough to say that phrase out loud.

Carlos lost his cigarette out the window while Dan fumbled a stack of papers he was holding right into the sink. The two friends exchanged a glance and then slowly looked toward Adam in unison, but Paul and Mercedes were already glaring at him.

They looked at him like he'd suggested they all sprout wings and fly to the moon, and honestly, that would be just as likely as ever successfully carrying out his revenge plan.

"Whoa, I thought we were just going to find a way to get you back in without dying?" Dan mumbled.

All eyes were on Adam, but his eyes were on Mercedes. Her expression was vacant, head down and staring with narrowed eyes, the same hard look she'd been giving him all day.

"You want to fucking kill Dorian Blake?" said Carlos. "You're madder than you used to be. Paul, did you know about this?"

Paul drew a sharp breath and scrubbed his hands over his face.

"You did!" Dan sprinted toward Paul, placing an accusatory finger on his chest and pushing him back with it. "You knew about this when you talked us into coming here."

Adam let his crew argue among themselves, allowing Paul to take the lead in turning Dan and Carlos around, because he knew they eventually would. Selling them on the plan was never going to be a problem.

Mercedes was the full focus of Adam's attention in that moment. To him, it felt like a turning point. Sure, she'd kept all his secrets, but how far would she go for her new fiancé? Which one was it going to be? Did she love Dorian Blake? Or did she want him gone just as badly as Adam did?

"Yeah, okay. I did know," Paul said.

"What the fuck?" Carlos said. "Even talking about this puts our heads on the chopping block!"

"Our heads were in jeopardy as soon as we agreed to come here...and let's face it, working for Blake has our necks moments away from the guillotine as it is," Paul said. "And our balls were *already* snipped."

The friends continued arguing in what seemed like background noise to Adam. He watched as Mercedes's breath heaved from her chest, her body growing stiffer, her brown eyes growing blacker.

Adam could only make out the brief sounds of Paul turning his friends in his favor. Whether they wanted to or not, the only way to take down Dorian Blake, and ensure he stayed down forever, was to take him out.

Mercedes would have to wait.

Adam turned back to his friends. "Blake has this city now because I fucked it up and underestimated him the first time. Dorian Blake has to die. That's how we secure our future."

Carlos and Dan exchanged a look, an eyes-only conversation passing between them. They had to realize that with how deep this rivalry now ran, between Adam and Blake, only one could live.

"Fine," Carlos said. "I see it. I see your point. In that case, let's just have Mercedes slit his throat while he's sleeping, hey?" Carlos looked to Mercedes with an easy grin.

"No!" Paul shouted. "We have to make sure we're in a prime position to take that spot when he goes down. There's always a next in line. T.B., Yani, Antonio. Somebody else will just take his place...and quickly."

"They will have to die, too," Adam said.

"Blake has leads in all the legal systems. Lawyers, cops, feds, all of us on his books," Dan reminded them, pacing around the room manically, drifting between bursts of fear and bursts of psychotic excitement.

"I know," Paul said. "But he thinks Adam is dead. That's an advantage if there ever was one."

"Are you sure we can't just kill him in his sleep?" Carlos sighed.

"No," Adam said. "I'm going to be the one to kill him. And I want him to look right in my eyes while I do it."

"Fuck yes!" Dan said, jumping on the spot. "Let's fucking go, then. Time to fuck shit up!"

Adam had to hand it to himself, he was one lucky son-of-a-bitch. How he'd lucked out with the best, most loyal, family on the planet, he didn't know. He sure wasn't worthy of them.

"So we're all on board?" Paul asked.

Carlos and Dan nodded back. In perfect unison all four boys turned their heads to look at Mercedes, who still hadn't stirred even an inch, but her evil eyes followed Adam every step he moved.

Looking back at Paul, the two exchanged a worried glance.

"M?" Paul prodded.

At the mention of her name, her eyes jumped to Paul, then to Dan, then to Carlos. Gauging from the tension in the room, Adam guessed her affections toward Blake were not just a mystery to him.

"No," she said, so quietly it was almost hard to hear.

"M..." Paul said.

"No," she said, this time sternly.

Rising from her chair, she picked up her coat and calmly walked toward the door. Just as Adam thought she was about to leave, she turned and shot him a filthy look, filled with so much venom that he actually jumped back. She was gone in a flash, slamming the door behind her so hard that it rattled the windows.

Adam's sense of self-control slowly shed from his body. Like he was physically on fire and steam was rising from his heated flesh.

He chanced a look over at his friends. They just looked shocked, watching him to see what he would do.

Every piece of himself that he was keeping closed in, to remain calm, was bubbling up to the surface, and ready to explode. Two choices. She either loved Dorian, or she was going to kill him. And Adam jumped recklessly to the conclusion that if she wasn't against Blake, then she must be in love with him.

With that thought, he was gone, all the restraint he gained blew right out the door with him. He charged down the stairs just as furiously as she did, letting out a low rumbling as he chased her.

Throwing the glass doors open, he caught her on the street.

"Hey!" he yelled, the anger consuming him, rising from his gut and exploding out his mouth. "What the fuck?!"

"You want to fucking murder my fiancé?" She yelled right back, the fire from her lips just as passionate and furious as his.

Suddenly realizing his public surrounding, Adam grabbed Mercedes by the arm and dragged her into the quiet, wet and dirty alleyway behind the hotel until they were covered by a shade of darkness.

"You want to kill the man I'm going to marry," Mercedes seethed, her rabid face twisting with rage.

"You're *not* marrying that idiot," Adam said, eyes bulging out of his head, feeling like they might pop like a balloon.

She came within inches of his face, until their chests were pressed flush against one another. "You're asking me to join a murder plot against the man I sleep next to every night."

"What *are* you doing sleeping next to him every night?!"

Pushing off him, Mercedes retreated farther into the alleyway.

Adam followed, the embers spitting from his mouth like little flames from a fire. "Hey! You gonna answer me?! What are you doing up there in that fucking mansion? Sleeping next to him? Fucking him? Wearing his ring on your fucking finger? You don't love him, you don't even like him!"

"I'm protecting my friends! I'm protecting this fucking family," Mercedes screamed back, her hair twirling as she turned. "Being next to Dorian in that bed every night keeps them alive. *That's* how we secure our future."

She looked at him like he was the biggest idiot on the planet. Like she couldn't possibly loathe him more if she tried.

"You think I don't want to protect this family?" Adam kicked the garbage container next to him, its contents spilling out on the concrete. The alleyway echoed the sound of shattered glass and reeked with the smell of alcohol.

"So you love him?" Adam shouted again, his yell scratching at his throat.

"I'm doing what I have to do to keep everyone—"

"Do you *fucking love him*??" Adam said.

"*No!!*" Mercedes said, launching forward as if she were throwing the words at him with force, her breath coming out like a deadly strong gust of wind.

Hearing it, though, he wasn't sure if that admission made him feel any better. He hadn't been that angry in years, and as violently pissed as he was with Blake, only she could make him so passionate. Aggressively or otherwise.

Her face twisted with regret, as if she hadn't meant to say that and the words were sour on her tongue.

She stepped back until they were staring at each other with panting breaths from a few feet away. Eyes shuttering, she shrugged as she tucked a loose hair behind her ear.

Calming down, Adam said, "Then are you gonna fucking help me kill him or not?"

She only shook her head, not as if she wasn't agreeing, but as if she couldn't take any more questions.

Walking to his side, she shoved her hand into his pockets. "Give me this," she spat, pulling out the keys to his car and striding off in the opposite direction from him.

"You can't take my car," he called to her.

But it was no use, she'd already left.

***

"I have to say, when you said you had a plan I thought you'd, you know, actually have a plan." Dan gave him a disapproving look as he read through the files laying across Adam's dining table.

Adam had come back up from his argument with Mercedes to the friends who were actually still on his side. But his heart felt hollow, and his regret was a sinking ship in his stomach. "It's a little lite on–"

"Fucking hell, this is just a bunch of useless notes, Adam. This isn't a plan," Dan said.

"Look, it is a plan. It's a list of everything we need to take from Blake in order to be powerful enough to take over." Adam paced around his room, pointing out items on the wall, but noticing that Carlos and Paul, who were sitting on the end of the bed, shared a nervous glance between one another.

"See this—this is what we need to control—you've got the prostitutes, the arms trade–" Adam continued about the room. Though he could tell the erratic nature of his movement wasn't inspiring confidence among his friends. "Um, and the drug trade, and his property, and—wait, I'm sure there's more around here somewhere."

Adam flicked through papers, throwing them about to find the one he was looking for. He looked over at Paul, who merely shook his head, giving him a very clear signal to stop talking.

"It's a little undercooked, I'll admit," Adam said, running his hands through his hair. "But I had to come back here before this was all fully fleshed out. We're running out of time. Blake is about to become the mayor."

"A great point," Paul said. "Once he becomes Mayor, the city budget will fund whatever he wants. The law will officially be in his hands. There won't be anything he can't do."

"Maybe he won't get in," Carlos shrugged, leaning back farther onto the bed.

"He'll get in," Dan scoffed, pushing papers about the table. "And if he doesn't, he'll just rig the vote so he does."

"It puts a definite timeline on things," Paul said.

"It means we can't let him become Mayor," Carlos said.

"Or we have to kill him before he does," Dan suggested.

Adam nodded. "See? The plan is simple. We have to steal all these things, and then kill him, and then we take over."

"Oversimplified." Dan rolled his eyes.

"It's all about power. The people will follow whoever has it," Adam said. "Guys, come on, trust me here. Imagine what we can do when we set our minds to it. Fully fleshed plan or not."

Paul's face gave away that he wasn't full convinced, but he still came to the rescue. "He's right. Last time we very nearly took Blake down. And we... kind of helped take down the Cortez's."

Carlos stood up and smiled. "If anyone could do it, it would be us."

"It will be us," Adam smiled back.

Dan rested his arms on the table. "But you walked back up here alone, so it's not really all of us, is it?"

Paul looked directly at Dan and waved his index finger in a throat-slashing gesture.

"She'll come around." Adam folded his arms.

"She never really did tell us why she's with him. What if she actually does lo—"

"She's not in love with him," Adam snapped. He looked down at the floor. "I would know."

"She'll come around," Paul agreed, standing behind Adam to intimidate Dan into stopping that conversation dead in its tracks.

"Alright," Dan said, he stood to survey the core pieces of evidence that Adam had collected. "So we need to find a way to steal all of *this*, which we failed to do last time, by the way, and we need to do it in half the time, without Blake realizing that we're doing it, all before he gets elected as Mayor."

Adam cocked his head in a smug smile. "Exactly. Piece of cake."

CHAPTER 6
FOR YOU I WILL

Motor off, the boat rocked with the waves of the river. The water sparkled like crystal underneath, the breeze humming as it blew hot Ridge City air around them.

They were alone on the water with a perfect view of the city, and only the crashing of the waves to keep them company. Dressed for the tropical weather, Adam pulled at his pastel Hawaiian shirt to create a breeze toward his chest. With him, Dan, Paul, and Carlos gathered at the bow, waiting. Far in the distance, a three-story Ferretti Yacht, owned by the Blake Family, served as the location of a party.

Adam surveyed his assembled team, one person down, unable to shake the feeling that without her not only his team, but his life, was incomplete. Forcing ahead without her felt wrong, but what choice did he have? He wanted more than what could be done with only the four of them.

Adam watched the party through binoculars, spying as guests enjoyed champagne on the top deck, and seedy businessmen with bikini-clad women on their arm closed curtains on the lower levels.

Dan yanked the binoculars from Adam's hand. "Would you look at that. Who knew this was how the other half lived?"

Paul held a second set. "I don't see anything yet. Nothing that looks like a deal is going down. Any of these people look important?"

Paul deferred to Carlos, who took the spyglass in turn. "No one so far."

"Drop me in," Adam said as he headed to the stern.

"You wanna go in?" Dan asked. "This is only supposed to be a recon mission. We're not meant to actually get on the fucking yacht."

"I can do recon from on the yacht just as well," Adam said, hitching his shoulder to start the motor.

"And what if you're seen?"

"Blake's at the range the whole day," said Paul. As if that excused it.

"Everyone on that boat is low level. No chance they'll know or even remember who Adam Vandemilio is," Carlos agreed, his eyes still glued to the binoculars.

Dan pushed Adam aside and took over his failed attempts to start the motor, managing to hit it first go before sailing off easily toward the yacht and giving Adam a smug look.

An approach from the east side was ideal, guests were arriving every ten minutes from the west, leaving the east side fully untended. Upon their final approach, Dan killed the motor, allowing them to silently drift toward the deck. Taking a gun and radio from within the plush back bench seat, Adam jumped onto the bow.

"We'll head back out and watch for any activity," Paul said.

"Buzz us when you want out…or if you're captured or killed. Give us a head start to flee, at least," winked Dan.

The height of the speedboat paled in comparison to the yacht. It had only brought him in at the lower enclosed deck. Not enough to get up to the open level. Adam couldn't even see the deck from where he stood. But boy, did he love a challenge.

Stashing the gun in the back of his pants, Adam cocked his neck and flexed his muscles to warm up. But when he jumped up onto the side of the yacht, grabbing hold of the window railings, he couldn't hide the smug smile that displayed the fact he hadn't needed to warm up his muscles at all.

He pulled himself to stand upright on the window rail and jumped once more to the above deck to join the party guests.

The unconventional entry earned him a few curious glances. He was well under-dressed, but it didn't stop him strutting confidently through the crowd. Confidence was key, after all. Fake it til you make it, right?

Groaning, Adam decided it was well past time to head below deck when "Ice Ice Baby" came roaring over the sound system. He'd had quite enough already. Especially when that particular song was playing.

After finding a door and making his way below deck, Adam landed in a large corridor with blue linoleum flooring and shut doors lining either side of the hall. He walked with his head down and his hand perched on his gun. The incoming light on his radio glowed red.

"Go," he said.

"Someone's pulled up at the back of the yacht, see if you can get close enough to find out what's going on," Paul said.

"Got it."

At the end of the corridor was an open door that housed a small storage room and bifold doors that looked out onto the open back deck. Adam ducked behind the door as he spotted men loading powder-filled white satchels into storage.

"Drug shipment," Adam whispered into the radio.

"Damn, right out in the open, Blake's are cockier than I thought," Carlos said.

"Drug shipment is bigger than we prepared for, we'll come get you out," Paul said.

Adam hesitated, looking back and forth between his radio and the shipment. He really wanted to take it. In the old days, he would've. But he knew better now, and he knew they needed a better plan before pulling off something so big.

"Adam?" Paul buzzed through the radio again, skepticism in his voice. Truthfully, Adam was just as skeptical as they were that he could really change his careless approach.

"Yeah, okay, I'm on my way ba–"

"You're not supposed to be down here! Who the hell are you?!"

Well, shit.

One of the drug shippers was coming right at him, angrily wagging a finger.

His team was going to be pretty disappointed with him, he had promised them he was no longer reckless. But it wasn't his fault, right? There was no other way out of this one. The thugs practically gave him no choice.

"You're gonna wanna get back here." Adam spoke slowly into the radio, and his capturer narrowed his eyes.

"What? Why?" Paul's panicked voice replied.

Adam rushed from behind his cover, giving the guy a pitied smile before drawing his weapon and firing three shots right into his head.

"Intruder!" Alarms began sounding on the lower decks, flashing red.

Bursting through the bifold doors, Adam stumbled out onto the back deck where the shipment was still being loaded into storage. Sliding over a wooden crate filled with cocaine probably, judging from the leaking white powder, Adam kicked one of the guards and spun quickly to land a punch to another.

The favor was returned, and Adam fell to the floor. He stumbled as blood poured from his nose. Recovering quickly, he snapped his hand around an approaching worker's neck, and with the other fired his gun at another who rushed him.

A rumble sounded in the background. Adam blanched, recognizing the sound of the drug boat starting up for a getaway. No fucking way were they getting away that easy.

Adam threw the guy he was holding down hard, stomping on his face to knock him out. He rushed toward the loading boat, ducking punches as he did, and once he reached it he jumped onto the bow, pushing forward.

A masked man, who had been frantically trying to drive the boat away, lifted his head with a fearful look as Adam grabbed his collar and threw him overboard.

With perfect timing, the last boat worker stilled, a gunshot wound to the chest. When that poor fucker dropped, Paul was standing behind him, gun in hand, and staring at Adam with a look of parental disappointment. "Really?"

"Bitch later. Fight now. No time to talk." Adam winked. There really was no time to discuss the recklessness of the plan, the fight was still in full swing, and Adam had every intention of taking full advantage of it.

Carlos and Dan were swiftly on the deck of the yacht, hastily picking up the plastic drug satchels and throwing them onto their own powerboat. Chaos ensued. Their movements were erratic and panicked, it was unplanned, and crazy, and it was *so much* fucking fun.

"What the fuck are we doing?" Dan asked, flapping about with the satchels.

"Fucking improvising!" Adam shouted back as he and Paul returned to the yacht. Heavy pattering footsteps arrived on the upper deck, giving the guards a clear height advantage, as they lined up in offense.

The first gunshot sounded—cracking through the satchel that Dan held above his head, splitting it open and throwing cocaine into the air. Raining down right into Dan's face. He fell to the floor, but somehow managed to inhale the coke like a madman.

Gunfire pooled from the sky like a rain shower.

Ducking behind a wooden crate, Adam returned fire at the deck above. They wouldn't make ground that way, though. A sharp nod to Paul gave the unspoken order to lay down cover fire.

As his friends did as instructed, raining bullets, too, Adam made a break to the port side, bolting upstairs.

That drew the guard's attention.

Oh shit, that drew more attention than he anticipated.

Adam dove behind one of the makeshift bars as guests ran wildly around him. He looked down to the lower deck, his friends were utilizing the distraction and ensuing chaos to load up the rest of the shipment.

Standing with a bounce, Adam found renewed energy as he fired, taking out five who attempted to circle him.

"We're loaded, man. Let's go!" His radio buzzed in his pocket.

Without warning, Adam's head banged sharply against the wall. Someone got the jump on him and was smashing his face into the wall. Adam buckled, face bloody. He drew his weapon and fired blindly, obviously hitting his target given the spray of blood splashing his face.

Panting and covered in blood, Adam spoke into the radio. "Drive to the front." He narrowly avoided the gunfire that chased him as he ducked inside the party. Guests were still lingering about, huddled under tables of champagne and delicious canapés dressed in all their finery.

Though his pursuers were right behind him. He spun, running through revolving doors into the galley. Kitchen staff scrambled as he dove through the fray, dodging him as he took the opportunity to knock pots and pans from the stove, causing little fires to ignite everywhere.

He had to feed the flames.

He began yanking cooking oils and supplies from the wall, throwing anything he could at the fire until it suddenly intensified with a bang, cutting his attackers off from him.

Peeling out from the galley onto the deck, he caught his breath, squinting into the sun before he pulled himself up to the highest level of the yacht. Making sure to keep an eye on his friends, Adam watched as they rounded the starboard side.

He wiped the sweat from his eyes and ran along the upper deck as the fire spread through the lower decks. At full speed he reached the end of the yacht's gunwale and jumped, hurling himself from the top into the depths of the water below, legs outstretched.

He held his breath, the rush of water blowing past his face as he was taken under by the current. He let the water roll his body underneath the surface until he could finally regain control.

Adam shook the water from his hair as he emerged in a spray from the depths of the sea. At that moment, his crew's powerboat shuttled past him, and Adam held his hand out in readiness. The powerboat sped past without stopping or slowing, and Paul grabbed Adam's hand from the water, pulling him from its liquid grasp and into the boat.

Lying wet on the floor, laughing at his success, Adam watched the sky circle until finally they leveled off the speed.

"Fucking scene that is," said Carlos.

Finally sitting upright, Adam stopped to admire his handiwork. Sure enough, Dorian Blake's prized party yacht was engulfed in flames. Almost like it had waited until it got his full attention, the yacht then exploded, leaving guests diving into the water below to save themselves.

"There must be at least a hundred thousand worth of shit here," Dan noted as he rifled through the drug cargo they'd stolen. "What the hell are we gonna do with all this?"

"I can move it," Carlos said.

"How?" Paul asked.

"I'll just run it with Blake's regular drug supply and take the cash for ourselves. Blake will never know, and the dealers will never know they're selling anything other than Blake shit."

"That's... actually a really good idea," Adam smiled, sitting up with his elbows resting on his knees.

"It's called having a plan," Carlos teased.

***

DECEMBER 1985

It was a December tradition in Ridge City to celebrate the holiday season with a string of festivals on its rich sandy beaches. The biggest attraction

84

was the boardwalk, a wooden deck set up over the sand, with a tiki bar, tables, chairs and a row of seats along the back to look out over the water.

With high spirits, Adam and his crew came to the beach to celebrate the success of a small job they completed that day. When they arrived, the place was already packed tighter than a toy store on Christmas Eve. And had a similar amount of gusto.

Young partiers pushed past Adam, all wearing bikinis and shorts to display their beach bodies, as he worked through the crowd.

He found Mercedes nestled along the boardwalk, hands resting on the wooden bar, sipping on a cocktail as she gazed out over the ocean. It was as if the sky opened only to let the sun shine onto her golden hair, and the crowd parted like the sea to clear his path to her.

"Hello, you." He sounded breathless. Like he'd run a marathon sprint to get to her side, and while he felt like that could be true, his breath was lost to her because his heart was, too.

He placed his hand on the small of her back, and Mercedes pushed back her mirrored sunglasses to kiss him with passion, pulling away with a smile that made him feel like the world rested directly in his palm.

"What're we drinking?" Paul popped his head in between them, killing the moment. Perhaps intentionally, Adam thought, judging by the smug look on his face.

"Any kind of whiskey," Adam replied.

"Another, please." Mercedes waved her cocktail glass, handing it to Paul, who moved off to take more orders from Dan and Carlos who were sitting at a table nearby.

"I'm already feeling a little buzzed, you know," Mercedes said. "I don't think it's the booze."

Adam smiled at her gentle tone. "And why might that be, baby?"

"You seem to think you have all the answers. Can't you guess?"

For a moment he lost himself in her eyes, twinkling in the sunset. Not dreamy, but mesmerizing and hypnotic, like a thunderstorm. Then her lips, peachy and pink, but thin and taut like a predator's. God knows, Adam knew she liked to bite.

"Come help me carry the drinks," Paul ordered, clasping Adam on the shoulder, and, for the second time that day, ruining the moment. Once again, that bastard was smirking.

Only having been at the bar for a few moments, leaning against it with his elbows, Adam chanced a look over his shoulder at the girl to whom he had a serious confession to make.

But what he saw dropped all those floaty, airy feelings right out of him. Back at the boardwalk, Dorian Blake was approaching Mercedes, leaning over her and smirking like she was the most delicious meal he'd ever eyed. And he was simply waiting to devour her.

Adam's smile turned into a wary frown, and the way Blake stroked Mercedes's upper arm was enough to make him forget all about the drinks being piled up in front of him and strut right over to where they stood.

Adam sidled up next to Mercedes on the deck and kept his eyes trained forward. Listening, but poised to back her up. Blake didn't know who Adam was, *yet*, and wouldn't sense the threat until it had him in a choke hold.

"You are a vision today, darling," Blake said, his finger stroking her tanned skin.

"You're a shameless flirt," Mercedes replied with a smile, but still she subtly removed Blake's hand.

"You enjoy my parties?"

"You throw a good party, you know that," she agreed, and Adam cringed at the sound of her flirtatious voice.

Even at the beach, Blake still dressed in his business suit with the sleeves pushed up to reveal the expensive watch on his wrist and the diamond rings on his fingers. His clean white skin was a far cry from Adam's rough, olive-toned and heavily tattooed sleeve. Watching Mercedes with him, he realized that he and Blake were polar opposites, two ends of a completely unrelated spectrum.

"Maybe you come by my place a bit later. After you're done messing around here."

Adam stiffened.

"Was that a question?"

"More like a command," he smiled. A man of power, he was used to getting what he wanted. There was no one who would refuse him anything. Except the fiery girl whom Adam had come to fall in...*care for.*

"Oh, please," Mercedes scoffed. "I won't fall into your bed that easily."

He laughed at her rejection. "Then I'll consider it a challenge." He winked before walking away and disappearing out of sight.

"Thanks for the help," Paul said in jest, pushing between them to set their drinks down. Cocktail for Mercedes, whiskey for Adam, before he went to sit with Dan and Carlos.

"What was that?" Adam asked. The anger at seeing Blake's face eclipsed by a different emotion this time. He was jealous. *Fucking jealous.* But all the more was his curiosity at the bashful woman who was bold enough to turn down Dorian Blake.

"Oh, that? A frustration," Mercedes replied. She removed the lemon from the edge of the glass and took a sip. A frustration was a start. He could work with that.

"Flirting with Dorian Blake? In broad daylight?" Adam teased. "Do you know him or something?"

"Just from the club. He's been... *pursuing* me for a while." Her body contracted like she was allergic to the thought.

"I understand where he's coming from," Adam smirked.

"It's just smart to play his game."

"Good girl," Adam said, holding out an outstretched hand. "Come with me for a minute."

Mercedes hesitantly put down her drink and stared at him with playful intrigue, but still she didn't accept his hand.

"Trust me." Adam cocked his head.

She slipped her hand into his. Dragging her away from the boardwalk bar, he drew her from the crowds to a spot where they could be alone. They walked through the sand dunes and over the hill until the party music was just a low whistle in the distance.

Sitting down on the sand and brushing remnants of the grit from his thick, hairy legs, Adam patted the spot next to him. She tucked her dress under her legs and joined him, sitting up on her knees.

"I have something for you," he said.

"You do?"

"It's your holiday gift."

"Is it?" She leaned closer into him and let him brush her long blonde waves from her face. There it was, that magic spell of hers again. It did something to him. Made his heart feel like it was both beating faster, and like it had stopped completely. He knew without question that he would never feel that way about anyone else. Every time he was around her, all rational thinking went out the window.

"You had something for me?" She laughed when he had gone a period of time without speaking.

Oh right, the gift.

Clearing his throat, Adam retrieved a small gift box from his pocket and held it in his outstretched hand. Her expression turned serious as she accepted the gift, holding the box in both hands. "You stole it for me?"

"No, baby," he said, laughing. "I bought it for you. It's not much, but I wanted this gift to be real."

She opened it slowly. The edges creaked as it snapped open, and laying gently on a cushioned bed was a delicate diamond necklace in the shape of the infinity symbol. Mercedes gasped, frowning as if she thought the gift was far too much to accept.

Adam watched her closely, losing himself in her nervous smile. He ran his fingers over her hands, which were still clutching the box, and then over the diamond necklace. "It's for infinity," he explained. "How you and me are forever. How I will always protect you and be there for you... How I *love* you. How I will love you now and forever. For infinity."

It was the first time he'd ever told her what he knew in his heart from the moment he met her. Frankly, it was the first time he'd ever said it to anybody, and he hazarded an educated guess that she would be the only person he'd ever say it to.

He waited for what felt like an eternity for her reply, searching for an answer in her frozen expression.

"It's perfect," she finally said with a smile. His smile spread, too, the corners of his lips pushing at his eyes. He pulled the necklace from the box, and she lifted her hair to allow him to place it, letting it fall against her chest. She grabbed his cheeks with two hands and pulled him into a soft, warm kiss. Sweet and thoughtful and lazy, like melted ice cream on a hot summer day.

As their kiss broke, she whispered in his ear the words he'd hoped she'd repeat, "I love you, too."

***

FEBRUARY 1991

Adam watched Mercedes from across a crowded room.

He'd found her at the country club ballroom, mindlessly chattering with wealthy gang wives, each looking more high-pitched and screechy than the last. Their faces endowed with so much plastic surgery, it was as if they'd been whiplashed.

For a random Tuesday evening the country club was surprisingly full, so it'd been harder to catch her attention than he first thought.

Adam stood in the arch of the service corridor, disguising himself as best he could, but putting him in her line of sight. Before she could sit down, she finally locked eyes with him, and he inclined his head in signal.

He saw her raise her finger to her friends, a universally recognized gesture as the polite signal for *fuck off*... Or maybe it was just *give me a moment*.

When she made her way deep into the service corridors, Adam pushed through the bustle of waiters carrying trays and clasped her wrist to pull her aside.

She flicked his hand off of her. "What do you want?" It seemed she was in no mood for small talk.

"I just wanted to apologize," Adam said.

"Oh." She relaxed her body but not her face, keeping her chin high.

"For the fight. I don't want to fight," he said.

She pinched the bridge of her nose. "You need to go. Before someone sees you."

Over her shoulder Adam spotted one of Mercedes's dinner guests rounding the corner and heading right toward them, eyes slitted with suspicion like she was searching for something. *Probably for Mercedes tangled up in her ex-boyfriend's arms.* Wouldn't that be delightful.

"First–" He grabbed her arm, pushing her with him into a supply closet just as the dinner friend rounded the corner.

He pressed her up against the wall and shielded her with his body, focusing his sight on the hallway but purposefully, and a little deviously, making sure every part of him connected with every part of her.

The guest hadn't spotted them, only searching the hallway briefly before disappearing as quickly as she came.

Mercedes shoved Adam away, carefully stepping over brooms, mops, and buckets in the supply closet as he tripped backward. "Always an agenda with you."

"What? I was just saving you."

"Pretty sure I warned you not to do that on more than one occasion." She brushed down the ruffles in her dress.

"Being close to me doesn't suck, though, does it?" he said. "You love it."

"Really," she smirked, advancing on him and forcing him back against the adjacent wall. "I'm the one who loves it?"

She spread her hands across his chest and licked her top lip, her face close enough to his to feel her breath. The look in her eyes was wild and lustful, his one of absolute weakness. And he wanted *more*.

Panting out some nonsensical words and becoming suddenly weak, Adam decided against averting his gaze, despite the swelling in his pants.

She must've felt it, though, because she pulled away with a victorious smile, like the excited little traitor in his pants had proven her point. But her eyes caught on the bruises on his face for a second too long.

"You know, one of Dorian's yachts caught on fire earlier today." She raised her brow.

"I heard," he said, cockily running his hands through his hair.

"He lost a lot of product. He's very upset. It's dangerously... unattractive."

Adam shrugged. "So having second thoughts?"

"I thought you were only going out there to do recon? Not blow up his favorite yacht."

How did she know they were only there to do recon? She hadn't tagged along.

"Paul told you." Adam realized and folded his arms, feeling smug. "Can't help but check up on me, can you, baby?"

She huffed with a sharp exhale through her nose, like she was one step away from breathing fire. Throwing the door open, she stalked up the hall. She was a few paces ahead, but still he called to her.

"Come on. Please. You want to take him down, don't you?" She stopped, but didn't turn. "Help me. I can't do it without you, baby."

"My God, no," she yelped. "You're putting everyone in danger, ruining everything we've done to build lives without you. To be safe."

"Baby," Adam said. "A safe life isn't a great life. Nothing worth having ever comes easy."

"My life is fine just the way it is."

"Is it? I don't know why you're sleeping next to Dorian Blake every night, I really, really don't. But I'm sure there must be a reason."

She shrugged and shook her head, but the gesture was more annoyed than anything else.

"Whatever the reason is, I'm sure it wasn't so that Dorian Blake could get everything he ever wanted. Was it?"

She paused, staring at him, her eyes intense and angry, but also giving away slivers of hurt. She had built up such a hard shell, if Adam didn't know her so well, the pain could very well be mistaken for anger.

"Fine," she relented. "Not for you, though. I won't do it for you. But I will help."

"You will?" he said, failing to hide his surprise.

"Yes, I will fucking help you take him down. But be certain that I'm only doing it for Paul, Dan, and Carlos. *Never* for you."

Adam smirked, breaking past the façade and getting straight to the point. *Why* she felt it was so important to specify that. "Oh, it's all for me, isn't it, baby?"

"Fucking hell," Mercedes sighed. "Just tell me why, Adam?" She closed her eyes. "Can't you just leave well enough alone?"

Adam exhaled sharply, clenching his jaw and shaking his head. "You know exactly why."

At his hard stare, she nearly softened. But he'd been holding this pain and this grudge a lot longer than five years. And he couldn't stop the words from forming. "Where is the honor in what he does? In how he takes and takes without reason. What is loyalty if it is bought with a paycheck? When I am on top, everyone will be beside me out of respect. And no amount of money will buy them."

She raised her brows, though she shouldn't have been surprised. That was their mantra, after all. Hers and his. Back when they were still partners in crime. Back when he had her whole heart. And he *would* win it back. In a fight to the death with Dorian Blake.

"You've apologized, so you can go now."

"Can I have my car keys back, please?" he asked nicely, holding out his hand.

She shoved through her silver clutch and placed the keys into his hand, their touch lingering before she flicked away.

"Mercedes?" he called out softly behind her. She flipped her head to him, her wide eyes filled with disdain. "I like your necklace."

Her expression changed so quickly, it was like she had been slapped and had to take a physical step back to deal with the blow. She clutched at the space where the diamond infinity necklace was still resting against her skin.

She stared at him for a moment, meeting his gaze, before frowning again like she'd caught herself misbehaving. Then she walked away, leaving him alone with his heart in his hands. And hers around her neck, in the shape of infinity diamonds.

***

The mansion filled with the smell of rotting bodies and blood. One of Dorian's most favorite aromas. It reminded him of all his greatest victories. All of which inevitably ended in bloodshed. Out on the back terrace, those who were lucky enough to survive the yacht party fire now had him to deal with.

It was nearing nighttime, at the lowest part of the sunset, and Dorian Blake strutted down from the pool deck onto the terrace to interrogate his final witness. Four fresh, bloodied corpses already poured red, and all that was left was one lone survivor on his knees.

Dorian stood over him, staring with his infamous murder-filled gaze. Yani, the most blood thirsty and ruthless of his Seconds, approached from the house, loading a fresh clip into his gun. It went like this: if he wanted someone chased, T.B. was the driver. If he wanted someone drugged or bullied, Antonio was the muscle. And if he wanted someone brutally murdered, killed, or shot, then Yani was the hitman.

"Fresh clip is in, locked and loaded," Yani said.

"See? We've already used a full clip of bullets on your friends. Talk." Dorian kicked the survivor in the chest with careless regard.

Dorian felt his shoulder pull back and Yani came into his direct view.

"We've killed four people already, all of them saying the same thing, maybe–" Yani said.

"They're full of shit," Dorian said. "Their story is bullshit."

"So you're just going to keep killing them?"

"Got a problem with that?" Dorian said, leaning in. He would not be questioned. They were called his *Seconds* for a reason. Because he was and would always be number one.

"No, not at all." Yani backed down, and together they turned back to the survivor.

"I suppose you have the same story," Dorian said.

"I swear," he panted. "I've never seen these guys before in my life. They raided the boat, killed our guys and our suppliers, and took the shipment."

Dorian pointed to the dead bodies. "That story didn't work out too well for these guys, did it?"

"I swear," he cried out again, dropping his head to the floor. The breeze was getting cold as the sun slowly set, quickly setting Dorian's patience with it.

"Feds?" Yani asked, addressing Dorian.

Dorian frowned, answering honestly. "No one in Ridge City would be stupid enough to steal from me. And we've greased the feds. No way no one's seen these guys before."

"It's the truth! There were four guys. New! One of them snuck onto the boat and led the rest. He set the boat on fire! I swear!"

The survivor fell onto his hands, beginning to cry.

Dorian narrowed his eyes, remembering a story from his past that had started very much like this. Like déjà vu had just bashed him across the head. Surely not...

"Four guys, huh," Dorian asked again.

"Yes!" The survivor smiled. "Four guys!"

Dorian took a breath to consider the story. But just as quickly as the thought had popped into his head, he dismissed it. It was impossible. He had dealt with that threat years ago, it had long since passed.

"I don't tolerate liars." Dorian nodded to Yani as he walked away from the terrace. "Kill him. Burn their bodies."

The survivor cried out for mercy before a single gunshot deadened all other noise.

CHAPTER 7
READY OR NOT

Adam paused with his hand on the door. Mumbled voices inside his hotel room told him his friends had already arrived. He turned and looked over his shoulder at Mercedes. He'd picked her up early from the mansion, bringing her back to him and them. Where she belonged.

He cocked his head at her, his way of checking that she was ready to go inside. They'd pounce the second they saw her. She had to know it.

She rolled her eyes and nodded. "Yes. Don't look so smug."

He couldn't help it. Having her back felt very much like a giant check in the win column. He gave her a wicked grin, sending all his dirty thoughts to her through his gaze.

Her eyes widened. "And stop fucking looking at me like that!"

Chuckling, he pushed open the door. He stepped inside, probably still looking smug given the confused looks on Dan, Carlos, and Paul's faces.

It wasn't until she stepped in behind him that their confused looks morphed into hope.

"Mercedes!" Carlos jumped. "You're here!"

Paul, Dan, and Carlos wasted no time in rushing to her, sweeping her into a group hug. Adam moved aside to let them crowd her, but her eyes trailed him.

"You came," Paul said, gently frowning as if he, too, had been heartbroken without her. "I almost didn't think you would, given how long it's been."

"Well," she said, finally pulling from Adam's stare to focus on the others. "Couldn't let you lot have all the fun, could I?"

Paul smiled, then, and Mercedes softened her eyes for him. For him only. Fuck, if that didn't make Adam die a little inside.

"About time," Dan said, making Paul shake his head. "What changed your mind?"

Mercedes smiled tightly, her eyes darting to Adam and holding a second too long to be coincidence, but she said nothing in reply.

"So, you're in, then?" Carlos said, his tone fluttering with child-like hope.

"Absolutely." Mercedes nodded. "In for life, remember?"

When Adam chanced a look at the infinity necklace still settled on her chest, her cheeks pinked.

"So you... and Blake?" Dan asked, stuttering over the words. God, he was trying to ask her if she loved Blake. See if he could get a better fucking answer out of her.

Aiming to confirm a suspicion of his own, Adam watched Paul. Paul's jaw tightened. Judging from his strained reaction, he certainly knew something, if not everything. The others obviously weren't as clued in. Not surprising, if anyone knew why Mercedes had agreed to marry Blake, it would be the ever-trustworthy childhood best friend.

"Still engaged, obviously." She wiggled the obnoxious diamond on her finger. "But it's you all that I love. For you, I'm in."

"All of us that you love?" Adam winked. He knew it wasn't the case, but he couldn't help himself. Something inside him felt like it'd just come back to life.

Mercedes glared and Adam chuckled. Ah, contempt. There she was. He should've known that little reprieve wouldn't last long.

"Someone fill me in, then," she said. She shrugged off her coat and they all moved back into the room, spacing out and lounging casually, integrating her back into the fold without a second glance. Why would they need to? The team fit together perfectly at every edge, and now it was whole.

"Well, you obviously know about the yacht," Paul said. She nodded.

Adam narrowed his eyes at his friend. He knew Paul had spilled the beans. Adam moved to the window to stare down at the street.

"Well, now we're intercepting all the drug trades we can," Carlos said. "Funneling them through my regular channels but skimming the profits."

"Smart," Mercedes said. "And what's the next move?"

"More people," Adam said. "We need to grow." He rubbed his jaw but didn't look away from the street below.

"No way you're getting people on your side," Mercedes said.

"You're on my side." Adam shrugged, smirking over his shoulder.

"Begrudgingly," she frowned. "Because I love *them* and they're dead set on riding headfirst into this fuckery right alongside you."

"You love my fuckery," Adam said. It had only been minutes back in his presence, but she already looked exasperated with him. "Some might say I was the best fu–"

"Alright, enough, children," Paul said, cutting him off before he could finish. Once a cock-blocker, always one.

Mercedes looked like she could rip Adam's head clean off his body. Her fingers even twitched like she was daydreaming about it. He couldn't help but laugh, even when she was irritated and insulting him—*hell, especially when she was irritated and insulting him*—he craved her like an addiction he would never want to quit.

"Fine. More people. How do you suppose we do that?" Dan asked. Adam didn't need to look to know Dan would be making a sarcastic gesture behind his back.

"I've got some old Cortez Cartel recruits in my sights. Old Blake exiles too. With Blake getting the monopoly on the only crime empire in the city, there's got to be some seriously pissed-off people in hiding. With serious skills, too. And they've got no one to work for."

"Huh," Paul said, giving him an almost flabbergasted smile.

"What?"

"Well, recruiting old Cortez guys and Blake exiles? It's pretty smart... and it almost sounds like a plan," Paul said.

Adam rolled his eyes. "Dan, reckon you can put some feelers out— subtle feelers—see if any of the old fishies want to bite?"

"Well, fuck, I mean, sure, but that's a risky task," Dan said.

"We just need to grab their attention. Let those who are hiding know that someone else is rising," Adam said. He joined the rest of them around the table, resting his hands on the back of one of the wooden chairs.

"I... might know how we could make some noise," Mercedes said. She grimaced, like it physically hurt her to help him.

"I'm all ears," Adam said.

"Tia," Mercedes said. "Let's go after Tia."

"Jesus Christ, baby." Adam straightened, his eyes wide. "That's a fucking bold move."

"I know. But with Tia, we get people, we get her. Done."

"What?" Carlos frowned. "What am I missing?"

"Tia, the one I used to work with at the Neptune Club," Mercedes reminded him.

"I know that," Carlos said. "You were a bartender, she was a stripper, I've met Tia."

Adam and Dan chuckled, but Mercedes silenced them with a scowl.

"Hon, she was *not* a stripper. That was a front. She's a prostitute, and now she's club manager," Mercedes explained.

"Club manager? She—she *leads* the prostitutes…like, a madam?"

Adam smiled, there was Carlos catching up just in time. Yep, Adam had called it, it was a fucking bold move. And he was more than ready for it.

"You know, getting Tia on our side means we have to secure the Neptune Club, too." Adam stood to face her, their toes nearly touching.

"So?" Mercedes scowled.

"Pretty bold for someone who has done nothing but warn us of how stupid the plan is."

"Let's face it, you'd have to have a plan in order for to me to mock it."

"Eh," Adam shrugged. "We figure it out as we go. You know I like to think on my feet, baby. Take my time, make it last."

"Oh, I don't recall anything you ever did lasting a long time," Mercedes said.

"Liar," he smiled. She was a dirty little liar, if passion had its own magazine, they'd have been the centerfold. Every. Single. Month.

"Urghkkk," Dan wretched. "Enough sexual innuendos."

She was cruder and crueler, sure, but Adam couldn't help but feel like it was old times all over again. When they were together, the air was so formidable with heat and electricity that it left very little room for anyone else to breathe.

"I want Tia," Mercedes said. "She's done a lot for me, I want her off Dorian's books, on ours, and getting the protection that she and the girls deserve."

"I couldn't agree more," Adam said.

"Better," Paul rewarded, like they were children who needed a chaperone and got a treat for using their nice words. "But we still need the Neptune Club."

"Get Tia first," Adam said. "If she's in, we will find a way to take back that club. After all, it's meant to be mine anyway."

***

The first pins of early morning light were just filtering through the sky when Adam, Dan, and Carlos arrived on Ridge City Bridge. Approaching slowly, Adam rested his hands on the railing, looking out across the small gravel parking lot under the bridge where a deal was about to take place.

"Mercedes didn't take you as her backup to see Tia, huh?" Carlos said, following closely behind and puffing cigarette smoke into the sky.

Adam frowned. "Nope. No skin off my back."

Carlos shot him a knowing look. Dan sauntered behind them, dropping his forehead onto the metal railing and groaning. He didn't take well to mornings. Or being sober.

Adam rubbed his chin while he waited for the shipment to arrive. It was only meant to be small, so he relaxed his shoulders and cracked his neck, looking forward to a simple steal.

It had started off with stealing the shipment from Blake's yacht. Then another from his underground garage. Then another from the beach. So on and so forth. Until they'd made a reckless habit of stealing from Dorian Blake, all while staying under the radar.

It wasn't that it was hard to steal from him per se. Just that most wouldn't, knowing the consequences and the high price of doing so. Thing was, for Adam, he'd already paid it.

Two Blake goons were standing under the bridge, failing to be inconspicuous. It was like they'd given up all pretense trying to be discreet. Now that Blake's sticky fingers were in every cop's pocket, there was no need.

"What time are you due back at the club?" Adam asked Carlos as he knew he made a morning delivery every day at the Neptune Club.

"Not until nine," Carlos said, checking his watch. Since the sun was only starting to rise, it couldn't have been any later than six. Plenty of time.

Though Carlos dropped the line of questioning, it still lingered in his head, eating him alive. She *couldn't* have taken him to see Tia. He was supposed to be dead. Logically, he knew that was sound, but his heart was a stupid little fuck that couldn't see sense, apparently.

Under the bridge a single purple Camaro pulled up to the site. Nice car. Far too expensive to be running a low-level deal, but whatever.

"About fucking time," Dan said, scraping his drool-ridden cheek off the railing. "It's way too early in the morning to be getting up."

"Dude, you haven't even been to bed yet," Adam said.

"So?"

"Well, you have to have actually gotten up to complain about getting up early," Carlos said, laughing as he tossed his cigarette into the river.

Three guys got out of the back of the Camaro, like a clown car, and from the vantage point on the bridge, Adam could see it was stuffed full of drugs. Curiously, though, the driver and passenger of the vehicle stayed put.

"Take the shot," Adam said, yawning and almost bored by the ease of it.

Doing as he was told, Dan pulled a remote from his back pocket. He had a brain for explosives, and loved to see shit burn, so he'd rigged up a small explosive device that would knock the enemies off their feet just long enough for a steal.

"Something's not right..." Dan said, repeatedly pressing the button on the remote to detonate, but nothing was happening.

"Blocker or something?" Carlos queried.

"Probably nothing," Adam said. "But if you want something done right..."

He made for the meeting when Carlos clapped a hand on his shoulder. "Stay here, let us check it out. And maybe put your mask on. Safety first and all that."

Honestly, Adam thought it was a bit excessive, but he complied nonetheless, placing a ski mask over his face before Dan and Carlos did the same. Making quick work across the bridge, they walked toward the parking lot and jumped the few feet from the bridge into its sunken hole where the deal was taking place.

Adam watched them make quick work of the three guys from the Camaro and the other two who had shown up to take the deal. It looked like they had it in the bag. But the driver still hadn't gotten out of the car, and that had Adam's back up. He narrowed his eyes.

Dan and Carlos approached the Camaro. Out of nowhere, five more dark gray cars roared in to form a circle around them, trapping them in and completely blocking the view of the drug-filled Camaro.

Adam's jaw tensed. But he was more annoyed than afraid.

It was a fucking setup.

A nice easy setup wrapped in a little bow, and Adam had let them walk right into it.

Finally, the driver poked his head out of the window. A cold settled over Adam's spine. Fucking T.B.

T.B. smiled, mouthing off like he was making some sort of witty remark—knowing him, probably not—before getting back inside the car and revving the engine in a taunt.

The men advanced on Dan and Carlos, and Adam took off running toward them.

He reached the edge of the parking lot and dropped the rest of the way, landing in a crash, and catching enough of a break to cause a distraction so Dan and Carlos could make cover. Running through the carnage, Adam slid over the hood of one of the backup cars and fell into position beside Dan and Carlos.

"Setup," Dan said, his voice muffled behind the mask.

"Yep, got that," Adam said.

Even pinned behind the car, the three of them made good work of the backup men. Taking them down with ease and practiced skill. With two-thirds of the men down, Adam sat back into cover to rest.

"Why hasn't he left yet?" Carlos said, sinking to Adam's side.

Adam chanced a look over the hood, seeing T.B. standing outside and frowning at all the fallen men. He looked like he very much wanted to join the fight. "No fucking clue."

A rain of gunfire forced them back into the fight, each of them shooting in different directions.

T.B. had left the car and was standing at the hood, watching with folded arms and still looking very confused as to why the thieves weren't dead yet. And he'd left the doors of the Camaro wide open.

Oh, this was too fucking good. Seriously. Why should he need a plan? You couldn't plan for this shit.

"Guys, you got this?" Adam asked, staring at the Camaro.

Dan followed his line of sight and saw the opening T.B. had just left them. Smirking, Dan said, "Oh yeah, we do. Make a break for it, I'll cover you."

Dan did, in fact, lay down cover fire and Adam took that opportunity to bolt straight from their hiding place and dive into the driver's seat of T.B.'s car, slamming the door shut and revving the engine. He circled the lot in donuts, thankful for the tinted windows, but laughing his head off as he burned rubber.

When he felt satisfied he'd caused as much carnage as possible, he broke away with speed, taking the entire shipment of cocaine with him.

He was still laughing when he checked his rear-view mirror and saw that T.B. had commandeered one of the other vehicles, spinning and drifting and catching up to Adam in no time.

His smile dropped.

Oh fuck, going up against T.B. in a race? Maybe he hadn't completely thought this through.

***

Paul and Mercedes sat shielded in Paul's white van as the sun began to rise over the city. Across the road from the Neptune Club, they waited for Tia to finish her shift. They couldn't risk going in, not when Dorian still owned the joint. The best chance they had would be to catch her on her way out.

"Any of these?" Paul asked as more girls bolted from the sidewalk to their cars.

"Not yet," Mercedes said. The girls ran to their cars with their keys in their hand. Shameful, really, because Dorian should have been protecting them. Sure, she wanted to protect Dan, Paul, and Carlos, but that more than extended to Tia. And now that she had the chance to do something about it, she wouldn't miss the chance.

"You sure she'll be here?"

"Eventually," Mercedes said. "We have to wait. We can't come back another time."

"Your future-husband won't let you out more than one day a week?"

"If we're successful here, he won't have to be my future-husband."

When she looked back at her friend, he was staring at her again with wide, guilty eyes. But fuck, she really didn't need to hear it. He knew *exactly* why she had agreed to marry Dorian Blake, and she wished he would stop dwelling on it. The past was the past and she couldn't change it now. She could only move ahead.

"Are you doing okay?" Paul said.

Damn, here it came.

"Plotting with your ex to murder your fiancé, I just thought you'd have more feelings about it," Paul shrugged.

"Adam being back has no effect over me," she replied, so casually it was as if she meant it. No, she did mean it. Dammit, she did.

"Remember who you're talking to," Paul said, giving her the older brother stare.

Fuck, it was not her night.

"That won't get in our way," Mercedes said. "I have no feelings for Adam."

Paul arched his brow and she sensed she wasn't getting away with the usual shut down response she'd grown so comfortable with over the last five years.

"I'm still angry."

"He had to leave. He had no choice," said Paul, empathy in his eyes.

She wished Paul would just shut up. She knew the stakes. Losing an epic love, like hers and Adam's, ripped away part of your soul with it. She'd never get it back. It'd always belong to him.

"There were plenty of choices. Hard choices, but choices nonetheless," Mercedes said. "And he left us to make them all."

Inclining her head, Mercedes nodded toward the familiar silhouette of her tiny, black-haired, spicy friend. "There she is."

Paul and Mercedes left the van and headed across the street, stopping to let cars pass before approaching the dark space out the back of the Neptune Club.

"Tia?" Mercedes called out.

Whipping around with her keys between her fingers, Tia shouted, "What the fuck do you–... Oh, damn! Mercedes, is that you?" Her expression instantly softened.

Mercedes hugged her friend. "How are you, Tia?"

"Not as good as you, honey. Look at that diamond." She leaned down to admire the six-carat diamond on Mercedes's finger. "So, what're you doing here? And who is your handsome friend?" Tia waved.

"Tia, you remember Paul," Mercedes said, laughing in surprise.

"Paul!" Tia realized. "You grew up nice." She ran her hands along her red miniskirt to secure her fishnet stockings.

"I'm taking it you're not here for my services," Tia said.

"No, but it's not a social call either. We need a favor. A big one."

"Of course, you do," Tia said, eyes stiffening. "I don't hear from you in months and now you want something."

"I know, it's a shame we can't meet under better circumstances."

"Do I want to know?"

"Probably not," Mercedes said.

Tia held up her finger to shush them as some of her girls went past to greet her. When Tia gave the okay, Mercedes continued. "We want to make you an offer... to stop working for Dorian Blake and come work for us instead."

"Don't the both of you work for Dorian Blake anyway?" Tia raised her brow.

Mercedes looked back at Paul for guidance and then again to Tia. "Not exactly."

"Fucking hell," Tia sighed as she realized. "What the fuck, Mercedes? What are you up—actually, don't tell me, I don't want to fucking know."

Tia started pacing away, pushing past the litany of girls only just arriving. Mercedes and Paul followed her up the street.

"We need your help," Mercedes said, chasing her.

"Why would I help you? Especially with this."

Tia stopped and turned with her hands on her hips, almost demanding of an explanation, but Mercedes's mind drew a blank.

"Bigger cuts of your earnings," said Paul. "An even split. Fifty to you, fifty to us. No more paying the Blake's more money than they need."

"That's it?" Tia scoffed, throwing her jagged black hair over her shoulder.

Paul continued, "And better protection. For our share we'll have bodyguards for each of your girls, and we'll protect you from the goons that Blake will send."

"Is he serious?" Tia asked Mercedes.

"Tia, how many times do you see girls bruised and bloody from a night with a client? Or worse, from what Dorian's men do themselves?"

Tia closed her eyes, looking supremely frustrated, but if the two of them had anything in common, it was an inherent desire to protect the friends who had become family.

"Tia, you know we're legit. We will protect you from Dorian and from any shit the clients throw at you. That way you can do your work and earn your money in peace knowing you and your girls are safe."

"You're fucking crazy," Tia said. "Anyone who goes up against Dorian Blake dies. Both of you should know that. I've already kept plenty of secrets for you, Mercedes, but I won't put my girls in harm's way for your ulterior agenda."

Mercedes rubbed her head in her hands, trying not to lose her shit. What was with people insisting on being more stubborn than even she was lately? "Tia–"

"Get the fuck out of my face before you get me killed, too."

Tia clenched her keys back between her fists and stalked off, leaving Paul and Mercedes standing alone.

"Well, that could've gone better," Mercedes spat, kicking her boots against the puddles of rain on the pavement. "Goddammit!"

"You can't blame her for being scared," Paul said. "As far as she knows, the last person who tried this got themselves killed."

"Yeah, fine," Mercedes said.

"Come on, let's get out of here," Paul said, placing his hand on her back to lead her away.

Before they could get too far, Paul's pager started beeping incessantly. And then Mercedes's did, too. As if on cue, tires began screeching in the distance, squealing like they were getting closer. And closer.

Checking his pager, Paul grimaced. "Well, that can't be good."

A purple Chevrolet Camaro slammed to a stop in front of the club, and Adam's head hit the headrest from the force of the slam. He was up, hanging out the window in a second. "Get in the car, baby!" He ran a panicked hand through his hair as he scrambled to the passenger seat. "Get in the fucking car!! I need you."

CHAPTER 8
HERE I COME

"What the hell have you done now?" Mercedes tightened her seatbelt and slammed the gas of the purple muscle car, leaving Paul gawking on the sidewalk as they raced away against the morning sun rising over the tropical city.

"It wasn't me." Adam held his hands in surrender. Mercedes glared at him from her side profile.

She'd bet anything that it was him.

Hands gripped tight on the wheel, she used her mirrors to survey the interior of the car. It wasn't one of theirs, obviously, and it was filled to the brim with packs of cocaine.

"Shit," she said.

"What?" Adam shot her a shit-eating grin. "It was a golden opportunity, T.B. walked away from his car, I made a run for it."

"Dammit, you're exhausting, you know that?"

Like a rattling reminder, the car jolted forward as the bumper was slammed.

"You said this was T.B.'s car?"

Adam nodded.

"So I take it that's T.B. behind us looking angry as fuck?"

Adam nodded again. "Lucky the windows are tinted, right?"

Christ. She'd been back in the thick of it for two weeks. Two weeks! And he'd already dragged her into a world of reckless shit. Reckless shit she wasn't sure she could stand up to. Not now. Not anymore.

"Adam." She squeezed her eyes tight shut. "I can't race T.B. I haven't driven in five years, he'll destroy me. He's the best driver in the city."

Adam gripped the headrest of the passenger seat as he twisted in his seat to look out the back window. "Second best, baby. He's always been a Second. Especially to you."

She chewed on her lip. Fussing between the rearview mirror and the tight suburban streets ahead of her. T.B. hit the bumper again and they rattled forward. She'd have to get out of the suburban streets of the city if she stood any chance. Why the *fuck* had Adam roped her into this? It had been years. She couldn't drive like she used to.

She removed her hands from the wheel long enough to slap at his chest, annoyance overwhelming her.

His pointed glare bounced from the unmanned steering wheel to her hand fisting with anger in his shirt. He smirked at her. Her hands had left the wheel long enough to slap him, which meant whether she believed it or not, she felt totally in control.

"Ughhh." She pushed the wheel back on course, removing her hands again just to make a strangling motion with her fingers. "Fuck, I could just–"

"Kiss me?" Adam turned in his seat to stare menacingly at her. "Love me? Never get your hands off me?"

"Strangle you," she clarified.

"I figured." Adam chuckled lazily and turned back to face forward, relaxing in his seat. "Show him who he's up against, baby."

Her eyes flicked down to where his seatbelt remained unchecked, where he rested like the fight was over, like it was an easy escape.

If he still believed like that, the least she could do was try. She placed one hand on the wheel, and the other on the gear shift.

Mercedes shot from the suburban side streets, leaving smoke across the sky as she sped along the overpass that connected to the eastern freeway. Hitting speed bumps that Mercedes refused to slow for, they jolted up and down with the car.

But she knew they could go faster.

She beckoned up another gear, the ball of her foot pushing the pedal to the floor.

She eyed the mirror, T.B. sped up to match her pace. He wouldn't easily be outdone.

The sunrise threw pink and orange hues across the water under the overpass as she raced for the on-ramp. T.B. snaked out behind her, coming parallel to her and swerving to ram into her side, but she swerved, too, dodging him and pulling ahead.

Hitting the incline's edge, the car banged as she made it to the on-ramp and up onto the freeway, speeding past the idling cars that were only getting in her way. Mercedes watched as the speedometer continued to climb and she planted her foot farther down on it.

There was a fire growing in her gut, the higher she climbed in speed, the more her stomach dropped. The more her heart raced to grow three sizes in her chest.

That feeling. *That* was the feeling.

The rush of adrenaline. Deadness in her stomach like she'd left it behind to find again later. The velocity pinning her to the back of her seat. Their lives literally in the palm of where her hands tugged at the wheel.

With the world blurring past her, high on the rush, she couldn't remember why she hadn't been behind the wheel in so long.

This was where she was meant to be. Crushing the asphalt and fucking up T.B.'s day by being better. Always better.

"He's gonna love this one," Mercedes smiled, violently drifting the car across the median into the opposite lane of traffic. It was the last point that was covered by grass and not concrete, so if T.B. wanted to keep up, he would have to head into oncoming traffic with her, or risk losing them.

Mercedes drove turbulently left and right, darting between the three lanes to avoid the traffic coming at her. She checked her rearview mirror to see T.B. on her tail, also swerving violently to avoid the traffic as he approached.

Adam grabbed onto the edges of his seat, steadying himself as they bounced along with the thrashing of the vehicle. Her foot pushed harder and the speedometer inched higher until T.B. started to look small in the mirror.

As they rallied down the highway, into the path of oncoming cars, Mercedes readied herself to take T.B. to her favorite trick spot. With an intentional drift, she bolted from the highway and into the parklands, thrashing even more under the uneven terrain of the grass. She swerved to avoid trees, banging her head against the roof and crushing her down again as T.B. rose to be hot on their tail.

"You'll wanna hold on tighter," Mercedes said to Adam. He looked her dead in the eye, holding her stare for a few fleeting moments and looking like every fantasy he'd ever thought of had materialized in front of him.

She gripped the wheel purposely, changed gear, and pushed the gas, sending them flying forward faster and more wildly than they had before.

They were pinned against the back of their seats as Mercedes sped toward the edge of where the parklands met the river. T.B. so close, he was nearly touching their bumper.

Mercedes squinted and braced as she tugged to the left suddenly where they met with a slight grass hill. The wheels left the ground and the car glided through the open air, crystallized waters passing beneath them. They lingered mid-air over the waters for what felt like an eternity, pushing closer and closer to the riverbank ground.

Only making it by an inch, the purple Camaro settled with a bang, hitting Adam and Mercedes's faces on the dash upon landing. Mercedes leveled off and drove calmly away. Why did she ever think she couldn't do this? She was made for this.

She watched Adam wipe the blood from his cut lip and smiled as she felt the hot sting of blood dripping from a cut on her head. She checked her rearview mirror to see T.B.'s car smoking and crumpled on the bank of the river, half of it slipping into the water. They had lost him. She had won. She'd beaten the unbeatable and reconfirmed that she was, in fact, still the best driver in the whole of Ridge City.

"Fuck. Yes," she said in low tone. "Take that, motherfucker!"

"I never doubted you for a second, baby," Adam said, grinning like a lovesick fool.

"I know," she said, shaking her head but pressing her lips tight to avoid smiling as bright as she felt inside.

"Still the best fucking driver in Ridge City, baby."

"Damn right," Mercedes smirked.

***

JANUARY 1986

The bullet shattered the blue glass bottle. Adam and Paul ducked to avoid the raining spray of glass off the roof of Paul's trailer.

"Fucking good shot," Paul said, handing Adam more ammunition.

Adam shot again, this time at green bottles, and in several firework-like explosions, they shattered, too. Ducking again, Adam and Paul crouched into the light brown dirt as it rained green glass.

"What's the verdict? You gonna leave the lot?" Paul asked, standing to brush the dust from his pants.

"Not yet," Adam said. "Don't want to leave this little trailer, I love it too much."

"Thought you wanted somewhere bigger now that you're a fucking drug lord," Paul said, ducking again as it rained red glass.

"I do have my sights set on something a little bigger," Adam grinned.

"What have you got in mind?"

Adam checked his surroundings to be sure they were alone. He aimed again, his eyes settling on the target. "I want Dorian Blake."

"You want fucking what now–"

Adam fired his gun, this time missing and hitting an electrical wire in the space behind the trailer, sending sparks into the air, though neither of them flinched.

"Dorian Blake." Adam smiled and moved to sit in a plastic lawn chair, taking a towel from the table and wiping the sweat from his face. He knew Paul wouldn't like it. He didn't have to. He just had to agree.

"I fucking heard you, I just thought you might want the opportunity to take that back," Paul said.

Adam chuckled.

"God. You told the others this yet?"

"They don't need to know, right now it's just a pipe dream," Adam admitted, holding his palm as a visor against the shining sun.

"You're talking about starting a war here, Adam," Paul said. "And for what? Why Dorian Blake and not Ricardo Cortez?"

"You don't really expect me to dignify that with an answer, do you?"

"Look, I know what you think he took from you," Paul sighed. He picked up a bottle of water and drained the whole thing, throwing it on the ground once he finished. "But you don't want attention from Dorian Blake *or* Ricardo Cortez. Trust me."

"I think if we keep making as much noise as we have been, Ricardo Cortez and Dorian Blake will certainly hear about it," Adam said.

Adam had him there. Paul clearly couldn't argue with that because he said nothing despite looking like he wanted to deliver the verbal bashing of a lifetime.

"Hey, you wanna know a secret?" Adam smiled.

"That wasn't enough of a secret? Fuck, do I want to know?"

Adam nodded.

"Go on, then."

Out of his pocket, Adam retrieved a small navy box and handed it to Paul. Grimacing, Paul snapped the lid open. Sitting center on a navy cushioned bed, Paul would find a sparkling diamond engagement ring.

Paul looked at Adam with an incredulous expression, like he was sure he'd misinterpreted the gesture.

But Adam wasn't joking. About any of it.

"Here's my plan," Adam said. "I'm gonna take down that fuckwit Dorian Blake, maybe Ricardo Cortez, too, if I'm feeling up to it, and then..." Adam smiled to himself. He held a palm to his chest to settle the excitement and stop the nervous cracking from showing in his voice. "And then I'm going to marry her."

Paul snapped the box shut and handed it back. "And you need to take down all the gang leaders to do that?"

Adam laughed and secured the box safely in the pocket of his jeans. "I suppose I don't, but I want to."

"Do me a favor," Paul said seriously, so Adam did him the courtesy of taking what he had to say seriously, for once. "Think about what you're doing before you do this."

"Sure," Adam said.

"*Really* think about it," Paul warned. "And for fuck's sake, tell the others first. At least give them the chance to back away if they're not eager to join a gang war for you."

***

<u>MARCH 1991</u>

Mercedes parked the purple Camaro near the edge of the cliff at the Ridge City overlook. The place was always abandoned because it was such a rough drive up, but it had impeccable views over the city. For those brave enough to drive on the gravel slope to get to it, that is. But his girl was always brave enough. In fact, she dominated those roads. He fucking loved how wild she was behind the wheel.

The engine rattled desperately, like it was coughing. Which couldn't be good for a car. Adam winced as Mercedes killed the engine, and pieces of the side paneling fell off with a bang, the car grunting to a stop. It definitely was trashed and wouldn't be starting again. Shame. It was a nice car.

Adam brushed his fingers through his hair and exited the car, heading to the trunk.

Paul's white van screeched as it pulled up behind them, lifting gravel from the path. Dan jumped out of the van right onto Adam, embracing his friend in a hug.

"What a score!" Dan said. "T.B. never saw that coming."

Carlos wasn't far behind him. "I forgot how good it feels to be on top."

Mercedes patted Carlos on the shoulder knowingly, causing him to let out a rare smile.

"Let's load it up and move on." Paul tapped on the side of the van from the driver's seat.

"We're celebrating here!" Dan shouted.

"There'll be time to celebrate when the job is actually over."

Dan and Carlos rolled their eyes and began loading the shipment out of the wrecked Camaro and into the back of Paul's van. It was a struggle to pop the trunk with all the bumps and dents the race with T.B. had left behind.

Once the shipment was secure and Dan and Carlos were back inside Paul's van, Adam nodded to Mercedes and they moved to the back of the Camaro. Placing their hands on the trunk, they leaned all their weight into the sports car, pushing to roll it over the edge.

"That was pretty fun," Adam said.

Mercedes said nothing, keeping her expression grim.

"You know it was," Adam said again.

He grunted as they herded the car toward the edge of the cliff. It was harder than he remembered. He guessed in his absence cars hadn't gotten heavier, just harder for him to handle. Fuck, he wasn't that old. T.B. must've done some work on it or–

"You good?" Mercedes shot him an amused look.

"This is... fucking heavy," Adam admitted, puffing.

With a final push, the car disappeared over the cliff. They both rushed to watch it smash. It was fast to fall, landing trunk first on the grounds below and crumpling into a wreck.

Adam loved the look of the mess they'd made all broken at the bottom of the cliff, but Mercedes was chewing on her lip like she liked the look of it, too. Like she liked it a lot, so he couldn't tear his gaze away.

"Come celebrate with us," Adam blurted out. "Promise I'll behave."

She lost all that wicked beauty from her eyes in an instant. "Don't do that," she said, seriousness crinkling her features.

"Do what?"

"This... all of this, with us," she said. She folded her arms and brushed her hair from her face. "I'm not here for you, Adam, you're not going to change that."

Ouch. He supposed he deserved that.

"I told you upfront I'm here for them." She jerked her head over to the others. "One little win doesn't change that."

He genuinely had nothing to say to that. It was rare that he found himself rendered speechless. That he didn't have something snarky to say.

"Well stay for them," he said. "The team doesn't feel complete without you, they feel it, too."

"It's not like before, Adam," she said. "We don't. I mean, I can't."

"And if you could?"

"Then I wouldn't want to," she said, ducking her face away. "Let's not make this more awkward or any harder than it has to be. We're not it for each other anymore. You know that. Don't pretend this is something it isn't."

He squeezed his eyes shut, hearing her boots pound gravel as she walked away. He promptly pulled his heart out of his throat and smothered his emotions down.

"Take me home," she said to Paul.

Fuck—home should've been with him.

CHAPTER 9
WHERE THERE'S SMOKE

<u>MARCH 1991</u>

Mercedes was fast to rise the next day. Being back in the driver's seat, literally and figuratively, made her feel more awake and alive than ever. It was like a five-year fog on her brain was finally lifting. And once again she could see.

At the same time, her heart carried the weight of her burdens. Her friends had jumped so easily back into Adam's embrace. How could she possibly do the same? Not when she held so much resentment for the choices he'd made.

She knew it was hurting her team, to keep herself on the outskirts, but she couldn't bring herself to the forefront. Even as her stupid, dumb, foolish little heart pulled her back toward the person she'd once thought was the love of her life, her brain—sensible, smart—wouldn't let it take the reins.

She was coming down the marble stairs when she heard murmuring voices in the ground-floor living room.

"That sounds like more than a hiccup, T.B.," Dorian said. His tone was scathing.

She paused mid-step, listening intently but ready to move as if she hadn't heard a thing.

"It wasn't like I was trying to lose my favorite car," T.B. said.

"I'm not upset about the fucking car, it's the fucking cocaine that's pissed me off!" Dorian said.

Well, that made a good day better. She could almost see T.B. hanging his head in defeat. That would look fucking delicious. She licked her lips at the thought.

"You assured me that the supply wouldn't get lost again," Dorian said.

"It had to look like a real deal," T.B. said, whining like a child without his toys. Dorian's favorite didn't do well under pressure, it seemed.

"Shut up, T.B. You've fucked up. Just...shut up," Dorian growled. There were a few beats of silence before Dorian spoke again. "Yani, what have you got?"

"Not better news, I'm afraid," Yani said.

"Good God—what now?" The sound of glass smashing echoed roughly.

"Another dead prostitute," Yani said. "Girl was seen by a few people before we could get the body out of there."

Mercedes's heart squeezed. Another dead girl. One of Tia's girls. If she and Tia had anything in common, it was their deep protectiveness. Like Tia, there was nothing more that Mercedes wanted than to keep her family safe. And since a certain ex of hers insisted on being reckless as shit, that burden rested solely on her.

There was more silence. It sounded uncomfortable. Though she couldn't tell.

"Witnesses are taken care of." Yani cleared his throat. "The girls are proving to be painful."

"They always are when one of the little sluts dies," Dorian growled back. "Cut their pay in half until they stop whining. One dead girl doesn't stop the world."

But it should, Mercedes thought. It totally should.

The doorbell rang, startling her, but her body didn't react. If she didn't answer, one of the guys would roll out of the living room and catch her spying.

Peeling herself from the wall, she padded down the stairs at loud-enough volume to announce a fake arrival.

She opened the door to find a harsh-looking Blake associate holding a box of envelopes.

"I'll take those." She snatched it before he could object. His eyes darted frantically inside the house, so Mercedes knew she'd stumbled onto something important.

She slammed the door in his face and turned to find Dorian had come up behind her.

"Looks like a delivery for you." She plastered on her sweetest smile. Looking over his shoulder, she found T.B., Yani, and Antonio frozen, their shoulders tight with tension. Surely not from their conversation with Dorian. She shifted the box in her hands, and their eyes glued to it like cats following a laser.

Dorian held out his hand for the box, and Mercedes slowly slid it into his awaiting palm. As she did, the Seconds released their tension. Like she'd just diffused a bomb by handing over the package.

Dorian pressed a gentle kiss to her cheek before disappearing into the living room with the box, smiling at her as he shut and secured the double doors.

With a curious smirk, Mercedes pulled an envelope from her back pocket. Luckily, she had sleight of hand down because Dorian was acting suspicious as hell.

"Devious fiancé of mine." Mercedes laughed as she opened the envelope and pulled out five ballots. The papers were all preselected with the name 'Dorian Blake'. Little fucker was trying to rig the election. Probably by stuffing the ballots from the look of it. Well, she expected nothing less of him. Little did he know, though, he'd be dead long before he ever got the chance to win.

***

When Mercedes arrived at Adam's hotel room, her four friends were already there, sitting around the table with the TV playing idly in the background, and empty beer bottles lining the countertops.

"Hey, baby." Adam's smile brightened when she walked in. Like they glowed only when they settled on her. It made her smile, one that she tried to push away quickly. Dammit.

"I have news," Mercedes said, rolling her shoulders to loosen her tensing muscles.

"I heard no luck with Tia," Dan said, absentmindedly picking at the label of his beer bottle.

"Unfortunately not," Mercedes sighed. She went around the table and gave a tight, friendly hug to each of them, stopping awkwardly when she got to Adam. He opened his arms, but she rolled her eyes and went to sit next to Carlos.

"She'll come around eventually," Paul said. "Give her time."

Give her time?!

She shot a look at Paul and noticed Adam had done the same thing. His a look of amusement, and hers a look of disgust.

Paul responded with widened eyes that darted back and forth between the two of them. "...Tia. I mean, Tia will come around," Paul said.

Mercedes shook her head and brushed the comment away. "Thought you'd all want to see this." She pulled the ballot from her back pocket and slid it over the table.

Her friends leaned in to get a good look, where they'd find a list of candidate names with Dorian Blake's box pre-selected.

"Ballots," Dan said as he plucked it from the table to hold it to the light.

"He's trying to rig the election," Mercedes said.

"Well, he's going to need to stuff a heap of ballots then," Carlos said, flicking the mechanism on his lighter. "Diego Garcia is going to be hard to beat. The city loves him."

"Looks like Blake is making sure that's not a problem," Paul said.

"Who's Diego Garcia?" Adam asked.

Mercedes smirked. For all his bravado, he clearly didn't fucking know everything, did he?

"He's the *current* mayor. If he gets back in, it would be his second term. He'd be the first mayor to ever do that here. He is actually very popular," Carlos said as he leaned back in his chair.

Adam nodded. "This isn't the worst thing Blake could do."

"My thoughts exactly." Mercedes narrowed her eyes. "If he's focused on this, he's not looking at the threat that's readying to take him out."

Dan, Carlos, and Paul exchanged a confused look. As much as she hated it now, she and Adam had always been on the same page. Very little words were needed in order to say a lot between them.

"He thinks he's rigging an election, he doesn't know he'll be dead before he ever gets the chance," Adam said.

"So you're not going to do anything about this?" Dan prodded.

"No need to," Paul said.

"Anyway... you're here just in time," Adam said. "Dan, continue with what you were saying."

Dan looked slightly weary but continued on anyway. "Slight good news. All this mess we've been making has drawn the right kinds of attention. I've heard from some underground contacts. We've got some interested parties."

"To work for us?" Mercedes leaned forward in interest.

"Yeah," Dan said. "People who've been outed are ready to get back in. With all the drug-running, we've got more than enough money to pay who we need."

Adam frowned and Mercedes rolled her eyes as she caught it. Like she said, very little words were needed between them. She knew what he was thinking. *The people who worked with him would ally out of respect, and no amount of money could buy them.*

Dan seemed to know it, too. "I know what you're thinking." Dan held up a palm to shut Adam down. "You want respect without a paycheck. That's not going to happen right away."

"You have to earn the respect first." Mercedes flicked Adam in the ear from across the table.

"Okay, so... we'll earn it then." Adam shrugged, crossing his arms and sinking into his chair.

"Just start by gathering a group of people that are happy to be paid." Paul patted his shoulder reassuringly. "I know you're desperate to rush to the finish line–"

"Yeah, yeah, I get it," Adam pouted, waving his hand in dismissal. "Pay them off first, respect later."

Mercedes smiled as Paul and Dan shared a chuckle that made Adam's pout grow deeper.

"About Tia," Mercedes said. "I'm going to take another shot at her."

"So soon?" Carlos said. "Didn't seem she was open to conversation."

He was probably right. But everything changed when someone important to you died. And unfortunately for Tia, that was all too often. It was an effort to hold back tears as she glanced at her feet. "Another girl died last night."

"Oh." Carlos' smile dropped as he looked nervously around the room. "I hate to be the bearer of bad news... but will that be enough to bring her around?"

"It won't hurt. I know what I have to do now to get her on our side," Mercedes said, kicking away her chair and standing to put some distance between her friends and the reminiscent feelings of loss that were encroaching on her mind.

"I'm listening," Adam said, appearing over her shoulder like out of thin air to whisper in her ear.

She jumped, erotic shivers running down her spine before smothered the feeling and turned to face him. "You won't like it."

Adam just shrugged.

"Tia won't join us because she thinks we'll get her killed. Because she thinks we got you killed. So..." Mercedes said, flicking her thumb over her lip and smirking as Adam's hungry gaze followed the movement. "...Show her you're alive."

"What? Are you fucking craz–" Dan stuttered, but one short look from Adam had him shutting up.

"You want to tell Tia I'm alive?"

Mercedes nodded.

"You trust her?"

"I do." Mercedes didn't miss a beat before answering.

Adam searched her eyes. She wasn't sure what he saw, but it seemed to be something that pleased him. Because his eyes softened before focusing back on her again. "Then I trust her," he said. "My life has always been safest in your hands."

"Are you kidding me?!" Dan shouted. "This is a massive secre–"

This time it was Paul who pinned him with a glare.

"Okay, I'll just shut up, then, shall I?"

"Just tell me what you need me to do," Adam said.

***

The cemetery gardens were sparse and decadent, a paradise among grief. A beauty against loss, bringing life to the death. Tall pine trees hung shadows over the narrow gray roads and dropped fluffy green leaves over flowerbeds.

Underneath a grand oak tree, Adam, Paul, and Mercedes waited. Rain hit the trees above them, grouping raindrops that made a heavy splash on their black umbrellas.

"You sure now's the right time?" Paul asked, shuffling his umbrella into his other hand.

"I can do this," Mercedes said. "I have to remind her of who we are."

She fanned her floor-length, black cashmere coat to create a breeze, revealing the black shorts she wore underneath. The rain only increased the humidity in the city.

Adam bit down on his knuckles as he eyed her legs before snapping away. She rolled her eyes at him again. They seemed to be permanently fixed to the back of her skull these days.

Across the graveyard she finally spotted Tia arriving, strolling casually through the rows. Tia, with flowers in her hands, kneeled in front of a headstone and wiped at her eyes.

"You should both wait here."

Mercedes left Adam and Paul standing under the oak tree and crossed the short road to reach Tia. Passing a group of flowerbeds, Mercedes plucked a white rose and held it at her chest as she approached.

"Hey," Mercedes said as she came up at Tia's side.

Tia grunted as Mercedes' shadow loomed over her. "What the hell do you want?" She wiped a few loose tears, highlighting the bags under her eyes and the darkness of her bruised face.

Mercedes kneeled down at her side. "What happened to your face?"

"You know, same old." Tia laughed through tears.

"Bosses or customers?"

"A little of both."

Mercedes nodded and placed her white rose down on the dirt. "What's her name?"

Seeming surprised by the question, Tia glanced suddenly at Mercedes's eyes as if to see if they were genuine. Turning away to answer, she said, "Sophia."

"Did I...?"

"You didn't know her," Tia confirmed.

Mercedes shuffled on her knees, resting her hands on her thighs, uncaring of the mud hugging her calves. "What happened to her?"

Tia scoffed. "What didn't? She was too pure for this... Man, they didn't even give her a chance."

Mercedes bowed her head as Tia let a chorus of tears flow down her face, staring off into the distance like she didn't even know the droplets were there.

"It doesn't have to be like that, you know." Mercedes fought for Tia's gaze.

"Don't start with that shit again," Tia said. "You know I don't want to hear it."

"I know you just want to protect your girls, Tia, that's all I want to do."

"I'm not having this conversation with you," Tia said. "It's dangerous enough just being seen with you. I won't challenge Dorian Blake."

"You don't have to; we will," Mercedes said.

"My God, you are so naïve. You forget—I was there the first time. I watched you try and take him down. Look how that turned out."

"You come here a lot to visit your girls. So many of them dead on the job. Murdered. They don't deserve that, Tia." Mercedes kept her tone hard. She had come to understand that it took someone brave to stand up against the status quo. Somebody had to be the person willing to risk it all to change it all. Nothing great ever came from accepting things the way they were.

Finally, Tia broke. She hugged Sophia's headstone, most of her body covering her epitaph, arms open with her head hanging in between them. Through broken tears she gasped intermittently to say, "I...just wanted to...protect them."

"I know." Mercedes hugged Tia's shoulder and ran soothing circles up her arm. "Let us help you do that. Please, Tia."

Taking a chance, Mercedes rested her head on Tia's shoulder, but she only managed to hold it there for a few seconds before Tia straightened up and pushed her off.

"I want to believe that you can, honey, but like I said, I watched you fail the first time. I watched you lose everything. I watched you break down when the person you loved died. Why the hell would you four want to take another shot when it cost a life the first time?"

Mercedes sighed and flicked her tongue against her teeth. She looked back at Paul and Adam under the oak tree and remembered how she had felt the day before. Finally alive after years of hiding. Her stomach falling out of her gut with the sheer thrill of the chase and the memory of who she was truly meant to be. Not Dorian's wife, but a legend of her own making.

It was no longer going to be easy. If they wanted to win, they had to be willing to put it all on the line.

It was time.

God, she hoped she was making the right decision.

"Can I trust you?" Mercedes said to Tia, her face pained.

Tia's face dropped, like she could kill her with a glare. A fair reaction. Tia had kept more secrets than she should've for Mercedes in the past. Mercedes looked back at Adam and Paul, hesitantly waving them over.

"Adam's not dead, Tia."

"What?" Like turning off a tap, the tears stopped flowing instantly.

"He's al–"

"Shut the fuck up. God, if you're saying what I think you are," Tia panicked, reaching out to cover Mercedes's mouth with her hand.

Ignoring Tia's protests, Mercedes slapped her hands away. "He's alive, we—he never died. We just made it look like he did."

With wide eyes, Tia wrestled her wrists out of Mercedes's grip and covered her own mouth with her hands. "What the fu–" Her eyes flickered over Mercedes' shoulder.

The shadows of two men standing over them covered the sunlight. Slowly, Tia looked up, examining them from toe to top. Adam and Paul stood towering above, umbrellas over their heads, looking down on the girls. Mercedes stood up first, and then reached her hand out to help Tia up, too.

Mouth agape, Tia stared at Adam, casting her eyes over every inch of him as if to confirm his existence. "Oh my God, you really are alive."

Adam smiled confidently. "Takes a lot more than that to bring me down."

"Fucking hell," Tia sighed.

"You see? We can protect you, we hid Adam from Dorian Blake for five fucking years."

"And counting," Paul added proudly.

"Wow," Tia said, taking her sunglasses off to get a better look. "And the five of you are really taking another shot at this?"

Adam, Paul, and Mercedes nodded in unison.

"You really want to help us?" Tia asked.

"Absolutely," Adam nodded, but Tia turned to Mercedes.

"Don't give anything more to the person who keeps murdering your girls," Mercedes said.

Tia glanced between Adam and Mercedes, back and forth, back and forth. Finally, she nodded approvingly, and Mercedes had to wonder what the fuck that meant.

"I suppose you have kept this one hidden for a long time." Tia gestured at Adam. "Man, people really believe you're dead. Imagine what they would do if they knew."

"No one can know...not yet," Mercedes said.

"Element of surprise and all that," Paul said.

Tia stared into Adam's eyes again. And Mercedes just couldn't help herself, much to her dismay. She had to look. Jealousy pangs beat in her chest as she searched Adam's eyes for what Tia was looking for.

She startled like she was physically slapped when she saw it.

Adam's wild recklessness was replaced with wisdom and restrained confidence. His carefree stare had been replaced with a fiery shimmer.

Tia looked to Mercedes then, and after probing her own eyes for a moment, she smiled wide. What did Tia see when she looked at her?

"Okay," Tia agreed. "The girls and I...we're in."

CHAPTER 10
THERE'S FIRE

"Here she comes," Mercedes said, rolling her fingers together in a nervous tell that she tried to hide. Still, Adam saw it. This was an important job to her. More than a job, really. He'd make sure they didn't let her down.

Tia slipped inside Paul's white van and startled when Dan slammed the door shut behind her. Crouched down low, she struggled in her heels and eyed them all curiously. "That's it? Just the five of you?"

Adam gritted his teeth but restrained his comments. It wasn't just the five of them, but they were more of a force than any amount of people he could send.

"Hey, the five of us are pretty dangerous, love," Dan said.

Mercedes leaned over the front seat to hit Dan on the arm. "We've got people inside and out."

"I'm going out on a limb trusting you here, don't fuck this up," Tia said, jabbing her pointer finger at them.

"We won't," Adam said, not even bothering to look over his shoulder as he loaded ammunition into the guns on his lap.

"Head on in," Mercedes said. "We'll listen for your signal."

Tia sighed in doubtful agreement. Before disappearing out of the van she paused to give them one last glare. The subtext was clear. *You'd better be as good as you think you are.*

"She's still pleasant," Dan said, sarcastic undertones dripping from his voice. He slid the door shut again and took his seat in the back.

"Alright, team, let's rally," Adam said. He turned in the seat to look at his friends. "Paul, Mercedes, you're with me at the bar. Carlos, you're posing as security. Dan..." Adam rubbed at his forehead. "You're posing as a customer."

"Fuck yes!" Dan's eyes twinkled as he fist-pumped the air.

It was a wise move. Any other job and Dan probably would've been distracted anyway.

Dan piled out of the van, walking to the club entrance and nodding at the security guy. One of theirs now. The guy whispered something in his earpiece, and then all the red lights on the security cameras stopped blinking.

After Dan secured the entrance, the rest of them filed inside.

The Neptune Club was exactly as he remembered it. Red pulsing lights. Green neons. Girls dancing on tables and poles in the center of the room. Though they looked a lot less happy than when he had been in charge... No, he could put his ego aside. They were probably just mourning their latest dead friend.

Dan perched in the front row, smiling like a loon. Adam caught Carlos rolling his eyes before taking up his position as security with the others on their team.

Adam, Paul, and Mercedes headed to the bar.

A few minutes later, Blake's rowdy parade of goons came walking in, thrusting themselves at the girls unashamedly as they took up residence near the front bar. They managed to down two rounds while waiting for Tia, harassing as many girls as dared get near them.

"Something's not right," Mercedes said. "Tia should be out here by now."

Adam narrowed his eyes. The men looked far too comfortable to wait, which was unlike any Blake man, and wasn't a good sign.

"I'm going to check it out," Mercedes said. Adam pinned her with a frown, but she shook him off. "I know my way around."

"I don't like this," Adam said to Paul once Mercedes had disappeared behind the pink gossamer curtains.

"You don't have to tell me," Paul said, sipping his drink. Even Dan, from his position perched near the front of the stage, had stiffened. Tia was supposed to be out through the front as soon as they entered the club. She wasn't supposed to linger in the back, and more importantly, it was unlike her to leave her girls alone.

***

Mercedes rounded the back corners that she knew so well from her bartender days. The rooms had clearly been refurbished, but the layout was exactly how she remembered it.

Turning another corner, she nearly bumped into a young redheaded girl.

"You seen Tia?" Mercedes said, keeping her tone soft despite her distress.

The girl answered without hesitation, pushing her lipstick around on her lips and heading toward the entrance to the club. "Alley out back."

Fuck.

"Why?" Mercedes tugged at her elbow to stop her.

"Blake guys, regulars."

Double fuck.

Mercedes worked her way toward the back, pushing past the dressing rooms and the kitchen until she finally found the back exit and didn't hesitate before kicking the door open with her boot.

"What the fuck?" A large man dressed in all black shouted.

There were two of them, dressed identically but polar opposites of each other, one tall and skinny, the other short with an overhanging belly. They had Tia pushed up against the railing, one wrong slip and she'd end up in the river below.

"Who the fuck do you think—"

The tall dickhead didn't get the chance to finish the sentence. Mercedes acted fast, spinning a kick to his stomach. He dropped, clutching his gut and leaving Tia to slide down the railing to the ground, holding her own stomach.

Dodging an attack from shorty, Mercedes ripped the tie from around his neck and kneed him in the balls, snapping his neck as he fell to his knees. Tall guy rose then, swinging at her. She ducked under his arm and jumped on his back, strangling him with the tie. They thrashed for only moments before he slumped and they eased down together.

She pushed him away like the trash he was, finding Tia still slumped over, clutching her stomach with panic in her eyes. "M, you shouldn't have done that."

"They won't be the only dead bodies by the end of the night. What the fuck happened?"

"Let's just say they wanted a free sample."

Mercedes helped Tia up and she hissed when Mercedes's arms came around her waist.

"They broke your fucking ribs," Mercedes seethed as she supported her friend.

Tia pushed Mercedes off, steadying herself. "I have to get out there. We need to finish what we started."

"Tia—"

"No." Tia pinned Mercedes with her stare. "Let this be the last time."

Mercedes screamed internally before taking a breath. "Okay. But you're not going out there alone."

***

"What's taking them so long?" Carlos said, saddling up to Adam's side as he cautiously kept eyes on the Blake associates.

"No fucking idea," Adam said. He checked his watch. "Five minutes and we're going back there."

Paul waved a finger to order another round of drinks and gulped his back in one go. He looked just about as settled as Adam felt.

Finally, the curtain parted and Tia appeared, limping out of the back rooms. Adam's eyes widened, what he saw doing little to settle his racing heart. Mercedes followed behind Tia. She'd changed—now dressed in tiny shorts, a silk crop top, and wearing a red fucking wig. The edges curled over her face just enough to hide it. But it was definitely her.

"Oh, fuck," Paul said, echoing Adam's thoughts exactly.

"Tia's injured," Adam said, watching as she favored her left foot. Probably broken ribs, Adam remembered what that felt like. "Mercedes is backing her up."

"This isn't good," Carlos said. "As little bloodshed as possible, remember?"

Adam paused with his drink at his mouth. "Might not be an option anymore."

The waiting Blake associates moved as a group, leering at the club girls as they approached Tia. Stopping just within earshot of him, they crowded Tia, Mercedes, and the rest of her girls.

"Look at you," one of them said, a thick-bearded Viking-looking guy who was clearly the leader. He ran his hands over the waist of a Vietnamese girl who unsuccessfully tried to swat him away.

"Don't touch her," Tia said, grasping the leader's wrist and tugging. The bearded man just laughed, pushing Tia away and smacking the girl so hard that she floated to the floor like tissue paper.

"Should we go?" Carlos said, voice shaking.

"Wait for the signal. M knows what she's doing," Paul said.

Tia's face tightened as she bent to help the girl off the ground, her fingers twitching at her sides like she desperately wanted to clutch at her ribs. The girl was passed back until she was pressed firmly behind Tia and Mercedes's protective stance.

"We're here to collect, hand it over." Another one of them spoke that time.

"And I'll take her. For free," the leader said, looking Mercedes up and down. Adam nearly choked. But it wasn't that he was worried she would be recognized...since *no one was looking at her fucking face!*

Paul placed a warning hand on Adam's shoulder, holding him back.

"Nothing is free," Tia said.

"It is for us," the leader said, chuckling to his friends. "Cash, now."

"No," Tia said. She folded her arms, but her voice bounced and her eyes did little to hide her fear.

Adam shared a look with Dan, Paul, and Carlos to make sure they were all on the same page. The signal would be close. The Blake associates would either go quietly. Or...or Adam would have a helluva good time making them leave.

"Don't fuck around with me, whore. Give us the cash now!"

"I don't have cash, but I do have a message."

The bearded one looked like he'd just been told someone had shit on his pillow.

Tia gulped and then continued. "You can tell Dorian Blake that we don't work for him anymore."

"Backup, move in," Adam said, nodding at Carlos. The room suddenly turned. The Blake associates instantly stiffened, glancing around nervously at the new recruits, all on Adam's payroll, who had turned guns on them.

"Leave on your own or suffer the consequences," Tia said, defiantly raising her chin.

Viking guy smiled, shaking his head at his boys. "You'll pay for this, bitch." He grabbed at Tia, palming her ass in a way that had to be painful.

"That's enough," Adam said quietly to himself. He whipped out his pistol and fired. The shot hit the bearded fuck right between the eyes. The air felt suddenly heavy, all eyes locked on the dead body.

"So much for doing it the easy way," Paul said.

"Yeah, well, too late now," Adam said, as he readied his gun. He sure did start a lot of fights, but he could finish them too.

Paul and Adam lurched to fight alongside their new recruits, while Dan and Carlos led innocent customers from the building. Mercedes retreated when they arrived, slinging Tia's arm around her shoulders and guiding the girls into the back.

There were only six Blake associates, not including the dead asshole, but he'd have to avoid gunfire if he wanted to minimize the damage to his nearly acquired property.

Adam rushed ahead, slamming his hand into an elbow to disarm his opponent, and punching another down. Paul was right there alongside him, trading blows of his own as they disarmed the thugs.

Ducking low, Adam dodged a punch, ramming his foot behind him to send the assailant careening into Carlos, who finished him with a silenced gunshot. He blocked another assault with his forearm before he grabbed a second guy by the collar and head-butted him down.

Carlos and Dan were right there, clearing out the mess as Adam and Paul took down the fighters.

The remaining Blake guys must've sensed their odds because the three of them traded nervous looks before bolting toward the door. Charging after them, Adam shook his head as he grabbed two collars and hurled them back into Dan and Carlos's waiting arms.

Adam kicked out a leg to trip the last one.

Sprawling on the floor, he looked up at Adam with wide eyes as he backed away in a crawl. "Who are you?"

Adam raised his brow, giving the guy a frown before he smiled. "Very good. You'll do." He leveled him with a harsh glare. "Guess you're the messenger. Congrats! Thanks to your dead buddies, you're our winner by default. Tell Blake this club doesn't belong to him anymore. And the girls don't work for him."

The thug whimpered as Adam kicked him in the face, hard, to knock him out. Three of his new recruits stepped up to Adam's side. Old Cortez guys if he recognized them correctly.

"Drop him on Blake's front steps." The recruits obliged, picking up the messenger and dragging him out of the club.

Tucking his gun away, he joined the others near the back curtains where Mercedes, Dan, Paul, and Carlos were standing with Tia.

"He'll deliver the message," Adam said. "You good?"

"I will be," Tia said.

Adam cocked his head when he saw the state of Mercedes' shoulder. There was a large gash along the end of her collarbone that was dripping blood all down her shirt.

"What happened to you?"

"Jumped us when we tried to get away," Mercedes said, gesturing to a man who may as well have been missing his face for how mangled it was. Well then.

"The hard part is over," Adam said to Tia. "We can't be seen around here, obviously, but this club is ours now and our people will be here permanently."

"And I'll be by once a week to take our share," Dan said.

"*I'll* be by once a week to take our share," Paul corrected, sensibly. Dan would be up to play. Paul would be all business. A much smarter move. The girls seemed to know it, too, because some of their faces slackened.

"50/50?" Tia said, raising her eyebrows at Adam.

"50/50, I promise."

144

***

Carlos ran from the dining table to the bathroom. "Don't touch my cards while I'm gone!"

Adam chuckled. The mood had been high after their win for Tia, and he'd managed to convince them, and even Mercedes, to stick around at his place for a game of poker that had quickly turned into a night of it.

Sure, he'd lured her back under the guise of patching up her shoulder. But—*but*—she'd stayed. It was the first thing that had gone right, and it gave him fluttery feelings in his belly. Just like the old days.

"Grab his cards!" Dan whispered.

Like magnets to metal, they launched over the table, snatching at Carlos's cards. A toilet flushing in the background jolted them in their seats in a way that couldn't possibly look natural.

Carlos reclaimed his place, narrowing his eyes on them before studying his cards. "I knew it! You fucking messed with these!"

Dan, Paul, and Mercedes burst into laughter, insisting through ragged breaths that they didn't touch his cards, and Adam couldn't help but join them. He hadn't felt unburdened in...well, five years.

"Yes, you did!" Carlos said. "I had it laid out Queen, Joker, Three and now it's Joker, Three, Queen!"

"Maybe," Adam said, as Carlos punched his arm. "It was a losing hand anyway!"

Carlos sank into his chair with an eye roll.

"I think we're done here anyway," Dan said, standing calmly. "And I need to go throw up." He padded to the bathroom and slammed the door behind him while Carlos took the opportunity to jump up and open the window for a smoke.

Dan made a yelp as he emptied the contents of his gut into the bowl.

"I got it," Mercedes sighed, going to help Dan and leaving Paul and Adam alone at the table.

Adam watched her leave. He couldn't stop looking at her, stealing every chance he could get without her noticing. He had to keep that locked up tight. So that nobody could see how terrified he was whenever he thought she might not forgive him.

"Let me ask you something," Paul said.

Damn, he'd clearly seen.

Paul shuffled the cards on the table, not to deal, but just to perform tricks. "You might not like it."

"Then don't ask it," Adam said, raising his brow.

Paul spread the cards and took a puff of his cigar. "I'm gonna ask anyway." He blew the smoke in circles. "Are you still in love with her?"

Adam thought for a second, holding Paul's gaze before glancing to the bathroom, switching back and forth between the two.

"No," said Adam. He clenched his jaw like it could hold his mouth shut. "I didn't come back for her."

"You've got a good poker face," Paul said, though if he was surprised by the answer, he didn't show it. "If I didn't know better, I might believe you."

Adam quietly watched Paul perform trick shots with the cards. He didn't want to let anybody see what he was feeling. He didn't want them to notice his anguish. Getting close to her again was harder on his heart than he imagined. The thought of Blake's hands over her body...kissing her, sleeping with her, touching her; it made him feel like he'd swallowed lead, inducing panic every time the images assaulted his mind.

He needed to get some air or he might explode.

146

"I'll be right back," Adam said. He downed the last of his scotch and bolted. He jogged down the stairs to the street and into the alley behind the hotel.

Leaning against the brick wall, he rested his hands above his head, taking care to control his breaths. His fear was like a shadow. Always hanging in the background, its presence usually unnoticed but not forgotten.

When he was younger he feared nothing, and that was stupid. There was plenty to fear. Now he was terrified, every moment of every day. He worked so hard to control it, to harness it, to feel the fear, and do it anyway. Sometimes it wasn't so easy.

He took a few minutes to catch his breath and let the night breeze slap sense into him like a mallet. After composing himself, he headed back upstairs.

When he looked up, Mercedes was standing there over him. She closed the glass front doors behind her.

"You taking off, baby?" Adam asked, through heavy, unsteady, breaths that had her frowning at him.

"What's up with you?" she asked, coming down the stairs to be level with him on the sidewalk.

"Nothing."

"You look pale, and you're sweating." She placed the back of her hand against his forehead, the concern in her eyes reflected by the hotel's glowing pink neon signs.

"I'm fine."

"Well, I have to go back. I'm just waiting for a car." The lone glow of lights poured shadows over her face. The directions pointing like an arrow to her thin lips. He needed to get a hold of himself.

Adam took a deep breath and began walking up the stairs.

"You can wait with me," she said. "If you want."

He whirled back around to face her, cocking his head. Surely, he'd misheard. But looking in her eyes he found her expression open. Without the anger that had been forefront since he'd returned.

He descended the stairs and stood at her side on the curb, eyes forward to not spook her.

"I almost don't want to go back."

She could've knocked him down with only a finger. He composed himself before speaking. "It's good to have the old crew back."

"For me, they never left," she said, her jaw tightening. She winced, like she was catching herself doing something she shouldn't, before speaking more softly. "But you're right. It's good to have everyone back together again."

"Even if things aren't the way they used to be," he said.

"Maybe they're better this way. Maybe we'll distract each other less. Not cause so much conflict in the group." She turned to him with a sympathetic smile.

"Maybe." He nodded in agreement. Inside though, he knew things would never be better this way. A world where they weren't together would never be favorable to one where they were.

A taxi pulled up across the street and Mercedes pointed in its direction. Adam nodded and waved with just a flick of the wrist.

For the umpteenth time that night, she surprised him, stopping suddenly before she could cross the road.

She was still, her head turning back and forth like even she was unsure what she would do next.

Adam waited patiently. Watching. Hoping.

After what seemed like forever, she whipped back toward him to stand eye to eye.

She had a nasty scowl on her face, but he wasn't sure who it was directed at. Him or herself. She collapsed into him, stretching up to wrap her arms around his neck.

It took him a second to relax, but when he did, he sank down with her, placing his hands around her waist. Her head twisted in his hold, and she ran her nose up the column of his neck. It must've been an assassination attempt because that move? He was seconds from dying.

They held each other for an impossibly long time. He held her like his life depended on it, knowing if given the chance, he would never want to let go.

Just as suddenly as she initiated the embrace, she pulled away, unable to look at him.

"I suppose we can be friends," she said.

"You think?" Adam laughed. "How generous of you."

"Don't make me regret it." Her eyes brightened.

"I am a good friend," Adam said.

"I know." Staring into his eyes and flashing him a crooked smile, she reached out her hand to shake. "Just friends?"

For now, sure.

Looking down on her outstretched and open palm he grinned, grabbing her hand with his and shaking. "Deal," he said.

***

Dorian arrived home in a sleek black limousine, his most preferred mode of transport. If he was going to be the mayor, he needed to act like it. It'd take one hell of a show on his part to expunge the dirt from his fingers.

His shoulders dropped when he headed up the stone front steps to find three men surrounding a bloodied man sitting on his porch. He was about to be thoroughly pissed off, he sensed.

Yani and Antonio followed behind as Dorian loomed over the inconvenience.

"Who the fuck are you?"

"This guy works picking up cash from the prostitutes," Yani said.

"Right, right, right." Dorian brushed Yani away. "Then *what* the fuck happened to you?"

The guy was blubbering, looking right over Dorian's shoulder at Yani. Dorian's jaw ticced as he looked back at his Seconds, at Yani who seemed to be imploring the imbecile to speak with just his eyes.

"Everyone is dead." The man whimpered. Fucking pathetic. "They're all dead."

Dorian massaged his temples as he pulled up his sleeves. He really didn't fucking have time for this today.

"Get him in the house," Dorian said.

Doing as instructed, Yani and Antonio dragged the broken man inside the mansion foyer. They dropped him at Dorian's feet right in front of the decorative flower vase that stood center against black-and-white checkered tiles.

Continuing to remove his watch and tie and primp in the hall mirror, Dorian said, "So, who is dead?"

"Everyone." The man whimpered again. "We were ambushed and they killed them all."

Dorian snapped his fingers and Yani held the man up by his hair, forcing his eyes high. Dorian straightened his suit pants, pulling them tight so he could bend to look him in the eye.

"Start from the beginning."

When again the man was too nervous to speak, Yani slapped him to bring back his attention.

"We went to pick up our usual cut from the working girls. When we got there, they refused to hand over our money, so we went to beat them down, and out of nowhere these guys jumped us."

Dorian turned away before he did something stupid like shoot this dumb fuck in the face before he got all the facts. How dare someone try to embarrass him with such disrespect in front of all his men.

"The girls said they were working for someone else now."

Dorian paused for a moment, taking in the story word for word. "They're working for someone else?"

"It's what they said."

In a violent huff, Dorian stood upright. He'd taken down every enemy he'd ever had in Ridge City until the city's crime empire rested solely in his hands. Add to that the fact that he was about to become the city's most powerful official, a near unstoppable force. He didn't know a person stupid enough to try and challenge him, let alone steal from him.

Add this to the continuous stolen cocaine supplies...

"Get this guy out of my sight," Dorian said. He looked away as Antonio grabbed the broken man by the shirt and dragged him back out the front door. The sound of the gunshot was almost comforting.

"Boss?" Yani prompted.

Dorian began to laugh, an angry chuckle, which turned into a full-blown manic shout.

"The fucking yacht," Dorian said, scoffing at his own stupidity.

"The yacht?"

Yani kept his arms clasped behind his back. His Second was a man of few words, but he was smart and had a brutal flair that came in handy. Like it would now.

"First, the yacht. Then all our drug shipments go MIA. Now, we've lost control of the prostitutes and my fucking club." Dorian paced as his mind raced to put all the facts together. "These are not little coincidences. These are not small-time thugs making bad calls."

He picked up the beautifully crafted flower vase from the front hall table and smashed it, scattering red roses along the tile.

"Somebody is coming for me."

Dorian pulled Yani in, wrapping his hand around his shoulder to make sure what was said was for their ears only. "And we know exactly what we're going to do about it."

Yani obviously caught his drift because he visibly paled.

"Isn't it a bit early to—"

"Do it. Now."

CHAPTER 11
HUSTLING

The doctor's office was busier than usual that day, but even so, Mercedes sat alone. The chairs, lining the walls and a little worse for wear, sat only inches apart, yet still she might as well have been a pariah.

She plastered on a confident façade, though she felt anything but. All eyes were on her and it was obvious. They stared when she wasn't looking and looked away when she did.

"Mercedes Preston?"

Mercedes sighed in relief and followed the doctor into her office. Inside, she hoisted herself onto the center table and steadied herself by gripping the edge of the vinyl. The doctor, Brooke, closed the door, her face buried in paperwork.

"Good to see you, honey." Brooke smiled as she looked up from her clipboard.

"Brooke, it's been too long," Mercedes said.

"You certainly drew some attention in my waiting room," Brooke laughed, putting her clipboard down and leaning back against the bench.

"I was just sitting there... they were the ones rude enough to stare," Mercedes said. "Is it because of Dorian?"

"That, maybe. But rich little white girls make my patients uncomfortable," Brooke said.

"Sure, fair shot," Mercedes said, grinning as she bowed her head.

Brooke pulled up a stool and sat in front of Mercedes to examine her. "What can I do for you?"

She tussled the collar of her white dress shirt down her arm, revealing a deep cut on her shoulder. It was packed with tissues that had filled with blood in a poor attempt to keep the wound closed. "I think I need stitches."

Wheeling back to the bench, Brooke put on blue latex gloves and grabbed some cotton pads. Settling back in front of Mercedes, she safely removed the tissues from the wound and winced. Must've looked pretty gross. Mercedes had only stuffed it once to keep it from pooling, but she imagined it had to be caked in dried blood by now.

"You do need stitches." She dabbed the cotton pads in antiseptic wash and prodded at the edges. Discarding the waste in the bin, she went back to the bench, returning with a horrid-looking needle and kit. "What happened to you? Dorian?"

"Nah," Mercedes said. "Got into a little fist fight, scratched myself up on some broken glass."

Brooke spun to face her, looking concerned. "And what are you doing in a fight? Aren't you supposed to be First Lady material now?"

"You don't want to know."

Brooke gave no warning before she spread a cold cream over Mercedes's arm, which made her shoulder tingle until eventually she could feel nothing, only watching as the needle and stitches pierced her skin.

"And are you bringing my brother into this? God knows, you never do anything without him."

"Don't worry about Paul," Mercedes said. She winced as Brooke pulled the needle again.

"M, if my brother–"

"Paul won't get hurt. You know I'd never let that happen."

Brooke studied Mercedes's face like it held the answers to life. Surely she didn't need any more proof that Mercedes wouldn't let anything happen to Paul. She'd proven that enough times to earn the benefit of the doubt.

"Tell him I said hello," Brooke whispered, her pain-filled eyes drifting to the floor.

"He keeps his distance to protect you."

"I know," Brooke said.

Mercedes tried to apologize with her eyes, knowing the actual words wouldn't do much. After all, it was the mess that she and Adam had created, which meant Brooke had to hide. Brooke and Paul hadn't seen each other in years. Maybe if they could pull this off, then all the hiding could stop. "Maybe it won't be too long until you see him again."

"What? Why?" Brooke said, narrowing her eyes. "What are you up to?"

"Nothing, I'm just saying it might not be long." Mercedes smiled, one that she couldn't contain, so she turned her face away to keep it hidden. But that just gave it away even more.

"He's come back, hasn't he?"

"What?"

"I can see it in your face."

"You couldn't possibly tell that from just my face," Mercedes scoffed.

"Don't try to lie to me." Brooke dabbed the blood away from Mercedes's arm and continued stitching. "Your silence tells me everything I need to know."

"You've got nothing to worry about, I swear," Mercedes said, jumping at the pull of the suture.

"I don't want to see a repeat of last time," Brooke said, concentrating on the stitches like she couldn't bear to look at her.

"Neither do we," Mercedes whispered. "This time it's different. If we get it right, you can see Paul whenever you want."

"I won't get my hopes up," Brooke replied with a skeptic grunt.

"Ouch!" Mercedes winced at the final prick of the needle.

"Sorry," Brooke smirked. She dabbed the last bits of blood away and placed a bandage over Mercedes' skin. "You're good to go."

Mercedes slid off the table and fixed her shirt into place. "Thanks, honey."

"Whatever you're doing, be careful. I can't—I mean, *can't*—lose my brother," Brooke said.

"You won't," Mercedes said.

Brooke folded her arms, pinning Mercedes with a warning look.

"Brooke, I promise. Dan, Carlos, Adam, and your brother are all going to come out of this alive. I fucking promise."

"Fine," Brooke said, turning back to the paperwork laid out on her bench. It was all the acceptance Mercedes needed to know that Brooke was trusting her with their friends' lives. Without another word, she left Brooke alone, closing the door to the office behind her as she left.

***

"Are you sure you want to hang out here?" Paul asked, looking around nervously. He was too nervous these days, in Adam's opinion. He was wound tighter than a corkscrew.

"Why not?" Adam said, taking a swig of his scotch and swirling it around to relish the taste.

"It's out in the open," Paul shrugged.

Adam rested his hand on the booth behind him, gripping it so he could survey the room. The bar in question was only a block from Adam's hotel room, and was one of the most run down, worn-out, dodgiest dive bars that could be found. The room was nearly pitch black, with only the glow of red neon lights that gently dimmed the atmosphere. Despite the smell of body odor and spilled alcohol, Adam had been making a habit of taking up the darkest booth at the back of the bar almost every night.

While taking back the Neptune Club had been a win, it wasn't smart to frequent it. It was a business he had to love and leave behind, trusting that Tia would keep the asset under control.

"I think we're fine," Adam said, turning back. He fanned himself with the drink menu, the lightly blowing fans on the ceiling a useless addition.

Dan and Carlos joined them, sliding up onto the sticky leather.

"Heaps of our people in here tonight," Dan said, enthusiastically surveying the force of people enjoying drinks.

"Our people?" Paul frowned, shaking his head but trying to hide his smirking grin. In response, Adam gave him a wicked smile of reckless unconcern.

Adam's pale pink and green Hawaiian shirt blew lightly as he continued to fan himself. He'd opened his shirt in the front to let the breeze in, aware of his muscled chest on display and the droplets of sweat riding down his neck. If a certain someone happened to notice, so be it.

"Cheers to us!" Dan said. They clinked their glasses and chugged. Before the drink even went down his throat, Dan lined his coke up on the table, sniffing it in.

"Not without war wounds," Adam said. The press of the glass had cut his lip open again, leaking droplets of blood that he wiped with his thumb.

"Victory wounds," Dan corrected him, his voice high and nasally from the coke.

"That's right, a fucking win!" Carlos said.

The front door of the bar swung open, letting in a hot breeze. Against the red light all Adam could see was her silhouette in a skin-tight black mini dress and heels. It was rare to see her in anything other than leather, for fighting, or elegant sundresses, for pretending she was someone she wasn't. He hoped this was the proverbial letting down of her hair.

"Scoot," Mercedes said as she reached the table. They shuffled around to make room as she slid into the edge of the booth next to Carlos.

"What happened to your shoulder?" Paul asked.

"Oh, I needed stitches," she said. She waved down a bartender, but slapped her hands down on the table when she got no response.

"Who gave you stitches?" Paul said.

Still getting no response from the bartenders, Mercedes threw her hands defeatedly in her lap. Adam held the cool glass against his cut lip, watching the exchange with interest. It was pretty fucking obvious who would've given her stitches.

"Who gave you stitches?" Paul repeated.

"Hmm? Oh, a doctor, obviously," Mercedes said, rubbing her hand over her neck and looking over her shoulder to the bar.

Paul sniffed and stared down into his drink, his smile still wide but his tone giving him away. "How is she?"

Mercedes looked like she was surprised to find herself not in trouble, and Adam cocked his head. Paul had always been over the top in keeping Brooke out of the dark parts of their lives, but he must've seriously gone into overdrive the last few years.

Mercedes reached her hands across the table to comfort him. "She misses you."

"I'll get your drink, what do you want," Adam said.

"Oh, thanks...Mai Tai," she said.

As he left the booth, he could see Mercedes and Paul deep in conversation. Immediately being served, he asked the bartender for another scotch and her Mai Tai and rested his elbows on the bar while he waited.

"These guys yours?" the bartender asked, throwing a dish towel over his shoulder and grabbing bottles from the shelf.

"Who the fuck is asking?" Adam squared his shoulders.

"Whoa." The bartender raised his hands in retreat. "Settle down, it was just a question. I have no loyalties."

"Right," Adam said, doing his best to relax. "Sure." It was hard to take anyone at face value or consider a question as anything other than a threat.

"So, are they yours?"

Adam glanced around the bar, it wasn't only his four friends. There were dozens of his people, playing pool in the back corner, drinking on bar stools, laughing in booths. A whole litany of Blake exiles and Cortez Cartel stragglers, no idea who they were really working for, but just knowing this place would be safe.

"Yeah."

"Big group," the bartender noted.

"You're a bit too mouthy for my liking." Adam squinted his eyes.

"Not trying to be. I'm good at secrets," the bartender said. "I just thought I'd let you know the bar won't be open for much longer."

"Oh?"

"Owners have backed out, so we can't keep the place running much longer. With a crew your size, I thought you'd appreciate the heads up to find new digs."

Adam looked over to his four friends in their booth, finally smiling, and then at the other outcasts. It was kinetic in that moment. Like he could see in them what he felt inside. He'd spent five years without a home. He recognized one when he saw it. And he certainly recognized the potential to create one for others.

And then he had an idea.

"Hey, Dan…get over here."

Obedient as ever, Dan jogged quickly to Adam's side, wiping the coke from his nose and bouncing his curls as he shook his head clear.

"You need someone to buy the place?" Adam asked the bartender.

"We do."

"How much?"

"Five-hundred thousand."

Adam turned to Dan, smiling and raising his eyebrows suggestively.

Dan squinted, looking back and forth between the bartender and Adam. When he caught up, he smiled, reaching into his back pocket for the checkbook. "Cash or check?"

***

JUNE 1986

Adam eyed Carlos and Dan fondly from where he sat in a private booth at the back of the Neptune Club. The two were standing alone at the bar among an array of broken glass.

Mercedes shifted into Adam's side. He pulled her close just as two more shot glasses smashed with a thunder, followed closely by manic giggles from Carlos and Dan.

"Stop throwing glasses on the floor! We have to pay to replace them now." Paul pinched the glasses out of his friends' hands and placed them on the bar top.

None of them were quite sure how they had managed, in all their heisting, to steal the Neptune Club from Dorian Blake. But they had. Adam had taken ownership right out from under his nose. It was their biggest win to date, and as much as they said they weren't trying to draw attention, Adam knew that he, at least, most certainly was.

Trouble would soon follow, but for now he was just enjoying the high. The neon green strobe lights pulsed throughout the club with "Spirit in the Sky" by Doctor and The Medics humming softly. With no one else in the club, this was just for them to enjoy.

"I still can't believe we did that," said Paul. "I can't decide if that's the smartest or stupidest thing we've ever done." He joined Adam and Mercedes in the booth, his the only face not filled with wonder, just caution.

Carlos and Dan were both close behind, each sliding into the booth at either end. Dan banged a bottle of scotch loudly onto the table as he said, "Another round, my friends!"

They had broken all the shot glasses, so Carlos served scotch from tall glasses at four times the strength recommended.

"What a steal!" Adam shouted as he toasted.

"The repercussions of this should be interesting," Paul noted, the alcohol choking his words.

"Who cares?!" Adam laughed. "Let's just enjoy it, okay?"

Mercedes retched as she downed hers. "No good." She spat the contents back into the glass and climbed across the table to leave. "I need tequila and lemon," she said before disappearing behind gossamer curtains to the back of the club.

At that moment, the front doors burst open, causing Carlos to jump in surprise. Adam squinted to see through the strobe lights at the interruption to their victory party.

It was the shiny business shoes that Adam noticed first, and then he knew exactly who he was dealing with. Through the doors entered Dorian Blake with a posse of guards holding rifles at the ready. Dressed in a full suit, Blake adjusted his cufflinks and waited at the entrance, seeming uncharacteristically relaxed.

Adam thought it would take much more to get Blake's attention, but he had asked for it. Patting the table, he signaled his friends to stay low. He then climbed over the table to exit the booth.

Still drunk, Adam fumbled to draw his gun as he approached Blake, who in turn approached him.

"No need for that," Blake smiled. "This one is a friendly visit."

Adam stopped patting his pockets for his gun and shrugged, he couldn't find it anyway. He figured if Blake wanted to fight, he would've started one the second he walked in.

"Let's have a drink."

With caution, Adam followed him to the bar. They sat adjacent on the black bar stools while one of the remaining club girls poured drinks.

"So, you must be Adam Vandemilio," said Blake, natural charisma and charm oozing from his voice. In the neon lights, Blake's manufactured smile looked whiter than snow.

"In the flesh." Adam winked. "I don't believe we've met."

Blake thanked the waitress and took a sip of his drink.

Glancing over his shoulder at his friends, Adam made sure their faces were hidden by the pulse of lights.

"Did you come to congratulate me on my new digs?" Adam said.

Surprise assaulted Blake's face and he nearly choked on his drink. "Well, you are ballsy, aren't you?"

"Pulled one over on you, didn't I?" Adam downed his entire glass in a show of power and slid it forward to request another.

"You've got my attention, that's for sure," said Blake. "I'm glad you're proud. Right now this is just a friendly warning."

The waitress delivered another drink to Adam. Cocky and confident, Adam surveyed the room of Blake's men, certain they could take them if it came to it.

"Is it?"

"Right now, I've just come to get acquainted...and, of course," Dorian laughed as he paused, "wish you luck."

"With?" Adam taunted, trying to sound genuinely confused.

Blake's nostrils flared as his hand tightened on the glass. "You stole money and property from me. A lot of money. Nobody steals even a shoelace from me without punishment."

Adam snorted, still not afraid of the threat and hoping his daring smile would only provoke Blake further.

"Well, I thought it was only polite that I introduce myself." Blake stood up. "Since I'm going to kill you, Adam Vandemilio."

"I look forward to it," Adam said, turning away to give Dorian his back. "Because I'm coming for you, too." A fucking boss power move, one that he probably would've been too smart to try if he wasn't so fucking smashed.

Blake exhaled sharply before sounding footsteps told Adam that he and his men were leaving.

If Blake did anything best, it was build up fear, and that surely had been the intention of his visit, however unsuccessful it was.

Mercedes burst from the back of the club while Carlos, Dan, and Paul rushed to Adam's side. He continued sipping his drink, acting as if he was not affected by the visit. And the thing was, he really wasn't acting.

"What the fuck was that?!" Carlos said.

"He wants to kill me," Adam laughed. He met four sets of panicked eyes. Adam, apparently the only one unfazed by the visit, took another sip of his drink. "Oh, come on, he won't."

"Are you serious?!" said Paul. "Yes, he will. He's Dorian Blake."

"Did I say won't? I meant, can't." Adam spun his stool to face them, resting his arms along the bar behind him.

His friends stared him down blankly.

"Guys," he laughed. "Whatever they throw at us, we'll deal with it when it comes."

He was still faced with vacant expressions. "Right?! Big fun! Big Five!"

He managed to get Carlos to crack a smile first, followed by Dan, and then Mercedes, though he couldn't manage to get agreement from Paul. Hindsight was a blessing.

***

<u>MARCH 1991</u>

Mercedes pressed her bedroom door closed behind her, securing the locks. She exhaled with relief and leaned against the door. In here, behind the locks, she could finally breathe.

At the mirror she checked her shoulder, pulling down her pink camisole to reveal the bandage which had now turned red at the edges, wincing as she ran her fingers over it.

Knowing that hard and fast was better than slow and cautious, she ripped it from her skin, writhing in place to hold in a yelp. Blood seeped from the wound, begging for cleaning.

"Hey, baby." Adam's head poked through her bedroom window.

She startled, jumping high at his voice. "Fuck! Why do you do that?"

"It's funny," he shrugged and helped himself through the open window, shutting it behind him. He frowned at her shoulder and paced to her side, hovering behind her in the mirror and holding his hand against her arm.

"This looks like it needs cleaning," he said as he touched the edges with his finger and she winced in pain. "Let me help you."

"I can do it," she said, reaching to the dresser for the bottle of antiseptic and cotton swabs. Stopping her, he took them instead and kept his focus on her as he dipped the cotton into the liquid. When he reached out to touch her, he hesitated at first before lightly pressing the cotton against her wound.

"Not used to injuries anymore," he laughed.

"Piss off, it's deep…look at it!"

"It is deep," he smiled again, then frowned as he wiped dried blood from her skin. "It looks really bad, actually."

"Not as bad as your face," she said.

He chuckled.

"I'm serious," she said. "You've got really black bruises. Here." She pressed her index finger to his temple. "Here." She brushed along his jawline. "And here," she said, holding his gaze as she brushed her thumb over his lip. When did she up and lose all her sanity? She blamed the man carefully doting at her wound for her loss of brain cells.

Suddenly, a gunshot rang out in the background, likely from the back terrace, far away and not leaving them in immediate danger. Though it was enough to tear their attention from each other. Mercedes dropped her hand from his face.

"Blake?" Adam asked, frowning toward the gunshot sound.

"He's not home," Mercedes said.

Adam thoroughly cleaned her wound and pressed a fresh bandage over her skin. His thumb ran circles over her bare shoulder, and she suppressed the urge to shiver at the pleasant tingles spreading over her.

Before Adam, she didn't believe in it. That feeling that one person could actually make your skin sing and your soul breathe. After Adam left, she stopped believing in such novelties. So what was this feeling? She frowned down at her wound, traitorous skin celebrating with every skim of his finger.

When she looked up their eyes connected.

Agreeing to be friends was already proving to be a horrible mistake. If she didn't have hatred for him, then her feelings swerved dangerously into other territories. Ones that she had no control over.

At that moment, the lock at the door wriggled and she nearly jumped out of her skin.

"Fucking locks on the doors." It was Dorian's voice.

"Fuck," she said, looking at the window like it had the potential to save her life. But Dorian was already opening the door, and they were on the opposite side of the room.

Adam bolted for the walk-in closet, but she grabbed his shoulder to yank him back. "No, linen closet."

She pulled open a small closet, shoved him inside and then followed, closing it softly when Dorian slipped into the room.

Then silently cursed herself.

If she ended up in one more fucking closet with Adam Vandemilio she was going to lose her sanity.

"You're awfully calm." T.B.'s voice.

"You're awfully fucking twitchy," Dorian said.

"You're not worried about the heat this might draw on–"

"Enough!" Footsteps creaked until it sounded like he was right outside the door. "Fucking stolen drugs, fucking prostitutes, in two hours it won't matter. Shut. Up."

Mercedes looked to Adam, a panicked expression on his face that she was sure was mirrored in her own.

"And get the fuck out so I can shower."

When the shower started and both the bathroom and bedroom door clicked closed, she dared venture out. Tiptoeing to the window, she paused to open it for Adam. He went through, perching on the ledge to hold out his hand in silent invitation, a tic in his jaw telling her he wasn't taking no for an answer.

She sighed and took his hand, following him down the trellis.

***

Adam managed to keep his cool for the car ride back to his hotel and not a moment longer. Once he arrived all bets were off, his temper loose and unruly like a wiggly water hose with the pressure turned all the way up.

Adam smashed the door of his hotel open and rushed in, pulling drawers open and throwing paperwork everywhere.

Dan, Paul, and Carlos, who were all sitting calmly around the dining table, jumped in alarm. Only a few seconds behind, Mercedes rushed in after him.

"Adam, what are you looking for?" she said, out of breath.

"What's going on?" Dan asked.

"Not sure yet," Mercedes said, she closed the door behind her.

"God fucking dammit!" Adam shouted when he couldn't find what he was looking for.

"What is it?" Carlos asked again.

"Something's going on, I swear," Adam said.

Dan, Carlos, and Paul all turned to Mercedes.

"We overheard Dorian and T.B. talking, something is going down today, in–" she checked her watch, "–well, an hour and fifteen minutes now."

Paul looked toward Adam and gave him an authoritative stare to signal that he needed to calm down. But Adam was having none of it.

"I cannot let Blake get the upper hand," Adam said. "We have to be smarter, better, stronger than we were last time. He cannot surprise us."

"Seriously, what is he going on about?" Carlos said.

Mercedes sighed, a chair scraping to indicate she was sitting, too. "Dorian said something about the stolen drugs and the girls not mattering. Not after—an hour and thirteen minutes now."

Adam sank into his lounge chair and held his head in his hands. The weight of his obsession with Blake hung heavy over his shoulders and imprisoned his mind.

"He's planning something," Paul said.

"Obviously," Dan said, rolling his eyes. "But how the fuck are we supposed to know what?"

"Wait a minute," Carlos frowned. He'd been silent so far. Adam lifted his head hopefully. Carlos was always observant. If there was something, surely Carlos, always pushed to the shadows but with his eyes and ears open, would know something. "What's Blake doing today?"

"Uh," Mercedes said. "I don't know—ribbon cutting at some opening, and then fuck knows what."

The others were intrigued now, too, judging from their wide eyes. Even Mercedes paled a little bit as she realized what she said.

"When has he *ever* done a ribbon cutting?" Paul said. "*Ever.*"

"It's a front," Adam said, picking up on the train of thought. "Blake's securing himself an alibi."

"For what?" Dan threw his hands in the air. "There could be thousands of things going on at that time."

Adam's shoulders dropped, even as the rest of his body tensed. An awkward combination. He squeezed his eyes shut, cursing his own fucking ignorance and stupidity. There, on the floor among the papers he'd already discarded, was a slip of paper.

"Fuck," Adam said, picking the paper up from the floor. He slammed it down on the table in front of his friends, imploring them to take a closer look as well.

They leaned in tight to read it. It was the ballot that Mercedes had stolen from Blake. It looked the same as it did the last time they saw it, with Dorian Blake's name pre-selected on all the boxes.

"It's the same ballot," Carlos pointed out.

"Read the dates," Adam said.

They synchronously whipped their eyes back to the paper and read again.

"June 17th," Paul stuttered. "That's five months too early."

"Which means..." Adam couldn't finish the sentence.

Lucky Dan was right there picking up on his trail. "Blake is about to make sure this election happens five months early. On June 17th."

And just like that, the whole revenge plan—hinging on his 'before the fucking election' timeline—was shot straight to hell.

CHAPTER 12
HOURGLASS

"Hang on a minute," Carlos said, his eyes still scanning the ballot. "Not everyone's name is on this list."

"What?" Paul rounded the table, leaning over Carlos' shoulder.

"How could he possibly get the election moved to an earlier date?" Mercedes mused, tapping on her chin.

"He couldn't," Dan said. "It's not possible."

Paul and Carlos were whispering over the ballot, but Adam's focus was on Dan.

"If anyone could, it'd be Dorian," Mercedes said.

"Pfft," Dan scoffed. "The only way to get an election moved up is if the current mayor is dead and that–"

"Guys," Carlos's voice tensed. "Diego's name isn't on this."

Mercedes snatched the paper from Carlos with wide eyes. "What the fuck?"

Adam read it over her shoulder and cursed himself internally again. He was such a fucking idiot. This paper changed everything, and they'd tossed it aside in his fucking nightstand! "Because he knows by the time the election will roll around, Diego will already be dead. He's going to kill him. That's why he needs an alibi and why he knows the election will be moved up."

Adam paced the room, his emotions growing in panic.

"What the fuck are we gonna do?" Carlos huffed.

"June 17th is less than three months away! If Blake succeeds here, we're fucked. Fucked," Dan said.

Carlos thumped his head onto the table.

"We can't afford to have our timeline shortened by that much," Paul said. "We were pushing it as it was."

"Pushing it? We were trying to pull off the impossible, if we lose half our timeline, it cannot be done!" Dan shouted.

Mercedes glared him down, so he turned to Carlos for support.

"It can't be done," Carlos agreed. "If we lose time, if the election gets moved up. We cannot beat Dorian Blake. He wins. Instant. Automatic."

"Then we have to stop it," Adam said, his thick brows smothering his frown. "Where is Diego right now?"

Dan checked his watch. "He has a regular golf game."

"Then we really are fucked," Paul said. "Out in the open like that? It's a sniper's wet dream."

"Gear up," Adam said. "We're stopping this fucking hit."

***

Adam was the only one left sitting in Paul's van across from the golf course. When they'd arrived, Diego had been on the twelfth hole. Alive, still. Luckily. Dan had worked his way into a security position, and Carlos had slipped in as an extra caddy. No one had noticed. Which meant security was lax and he had his work cut out for him.

"Am I good to go?" Adam buzzed into his radio.

"You're good." Mercedes's voice came back. She and Paul had positioned in a tower opposite the course, him sniping and her spotting.

Adam approached the entrance, sporting his own disguise in a green-keeper's uniform, and floated past Dan who waved him in.

He positioned at the edge of the fourteenth hole, thanking all his luck that holes one through thirteen had obviously been a bust. He couldn't keep still, fiddling with anything he could. Buttons on his jumpsuit, grass, random assortments of tools.

"Incoming," Dan said. Adam turned over his shoulder to see Diego, his team, and several city officials move onto the fourteenth. Carlos was staying back, far enough away to be unthought of, but not so far that he would fall behind.

Careful not to rouse suspicion, Adam tailed Diego and the officials around the course. With each new hole that was completed without any activity, Adam grew more and more nervous. They couldn't afford to miss their opportunity to intercept a potential shot.

By the time they hit hole seventeen, his skin was practically on fire with irritation.

There was a chance they were wrong. That Diego wasn't the target. And he'd wasted the better part of forty minutes trudging up a golf course, sweating his balls off.

"Are we sure this is where it's going down?" Adam asked into the radio.

"It's where I'd do it," Paul said. That did a lot to settle his nerves.

"Hang on, I have something," Dan said. "Got someone approaching, check the pro shop."

There was a lone golfer approaching the entrance where Dan was stationed. He brought his own clubs and declined a caddy. Adam listened over the radio as Dan greeted him and let him onto the golf course.

"Did you get that?" Dan said.

"Got it." Adam watched as the man bypassed hole one and moved farther through the course. He didn't take out any clubs, and he didn't appear to head to any specific hole. He was moving completely out of order.

"We've got him in sights," Mercedes said.

The man disappeared underneath a shade of trees, crouching low and taking out a cigarette. His general demeanor made him seem suspicious, but somehow Adam felt this wasn't the threat they were searching for.

"It's not the guy," Paul sighed. "He's just having a smoke."

"Well, we're at hole seventeen now. If it's happening, it's happening soon," Adam said.

"Do you guys see that?" Dan's uncertain voice came through the radio. Looking back at his friend near the entry, Adam found Dan cocking his head, looking curiously out to where Diego was pushing up to tee on the seventeenth.

"What is it?" Adam said.

"There's a red dot floating around out there," Dan said, his voice rising in alarm.

"Oh, shit," Mercedes said.

"Do you see the source?!" Adam said.

"We don't have a source," Paul said, his tone indicating he was deep breathing to steady his weapon in case he had to make any hasty shots.

Fuck it. They couldn't wait.

Adam started a run toward Diego's location. "Carlos, I need you to create a distraction. Make sure they can't get a clear shot on Diego."

"Fuck my job," Carlos muttered.

Up on the green Carlos twitched on his feet, his shoulders slumping before he trudged to where Diego stood with his golf club poised to strike. Shaking out his hand, Carlos made a fist and calmly punched Diego square in the face.

His companions immediately ceased their chatter.

"What in the—" were all the words Diego could get out before his security team tackled Carlos to the grass. Diego was ushered away and pressed against the golf cart for safety.

"I see something!" Mercedes announced suddenly. "Sniper, fifth floor of the parking lot."

"He has a clear shot. I don't have a shot on him," Paul shouted.

Adam, approaching Diego at a run, noted the general location of the parking lot.

His friends must've been watching because Paul said, "Shot likely incoming northeast at 34 degrees."

Adam made an incredulous face that he was sure they couldn't see. Fucking northeast? Degrees? What?!

"Left leaning shot to the heart, center of mass, angling downward," Mercedes said, somehow knowing that she had to translate without Adam needing to ask.

Adam rushed past Diego's security, who were far too easily distracted by Carlos, and fisted Diego's shirt, tugging him down and to the right just as a bullet punctured the golf cart where Diego had been standing upright not five seconds earlier. Not letting go, Adam pulled Diego around the side of the cart and sheltered them low. Two more missed gunshots punctured where they'd stood.

Security swarmed around Diego, leaving Carlos to make a run for it.

"Do you have the sniper?" Adam said into the radio.

"No, he's on the move," Paul said.

Leaving Diego with his security team, who were calling in police and ambulances, Adam made a break for the front entrance where Dan was waiting for him. They each pulled out a pistol and headed for the parking garage.

They arrived at the ground level, guns at the ready and moving through the concrete structure dodging cars. But the hitman was nowhere to be found.

"Empty," Dan said as he surveyed the area.

They passed shadowed areas and jumped over railings, but still nothing. At the other end of the building they exited the parking lot into an empty open plaza.

"We can't let him get away, who knows what he saw," Adam said.

Dan's mouth tightened and he nodded in sharp agreement.

They split up to search for any sign of their opponent. Each of them knew that they couldn't take any risks in the hitman identifying them or breathing a word of their intervention.

Adam jumped back in a huff after checking another hiding spot to no avail. That was until he felt the cool tip of a gun pressing against the back of his head and froze. His mind betrayed him, his heart hammering as it recalled the horrific memory of standing on a cliff face watching a train grow smaller in the distance. Only then it was a different gun at the back of his head all those years ago.

Adam raised his hands and dropped his pistol, purposefully making a loud clank. Dan spun to face them, eyes widening even as he kept his weapon drawn.

"You have caused a big problem for me," the hitman's deep voice bounded.

"Take the shot," Adam said.

"You are not fast enough. Either way, today you die."

"I'm afraid that's not an option," Adam said. "I'm actually quite hard to kill."

"You have much confidence," the hitman said. "It is unfounded. If Dorian Blake wants someone dead. They are already dead."

The hitman's barrel clicked.

With a crash, blood sprayed like a party popper, and a deafening ringing echoed across the open plaza. The hitman's body hit the floor.

Adam, his back covered in spray from the hitman's blood, turned to face the dead body. Bending over to catch his breath and slow his racing heart, he released a deep exhale before speaking into his radio. "Nice shot, Paul."

***

"Cheers!" They raised their glasses in salute, none more excited than Adam to have foiled Blake's plans. He'd celebrate the wins where he could. One very alive mayor. One very dead hitman. Timeline crisis averted, for now.

Their new bar crowded as night drew near, filling up with other unsuspecting revelers as they relaxed, playing pool and shooting back drinks. The news played on a loop in the background, reporters swarming for every gory detail of a near-miss murder plot against the Mayor of Ridge City. A lucky escape for the incumbent, they were calling it.

Adam smiled. Yeah, luck. If luck's name was Adam Vandemilio.

"You're still as sharp as ever!" Dan patted Paul on the back. "I really thought we were done for there."

"Yes, here's to you." Mercedes hugged her childhood friend.

"So you're a good shot, but let's see how sharp you are in pool," Carlos laughed and dragged Paul away for a bet on a pool game.

"Don't bet him any money you aren't prepared to lose," Adam called out. Dan excused himself to the bar, eyes lingering a little too long on a leggy brunette who looked pleased with the attention.

"That was a close one," Mercedes said.

"Too close," Adam said. "You know, I never did like being held at gunpoint."

"Could've fooled me," Mercedes said, swirling her drink.

He could easily fall with her into this abyss of flirty banter and die happily. He watched her swirl her drink where the diamond ring on her finger was creating light circles. It was certainly bigger than the one he'd had for her. But he sensed Dorian's was too weighty anyway, holding her back in more ways than one.

"So, what do you think Blake is doing right now?" Adam settled back into the booth, resting his outstretched arms across the back of the seat. Feeling rightly smug, if he said so himself. "Crying in the corner or raging at the impossibility of being outwitted?"

"Wow, you really hate that man, don't you?" Mercedes laughed. What planet had she been living on?

"The man who nearly murdered me, ruined my life, and stole my girlfriend?" Adam hardened. "Just a little bit."

Mercedes chugged her beer and slammed the bottle down. "He didn't steal me. You gave me away." Her tone lacked any semblance of menace, holding only resignation.

The less-than-subtle indication that he had given her away tore strips into his already bleeding heart. "So you think it's option one, too? He's definitely crying in the corner?" he said, trying to lighten the mood.

"Actually." Mercedes pointed toward the TV with a frown. "Looks like he's about to tell you himself."

He focused on the screen, where apparently Blake was about to speak to the media. Which didn't make an awful lot of sense. Something in his gut tingled in nervous anticipation.

"Thank you for being here," Blake began, speaking as camera flashes burst in his face. "It is with great regret and sadness that I must inform you of the tragic death of my opponent and colleague Diego Garcia." He paused, like he was waiting for gasps, or fuck, probably just for psychotic dramatic affect. "While recovering in the hospital from the attempt on his life, Mayor Garcia unfortunately succumbed to his injuries."

Adam's eyes widened as Mercedes leaned forward.

"What fucking injuries?" Dan said, appearing back in the booth like his legs had slipped out from underneath him.

"The sudden death of Mayor Garcia has rocked us all. Taken far too young. A good man who was devoted to his wife and his children, and to the people of the city. From personal experience I can attest to the fact there was no better man than Diego Garcia. Rest assured, the culprit of this violent and vicious attack will be punished, and Diego will dearly be missed. Our thoughts are with his family, who have asked for privacy at this difficult time."

He'd lost all sense of his surroundings, his eyes glued to the TV in disbelief. "He... He killed him anyway," Adam said, dread wrenching his heart.

"It's an absolute tragedy what has occurred today. It shows a demonstration of the violence that has been a cornerstone of the culture in Ridge City for many decades now. As a city and as a people, we need to send a clear message to those who would do us harm. To them, we stand up and say: your violence will not be accepted. Their destructive will cannot control the outcome of this election."

Blake signed off with a sinister smile straight to the camera that sent Adam's gut dropping.

After a few moments, an older looking man—who was clearly a city official from how he dressed—took the mic. It squealed as he tapped it, and then the man began his announcement, with much less charm than Blake had Adam could begrudgingly admit.

"For as long as we continue to draw out the election... is an... is an amount of time longer that we continue to place the lives of our candidates and their families in harm's way. For that reason, I would like to announce... on behalf of my esteemed colleagues, that the election will be moved forward. In the interest of candidate safety and stopping the perpetuation of... of gang violence in Ridge City, you will now be asked to cast your vote five months early, on June 17th."

Frozen in shock, Adam only briefly made out his friends' panicked murmuring. He couldn't hear them, like his internal rage and disbelief had blocked all ability to hear sound. Unable to tear his gaze away from the screen, his fingers tightened on his glass to the point of pain, until it smashed underneath his hand. And even the blood that dripped from his hand felt like it had gone cold.

***

"Adam? Adam?" Mercedes snapped her fingers in front of his face. Adam sat in his hotel room at the end of his bed, shoes still on. He could barely make out what she was saying. Though his name was like a prayer on her lips.

"Adam?" she snapped her fingers in front of his face again. Suddenly his eyes darted toward hers, making her jump back quickly, hand on heart.

"Where are the others?"

"Still at the bar."

That's right. After the announcement of Diego's 'sudden death', the two of them had rushed out of the bar. Leaving Dan, Carlos, and Paul behind at Mercedes's instruction. She seemed to sense it was her he needed.

She had always had a way with words, a nurturing instinct, and so of course, none of them had argued when she asked them to give her space.

"Diego is dead," Adam said. Mercedes nodded. "I couldn't save him."

She knelt down in front of him, dropping her head to find his eyes under his downward gaze. "There was nothing we could've done."

"I let him die."

"You didn't let him die," Mercedes said. She placed her hands on his knees and caressed him lightly.

"I could've saved him if I'd figured it out sooner." Adam rubbed his head in his hands and pushed his fingers through his hair.

"Nobody could have saved him," Mercedes said, but she sounded like she wasn't sure if she believed it.

"He has three kids, Mercedes. And a wife, and now he's dead."

Standing up tall, she brushed the hair out of her eyes and tucked it neatly behind her ear. "We did everything we could."

"We could've done more. Now Blake has the upper hand," Adam said. "I don't know how we let him get the jump on us. And we were at that fucking bar celebrating our win like amateurs."

The bed sheets wrinkled as she sat down next to him and drew comforting circles on his back. "Dorian is always one step ahead. He's smart, and cunning. There's a reason people are afraid of him."

Adam looked up at her, barely containing his annoyance at that statement. The whole point was to pull one over on Dorian Blake.

"I just mean we can't beat ourselves up when he gets a little bit ahead. That's what he does. He gets ahead. He may not be much in a fight, but he's smart, and he always does things you never see coming."

Dan gently pushed open the door of Adam's room, peering in with only his head like he was checking if the coast was clear. "Can we come in?"

Mercedes nodded, though he wasn't sure if he was ready to face the others. Somehow back in the day he'd become the leader of this group, and now every win and loss felt like it rested solely on his heavy-hung shoulders.

Mercedes stood up from the bed as Dan, Carlos, and Paul filtered into the room, looking at Adam like he was a wild animal that could scamper off into the woods at any sudden movement.

"Every news station is playing the news about the election move up," Paul said.

"Three months to go," Mercedes said. "That's more than half our timeline. Gone."

"What the hell are we gonna do now?" Dan said, flopping down at the dining table.

"Turns out it didn't matter what we did. Blake's plan was going to be a success anyway," Carlos said.

"Now just hold on, it's not over, we've still got three months," Paul said.

"We're screwed. We're totally screwed," Dan said, growing panicky. "We've started something now and we can't wind it back."

"It's way too late to wind anything back," Paul sighed, clearly also sensing the tension rising in Dan's throat.

Bad news did terrible things to his friends, they always retreated into panic and despair before conviction. Setbacks didn't have the potential to steer himself off course...well...usually they didn't, at least up until five years ago, he supposed.

"What the fuck are we gonna do if we can't actually pull this off? All of us flee the city this time?" Dan said, standing to round out a circle with Paul, Mercedes, and Carlos.

"Oh, shit," Carlos agreed. "Are we all gonna have to up and leave now?"

"No one has to leave the fucking city." Mercedes rolled her eyes.

The four of them started shouting among themselves, Mercedes and Paul reasoning that they didn't have to flee, and Carlos and Dan becoming more agitated and afraid by the second. Fingers pointed across the circle as their words grew loud and fidgety.

"Adam, tell them that we're not gonna have to up and leave the city." Paul held the trump card, turning to Adam as a tiebreaker.

He stared Dan and Carlos down, like he was expecting that at any second Adam would jump to his defense. When he got no response, he turned back to Adam, still sitting silently at the edge of the bed. "Adam?"

Adam stared at his four friends standing in a circle, looking to him for guidance. But how could he possible assure them when he couldn't push away his own fears. He closed his eyes and took a deep breath.

He'd made a colossal mistake five years ago, letting the setbacks make him think he should give up. He wouldn't make that mistake again. He was never giving up. So he couldn't afford to be afraid. His friends needed him.

Slowly, he stood, folding his arms and rising. "We're not leaving the city. We're not going anywhere."

"Then what're we gonna do?" Dan asked.

"We knew this was gonna be hard. We're not gonna quit now," Adam said. "We've got less time than we thought, but we've still got time. It's not over until it's over. I still believe we can do this. I still believe in us, and I still believe in this team. We will succeed."

Adam checked around the room, making eye contact with each of them, to make sure that he had their full attention.

"We're not giving up?" Dan asked. Adam shook his head.

"But it's impossible to stop him now," Carlos argued.

"No, it's not. It's just harder," Adam said. "And I don't know about all of you, but I've never been afraid of a challenge."

Adam smiled. "Okay, the election is in June. It's now March. So we've got three months to make this come together, and we can. It's time to get serious. We can't go half-hearted, we have to go hard, we have to go big, and we can no longer be afraid. Nothing great ever comes from staying in your comfort zone."

"Damn," Mercedes smiled her approval, looking at him like she knew how he felt. Like he'd found himself.

"So let's lay out a plan, a real one this time," Adam said. "Carlos—we can't keep running supplies out from under Blake. We need something of our own. See what you can come up with. Dan—we need to get the law on our side. See what you can do about getting some officials on our books.

Even better if you can steal them from Blake's side. Paul—we need to expand into the arms' contracts, I want to know everything you know about Blake's gun supply chains. Mercedes—you're the eyes on the inside," he said, even though it made him cringe to admit the advantage. "I want to know what he's doing and when he's doing it."

Adam looked around the room at his friends. His heart was beating fast and heavy, he was terrified, but he knew some things were bigger than fear. His dreams were bigger than his fears. Somehow, he truly felt like he didn't have to push his fear away, that he could harness it, build it, grow it inside of him until it turned into nothing but inspiration.

"We all get that?" Adam asked, noticing each of them nod their heads in approval. "Good. Let's get to work."

***

When Mercedes arrived home, the maid informed her that Dorian had requested her presence on the back terrace. So she'd walked straight through the house, through the bifold doors at the rear, and down the Mediterranean stone steps to the terrace overlooking the water. It was only once she saw T.B., Yani, and Antonio all gathered around in a circle and the powerboat floating on the private deck, that her suspicions raised.

The powerboat always meant Dorian was in the mood for murder. Whose, though? That remained to be seen.

"What's going on?" she asked as she approached them.

"Couldn't tell you," Antonio said as he flicked a cigarette from his hand into the open waters.

"He's pissed about something," T.B. said. "Don't fucking know why, it's not like he just successfully killed Diego or anything."

Mercedes raised her brow in T.B.'s direction.

185

"Oh, right," T.B. winced. "I wasn't supposed to tell you that."

As they heard the click of Dorian's footsteps approaching from the house, they turned expectantly.

"Honey, what's going on?" Mercedes asked.

"Something big is happening," Dorian said, eyeing them all. "Get onto the boat."

She hated when he kept his face blank like that. It made him so difficult to read. But obviously he wasn't the biggest fucking crime boss in the city because he plastered his face with his emotions twenty-four-seven.

Mercedes glanced again at the powerboat. T.B., Yani, and Antonio all exchanged nervous and defensive looks. Like they also knew powerboats meant murder, and one of them would be returning as shark food. Upon closer inspection...nope, this motley crew looked like they'd feed each other to the sharks to save their own skins.

Antonio started, "Is that really—"

"Get on the fucking boat!!"

Doing just as they were told, one after the other, they all embarked, waiting patiently with only the splash of ocean breaking the silence. The tension was thick as Dorian drove erratically out into the open ocean. Once they were far enough from the mansion that it appeared as only a distant speck, Dorian turned off the motor and came to face them.

Sitting at the front of the boat with her legs crossed while the others stood around her, Mercedes asked again, "What's going on?"

He paused and, interestingly, hesitated before he spoke. Unusual for him, Mercedes thought.

"Somebody is coming for me," Dorian said.

"Somebody's what?" Antonio's voice quivered like he didn't believe what was being said. Surely nobody out there would be stupid enough to challenge The Great Dorian Blake.

"That's crazy, boss," T.B. said.

"Nobody is that stupid," Antonio agreed.

"Sorry, what? You think someone is coming for you?" Mercedes said, placing her hand on her chest. It was meant to be an attempt to appear shocked, but it *was* actually shocking news to hear. Had they been figured out? Did he suspect that she was a part of it?

"If they're coming for me, they'll be coming for you, too, darling," Dorian said. Perhaps he was still in the dark for now.

"That's impossible," she scoffed.

"It's not only possible, it's happening," Yani said.

"What the hell do you know?" Antonio said, squaring up (stupidly) to the much-larger Second.

"Shut the fuck up," Dorian said calmly. "This isn't time for infighting. We are under attack."

"Who?" Antonio said.

"I don't know," Dorian said, and Mercedes breathed a silent sigh of relief. "But our drug supplies keep getting stolen, T.B. was run off the road, now the whores have sent a message that they're working for someone else."

"But you got Diego? We moved up the election. This is time for celebrating!" Antonio said.

"Yeah, we got Diego. As a fucking improvisation. Greedy fucking hospital nurses cost me thousands administering that unfortunate death. Someone murdered my fucking sniper," Dorian belted, scrubbing a hand over his jaw. "Which means someone figured out what I was trying to do, and tried to stop me."

She steadied herself against the rocking of the boat along the water. It all made perfect sense. Dorian's conclusion was obvious, and it was correct. Fuck.

"Oh, God," Antonio said, dropping into a seat like he had followed her thoughts exactly. But was panicking for a completely different reason.

"No way, it's not fucking possible!" T.B. shouted.

"It is," Dorian said. "Someone is plotting to take me down. Now I don't want to tip them off that I have any idea…business as usual, so nobody else can know about this. The three of you are going to find out who is coming after me, and fast."

Great, so the powerboat would mean murder. Hers… if she couldn't keep one step ahead of him.

CHAPTER 13
BY THE BOOK

T he blinds drew suddenly, the scorching sun streaming in through exposed glass windows. Jolting from his sleep, Adam sat up in bed, shielding his eyes with his forearm and clutching the black bedsheets in his other hand.

"Rise and shine." Mercedes's jovial laugh found him long before he saw her standing at the window, hands on hips.

"How did you get in here?"

"You're not the only one who can scale walls and get the jump on people," said Mercedes. "It's annoying, isn't it?"

Rolling out of bed with a grumble, Adam stalked to the window. He grabbed the curtains and pulled them shut again, reaching past Mercedes' shoulders to hold the drapes sealed, his lips only inches from hers as he held the fabric still.

"Carlos and I need you for something," she said. "He's waiting downstairs."

It was far too early in the morning for the intrusion. He'd never been a morning person.

His sleep attire was only light gray sweatpants, and though she clearly tried not to, her eyes betrayed her and settled on his bare skin.

Pride had him puffing up his chest. He wanted her to take him in. To remember. But, to his surprise, the wicked smirk playing on her lips dissolved in an instant.

"Those scars," she said, eyes pained. "You can see the holes from the stitches."

Right, the scars. He had forgotten about them, honestly. He certainly wasn't ashamed of his body, even less so of the white, raised tissue that healed over his bullet wounds. But he forgot that she'd never seen the scars before.

"Three shots," he said. He took her hand in his and placed it over the scars one by one. "One." He pressed her fingers into his sternum. "Two." He let her fingers slide down to the left side of his ribcage. "Three." He slid her fingers through his abs to his lower torso.

Her palm shook when she withdrew it, her breathing quickened, the glint in her eye making it seem like she could feel the bullets. Something stirred in her eyes that she was trying to keep hidden. Adam could see it.

"I should be dead," he said.

Leaving her, he picked a white t-shirt from his drawer, sliding it over his muscled chest. "I would've been, if it weren't for you."

He slid the drawer shut, watching her for any willingness to discuss. He didn't find it, and he wouldn't push it.

"After you," he said, opening the door and bowing to wave her through. She wouldn't look at him the whole way down to street level. She was still his Mercedes. Always. But something had changed. He feared he'd been the one to change it. He just hoped it wasn't permanent.

Down on the street, they found Carlos leaning against the side of his car. "Bro." Carlos jumped when he saw them. "You gotta check this out."

Opening the back door, Carlos revealed an assortment of chemicals, beakers, and metal drums scattered along the seat.

"What is it?" Adam asked.

"This... is the future," Carlos said. Well, at least someone was excited about it. Grabbing a beaker, Carlos presented it forward and beamed like he was holding proof that unicorns existed. "We can use this to turn our regular old cocaine hydrochloride supply into crystallized rocks. Apparently, it's a big seller, we'll edge Dorian right out of the market."

Science, science. Chemicals, chemicals. Nonsense.

"Rocks?" Adam said, smothering his laugh.

"Yeah, man," Carlos nodded. "The effects are instant, and it sells for more than coke does." Nobody should've been excited about cooking up drugs, but Carlos was. Sweet little Catholic Carlos.

"You're gonna cook this?" Adam shook his head, finding Mercedes suppressing a giggle of her own.

"Yeah, easy," Carlos said. "This is the shit they've been making in Darton. Bet I can make it a whole lot better though."

"Fucking hell, alright." Adam finally succumbed to his laughter. "Let's get the kit upstairs then."

Carlos scooped the equipment into his arms, piling it high and struggling to see over the top of his loot as he hobbled up the stairs. Like a kid on Christmas.

Adam made to follow him, but stopped when he felt his arm being tugged back. Mercedes held him at the elbow.

"There's something else," she said. "Something bad, possibly."

"What is it?" he frowned, letting her drop his arm from her grip, though he instantly missed the touch.

"Dorian knows someone is after him," Mercedes said, adding before Adam could explode with panic, "He doesn't know who yet."

Damn.

"He's catching up," Adam said, more resigned to the fact than worried.

"He's catching up," Mercedes agreed.

"Okay, just keep an eye on it," Adam said, and Mercedes nodded. As he'd always said, if his life was safe in anyone's hands, it would always be hers.

***

"What do you think?" Adam asked, raising his arms and feeling more impressed with himself than usual. He was usually pretty impressive, too, if he did say so himself.

It was the middle of the day, so the bar was closed, but still as dark and dingy, not managing to filter in any natural light, and somehow smelling more odorous with nobody in it. Dan had paid cash, and so their purchase had settled the week prior. Now it was officially theirs, and since they had decided not to give up and flee Ridge City, it was the perfect place to plot to take down Dorian Blake in three months or less.

"It's a shit hole," Paul said.

"Yeah, but it's our shit hole." Dan bounced around.

Adam followed Paul's eye over the rotting walls and broken tabletops. He needed to stop overthinking and see its potential, instead.

"And why did you buy this?" Paul said.

"We've got a big group of people now, they need a place to cool off," Adam said.

"And this was that place," Paul cringed, but Adam saw through the façade and found the tease for what it was. Sneaky prick. He liked the place, just didn't want to admit it.

Dan rushed from wall to wall, throwing pool cues around the place for seemingly no reason other than for the hell of it. Adam watched on in amusement while Paul just frowned. The same thing had happened last time they owned a place. They'd never had much respect for property, so Paul always had to remind them to at least respect their own.

Dan threw a striped ball across the room where it lodged in the wall.

They'd never learned. Obviously.

"How are you doing with the arms' supplies?" Adam asked, ignoring Dan running across the bar top.

"It's rough," Paul said. "I only get the supplies once a deal has gone down, no idea where they come from."

Adam frowned, disappointed, but let it go for now. "Dan?"

Like a kid who had been caught with his hand in the candy jar, Dan halted on the bar top and climbed down sensibly.

"How you doing with the officials?"

"Not great," Dan admitted, coming up to join Adam and Paul. "I don't know who's who, Blake keeps all that locked down. I mean, Blake keeps the paperwork in my office. So access isn't an issue, but it's all written in gibberish. Some kind of code that I can't read."

"Same for me," Paul agreed. "Got all the docs at the range, but no way to know what the fuck they say."

It was as if a lightbulb appeared over Adam's head and dinged the answer right into his brain. Excitedly waving his finger at Dan, he said, "We need Blake's encryption key."

"Oh, fuck no." Dan rolled his eyes, obviously seeing where Adam was going before Paul had caught up.

"And where can we get this key?" Paul narrowed his eyes but patiently saw the question through.

"White book," Adam said, smiling so widely his teeth could fall out.

Paul's face dropped. "No fucking way."

"Come on."

Paul and Dan seemed to realize at the same moment that Adam was far from joking. "You've got to be kidding," Paul said. "The fucking white book?"

Shrugging, Adam said, "Why not?"

"No way! Blake's white book is locked up in the safe, in his office, that's three levels of protection to get to it. We'd need to get into the mansion, unlock his office, and then crack his safe. No way!" Dan said.

What a challenge. That would be fucking ecstasy.

"We need that white book," Adam said, lips twitching up.

"Not this fucking badly!" Dan said.

"Yeah. That fucking badly." It was a struggle for Adam to remain steadfast. This would be a heist, dangerous and stupid and fun, all the things Adam lived for. He had to convince his friends it was the best plan, not just Adam running off for the sake of stupidity. Which, admittedly, he did often do.

"I'm serious," Adam said. "Three months to go. This is an advantage and an opportunity we can't ignore."

To his surprise, Dan and Paul stared him down. It wasn't often that his team disagreed with him, and it definitely wasn't often that Paul felt strongly enough about something to drop his always-reliable support.

"No way, it's ridiculous and it's dangerous. Find another way to get your shit done," Paul scoffed, storming out of the bar and leaving Adam and Dan in the dust. Adam raised a brow to Dan, turning down his mouth as if to prod him further. This time, Dan cracked a smile, but still walked away before Adam could get to him. But that smile said more than his words could.

That he'd wear them down eventually.

***

JUNE 1986

Mercedes was wrapped tightly in his arms as they laid on the couch in Adam's trailer. So close that he could hear the soft contented beats of her heart, smiling when she sighed happily into his shoulder.

He slipped one hand into the back of her jeans, and with the other brushed the hair away from her jaw, lifting her chin to his ever so slightly as he reached in to taste her.

The doors to his trailer burst open with a crack, and their faces snapped apart, eyeing the door.

Paul raged inside with clenched fists, followed closely by Carlos and Dan.

"Dude, knock much?" Adam scoffed as he stood up.

Paul, looking violently enraged, snatched the TV remote and turned to the local news.

Mercedes sat up from the couch, and looked to Adam nervously. They all turned their heads to watch the screen while Paul's eyes fixated solely on Adam.

On the screen, footage played from the view of a helicopter. The grass below blew against the blades, and a newswoman narrated the devastation. A prison van had crashed in the middle of the highway, guards near dead, and the high-value, most-wanted prisoner no longer alive on the side of the road. The news obscured the view of the body, but she described it in such gory detail that it sounded worse than it looked.

Great for tourism. Adam chuckled.

She finished her story with the obvious, as if she had to explain it to the people of Ridge City. "Police say they are investigating links to organized crime as the prisoner was due to face court on gang-related charges later this month."

The TV played out the reactions in the studio as mere background noise. Mercedes, Adam, Dan, and Carlos all turned toward Paul, who was still glaring at Adam like he could bore holes into his skull.

"Fuckkk," Dan sighed. "Blake has been trying to free that guy for years."

Adam returned Paul's deadly sharp stare.

"What the fuck did you do?" Paul spat.

"Chill out, I sent Dorian Blake a little message," Adam said, sliding his crossed arms against his chest.

"That's—God—what? A message?"

Adam laughed before shutting down and turning to anger. He placed his hands firmly in his pockets and looked up from his lowered head. "He threatened me. In my club."

"Goddammit, don't make this personal!"

Adam narrowed his eyes. How could this be anything but personal?

"Alright, that's enough." Mercedes rose to stand in between Paul and Adam. But Adam knew he was being a bit of a shit, so he would've let Paul get in one good punch before he clobbered him.

"Don't," Paul warned her, all sense of reason gone from his voice. "I know you helped him. He could not have chased a prison van down and outrun T.B. without your help."

Mercedes dropped her eyes to the floor, as good as admitting her involvement.

"This time it was business," Adam said. "Blake needs to know that he can't threaten me and get away with it."

"Blake can do whatever he wants and get away with it!" Paul shouted.

"That's exactly the fucking problem!"

Paul's eyes shuttered, the room silent until Carlos dared to speak. "You weren't there with us all those years ago. You didn't see what we saw."

"Lose what we lost," Dan chimed in.

"Dorian Blake may be a scary fucker," Carlos admitted. "But after everything we've been through, I want to see him burn."

Paul had made Adam promise he'd ask the others before he started a gang war with Dorian Blake. And yes... he *had* forgotten. But it looked like they were on board, so Paul needed to back down.

"You don't get it." Paul shook his head, calming enough to let the pang of fear show across his dark eyes. "None of you worked alongside Dorian Blake for as long as I did. This isn't how he operates, it isn't how he works."

"We know how we works," Dan said solemnly. "Bribes and dishonor and murdering innocent bystanders. When he paid off one of our neighbors to give up someone who happened to be hiding on our street, do you think he took his target and stopped? Or do you think he slaughtered our entire neighborhood until there was nothing left."

"Nothing left but the three of us," Adam finished for him.

"I used to have three sisters, did you know that? These two were my brothers, sure," Dan said, gesturing at Adam and Carlos. "But I used to have three sisters."

"Six cousins, two aunts, and a mother," Carlos said.

"So yeah, we know how he works," Dan said.

"And when someone pledges loyalty to me, it won't be able to be bought away with a fucking bribe," Adam said. The mood in the room shifted dramatically, all three of them staring Paul down. And though Adam knew it wasn't fair to put that on Paul, he did need him to understand. Because Dorian Blake was a fucking dead man, and he didn't care how long it took. It was happening.

Paul shared a loaded look with Mercedes.

"I'm sorry. You know I'm sorry for everything you've been through at his hand. But I've been under this thumb, too. I was nearly a Second. I know how he operates. Much better than any of you do. And regardless of what *he's* done to *us*, what *you've* done," he squared his jaw at Adam, "you just signed our fucking death sentence."

***

APRIL 1991

Adam had begun to find solace in the old lot. Their trailer park, the place that they once called home. Though now it was reduced to ashes, nothing left but rubble and brown, overgrown grass.

More and more often, he found himself spending time there. There was a wholesomeness to ending up back where he started. That day, he'd brought Paul to spend the afternoon shooting cans off broken brick walls.

Paul took care when lining cans up on the bricks, placing each with the delicate embrace of a lover. Adam smashed that all to hell when he shot it out of Paul's hands.

"Can you wait until I'm done, please, before you start," Paul huffed. "You're a terrible shot. Could've hit me."

Adam laughed and reloaded his gun, waving to usher Paul out of range. Sure, he was a little impatient. Call it a character flaw. Though he'd always thought impatience was more of a virtue.

He downed two more cans in the time it took for Paul to walk back to his side.

"Your shot." Adam handed Paul the gun, covering his mouth with his palm to hold in another laugh. It was a taunt, always a taunt. Paul *was* the better shot, so Adam's only hope was to psyche him out.

"That's how it's gonna be?" Paul gave him an incredulous look, rolling his shoulders like he'd only just decided to take this seriously. Taking only seconds, Paul focused the gun, shot seven times, and killed each can in succession. So quickly that smoke still hung and the shrill of gunfire rang into one long hum. When he turned back Adam greeted him with nothing but humility. "That's what I thought."

They both turned to look as Mercedes's car pulled in, blowing the brown dust into a whirlwind. She was quickly out of the car, followed by Dan and Carlos.

When Adam saw her heading to him, his heart flashed with memory. One of her running into his arms in this very spot, five years earlier, with her hair flapping in the wind. Wrapping her arms around him and looking at him like the stars were born behind his eyes.

But it was just a memory. One that seemed less like reality with each passing day.

Carlos was the first to reach him, waving a small plastic bag like a flag. "Look at these!" Carlos said. "Beautiful, aren't they?"

"Is this the crystallized coke?" Adam asked, snatching the bag and holding it to the sunlight. "Is it any good?"

Now having caught up, Mercedes lingered next to Paul while Dan sank himself into a camper chair and pushed his sunglasses over his face.

"I can personally attest that it is fucking top notch shit," Dan smiled, clearly baked and out of his mind. He retrieved another bag from God knows where, his hands jittering as he attempted to light it.

"Fucking hell." Carlos knocked the lighter from Dan's hand. "Don't have more so quickly, you moron."

"Well, the focus group seems to like it," Adam said, frowning in mild concern for Dan. He couldn't judge his friends for their vices though. After all, Adam's idea of a good time was *murder*, so… "Can we get it on the street?"

"I think we need richer clientele for this one. If we really want to make a splash," Carlos said.

Adam grinned wickedly while Paul sighed and rubbed a hand over his face. Oh, Carlos. He'd just walked right where Adam wanted him, and Paul knew it.

"Richer clientele?" Adam said.

"No." Paul rushed forward. "Don't even–"

"Like clientele that could be found in, I don't know, maybe Blake's white book?"

Carlos seemed to catch up, dropping his face into a scowl. "I've missed something here. What's got this idiot trying to plan another suicide heist?"

"Hey," Adam said, aiming to defend himself, but somehow even he knew he was coming across more arrogant than usual. "The white book would be an undeniable advantage."

"Fuck, I swear." Paul pinched the bridge of his nose. "It's like you're actually trying to poke Blake with a stick."

"Come on, can we just accept that–" Adam began.

"No," Paul said. "We can't afford–"

"We don't have a choice," Mercedes interjected. "The situation is progressing faster than we can keep up with."

"What does that mean?" Dan asked, somehow sitting upright—even in his condition—and pushing his sunglasses into his curls.

Adam frowned, looking to Mercedes for support. "Fine, fine," Adam said. "We have some pretty good intel that Blake suspects someone is after him."

Dan, Paul, and Carlos all looked to Mercedes. Her word was golden if they couldn't trust that he was doing it for the right reasons. *Because he wasn't.* Fuck! Yes, he was, okay, *he was.* It was for the greater good of the group. Not his own reckless entertainment.

"He doesn't know who," Mercedes said. "Yet."

Adam wouldn't dare leave that hanging out there long. "We've had our timeline cut in half, so we have to keep moving. We can't afford to slow down."

"We need that white book," Mercedes agreed. "Antonio keeps a key to the office, and there's a party at the club next week that he'll be at. I can distract him. Adam can make the pick."

Fuck yeah, he could make the pick—wait, what? Him? In the open?

Adam held his jaw in his hands. "That will be out in the open, though."

"I know, it's risky," she said. "But only you can make this pick."

Fuck if that didn't make his trousers tight.

"You don't have to convince me, baby." He folded his arms and smiled wide, nodding at his friends. But it was them she needed to convince.

Turning her back on him to face their friends, Adam's heart grew three sizes when she stepped back into him, flushing her back with his front. Perhaps just a show of solidarity that would convince the team, but it still did special things to his gut. That was how they were always meant to be. Partners in crime. If only she'd acknowledge that.

He had his friends' full attention now.

"We need this book," Adam said. "Time is running out and Blake is catching up. We need to act."

Dan and Carlos reluctantly nodded.

"We'll need everyone for this one," Adam said, giving Paul a meaningful look. But the former hitman had a softness that played in his eyes before he nodded tightly. An apology lingering in his gaze for stopping it in the first place. An apology that dried up into a warning frown when Adam's smile widened.

Adam smirked and said, "Listen carefully, here's what we're gonna do."

CHAPTER 14
SLICED AND DICED

Adam and Paul dressed in waiter uniforms to blend into the atmosphere of the country club kitchen. Kitchen staff, waiters, and chefs alike bustled around them, too preoccupied to notice a couple of tatted-up gangsters snatching canapé trays off metallic countertops. Then again, perhaps they did notice, but actively chose not to. Smart.

Adam's nerves were a jittery mess. It'd been his idea, sure, but it didn't mean he wasn't nervous as fuck to be out so brazenly in the open. Every single eye that lingered too long on his face had his teeth clenching.

Paul bumped Adam's shoulder with his own, giving him a meaningful look that was probably meant to calm his nerves but didn't. Dan needed to hurry the fuck up.

"I'm in. Thirty seconds, and then head out." Dan's voice clicked in through Adam's earpiece, thank fuck. Dan's job was to break into the security office and act as monitor and guide. Their all-seeing, overseeing, bird's eye...he would oversee things. Adam would listen. For once.

Making sure to wait the allotted amount of time, Paul and Adam made their way through the kitchen until they sidled out the double doors into the party.

The main floor was a sight to take in. There had to be hundreds of people crowding the club dressed in finery and likely stolen jewels. The large, octagonal-shaped dining area had been cleared to create a cocktail function atmosphere. The middle of the room was sunken in, with floor-to-ceiling windows at one side, leaving the edges on a raised platform.

Adam split from Paul, each of them going a different way and moving through the crowd at seemingly random intervals. It wasn't, though, it was timed and calculated. Because they planned shit now. *Planning*. Now there was an annoying word. It was code for extra work.

A spot of baby blue had him stopping. When he saw her, Adam's breath caught.

He'd spotted Mercedes from across the room, mingling in the middle of the sunken party floor. She wore a baby blue ball gown, the fabric hugging her curves, her long blonde hair curled and blowing against the dress's open back. He stopped in his tracks, trying desperately to release his lungs but finding they wouldn't comply.

A diamond choker hung at her neck which made Adam frown. Like she knew he was looking and what he was looking *for*, she brushed a lock of hair from her face, showing the diamond infinity necklace hanging off her wrist.

"Ugh." Dan's annoyed voice came over the earpiece. "Focus, dickhead."

Mercedes's eyes flicked to Adam's, a satisfied look on her face, but she kept her conversation going.

Adam finally coughed out his breath when Paul brushed past and elbowed him in the rib. He almost doubled over but managed to compose himself. Dick move. But necessary if Adam were being honest.

He began circulating the room again and Paul made to hide in the shadows.

This was surely a bad idea. If anyone were to ever recognize him and call the whole thing game over, it would be here. Among Blake's high-level associates, there were several who would certainly remember his face. Especially Antonio. He was there the day Adam died, after all. Even dressed down, purposefully keeping his face hidden, it wouldn't be enough if they came eye to eye.

Adam glanced at the security camera sitting above him as if he was staring directly into Dan's eyes. "Say when," he whispered. If he was going to get close enough to Antonio to make a pick without him seeing his face, he would need all the help he could get.

While he waited for Dan's instruction, Adam shifted through the crowd, head down serving canapés. Finding that for all his bravado, he rather hated crowds. He watched as Antonio moved into the middle of the room. Without T.B. and Yani nearby, he was the VIP and was peacocking like an idiot at the attention.

Adam barely suppressed the urge to roll his eyes.

But with Antonio schmoozing, now was surely as good a time as–

"Go now," Dan said.

Mercedes reached Antonio first, tapping him on the shoulder and giving him a polite kiss on the cheek that he grimaced away from. Dick.

Paul arrived next, serving canapés at Antonio's left. Close enough to hide the side view of Antonio's belt. It would seem unlikely that a six-foot, mountainous black man would be able to hide in plain sight, but Paul had a useful set of skills from his hitman days. Dude could blend in anywhere.

Less could be said for Adam, hence all the cover. He wasn't practiced in stealth. He liked to make messes. Big ones, preferably.

Adam slipped into place behind Antonio, brushing past without stopping. He nodded to Mercedes, who let out a playful laugh and slapped Antonio on the shoulder, jolting him enough that he wouldn't feel Adam slide the keyset from his belt buckle.

"Got them," Adam said when he settled along the edge of the room. Returning to the kitchen, he and Paul reunited behind the closed doors.

"That went better than I thought," Paul said.

Adam shot Paul a glare, he should know better than to call it before it was finished—that was the first rule of the game. "It's not over yet," Adam chastised as he bolted away, leaving Paul and heading for the staff bathroom.

The door swung open, showing Carlos grinning where he sat on top of the closed toilet, safety goggles in his hair, blue apron over his suit, and burners already stoked.

"Melt it quickly," Dan said. "Mercedes can't distract him forever."

Adam passed Carlos the key and secured the door before standing on the toilet tank to unhook the smoke detector, holding his palm over the fire sprinkler.

With a strong flame, Carlos lit up his burner and melted wax, setting the key in it and creating a mold in its shape as he fanned the flame.

The smell was pungent, not the smell of the wax, but memories. Memories of flames in his face and hot skin that felt like it was peeling. Hand still to the ceiling, Adam covered his nose with his jacket, trying not to gag.

Carlos seemed to notice, working harder to finish the mold quickly and covering the burning smell by lighting a tropical incense stick. Whether for Adam's benefit, who knew, but more than likely it was out of kindness. An acknowledgement of past trauma and a hand of support that they wouldn't speak of.

Just as Adam had the keys back in his hand, Dan spoke again. "We have a problem."

"A big fucking problem," Mercedes repeated, whispering.

Adam's hand stilled where it had been ready to open the locked bathroom door. "What is it?"

"Blake just got here," Dan said. "He's twenty minutes early."

Goddamn fucking prick. Had he never heard of making a fashionably late entrance?

Standing tall and tightening this chest, Adam jumped into action. With danger and the chance of conflict, his instincts immediately sharpened.

Adam burst through the door of the bathroom back into the kitchen, snatching a tray from a waiter who stumbled back in alarm.

"Everyone who isn't meant to be here, get the fuck out now," Adam said for those in his earpiece, briefly registering Paul slip out the back door. Back on the party floor, he held the tray to his face so he could move through the room quicker.

He flashed past Antonio, dropping the key into his pocket (messy, but he was out of time) and attempting to make an escape. He'd almost made it all the way through the room, back to the door, when he felt his arm tug.

"One second." An older lady held him up, clawing at the tray of food. She spoke softly to her friends while she picked through the tray, but raised her voice and gripped Adam's arm like a vulture in heat anytime he tried to pull away.

Shit.

There was no way he could leave her without making a scene. He needed help.

From across the room, he made eye contact with Mercedes, who gave him a strange look. Probably to say, *why the fuck are you still here?* Adam answered her with a tight jaw and narrowed eyes that glanced down to his arm.

With a confused frown, Mercedes followed the path of his eyes to the woman's sharp claws gouging into Adam's forearm.

Yes, now she had panic in her eyes, too. *Exactly.*

Adam watched her gaze flick to Blake. Following, Adam saw him held up at the front of the room. He widened his eyes to Mercedes, urging her to hurry the hell up if she didn't want to be caught.

She moved quickly but quietly as she rushed to Adam's aid, placing her hand over the old lady's deceptively strong, vise-like grip and tugging it away from the next piece of chicken that was about to be snatched and gobbled.

"These look undercooked! Absolutely unacceptable," Mercedes said to Adam. "Don't eat these, Mrs. Willow, we'll get you some fresh ones."

"Oh, dear. Disgusting, yes, please, immediately," Mrs. Willow said, throwing back the pieces of chicken she'd already acquired, and death glaring Adam like *he'd* slaughtered and deep-fried the chicken incorrectly.

Adam's lip tipped up in a soft smirk, earning another death glare from the greedy vulture crone.

Adam followed Mercedes's lead, making an escape through a long side corridor. It wasn't the way he had intended to go, so his only option was to improvise.

"In here," Mercedes said. She pushed open the door of the baker's kitchen, luckily finding it empty, and herding Adam through before closing the door behind them.

The metal door shut with a loud, securing thud, as if it were just as relieved to be closed as they were to be tucked safely behind it. Resting their heads against the back of the metal and looking into each other's eyes, they each let out a sigh of relief.

Adam couldn't tell why his temple felt so sweaty, not until he noticed that Mercedes's hand covered his where it rested against the cool metal door. The infinity necklace hung from her wrist between them like mistletoe. A reminder of how they'd once promised each other they'd stay locked together forever. Partners in crime.

"Well, well, well," a voice said from afar. "If it isn't Adam Vandemilio. Here I thought you were dead."

Adam knew that voice...*fuck.*

***

Adam pivoted to see the very person who had spotted them, who had discovered him, very much alive and well, and back in Ridge City.

Across the baker's kitchen, nestled behind the metallic countertops and stomping out a cigarette with his foot, was Yani, looking like a cat that'd cornered a bird. Smug, yet not surprised.

Yani remained calm and composed, his attention briefly holding on where Adam's and Mercedes's hands were clasped over the door. "I'd say we've definitely found the one trying to take Dorian down, wouldn't you?"

They shifted away from the door, and Adam rested his hand on the small of her back. Ready to push her to safety should Yani do something stupid.

Yani seemed to notice Adam's protective stance, because he looked even more pleased with himself than he had originally.

"Damn, you sat right next to us on that boat, and you actually seemed concerned," Yani laughed, hand on heart and smirking at Mercedes. "Genuinely concerned." He chuckled again, as if it was the funniest thing he'd ever encountered.

"Wait until Dorian finds out about this," Yani said. "That you're rolling around with Adam Vandemilio behind his back. That'll be worse than anything I could ever do to you."

That was Yani's best idea of a threat. He was Blake's hitter, after all. It was well known that Yani liked to kill almost as much as Adam liked making mischief.

Well, looked like someone was leaving the party in a body bag. So Adam rolled up the sleeves of his suit and prepared to do what he did best.

"You've just made a big mistake," Adam said, running his tongue along his teeth. "Now you have to die."

That seemed to amuse Yani even more. Clearly, he remembered Adam's face, but not how deadly Adam could be.

"Go back to the party, baby, I got this," Adam said, but Mercedes didn't budge.

"Go," Adam said, looking back to her. Yani was the most-worthy opponent of the Seconds, and would be a hard kill, but being found in this position by Blake would be much worse. Mercedes dug her heels in, raising her chin. "Trust me," Adam said, searching her eyes.

Mercedes grimaced, looking very much like she didn't want to go. But still she nodded and left the kitchen, giving Yani one last look of contempt before securing the door.

Then it was just Adam and Yani. It was time to fight. And Adam was never going to back down from a fight ever again.

Yani smirked and licked his lips, like a predator readying for a fight that he knew would end in a kill. In a win.

But Adam was more aware of death than he'd ever been. Nearly dying had had that affect. Adam knew that every fight was one that he needed to put his whole life behind. He had a lot more on the line to fight for.

"Guess three gunshots weren't quite enough," Yani scowled.

But Adam wasn't giving him a chance to move first. The air was heavy for only a moment. Then Adam bolted for a meat cleaver and launched it across the room. Yani jolted sideways at the shoulder, the cleaver embedding in the wall where it stuck.

Fuck, maybe Yani would be hard to kill? At least he didn't appear to have his gun.

The hitter advanced, swiping a bread knife and slashing at Adam as he jumped back each time, with only milliseconds to spare. *Too fucking close!*

They pushed around the kitchen, each slash getting closer until Adam backed into the metallic countertop. Cornered. In a wild panic, he grabbed an electric mixer from his back and belted it across Yani's face. Blood pooled at his cheek, but the psychopath still didn't slow.

Adam ducked as the knife slashed for his throat, grabbing Yani's arm mid-air as he cocked another hit. But before he could move, he was knocked in the gut and sliced at the forearm, tearing flesh.

"Jesus, fuck!" Adam said. Cuts still stung. No matter how deep. Though, this one was deep. And a fucking good shot, too, Adam needed to regain the upper hand.

Adam socked Yani in the belly and swung under his arm until he stood behind the overturned Second. Pushing his hand at the hitter's neck, Adam slammed him face first into the metal counter.

"Stop fucking wiggling," Adam said, holding Yani down but pushing harder so the force of his forearm held him still. The cleaver was still pronged in the wall above him. Oh, it'd be brutal, but thus was every aspect of this life. Reaching for it, Adam ripped the cleaver from the plaster and rocked in a smooth chop across Yani's fingertips.

"*Fuck!!!*" Yani said, crying out in pain that rebounded like an acoustic symphony.

Adam smashed Yani's face down on the counter again. He needed him to shut the fuck up before someone came to investigate. Couldn't he die quietly, for fuck's sake? Rude.

Adam doubled over when Yani punched him in the gut and kicked the cleaver out of his hands. He barely had time to breathe before Yani had wrapped his hand up in a towel and raised his fists again.

Damn, that was some stamina. Dude was obviously running on adrenaline. Adam would admire his tenacity if it weren't so inconvenient at that moment.

They rattled and banged throughout the kitchen, struggling for dominance. A punch from one, a dodge from the other, and so on as they smashed about the kitchen. Yani spit blood when Adam punched him square in the teeth. Adam hissed when Yani squeezed his cut forearm.

With his good arm, Yani rushed forward and wrapped his hand around Adam's neck, pulling him up off the ground before slamming into the counter. God, he had a good grip.

Adam struggled as he was held down, his throat closing so tightly that he saw stars.

Face to face with Yani, he could see the hatred behind his eyes. So vile and strong. The pressure on his neck was blinding, coating his vision so all he could see were lights. The sting of death that drew near was familiar, and against it, Adam found his heart beating faster, harder, compelling him to push it away.

Reaching behind him, Adam grasped a cooking tray and swung it across Yani's head. The mad man fell away, giving Adam time to heave in air and cough away the closeness of death.

A slice at Adam's cheek made him stumble back.

Where did that fucker get another knife?

Adam gripped Yani's good hand and tossed the knife away.

They each raised their shaking fists. Both of them bleeding too much to go on much longer. With swift movements they punched, blocked, and took hits as they moved around the kitchen. With fists flying left and right, blood flying just as fast, they fought until they both were left breathless.

Yani fought pretty well for someone who was down four fingers.

Clutching Adam at the shirt and smearing it with blood, Yani pulled him close. But just close enough for Adam to spot a blade hidden on one of the lower shelves. A fight-ending type of blade.

Their movements came to a sudden stop when Adam swung at his enemy behind him and dove for the carving knife that sat under the counter. As Yani advanced forward, Adam plunged the knife, spearing it into the hitter's gut and sliding so smoothly it was as if the guy was made of melted butter.

Yani puffed, a shocked and deadened look appearing as blood poured from his mouth. Adam held him still at the shoulder so they would lock eyes when he wrenched the knife in farther.

Yani gazed lazily down at his stomach, blood coating his teeth red. "Ouch."

Adam smirked.

"He's already…got…your girl," Yani panted. "He'll get…everything else…too."

Adam twisted the knife.

"He *will* kill you," Yani spat through his bloody last breaths.

"Not if I kill him first," Adam said.

"You will…never…get–" Would he ever shut up?!

Adam finished Yani off by swiftly removing the knife, and with one final blow, plunged it into his heart. With a short gasp, Yani was gone, sliding out of Adam's arm and thudding onto the floor.

You will never get the chance, Adam supposed were the last words he stole.

Adam wiped his own dripping blood from his face, stumbling to steady himself.

"Dan?" Mercedes' soft voice crawled through the earpiece. "Dan, are you there?"

"Here," said Dan.

"Did you clock the scene in the kitchen?" she whispered.

"Yeah, brutal," Dan said.

"Is Adam alive?" Mercedes's breath shook.

Adam dropped the knife from his hands and secured his own earpiece, huffing from the intensity of the fight.

"I'm here, baby. I'm alive." He didn't miss Mercedes audible sigh of relief. She absolutely still had a soft spot for him. *Just helping for their friends*, huh? Nah, it was all for him.

He left Yani's body on the floor, his blood staining the tile, and stepped over it to leave through the back entrance of the country club and slide into the passenger seat of Paul's van.

"Alright," Adam said, feeling like he'd had enough of this damn night. "Let's go get that fucking book."

***

Adam stood impatiently with Paul in Mercedes's bedroom. Fumbling up the trellis, Carlos landed in a heap at the base of Mercedes's window, brushing greenery and thorns off his clothes.

"Took you long enough," Adam said.

"You know this entry a little too well," Carlos scoffed, helping himself off the ground.

Adam smiled and made his way to the bedroom door, pressing his ear up against it. Satisfied, he nodded to his friends and slipped the old mahogany doors ajar, peering out into the hall. The three of them pushed through Mercedes's bedroom door and braved the corridors of the mansion.

The crimson and gold hallways had not a speck of dust in them. Nor did the elegant sculptures lining the walls. Useless, but they were decorations of someone who considered himself a king.

When Adam was king, he wouldn't need all these fancy trimmings and square footage to know how big his balls were.

Navigating the labyrinth mansion, they passed maids and other service staff, all of whom nodded politely but kept their eyes away—possibly thanks to Yani's blood drenching Adam's suit.

Meeting the stairwell, they rushed ahead to the next corridor, but Adam held up a palm to stop them, pressing his back to the wall as a couple of lingering associates wandered past.

Once they were clear, they made the final approach to Blake's office. Adam and Paul stood guard as Carlos moved ahead to press the key into the lock, kissing the cross around his neck before turning the key.

The locked popped open and Adam smiled as they rushed inside and secured the door behind them. Momentarily starstruck, Adam faltered. He was probably the only one of them who'd never been in this office. And it was incredible. Fucking ostentatious like everything Blake owned, and nothing like Adam would want for himself, but incredible, nonetheless.

Breathtaking floor-to-ceiling windows overlooking the gardens, giant mahogany desk, and a private bar with enough alcohol to drown a sailor.

"The white book is in the safe behind the desk," Dan said, jolting Adam back to reality.

Together, Adam and Paul rounded the desk, kneeling down where the empty spot revealed the hidden safe.

"Guys, you need to hurry up. T.B. is on his way back to the mansion now," Mercedes said from the voice in their ear.

Adam sat in front of the safe and started to turn the dial, reaching out behind him without looking where Carlos handed him a piece of paper with a written code.

"T.B. just got his car, and you know he drives like a fucking lunatic, you've got five minutes tops," Dan said.

T.B. might have been a useless piece of shit, but he had a great habit of turning up when he was least wanted.

His brow furrowing, Adam pinged the code in the safe and wriggled. But...nothing. All this way... and the safe wouldn't open?! Adam slammed his fist against the metal door. "It won't open. Dan, you said he keeps the code to all his safes the same?!"

He looked back at his friends from his position.

"I thought he did," Dan's panicked voice came over the comms.

"Try 10-14-46," Paul said. Blake's birthday. A guessing game it would be then.

Adam typed in the numbers to no avail.

"What about 10-19-86?" Carlos suggested. The day Dorian killed Adam. The keypad pinged harmonious tones as Adam tried the combination. But still, nothing.

"01-19-75?" Dan suggested. The day Blake murdered his last living cousin in order to take the reins of the Blake Family empire. More lyrical pings on the pad, but still nothing.

"Fuck!" Adam shifted on his feet. "It won't fucking open!" He jostled the door, trying with all his might to pull it open.

"T.B. just pulled up in the driveway," Dan said.

Adam was just gritting his teeth and preparing to rip the safe off its hinges with his bare hands (yes, it was a bad plan...no, he didn't care) when Carlos and Paul wrenched him back by the shoulders.

"We gotta go," Paul said as Adam resisted their pull.

"No!" Adam yanked himself from their grip and sat staring at the safe, once again trying to pry it open with just his fingertips.

Adam could feel Paul and Carlos gripping his arms at all angles, desperate to pull him away, but he wouldn't go. Not without that fucking book. It took enough to convince his friends to try this in the first place, there wouldn't be a second chance. He was getting that book now, goddammit! Even if he had to rip his–

"Victory day…" Mercedes's quiet whisper came through his ear, stunning them all to silence. "Um, December 7, 1986," Mercedes whispered. "So, uh, 12-07-86."

Adam shook the tightness from his chest and put the code in. His fingers shook with each slow input, each beep of the numbers. As much as he wanted it to open, at the same time he fucking wished it wouldn't. Because somehow he knew exactly what that date meant.

Adam, Paul, and Carlos tensed as the safe popped open neatly with a whoosh of air. Inside it sat Blake's white book, alone around empty shelving, resting softly against the dark metal.

"That was it," Carlos said solemnly as he rushed ahead to snatch the white book from the safe. And though it was a victory, it certainly didn't feel like it.

***

Dorian stood center in the country club dining room, tall against the sunken floor and looking out the large windows into the garden. Tired from a long night of campaigning at the very same club, he couldn't hide his annoyance at being called there so early on a weekend, not that he would ever have to hide it with his position.

Over his shoulders and down the hall he could hear the whispers of two lower-level associates. He couldn't quite make out what they were saying, nor he could see them, but he could hear their quick-whipped sentences and the shakiness in their throats.

"I can hear you out there. Get in here if you've got something to say," Dorian said. He folded his arms and turned his attention toward the door. "Get in here, now!"

The two lower associates sheepishly brushed into the room, their heads downcast, begging to avoid the frightening catch of Dorian's eye.

"What did you call me here for?"

Wide-eyed, they looked only at each other before quickly looking back to the floor.

"What is it?" Dorian said. "Don't make me ask again."

"It's about Yani, sir," one of them said suddenly, wincing as he did.

Dorian waited for them to say more, but they didn't. Fuck's sake. He enjoyed the fear, but right now it was just irritating. He rolled his eyes when he realized they weren't going to continue. "Hurry the fuck up and spit it out."

"Yani's dead, sir," the other one said. "We found him in the baker's kitchen this morning."

Dorian cleared his throat.

"Yani's dead?" Dorian asked, sure that he had heard wrong. A smile pulled at his lips. A nervous twitch of sorts.

"It looked like a struggle, sir...he was stabbed."

What in the fuck?! These two little lying shit faces were about to get their heads blown off. Dorian reached for his gun and charged at the two of them. "What did you fucking say?" He narrowed his eyes as he pressed the gun against the temple of the one who had spoken such heinous words.

"He's dead," the guy repeated, though he stuttered through it this time. And then the smell of piss soaked the air. Dorian dropped his glare. Seriously? The guy had pissed himself.

"Well, if lying wasn't enough, clearly you haven't got the balls for this kind of job."

Then he shot the guy square in the temple.

"Boss?" T.B. cleared his throat. "Letting off steam?"

"This little fuck just told me Yani is dead," Dorian said.

"Well, before you blow any more brains out, come see for yourself." His head tilted in the direction of the baker's kitchen.

Dorian straightened, collecting himself and swallowing before following T.B. down the deep hallway. Keeping a respectable distance, Dorian noticed the second lower-level associate following him. Huh, that one had balls. Who knew?

When Dorian pushed open the door to the baker's kitchen, the smell of decomposing flesh polluted the air. In the heat of this city, the decay had been sped up and the smell was unbearable.

The lower-level covered his nose with his shirt while Dorian kept a straight face and moved around behind the counter.

On the floor he saw it.

Yani laid dead and still, his eyes wide open and his flesh almost transparent. There were pools of dried blood on the floor. He was also missing his fingers that were still arranged on the chopping board above. He had two stab wounds to his abdomen, one fatal stab to his heart, and a multitude of bruises covering his face.

Dorian took in the scene and rubbed his head between his fingers to cover his eyes as he looked away. Yani was a good friend who had worked for him for a long time. If Dorian still had a heart, it might have hurt. "Fuck."

He turned to the lower-level associate and waved him out of the room. He scattered away gratefully, the sounds of him retching in the hallway as he attempted to hold in his vomit the last sounds that they heard as he fled. Weak as piss, after all. But Dorian didn't have time to shoot him too.

He held up an open palm to signal T.B. to stay in the room.

"This has got to be whoever is coming after us...and now they've got Yani."

"It looks that way," T.B. said.

Dorian squinted and turned to T.B. "I'm feeling nostalgic, T.B., take a walk down memory lane with me?"

T.B. twitched on the spot. "What are you thinking?"

"Tell me, you lost a race the other day..." Dorian said.

"I did," T.B. huffed, his face red with an angry embarrassment he obviously still held onto.

"When has that ever happened before?"

"Never," he answered, too quickly.

But that wasn't true, was it? Dorian folded his arms and stared him down knowingly, compelling him to think a little harder.

T.B. sucked in with a tight mouth as he answered. "Only once. Back when we lost the prison van."

To Dorian, the words seemed like an agreement from T.B. that there could only be one possible conclusion, one possible reason that all of this was happening, and that it was happening now. Again.

The rage grew within in him like a dark, all-consuming black hole, and Dorian let out a crude grunt that echoed the halls, though T.B. did not flinch. "And who did you lose to?"

"We can't say exactly, but..." T.B. hesitated. "Someone working for Adam Vandemilio."

"Exactly."

And that was all the confirmation he needed.

"Holy shit," Antonio nearly gagged as he came charging through the doors. "Is that...?"

T.B. nodded.

"Christ," Antonio said, but his eyes widened when he saw Dorian huffing and puffing on the spot, nearing a nervous breakdown. He hadn't felt this violent kind of certainty in himself since he had killed all his brothers so many years ago.

"Come in close," Dorian barked at his Seconds. "Somebody—I don't fucking *care* which one of you—somebody needs to go and dig up a grave right now. I want to see a fucking skeleton."

Though... he didn't expect to find one at all.

CHAPTER 15
DIG 'EM UP

"Hey, baby," Adam said, poking his head through the open window into Mercedes's bedroom once again.

"You have *got* to stop doing that," she said, startling where she stood at the dresser and knocking her perfumes over in surprise.

He helped himself inside, watching her as she collected the wayward perfumes into her arms. She scowled like she was annoyed, but the window was always open when he came by, and he was sure that wasn't a coincidence.

"Going somewhere?" Adam sat down at the edge of the bed where a half-packed suitcase laid open, surrounded by neat little piles of clothes, all of them hers.

"Just a last-minute trip," she explained, scurrying around the room with her diamond watch jiggling as she fluffed items inside. "Dorian is headed upstate to make some deal, wants me to go with him."

"Right," Adam said, a sting eating his chest. "You're going, though?"

"Why wouldn't I?" she asked, continuing to ignore him in favor of packing.

Why wouldn't she?! Several reasons... but none of which he could possibly bring up.

Adam shrugged in response and laid down on the bed, though his tense shoulders strained at the motion.

"It's a good opportunity to get back into his office and return the white book," she said. "Once you're done with it, of course. Dorian and all the Seconds are going, so there'll be no one here to burst in on you."

Moving over him, she slapped him playfully on the arm, shoving him to sit up. He smirked when he noticed he'd laid against and disrupted all her piles.

"Sorry." He wasn't sorry. "How long will you be gone for?"

"Just the weekend, one or two days."

One or two days. May as well be a lifetime.

He stroked the soft silk sheets of her bed, a horrible thought about what she and Blake did on that bed assaulting his mind. And then he was blurting out something that he hadn't meant to ask, but that nit-picked at his brain like a little bug. "What's December 7, 1986?" The date code that had finally popped Blake's safe.

She didn't answer right away, but he could see her jaw straining, as if she were trying to control her reaction. "It's not important."

"You can tell me," he said. Why couldn't he let this go? Did he really want to know?! *Yes.*

"You don't want to know." She slammed her dresser shut, fiercely avoiding Adam's eye. Then it occurred to him to wonder who the answer would hurt more. Him or her.

"I do want to know. Please."

Mercedes brushed her hair away and planted her hands on her hips. Her face contorted and rolled, the mask of her pretense slipping. "Fine, if you must—it was the first night Dorian and I, you know, it was when we got together, or whatever." She flicked away the words with her hands like she could push them out of her life.

Hearing it out loud made him feel so sick he felt he would rather eat glass. Though... he was sure that was what he was going to hear when he asked. Deep down, he knew. But why he needed to hear it said out loud? God knows.

He steadied himself on her bed, his arms behind him the only thing keeping him upright. "Blake remembers that date? He's a better man than I thought."

She shook her head. "No." Her face scrunched. "No. It's not about *that*. Victory day... it was the day that he finally... *won* me. After years of chasing. December 7, 1986, he finally took what he wanted."

Mercedes took in a deep breath and went back to packing, though she only seemed to be rearranging the same three piles in sequence. Whispering over her shoulder, she said, "We both knew he would, eventually. He wanted me. He was always going to have me whether I liked it or not."

Sure, but the girl Adam loved never did what someone else told her to. Never did what she was expected.

Adam held his tongue. He still didn't know why she was with Blake, and there was clearly a story behind it, but one he sensed she wasn't ready to share yet.

She removed a pair of lacy black lingerie from her drawer and dropped it on top of the pile inside her suitcase, quickly moving on to other tasks.

But once he'd seen it drop there, Adam couldn't keep his eyes off it. God, what was it about her that made him turn into a mindless zombie?

He stared at the piece of fabric, practically drooling at the mouth. His head chanting in rhythm. *Mercedes, Mercedes, Mercedes.*

Next thing he knew, Mercedes was laughing as she launched the underwear at his head and it went sliding down his face into his lap. "Come on, back to earth with you, please."

"That was a mistake. These are mine now." Smirking, he scrunched the garments into his pocket.

Her brows nearly hit the ceiling. "Sorry, what?"

"Mine. Now," he said slowly, mocking her as if she hadn't heard him properly. She obviously had. He gave her a dirty smile and projected all his lust into one look.

By the look of it, he almost had her for a second, her eyes glazing over with heat, and her knees twitching like she was one second away from pouncing on him. But sense took back control far too quickly, and she narrowed her eyes at him before raising her chin.

"Oh, really? Well, you picked the wrong pair." She pulled red silk underwear from her drawer. "Red was always your favorite color, right?" She smirked as she threw them across the room at him.

He caught them in his right hand and nodded. She may not have jumped on him, but if she wanted to play, he could play. "Oh yeah, red is good." Discarding the underwear on the bed, he folded his arms. "I always liked you in navy, though."

She averted her eyes and raised her brows like she knew something that he didn't, gently stroking her forehead to hide her smirking face.

"What is it?"

"I might be wearing navy now."

226

His eyes brightened. "Let me see."

She shook her head and bit her lip.

Oh, it was on.

He picked up his pace to try and grab her. She ran around the room avoiding his capture, using the sofa as a barrier and giggling as he fought his way to her. If he went right, she went left. They made a full lap with him on her tail, so close to reaching out and grabbing her.

Once they found themselves in their starting positions again, he rested his hands on the sofa back with a lazy sigh. Then, without warning, he dove, mounting it to reach the other side and throw her over his shoulder, both of them laughing as he did.

"What should I do with you now?" he said. He carried her from the sofa to the bed.

"Here?" He threatened to throw her down, but grabbed her tighter over his shoulder when she resisted.

Playfully, she slapped his arm to force her release. He did as she wished and set her down, letting his arms work their way up her body. Legs, behind—*don't linger too long on that one, Adam*—hips, and finally, waist.

When she was planted on the floor in front of him, he didn't let his hands drop from her waist, and she didn't remove hers from his biceps. The proximity was screaming between them, and he could see her looking from his eyes to his lips, wetting her own like she could already taste him.

But it was her stare he was fixated on. As hungry as her mouth apparently was, her eyes were soft. Like he could almost see the feelings they had five years ago flooding into her irises. Then, he wondered, had that emotion always been there, just hidden somewhere that she wouldn't let him see.

She ran her hands down from his biceps to the center of his chest as he leaned up to push her hair over her shoulder. He couldn't take it anymore, he had to be closer.

"Darling!"

His head snapped toward the door.

"It's Dorian." Mercedes's voice quivered as she whispered.

The moment they shared rocketed out of sight as she pushed him away, tugging him toward the window. He dove out onto the ledge, a little dazed. Her arms waved in front of her as she continued herding him out.

Adam looked at the door, then at her panicked eyes that locked on the entry, anticipating Blake's arrival.

The feelings in her eyes were gone. That beautiful look of love, gone. He couldn't let them go. God, *she* couldn't let them go. He had to see them again. This couldn't be it for him. He would always need more.

Adam stopped at the ledge before shutting the window. He grabbed her hand and steeled his voice, willing his words to pierce her soul. "Don't let go, baby."

When she turned to really look at him, her features softened, but in a way that gave away a sweet sadness. Not the burning desire he had been hoping for. Just pity, hollow, emptiness.

"I'm not the one who let go."

She pulled the window shut and fastened the latch, forcing Adam out just as Blake burst into the room.

"The car is ready, darling. Let's get going," he said.

***

A bell sounded as Adam pushed into his bar. He looked above, wondering who had placed that little bell up there. Either way, it was of no use because the party was already in full swing, the bell only a quiet tickle above the grunging metal of music. Hordes of his people were already deep in their drinks, with only a red whistle of neon light coating the atmosphere.

Somehow the underworld scene, all the people who had been hiding from Blake, too, just knew that this was a safe space now.

Adam sank into his shoulders, hands slipping into his pockets to keep his face low, but nobody even looked as he slinked to his regular booth. Right at the back of the bar, Carlos and Paul were already perched at the edge of the leather seats, engrossed in decoding the secrets of the white book.

"How is it going?" Adam asked as he slid into the booth. His muscular, tattooed sleeve spread out against the edge of the booth as he placed his other hand on the hip of his black jeans.

"My God, the shit that's in here," Carlos said, marveling like the pages were spun with gold.

"You made copies yet?" Adam asked.

"Not yet," Paul said.

"Well, do it soon. We'll drop the book back before M and Blake get back from out of town."

The little bell rang, and Adam looked lazily over his shoulder to see Dan approaching them with three girls at his side, his arm around two of them. The brunette at his left side whispered sweet nothings in his ear, gently nibbling on the lobe, and looking at him like he cured cancer for a living.

Dan was halfway through a conversation when he reached the booth, his eyes a stinging red. "Team—meet Tia's girls, Alyssa, Bronte, Leticia. Girls—meet team. You already know Paul and Carlos."

Adam shot Paul and Carlos a warning glare. It was bad enough that Dan couldn't seem to find the line between business and pleasure and stay on the right side of it. He couldn't have everyone losing their heads. Especially when he himself misplaced his own so often.

"They're very grateful for all the help." Dan winked at Adam. "They wanted to thank us."

Adam smiled tightly as he watched the girls' eyes rake over the colorful tattoos on his sleeve. He folded his arm away in response.

"It's a business arrangement, ladies, no need to thank us."

Dan huffed as he waved the girls away, and then jumped into the booth across from Adam.

"What the hell are you doing? They want to *thank* us," Dan said again, raising his eyebrows as if he thought that Adam didn't understand what he meant the first time.

"I know what you meant," Adam chuckled.

Dan exchanged a knowing look with Carlos. "Let the girls *thank us*, Adam."

"Not interested." Adam frowned in amusement, waving Dan away with a flick of the wrist. He turned to the others for confirmation that Dan's behavior was odd, but found none.

"Suit yourself," Dan shrugged. He was up chasing after the girls again before his body could even catch up with his feet.

Adam wasn't trying to be rude. His heart was simply somewhere else.

"You sure you want to pass that up?" Paul said.

"Hmm?" Adam's ears pricked as his mind had been absent. "Oh, yeah. Not interested."

"I hate to say it, but you know…you might not be able to get her back," Carlos said, matter of fact, not taking his eyes away from the book.

Adam glared at Carlos before catching himself and brushing his hands over his face as if he could wipe away the annoyance and the voice in his head that somehow knew Carlos may be right.

Paul, though, he looked over to Carlos and smirked, as if they shared a secret. "And why not? She doesn't love Dorian Blake."

"Well, she doesn't love him either, does she?" Carlos said, gesturing toward Adam.

"I don't want her back," Adam snapped. He couldn't have this conversation right now. "I just…I'm not interested. We've got work to do. I can't afford to be distracted."

"Yeah, alright, sure," Paul replied, his cheeks tightening.

Adam needed that particular train of thought to end. Fast. He couldn't afford to believe it. There was no scenario in his head where any of this would be a success if he couldn't prove to her what she meant to him, especially if she could never love him again.

Leaving Ridge City felt like the right choice at the time. But… maybe he'd chosen wrong. Maybe he should've come back sooner. Or better yet, never left. Ugh.

She didn't understand he wasn't off living the high life, if anything he'd felt dead. Rotting like a corpse in the ground. Adam hadn't felt alive in years. He would've given anything to feel the way he did five years ago. And that meant–

Carlos snapped his fingers in front of Adam's face, bringing him back to earth. "Do you want to look at this, or are you just going to keep daydreaming?"

***

AUGUST 1986

"I need to sleep," Dan whined.

"You can sleep when you're dead," Adam said. Though he wasn't quite sure if he was joking anymore.

They were all so exhausted that even Paul's sharp warning glance was weary. With Dan, Carlos, and Paul in the back seat of the SUV, himself in the passenger seat, and Mercedes driving next to him, he only huffed a laugh when he caught Paul's half-hearted stare in the side mirror.

"Not funny," Paul said with droopy eyes.

"I'm sick off fending off his attacks, I just need to get home to rest," Carlos agreed, sliding about like he was struggling to get comfortable in the middle back seat.

"We're almost home." Mercedes rolled her eyes, like an annoyed parent trying to control her children. Which in many ways, she was.

It was nearly the darkest time of night, but the closer they drove toward their trailer lot, their home, the brighter the sky seemed to get.

Adam checked the time. Yep, nearing midnight, so what the fuck...

Then, he smelled the smoke.

He sharpened to attention, his focus like a laser, mounted on the flickering orange flames that seemed to be gathering in the distance.

The guys in the back hadn't noticed, but Mercedes slid him a side eye, the smoke growing thick and swirling in the headlights.

Farther and farther, closer and closer, and only more smoke, more bright flame, and then scorching heat.

"Why is it so... bright?" Dan said.

"Oh God," Paul said.

Mercedes stopped the car suddenly. They bolted from their seats out onto the road. Displaced residents were gathering in the streets, sirens sounding in the distance as help beckoned, but it would be too late.

It already was too late.

The trailer park, their home, everything they held dear, gone up in flames.

The trailer that Paul owned, the one that Mercedes grew up in, and the one that Adam called home, all alight, turning black. The trailer that they all lived in, slept together in, and put all their best plans in motion was burning down right in front of their eyes.

It felt almost symbolic at this point. The last place that was his own, gone. After this, there would be nothing left for them physically, and very little left for any of them to give emotionally.

"No, no," Mercedes whispered, before launching into a shout. "No!"

"What could—how could–" Carlos stuttered.

Adam stepped in front of the group, his temper like a kettle rising to a boil, getting louder and louder until it whistled, knowing that all his reckless emotions were about to take control of his good sense. "Dorian Blake did this."

"All of our money, all our property was in there!" Dan said.

"What the hell are we going to do," Carlos said. "That was our one last hideout, there's no place to go now, we can't hide from Dorian Blake."

Mercedes dropped to her knees in the middle of the road, and Adam could see the control slipping from her face. After all, this had been her home much longer than it'd been his. Paul was the only one brave enough to approach her, placing a gentle hand on her shoulder as he tried to pull her upright.

"The photo albums, everything we—I have to get it," she said, and she started running toward the engulfed trailer. But Paul was there a second sooner, diving forward to grab her arms and stop her. She struggled against him, thrashing, fiercely trying to rip herself away, but he held strong until she whirled toward him and sobbed into his shoulder. He slid a gentle, calming caress down her back.

"We've lost everything now," Carlos said. "We're all gonna die."

Carlos didn't even sound sad about the fact. Just resigned. Like he knew that was always their outcome. And that broke Adam's already damaged heart. He'd pulled Carlos and Dan out of their neighborhood after the slaughter, away from the Cortez Cartel, specifically so that they *wouldn't* have to die for anyone else. Now... he'd basically asked them to die for him.

What a stupid, idealistic prick he'd been.

Words would simply not be enough for them to ignore the truth any longer. But Adam, oh, he still had a little bit of stupid left in him. He wasn't done yet.

"Adam," Paul said over Mercedes sobbing in his arms.

Reining in his wild rage with precise control, Adam attempted to quell his erratic breathing, his nostrils flaring and his eyes wide.

"Adam, I think it's time to run," Paul said.

"Never," Adam said. "Over my fucking dead body."

He meant it, too. The only way he was leaving Ridge City was in a body bag.

***

APRIL 1991

Mercedes had to play her part. She could very well be the First Lady of Ridge City, so she had to dress as such, no matter how much unlike her it really was. When she awoke in her hotel room in Darton, she made sure she had the tools to dress for the occasion. And a plethora of tools it did take to turn her rough interior into an exterior of elegance and grace.

Darton was a two-hour drive away, and hosted a heap of people more high class than could be found in Ridge City on a good day—Dorian included. Business with Darton was key to keeping the city running, which meant for one day she had to pretend to be classier than she felt.

Mercedes dressed in a set of baby blue sailor pants and a white beaded tank. She set her face with powder and her lips with a petal pink. Her dirty blonde hair was curled and waved. She had her six-carat diamond engagement ring on her finger, pearls on her ears, and as always, the infinity necklace at her chest.

She looked herself up and down in the full-length mirror and thought with a sigh how she didn't recognize the person staring back at her. Touching the infinity necklace, she smiled as she held it tight. It was the last piece of herself that she could carry.

Dorian burst from the hotel bathroom, wearing only a towel and steaming from the shower.

"Darling, you're friends with Paul, yes?" Dorian said, flicking the water from his hair.

What. The. Fuck.

She immediately froze, dropping her hand from her chest and wiping the lazily romantic look off her face. The game was on.

"Used to be friends with Paul." She did her best to correct him. As far as he was concerned, she hadn't seen Paul in years.

"Sure, and you used to bartend at the Neptune back in the day?" He was casual as he stripped out of the towel and dried himself.

"I did." She nodded as she completed her look with more pink lipstick, plumping her lips together in the mirror, though her muscles were tense.

"Do you remember all the people who used to hang around there?"

"I suppose."

He discarded the towel and slid his boxers up his body. She watched his face in the mirror, looking like he thought she couldn't see the devil's grin on his lips. "And do you know why Paul got in so much trouble? All those years ago?"

She prepared herself to lie. "I know he betrayed you, and he was in big trouble for it."

Dorian approached, sneaking up behind her to put his hands on her waist. He ran his fingers up the length of her body and kissed her neck while she watched him in the mirror.

"What about the club? The guys Paul used to hang around with, do you remember them?"

"Sure, they hung around a bit." Mercedes swallowed as he placed his hands around her neck and gripped. She was trying like hell not to seem uneasy, but he was getting incredibly close to home.

"Do you remember a kid named Adam Vandemilio?"

Her heart stopped with a flutter, but she made an effort to compose herself, and in her head grabbed tightly at the fringes of her apprehension and pulled it closed. "It sounds familiar."

"Mmm, it should, his was a famous name once upon a time," Dorian whispered in her ear. His hands tightened around her neck while he placed gentle kisses down her shoulder.

"Paul hung around with them," she offered, giving as little as she could. Playing the role of the mindless little lamb he thought she was. The mindless little lamb for the slaughtering.

"He did," Dorian nodded, meeting her gaze in their reflections.

"I think there were four of them, always together," she squeezed out through tough breaths.

"Four guys?" Dorian loosened his grip and stepped back only millimeters.

"Mmm, four guys," she said, catching her breath without making it obvious she was about to freak. "Why?"

"Really? Four?" Dorian sulked away.

She grabbed her stomach to steady herself, and then stood and walked to Dorian's side, taking his tie to help put it around his neck and strategically holding it in place in case she needed to use it.

"Four," she nodded again. "You think it's–?"

He grabbed the tie from her hands, huffing like he thought there was no way she'd know how to tie it. "Everyone I've ever talked to swears that there were five guys on Adam's team."

"What does it matter?"

He laughed, in that condescending way of his. "It's a bit above your head, sweetheart."

"You can't think that it's them who're after you?" she said, walking back to the dresser, mindless little lamb back in her rightful place.

"Of *course* not." Though, unfortunately, she knew he was lying. If he didn't know how much Paul meant to her, if she hadn't *proven* multiple times how important Paul was to her, maybe Dorian wouldn't have lied.

"Come now, darling, we'll be late for lunch," Dorian said, the venomous whisper now turned toward her, too.

***

Adam landed on his feet on the pavement outside the mansion. He brushed the sticking hedges from his arms with an exhausted breath, though he felt that climbing up the trellis and using Mercedes's unlocked window to enter the mansion got easier every time he did it.

He crossed the road to where Paul was waiting underneath a line of shade trees, leaning up against the car.

"Did you put it back?" Paul asked.

"Yeah, it's done, safe and sound back in its rightful place," Adam said, wiping his hands together as if to say job well done.

He saw Paul's shoulders tense and his eyes narrow before he saw why.

"Get down!" Paul whispered, grabbing Adam's back to lead him low and crawling behind their car to shield themselves.

Another vehicle approached from up the street, driving right past them and through the mansion gates. The rumble of a high-powered engine and the bright orange color gave it away immediately.

"T.B.'s car?" Adam questioned. "They're all supposed to be upstate."

T.B.'s car idled through the gates, sun gleaming off the orange paint, and parked under the carport. T.B. stepped out, lighting up a cigarette and leaning against the edge of the car. He was too tense to be smoking casually. He was waiting for someone. Biding time.

Suddenly the front doors swung open, and Antonio came strolling down the steps carrying bundles of garden tools in each hand.

"What the fuck? Did you know he was in there?" Paul's tense voice quivered.

Adam shook his head. He made sure to shelter his face as he peered over the hood, but he couldn't look away from T.B. and Antonio.

T.B. plucked the tools from Antonio and loaded them into the trunk, which had been cleared like they'd been planning this trip for a while. Together, T.B. and Antonio disappeared into the car and roared away at speed.

As the orange muscle car passed them, Adam and Paul stood, hands shading their eyes from the sun.

"And where the hell are they going?" Paul asked casually as they watched the orange speck get smaller and smaller.

"I don't know," Adam said. "But let's follow them and find out."

They were off in a flash, driving fast to catch up with the orange speedster. Adam leveled off when he spotted T.B.'s car ahead, ostentatious and obvious, not a very smart getaway driver.

For the drive they kept a low profile, making sure to hang back as they tailed T.B. and Antonio through the streets of Ridge City. They went over the bridge, up the freeway, and around the outskirts of town, passing the industrial district until finally the car peeled from the main streets and started slowing.

Adam recognized the road.

"They're going to the cemetery?"

"Paying respects to Yani?" Paul wondered aloud.

"No way, they all fucking hated each other," Adam said.

Across the street from the cemetery, Adam stopped his car as they watched T.B.'s roll inside. He gave it space, knowing they'd need much more than just a few car lengths to not be detected when the cemetery was so bare.

Once they were far enough away, Adam drove again. From a few roads over they glued their eyes to the window as they rolled past where T.B.

and Antonio had stopped, lingering over the trunk and emptying their tools.

"Shovels?" Paul raised his brows.

Adam frowned as he kept watching them but still, for the sake of safety, he did a short lap and pulled in around a distant garden row of epitaphs.

"What on earth are they doing?" Paul said.

Though it seemed an obvious next move, they both buckled in surprise as Antonio and T.B. took their shovels and began shoveling dirt from a grave. Ripping soil from the ground and carelessly shoving it into piles behind them.

Adam leaned into the backseat, fumbling around on the floor to find the binoculars he had left back there. When he found them, he wiped the dust off with his fingers before putting them to his eyes.

Squinting into the lens, he adjusted the focus, struggling to see the name written on the grave. The lens became blurry and then suddenly clear, and his vision settled ominously on the gravestone.

"Oh, fuck," Adam said. Paul's concerned glance cut his eyes, and he snatched the binoculars away as Adam's low voice throttled again, "They're digging me up."

Antonio and T.B. made quick pace as they dug in front of the tombstone that read: R.I.P. Adam Vandemilio. 1962 - 1986.

CHAPTER 16
IN THE NIGHT

<u>APRIL 1991</u>

It was a rare thing for Mercedes to spend uninterrupted time with Dorian anymore. The two nights and three days in Darton had felt like years, and it was like he was choking her with his presence.

When they were first together, before he had bored of her and had spent every second in her company, she was much better equipped to handle it. She'd been numb in those days, as dead as the lover who had left her behind.

She sighed when she reached her bedroom in the mansion again. Her safe haven. But soon Dorian followed her inside, so she willed herself to sit up a little straighter.

"I've got business to do. Don't wait up," Dorian said.

Thank fuck for that. He took a different pre-packed bag from his wardrobe. She didn't bother to reply as she laid on the bed and kicked her shoes off.

He didn't look back as he left the room in haste, but she knew what his overnight bags were for. It was a Monday night. A Shaundi night. He would not be home until well after dawn. Small mercies.

She heard a light tapping from her window and reluctantly sat upright. Curious at first, but not so much when she registered Adam standing at attention on the ledge. Of course, it was him. But he, too, seemed to want energy that she wasn't willing to give. The face she put on for him was much harder to keep in place. To pretend that she didn't still lo—

Nope. She wasn't going there.

"What do you want?" She opened the window with a snap.

"Came to say hi."

"At least you didn't barge in this time, I suppose." She shuffled away, turning back when he didn't follow her inside.

"We got a big cash injection from Tia, I used it to buy some new guns. Do you wanna shoot them with me?"

She was wearing a tiny black dress and sporting a nasty scowl, hardly shooting attire. She glanced down at her clothes, warning him away with just a look.

"Get changed and come with me," he hissed.

Slumping back down on the bed, she stared at the ceiling that was inlaid with flecks of gold too. Yeah, even the ceilings. Money really was nothing to some people. "Adam, I'm tired, I've had a big enough weekend as it is. I don't feel like putting on a face for you, too."

"You don't have to put on a face for me." She vaguely registered him jumping through the window like a cat and stalking over until his shadow covered her. "Unless you're trying *that* hard to hide how much you want me. In which case don't bother. I already know."

She lifted her head just enough to give him an incredulous look and see him chuckle in response.

Once he was done laughing at his own joke, he tugged on her hands and pulled her to sit upright, kneeling between her legs so that they could look eye to eye.

"Come on, a little fun might loosen you up a bit. You're always too tense," he smirked.

"You're always just a little too relaxed," she said.

He rolled her spite away with a laugh, hands still locked together and her weary eyes studying him.

"I've got a Beretta and an M19.'

Damn, he was temping her...those *were* something she'd always wanted to try...

She resisted at first, but he prodded her with a devilish grin, and though she combated acknowledging it, she couldn't help but crack a smile of her own.

He nodded, and in a sweeping movement he lifted her off the bed, her feet nearly missing the ground as he told her, "Change, please."

Like a gentleman he turned around while she changed. Which was odd, because obviously, he was no gentleman and had seen every part of her that a lover would. But when she was ready, he helped her out the window, down the trellis, and into the hedge maze and over the fence like teenagers sneaking out from their parents' house. Teenagers who were too obsessed with just being together to see rhyme or reason or sense.

***

As they shuffled over the mounds of dirt in the old lot, with Adam covering Mercedes's eyes with his hands, he wondered if he'd gone too far with his surprise. But then couldn't bring himself to care. If he was going to be caught tomorrow, he'd always want his last moments to be with her.

"Adam, how far are you taking me?" she said, sounding excited rather than hesitant.

"Just a few more steps," Adam said. He guided her over a piece of fallen debris. Steadying her from behind, he dropped his hands from her eyes down to her shoulders.

"You can open your eyes now," he whispered in her ear.

She opened her eyes, lifting her lids like they were heavy.

Across the old lot Adam had lined up hundreds of red and blue bottles, which now sparkled under the pale moonlight and covered everything in a sea of colors. They were in every tree, every fallen block of brick, every leftover table, all of them coating the sky in a soft glow, as if thousands of red and blue gems sparkled in the sky.

He could feel the tension squeeze from her shoulders with his grip, the gentle night wind rolling over his skin.

She'd been silent for a long time...

"Wow," she finally said, wriggling from his grip and turning to face him. He huffed in relief when he saw the look in her eyes.

"So here's the challenge: red bottles are good to shoot. Blue bottles are off limits," he said, handing her the M19. "Let's see how you do."

"Please. I think I can handle it."

He took the Beretta, and together they moved through the course, simulating a real fight. They ducked behind cover and jumped out to shoot. Dove behind pillars and rolled along the ground in advance. Feigned breathlessness and defeat when they sheltered together. Acting as if this was the fight of their lives. Which come morning, given what T.B. and Antonio had discovered, it very well might be.

Each smashing bottle sprinkled refracted showers, creating a glow like they were falling stars. They hadn't lost their touch, perfectly timing their shots into the red bottles while avoiding the blue ones.

Just about to win the game, Adam fired into a red bottle that caused it to drop to the side, knocking a blue bottle over in the process. He cringed as he caught her looking from across the field, smugness spread into her smile.

"Look at that," Mercedes laughed, approaching him. "Broke your own rule!"

"Hey," he said, holding his hands up in surrender. "That doesn't count. The bottle's not shot, it's just fallen down."

"Still," she said, advancing too close. "The bottle is injured. It's down. It may as well be dead."

He cocked his head and rolled his eyes. "The bottle lives," he said as he picked it up off the dirt.

"Let me see." She took the bottle from his hands and examined it closely, her eyes squinting as they scanned. Suddenly, a devious grin met her lips and she smashed the bottle at her feet. "It's dead."

"Because you killed it!"

"Just finishing what you started…putting it out of its misery," she laughed, flipping her hair and turning her back on him.

She reloaded her gun and lifted to aim, keeping her eye on the sight and taking out the remaining red bottles. She won the game, but he watched closely over her shoulder as she did, until his breath brushed off her neck and back at him. So close he could smell her lavender perfume. It gouged at his heart strings, reminding him of the last time he'd been so close. Reminding him of everything he'd lost…that they'd lost.

As if she noticed his nose lingering at her neck, his lips inching ahead, she said, "I think we need to watch Dorian more carefully."

The words were a sharp knife slitting through his affection. He took a startled step back.

"He asked me if I remembered Adam Vandemilio and the *five* guys on his crew."

Adam stepped farther away from her and rubbed at his neck, but she was already looking at him with narrowed eyes. He just wanted this night, one night with the love of his life, before it all went to hell. Before he had to face the fact that they could be dead by morning.

"What is it?"

He couldn't look at her long enough to say it. But he had to. "Yesterday, Paul and I followed Antonio and T.B. to the cemetery."

"Were they up to something?"

"You could say that," Adam said, pausing to take a breath. "They were digging up my grave."

"What?! They wer–"

"They had shovels, at my tombstone, dug right down to the coffin."

The panic that was squeezing his chest was written all over her face. "But that means–"

"I know, baby."

"But—this," she said, breaths coming in heavy pants. "Is this goodbye? Are you running again?"

"No."

"Then you're dea–"

"Don't say it. Not...tonight. Tomorrow. Please," Adam said, brushing her hair back over her shoulder.

Mercedes placed the gun in her sights again. She landed six angry shots in a row, hitting the blue glass bottles now and smashing them on impact. The rules were officially off the table, it seemed. "I can't lose—"

"You won't lose anyone," he said, but she just frowned. "Worried about me, baby?" Said to inject playfulness back into their conversation, but his voice broke on the words.

"What a stupid question," she huffed, throwing herself into his arms.

"Worry tomorrow," he said, placing a kiss on her forehead.

"Tomorrow," she agreed.

***

After he'd dropped Mercedes back at the mansion, Adam spent the rest of the night on the beach staring out into the waves. He returned to his hotel room the next morning to find Dan, glasses on, was busily working through paper files on the dining room table while Carlos was down in the far room cooking crystals.

Paul had been pacing at the window, and he startled, rushing forward as Adam opened the door. Adam shook his head sharply. "Wait until she gets here," Adam said. Paul returned to the window away from his friends, like he was afraid he would give something away.

Adam shuffled down the hallway, hands in pockets, to watch Carlos work in the far room. Adam was distracted when Mercedes finally entered, removing her leather jacket and hanging it up on the coat rack behind her.

"Drop that for a minute, Carlos, and come to the kitchen," Adam said. Smoke puffed but Carlos stepped out of it, removing his safety goggles and nestling them in his dark hair.

"Everyone, come sit down," Adam said. "We need to have a chat."

Paul, Carlos, and Mercedes joined Dan at the dining room table while Adam stood over them. He must've looked pretty skittish, because they were all immediately attentive.

"What is it?" Dan said, removing his glasses.

Adam caught a lump in his throat as he struggled to tell his friends the truth. He was a fun guy. An official 'fucker-up-of-shit', if that were a thing. Bad news wasn't his forte. How did he even become the leader? He was stalling. He sighed and ripped off the metaphorical Band-Aid. "We have good intel that Dorian Blake might know I'm alive."

"What sort of intel?" Carlos asked.

"Well, Paul and I–" Adam started, but his throat caught again.

"We followed T.B. and Antonio to the cemetery, and caught them digging up Adam's grave, right down to the coffin," Paul finished, in more of a blurt.

Hands resting upon the table, Adam looked over to Mercedes, who sat back in her chair with her arms crossed, their eyes locking as they waited for the roars they expected.

"I didn't know they turned to grave robbing," Dan mumbled.

"Or they know I'm not actually dead," Adam said, to remind them of the seriousness of the situation.

"It's not just that," Mercedes said. "Dorian was asking me about the four of you."

"Well, that's officially not fucking good," Dan said, his voice rising, but still bubbling below the surface of outright panic.

"We did a good job of faking your death, Adam, even if he does dig you up, he'll find a fucking skeleton," Carlos nodded, pointing his finger.

"He... will?" Adam frowned.

Dan sat forward, licking his lips, "We were terrified, to be fair, couldn't give him any reason to believe you survived."

"You buried bones in my grave?" Adam smiled.

Dan and Carlos nodded furiously, like bobbleheads that had just been struck.

"You buried *bones* in his *grave*? Like complete fucking skeleton-type bones?" Paul sat forward, frowning.

"Yeah, while you fucked off out of town for weeks after Adam *died*, we had to clean some shit up, didn't we?" Dan said, his tone accusatory but doing little to mask his pride.

"Damn right," Carlos agreed. "Spread charred bones at the site, chucked a few more in your grave. Threw in your gold watch for good measure."

"And the suit." Dan smiled, gleaming at Carlos.

Carlos looked excited when his eyes snapped up. "Oh yeah! Three-piece suit. Dressed that skeleton up real nice."

They burst out laughing, making the others smile in return.

"Huh," Adam said, stunned into submission. His friends had covered all their bases. All the worry he'd felt, the panic, was for nothing... But the feel of her in his arms last night. Her nose brushing his neck like she couldn't bear to lose him... Where fear was before, hope blossomed.

Adam cleared his throat. "Alright, that might take the heat off us a little bit, but he's still suspicious. He cannot—*cannot*—know I'm alive until it's in our favor."

"You're telling me," Carlos puffed.

"Well, I've got something more to celebrate," Dan said. "I've decrypted the keys from the white book. I've started compiling a list of city officials we can get on our side without alerting Blake."

"That is good news," Adam said.

"And Paul, I've decrypted your files from the range, no idea what they fucking say, but that has nothing to do with encryption. You should be able to read them now," Dan said, sliding a file over to him.

Paul took the decrypted documents from Dan's hands, the three of them turning to general conversation and boisterous laughter.

Stuffing back his surprise, Adam locked eyes with Mercedes. She appeared to think the same.

Were they... calm? His friends? No, surely not.

There was a time that any kind of information outside their favor would've put them in a spin. But now, they had calmly dealt with an issue. Kept pushing ahead despite the threat of conflict. To Adam, it only made him more sure that this time they were ready to win.

Mercedes floated from her chair and nuzzled up next to Adam, her arms folded but her mouth near his ear. "So...what *are* we gonna do about my lovely future-husband?"

Adam grinned, but chose not to taunt her this time. Blake wasn't her future husband. He already had plans for who would take that role. "We are gonna keep pushing forward, keep one step ahead, and keep outrunning him until it's too fucking late for him to catch us."

***

It was alone in his office that Dorian realized he was losing. He was casually reading over files when a papercut snagged his finger. Looking down on the blood, the slick redness coating his thumb, he realized it was the first of his own blood that had been on his hands in years. Was it decades, even? He couldn't recall.

He was losing his grip on the empire he fought so hard for. And he had fought hard for it. When he was twenty-one years old, he killed his oldest brother. Then, when he was twenty-nine years old, he tracked down and killed his last living cousin, who had been hiding from him for years.

So when he looked down upon the simple, small droplet of his own blood sliding along his thumb, he realized he was perhaps underprepared. So many years spent in power, so many years spent behind a desk, he had become distanced from the brutality he needed to foster in order to survive this life.

Three brothers dead. Six cousins. All for this empire. Every threat he had ever come up against he had squashed. Fiercely. Violently. So he wasn't going to let someone—some stranger—take it all out from under him this time.

Once he was mayor, there wouldn't be a power in the city that could stop him. He would have domain over the police, the courts, not to mention the streets he already controlled. The one and only thing he knew was that he had to get there, by any means necessary.

He wiped the blood from his finger across his stark white shirt, right over his heart, so it would stain and serve as a reminder to be harsher than before.

Antonio and T.B. appeared at the doorway just in time to witness the end of Dorian's revelation. They spied the blood on his chest and exchanged a glance, but ultimately ignored it. Smart Seconds.

"Boss," Antonio said. "We have the records for you."

Dorian waved them forward, and Antonio placed a file front and center on the desk. Through lowered brows, Dorian brushed his eyes over the file and then looked to Antonio before slowly picking it up.

He took care when flipping the pages, but there was a restless monster rising beneath the surface of his skin. Having not read so much as even a word, Dorian set the file gently on the desk in front of him before grabbing a dagger from his desk and casting it across the room, at the same time that he shouted, "I don't need to fucking read it, just tell me!"

The dagger landed in the wall to his left, vibrating with force.

Antonio cleared his throat and straightened his jacket. "Adam Vandemilio is definitely dead. The police report shows there were charred bones in the warehouse, and there were no hospital admissions within five-hundred miles for anyone matching his injuries that day, or even for the next few weeks."

"You're sure?" Dorian's voice was a quiet, poisonous whisper.

"Positive. He couldn't have made it out of there. Even if he did, there's no way he could have survived those injuries for any length of time without medical attention."

Dorian's eyes flickered with a glimmer of knowing, one that made his Second twitch on the spot.

"We dug up the grave ourselves—" Antonio stuttered.

T.B.'s voice was more confident, and behind his eyes was a glittering of wickedness. He, at least, would relish in the things they would have to do to make sure they stayed on top. He was almost taunting when he said, "What did you find in Darton?"

Ah, that little trip upstate with Mercedes... Yes, that was a fruitful adventure. Much more so than his usual business escapes.

"Darton revealed exactly what I thought it would," Dorian replied.

Though the evidence was to the contrary, Dorian no longer believed that somebody else could be after him. There was no one else he knew who had the power to put together a successful enough team to take him out. The other gangs in neighboring cities had all been dealt with through legacy agreements. He had killed his siblings. He had killed his cousins. There was no one else coming for him.

It had to be Adam Vandemilio.

Or someone acting in his interests.

"Fine," Dorian agreed, though his eyes said otherwise. "But if it's not Adam Vandemilio himself, then it's someone very close to him."

Antonio, wide-eyed, glanced to T.B., but T.B.'s look was just as feral as Dorian's.

"Get Dan, Carlos, and Paul up here first thing in the morning. We need to have a chat," Dorian laughed.

"Really? They're just low le–"

"I said *get them up here.*"

CHAPTER 17
PUSH THE TEMPO

Mercedes spotted Paul and Adam standing on the Ridge City Bridge before she even pulled her car up, parking on the right side of the bridge in a dense gravel parking lot.

She stepped out into the heat and wiped a dribble of sweat from the back of her neck. Casually dressed, she'd opted for white sneakers, denim mini shorts, and a black lace bralette.

Adam, she noted, almost matched. He was wearing white sneakers and denim shorts with a black linen shirt, and clearly unbothered with the buttons, leaving his shirt to hang open, exposing his chest beneath.

Mercedes approached them, her long, dirty blonde hair blowing aimlessly in the wind. Still not having noticed her coming, Adam tilted his head back in a laugh, exposing a tattoo on his neck that she'd never seen before. Feathers. Tucked just beneath the collar.

And once she'd started looking, she couldn't stop herself, looking down his neck to his chest, muscled, veiny forearms, abs, and the sprinkle of hair below his belly button. Adam turned to look at her, too, and the sun caught his eyes, the whiteness of his wicked smile bouncing off the sunlight as if he knew where her next look would go.

Snapping at Adam, she said, "What am I out here for?"

"Hello to you, too," Adam smiled, his eyes now lingering over the fabric barely covering her stomach.

She pushed her way in between Adam and Paul, folding her arms and glaring.

"We're going to intercept a truck with a new supply of weapons and ammo," Adam said.

"Is it Dorian's guys?" she asked.

"No, upstate suppliers," Adam said. "We just need to make the intercept."

Paul had become an awkward intruder, and his face was in a wince when Mercedes finally turned to him. "You decrypted the codes?"

"I did, every shipment Blake has coming in he can't hide from us now," Paul confirmed.

"Good."

She whipped back to Adam, looking over her shoulder with a harsh stare, but he only smirked at her. She was being harder to him than usual, and he was looking at her like he knew. Like he knew that her hardness meant she was really softening, and trying to hide it.

"And why are there two cars?" Mercedes asked.

"You'll see," Adam said. "Come on, let's go."

***

An hour out of Ridge City, Adam spotted the semi-truck on the freeway. Sent by legacies in Darton to Ridge City, care of Dorian Blake, to supply guns, inside the trailer was an arsenal. Blake's reach inside Ridge City was so vast that there was no other way to buy arms; even the police bought their weapons directly from Dorian Blake.

Corrupt motherfuckers. Like he could talk.

Next to him, Mercedes was at the wheel of a white RX-7 convertible, while Dan sat in the back. In the identical car traveling directly behind theirs, Paul took the wheel with Carlos in the passenger seat.

"Up ahead," Adam said. The stocked armory semi-truck was guarded by two smaller vehicles that traveled in front and behind of it.

"Got it," Mercedes said, her instinct clearly taking over as she pushed ahead, wind rippling over the fabric of the currently closed top of the car. Her movements were so swift, so fast, that the guard cars couldn't keep up with her or even anticipate her arrival as she slammed past them and settled in to drive parallel to the trailer.

Adam looked back with a laugh as the rear guard car swerved like it'd been hit. It hadn't, but its driver was panicking anyway. It wasn't until Paul roughed its bumper that it settled back into line.

"You got that?" Dan buzzed through the radio.

"We're on it," Carlos replied, and Paul's car slammed once more into the rear guard car to keep its focus away from the real threat.

Adam narrowed his eyes on the front car, which hadn't yet moved out of formation.

"You don't have long," Mercedes said. She pressed a button and the roof lowered, descending into a spot in the back of the vehicle.

The semi was trying to push them off the road, acting out since its guards were otherwise occupied, but Mercedes just swerved left and right effortlessly as if she were bored by the whole ordeal.

"Someone is panicking," Dan laughed as he peered into the cab of the semi.

"Well, if he isn't yet, he will be in a minute," Mercedes said, gripping the wheel so hard that the whites of her knuckles showed. With one strong rip, Mercedes slammed into the side of the semi.

Wouldn't matter how many times she did that, though, it was guaranteed to get the driver's heart moving.

With the force of the impact, it was like they were magnetically bound to the trailer, clutching as they drove in synchronous movements.

Taking the cue for what it was, Adam undid his seatbelt and stood upright, climbing over to straddle the driver's seat. One foot against the windowsill, the other balanced on the center console, Mercedes sitting between his legs and his hands braced on his knee to admire the mighty jump ahead.

Yes, yes, yes! He loved this. His adrenaline was practically screaming in his head and purring beneath him. He was a sick, sick man, sure, but he wasn't ashamed.

Gunfire whipped past his face, but he just frowned while Mercedes and Dan ducked. Even as the convertible swerved across the road, Adam remained standing on the windowsill with Mercedes controlling the car beneath him.

"That fucker nearly hit me...what a *dick!*" Dan said, trying and failing to scramble out of the back of the RX-7 as Adam pulled him in by the collar and held the reckless little idiot still.

Paul neutralized the threat, all while still driving his own car, and gave Adam a hearty thumbs up. He had to admit, it looked a bit weird on a man that big and dangerous.

"I'm going to let you go and you're going to stay in the fucking car." Adam shook his head at Dan and released him.

Adam nearly stumbled when Mercedes slammed into the side of the semi again, but she just smiled up at him with a look that said she really wasn't sorry.

Again, Adam braced for the jump.

He only allowed himself a sharp inhale before he leapt through the open air and onto the side of the cab. His grip secured him to the door by only the handle and the sheer might of his legs digging into the metal.

Holding his gun one-handed, he shot the passenger side window out, opening the threshold between him and the occupant's relentless screaming. He reached in to unlock and then open the door. It flung open, sending Adam flying along, too, holding on for his life.

It didn't falter him, though. He reached forward and pulled the passenger from the vehicle, throwing him out to fly away like discarded paperwork.

Adam slid into the cab and closed the door behind him. Leaning his back up against the door to brace himself, he stretched his legs and kicked, forcing the driver out of the other side of the vehicle. Smiling, Adam took control of the truck and continued its trail along the highway.

Okay, now all they had to do was get the truck back in one fucking piece. Couldn't be too hard, right? How difficult could it be to drive a semi-truck?

***

Mercedes swore when she noticed a parade of enemy vehicles rushing in. Fucking reinforcements. Darton people were too rich.

"We have company." Carlos buzzed into the radio.

"Yeah, we got that... thanks, buddy," Dan said sarcastically in reply.

The cars joined them on the highway in a matter of seconds, flanking them from all sides until they could only see black.

Gunfire wasn't far behind the pursuit, and Mercedes could barely see the road ahead as she ducked to avoid it. Carlos and Dan did their best to return the fire while Mercedes and Paul swerved to protect Adam in the trailer. But Adam was swerving all over the goddamn road, too.

Fuck, he had no idea how to drive that truck, did he? That was the last time she was letting him make the plan.

The return fire didn't slow the new enemies down. It was obvious that they would rather see the trailer burn than see it fall into the wrong hands. She had to think on her feet, or they'd quickly be outnumbered.

"Remember the spins we used to do?" Mercedes asked Dan.

He nodded. "I can do it."

"Move ahead, Paul," Mercedes said into the radio. "We got this."

Paul's car sped ahead to take direct defense of Adam. The trailer itself bumped and jumped along the highway as Adam tried to control it without running it off the road.

As Paul's car sped ahead, Mercedes dropped back and threw the car into a spin, drifting from forward into reverse and rolling backward past the enemy cars.

She held on tight to the wheel and the stick to maintain control, her tires smoking into the asphalt as easily as a cigarette butt stains fabric. Dan lined up his automatic and unleashed an onslaught of bullets while she drove donuts into the road, maintaining pace so some cars were forced off the road, and others were taken out by Dan.

With a spin from reverse back into forward, and a few steadying swerves, Mercedes's car settled nicely along the other side of the truck. All that remained was the original front guard car, the others had been flipped, tipped, and upturned on the roadside.

"Well done," Mercedes said as Dan joined her in the front.

"And you." He took his imaginary hat off to her.

"One more at the front," Carlos buzzed into the radio to remind them.

Mercedes and Paul came speeding up on either side of the trailer to reach the lone car that was left. The one that had remained in formation even as all the other shit went down behind it. Would've been smarter to run. What was there really left to guard anyway?

Mercedes and Paul were positioned on either side and sandwiched the loner in between their two vehicles. They squeezed so hard that they had full control over the vehicle in their center, leaving it nowhere to go but where they desired.

Carlos and Dan loaded their guns and simultaneously shot the driver and passenger just as Mercedes and Paul released it.

After more steadying swerves, they pulled in to drive alongside of each other, Adam following along in the struggling semi being driven by him. They were now alone on the road.

No more cars in front of them, no more behind them, just the five of them on the open road. And... needing to make sure Adam drove that fucking thing back in one piece.

***

The semi was brimming with wooden crates full of weaponry, almost too much to fit inside their bar. Paul had sworn he'd find contacts to pick up the pieces. Dan was also confident he could sell some as an aid to his plan to get city officials on their payroll.

Once they'd finished off-loading the guns in the back room of the bar, and had promptly ditched the trailer in the river, they settled in. Spilling drinks more freely than a burst dam and yelling so loud in their revelry that Paul had warned them to quiet multiple times already.

Through the bursts of laughter from his friends, with a giggle on his lips, Adam suddenly yelled. "Shut the fuck up!"

Dan ran behind the bar to the phone, his fingers tripping over themselves as he dialed a number they'd found courtesy of the white book. He signaled the group to quiet down, too, placing his finger over his lips. The others looked at Adam curiously, but Adam just shook his head and smiled. It would be worth it.

After several rings the person finally picked up.

"Who is it?" A strong Russian voice came over the line.

Now leaning over Dan, hands on the table, Adam said, "We have your guns."

Paul, Mercedes, and Carlos widened their eyes, the latter two pointing viciously and making slashing gestures at their throats.

"*You* stole my guns," the voice growled.

"We did, and we want to make a deal," Dan said.

"I don't make deals with anyone other than Dorian Blake."

Adam grabbed the phone from Dan's hands. "I think you'll want to make this one." His smooth voice was confident as his vocal cords caressed that phone line like an intimate lover.

"Who are you?"

Dan hushed the group again as Adam started to speak. "We're willing to pay you for what we took—"

"What is catch?"

Adam and Dan beamed at each other, the conversation heading down the exact planned path.

"If—and only if—you deal exclusively with us from now on," Adam said, keeping his eyes on Mercedes, Paul, and Carlos.

The voice on the other end was silent for a moment.

And then silent for a moment longer.

And another...

Dan shrugged at Adam. But Adam simply shook his head and smirked again, nodding at the phone, telling them to wait.

"You want us to deal with you, whoever you are, and cut the Blake Family out?"

"That sums it up," Adam said, a hardness in his voice.

"You are crazy."

"Maybe," Adam said. "But either you agree to do business with us, or we'll just keep stealing from you."

"Why give me the choice at all?"

"To make *my* life easier," Adam said. "I'm just as happy stealing from you if you want to do things the fun way."

Mercedes slapped his shoulder.

"The hard way... the hard way." Adam's jaw tensed.

"You cannot steal from me."

"Have you heard what's going on down here in Ridge City? Missing drug shipments? Millions of dollars on the loose?"

Once again, the other end was silent, whether from consideration or speechlessness Adam couldn't be sure.

There was a low grumble before the voice started to shake. "You are the guys who try take down Dorian Blake?"

"You've heard of me then. Excellent," Adam said. "Do we have a deal?"

"You are blackmailing us."

"Seems so," Adam said.

There was a hustling of arguing in the background, all in Russian. Adam heard rustling as the phone was obviously snatched and passed around the room. Finally, a different voice came on the line and said with a threatening kind of calmness, "You won't last long before Dorian Blake eventually find and kill you. Because he will."

"Everyone seems so worried for me. It's sweet. Maybe you should be less worried about what *he would* do and be more worried about what *I will* do."

The voice exhaled on the line. "*Piz-dets.* Fine, you have deal."

***

Paul made his way through crowded streets to Dan's office building. Directly across from the beach there was always a hurried buzz of people. Perhaps why Dan had requested it. For the view of the topless sun bathers on the open beach front.

When Paul walked up to Dan's building, Carlos was already waiting out in front, leaning against the brick with one foot rested at his knee. When he saw Paul, he dropped his cigarette, smothering it with his shoe.

"How'd you do?" Carlos asked.

"Guns are mostly sold, only got a few crates. You?"

"Crystals all gone, can't fucking make them quick enough. Fucking drug addicts in this city," Carlos said.

"Sorry, I'm here! I'm here," Dan said. He jogged from around the corner, the redness in his cheeks and the heavy sweat pooling at his jawline said enough of how far and fast he had run. When he reached them, he bent down to rest his hands on his knees and blew out long, heavy breaths.

"You have lipstick on your face," Carlos said.

From his rested position, Dan smiled up at them and then wiped the lipstick off his cheek with his thumb, rolling his eyes at Paul's disapproving stare.

Dan held the door open for his friends, and together they ascended the open glass stairs to Dan's third-floor office. Not high by the standards of the high-rises in the city, but it was still the top floor of that particular building.

"You're not paying for anything, are you?" Paul said. "You're just funneling our own money back to us if you are."

"I don't need to pay for shit," Dan smiled, winking back at Carlos. "Not that there's anything wrong with that."

"Don't bring me into this." Carlos shook his head, but Paul didn't miss how the corners of his mouth tugged into a smile. Being the voice of reason always meant Paul was short on allies.

They pushed through the doors to Dan's suite and reached the reception desk, but up front Dan halted so suddenly that Paul and Carlos nearly slammed into him.

Dan's eyes were locked with his assistant, her face tight with panic. Paul went to open his mouth to speak, but she shook her head in warning, as if she knew that they had been doing something wrong.

Paul peered behind her with pinched brows. The office door was almost closed, but ajar enough that he could just see in. It was a swarm of suits…and guns.

Blake men.

They needed to slowly start backing away. But before they could, Antonio smashed the office door open. And the opportunity had passed...it became too late to run.

Antonio spied them all. His smile that of a wicked servant ready to please its master, rubbing his hands together like he'd get a special treat for being a good doggie.

Shit, this was bad. The three of them were not supposed to be together.

Antonio flicked his head toward the office, urging them inside. Though he didn't want to, there were limited choices. Paul nodded at the others to follow him inside.

"What's this about?" Dan asked.

Paul's eyes were immediately on the office chair, where it seemed someone was sitting. With a painfully slow swivel, the chair turned, and sitting in it, hands folded at his stomach, was Dorian Blake.

He cast his eyes over the three of them, the same distasteful look Antonio had given them. But Blake didn't look surprised to find them together at all. In fact, his eyes glowed with satisfaction. Purpose. Like he knew. "Have a seat, boys, we've got a lot to talk about."

Still, Paul looked for his options, but found them slim. Blake's men were surrounding them. Some gathered to block the door, others were blocking the window. In front of the desk were three armchairs, which must have been brought in especially for this moment, because they hadn't been there before.

So they sat in the seats Blake had personally selected for them.

"Didn't think I'd find you three all grouped up. I thought I warned you about that," Blake said, giving them that tough voice that sounded like poison.

He moved around the front of the desk, leaning back against it to stare down at them. "This conversation is well overdue, I'm sure you'll agree," Blake said.

He was looking at them like he expected a reply. But come on, at this point, none of them were that stupid. Better to let him reveal what he knew than let something accidentally slip. Was Blake so arrogant he thought they'd spill the beans without a little torture first? And even then...

"Want to stay silent? That's fine. I can do all the talking." Blake smiled. He waved his hand at Antonio, who bounded forward with a gold wristwatch.

"Do you know what this is?"

Paul hesitated before he answered. "It's a watch."

Dorian smiled again, spinning the item on his finger. "It's Adam Vandemilio's watch. Dug it right out of his grave."

"Well, why the fuck would you do that?" Carlos said, casually, breaking his silence.

"Why don't you tell me," Blake said, closing in on Carlos's face. So close that his breath heaved and blew back Carlos's hair with each puff.

This was getting worse by the second. Paul knew how unhinged Blake was already, but now he looked like he'd busted the door open to Crazytown and thrown away the key, leaking the crazy all over the carpets.

Carlos shook his head and shrugged, trying anything to avoid eye contact—and the heat that came from being under Blake's suspicious gaze.

Blake turned his attention to Dan.

"Adam Vandemilio is dead, I don't know why you wanted to dig up his watch," Dan said, gulping so loudly that Blake snickered, until he noticed the red on Dan's chin.

Dammit, Dan. *The girls.*

"Mmm," Blake said, his poisonous tone now turning into an icy whip. "You've got some lipstick on your chin, Dan. Where'd you get that from, hmm? Not from one of the girls who no longer works for me."

Dan sank into his chair, pushing his shoulders high.

"Okay, how about this one?" Blake said, turning his back to them and motioning Antonio to come forward again.

Antonio pulled out a file and Blake held up a picture up with pinched fingers.

It was a picture of the hitman who was supposed to take out Diego Garcia, lying dead on the plaza pavement. The hitman whom Paul had killed. His eyes were still open.

"Sharpshooter shot, right between the eyes," Blake said. "You were a pretty good shot right, Paul? Back in the day."

"Not that good," Paul said, keeping his tone cool, the most casual of the three of them. "Plus, a trained sniper never goes for the head." Paul tapped his chest. "Always aim for the center of mass."

If he was careful, he might just get away with it. Commonly trained snipers never did go for the head, but Paul wasn't commonly trained.

"And this?" Blake pulled a bag of cocaine crystals out of his pocket and threw it over into Carlos's lap.

Carlos's eyes were wide and guilty as he plucked the bag from his lap and shrugged. But the movement was too robotic to look real.

"So you know nothing about any of this?" Blake smirked, crossing his arms.

They all shook their heads.

Blake dropped his head and his smile, turning his voice low like a soft caress that itched with the undertone of murder. "Then what're you all doing together?" He didn't even blink as he looked them over individually, stopping at Paul.

Dan and Carlos moved only their eyes, like they didn't dare turn their heads.

Paul kept Blake's eye contact, just as unflinching. He wasn't about to let a weakness slip.

"If I recall correctly, Paul, wasn't it also you who disappeared right after Adam's *death*," Blake said, emphasizing the word death in a way that sent shivers down his spine. Fuck. Shit. Fuck.

But despite his body begging him to do otherwise, Paul remained steady.

"Mmm, business in Darton was what you said at the time." Blake's smile grew. "But that wasn't quite true, was it? At least, not according to my friends in Darton."

Blake was far too close to the truth. To unraveling everything. Paul's eyes flickered and then dropped to his lap. He tucked his lip under his teeth and took a deep breath.

"Error in judgment, boss. We're sorry. We thought we could catch up for a beer since it has been so long. We were wrong. We're so sorry," Paul said, throwing the words into his lap with such breathless fear that he couldn't even look Blake in the eye. There was too much on the line for him if Blake found out where he'd really been, and the reasons why.

Blake tested them again, scanning their faces, and wisely this time, Paul made the decision to avoid Blake's gaze again. It was the test of his power. Whoever looked away first was the slave to the master.

"Don't let it happen again," Blake said, standing up from the desk and moving back around to sit in Dan's chair.

Paul nodded and encouraged the others to stand up and leave with him. They rushed out of the office, Dan's poor terrified assistant nowhere to be found, and didn't speak again until they were bolting down the stairwell.

"Phew, we got out of that easy," Carlos said.

"No, we didn't," Paul said. "No, we fucking didn't. He doesn't believe a word we said."

Dan tried to stop, Carlos slamming against him in the process, but Paul pushed him ahead, guiding him down the stairs again. "Run. Move. Keep moving. We need to get the fuck out of here. Before they come for us...or we're dead."

CHAPTER 18
SKIN OF THE TEETH

Word from Paul had sent Adam into alarm, enough to call Mercedes down to the bar in the middle of the day. Besides the on-duty bartender, they were alone. They huddled together, shoulders nearly touching as Adam held his jaw in his hands.

"What was so urgent? What did I have to rush down here for?" Mercedes whispered, pushing farther into Adam's space. Usually her closeness would be a welcome distraction, but this time he just shook his head with his eyes pointed at the bartender.

"Make yourself scarce," Adam said. The bartender nodded and immediately dropped what he was doing. Not bothering to pack up or even look in their direction, he just strode straight through the front doors and left.

Adam made sure the door was pressed shut and the little bell above it had stopped clanging before he relaxed his shoulders.

"I don't know, but it had Paul really freaked out," Adam said. "So much so that he wouldn't say it over the phone."

"Nothing good, then," Mercedes said. "Are they on their way he–"

The little bell crackled, and Dan, Carlos, and Paul came bursting inside, bringing all their chaotic energy rushing in with them. They were wild-eyed, looking simultaneously like they hadn't slept in days, and like they were more awake than they'd ever been.

Mercedes and Adam opened their circle to face the others.

"What's going on?" she asked.

"Dorian Blake," Paul said.

"Might need to elaborate, bro," Adam said as he ripped the toothpick from his mouth and folded his arms.

"He had us, man!" Dan shouted, jumping from foot to foot. "He cornered us at my office."

Adam shared a look with Mercedes before turning to Dan, who was starting to lose it. A quick side eye at Paul and Carlos informed him that while they weren't as outright panicked as Dan, they were rattled. Really rattled.

"He's fucking got us now! Caught all of us! We're done for," Dan shouted.

"Chill out," Carlos said, rubbing his temple. "It's not game over."

"Might as well be!" Dan said, spitting at them like his mouth couldn't keep up with his brain. "It was a threat!"

"It *was* a threat," Paul said. "But panicking won't save you from it."

While Paul and Carlos calmed as the conversation drew on, Dan remained manic. Judging from the lipstick on his chin and the white powder shining at his nostril, Adam guessed his demeanor could only somewhat be blamed on Blake.

271

"Stop...slow down. What the hell actually happened?" Adam said.

Dan launched forward to explain, mouth agape, but Paul pushed an arm across his body to take over.

"The three of us were headed up to Dan's office," Paul started, watching carefully as Dan settled back into line, still jumping foot to foot. "And when we got there, Dorian Blake was waiting for us."

"He caught the three of you together?" Mercedes said.

Paul nodded and began a half-strung sentence before Dan launched ahead again, cutting him off. "He had loads of evidence and he w–"

Paul threw him back more forcefully this time. "He had the watch that he dug up from your grave, and the picture of the dead hitman, and a baggy of Carlos's new product," Paul said. "We're not getting out of this one easy, he's going to do something. Probably to us. I know him, I can feel it."

Adam drew a sharp breath and ran his hands through his hair. Blake had cornered them, like he *knew*.

"Goddammit," Adam sighed. "He's so close to catching up."

"So much for outrunning him," Carlos sniffed.

"We're ready for him," Mercedes said, quiet as a whisper.

"We're not fucking ready!" Dan shouted. "I'm very, very fucking nervous!"

"We can see that." Adam rolled his eyes.

"I'm not feeling settled myself," Carlos said.

Adam gave Carlos a sad smile. "We've got to keep one step ahead, we cannot let him catch us." He rubbed his eyes violently to hype himself up. "Okay, how much does he know?"

"A lot more now," a voice said, and that little bell above the door sang.

Adam's gut dropped so hard he swore it was audible as he realized they were no longer alone. And that, fuck, he should've locked the door.

A tingle caressed Adam's arms, down his back, and into his legs. He swallowed the fear like it was a fire that ignited his insides and raged out of him like lava. Slowly, he turned to face the intruder.

"Fucking hell," Antonio said, grinning like a cat. "Adam Vandemilio—you really are alive."

Antonio paced the room, ten men with him chugging along in tow. He did a full lap around them before coming to the wall, wiping dust off the top of the booths.

"You know, I didn't believe it. When Dorian was going on about you still being alive. I thought he was insane. Had to be one of the other three who were after him," Antonio said. He leaned against their regular booth and angled his head to make eye contact with Mercedes. "Or...should I say *four* of you?"

"Adam..." Mercedes said in warning.

Antonio smirked and bounded upright. "Never thought there was a fifth either. But here you are with all of them, *and* sleeping with Dorian—you are a cunning bitch."

"Why, thank you."

Adam looked back at Mercedes and then the others, now lined up in a protective row at his back. They were probably thinking the same thing he was. Blake was catching up. They'd already killed Yani, killing Antonio would light an inextinguishable flame. Like a trail of breadcrumbs that led Blake right to their door. But leaving Antonio alive? That definitely was not an option.

"Paul, Dan, Carlos—head out the back and get out of here," Adam said, a soothing calm in his voice as he glared at Antonio.

"They're not going anywhere," Antonio spat, his tone making his men stand alert.

"Let's go," Paul said.

"What? We can't go!" Dan said.

"We can and we are. We're gonna go somewhere public and make our faces seen," Paul said.

"Why?" Carlos whispered.

"So that when all of these assholes die, Blake won't be able to pin it on us," Paul said.

Their footsteps prodded loudly on the sticky tile as they calmly paced for the back exit.

"Stop them!" Antonio ordered.

With small, unsure steps the men began a forward march. Adam blocked their path. Paul nodded to Dan and Carlos, and together they continued their slow break for escape.

Just as slowly, the thugs began another approach, attempting to sidle past Adam.

It was an intricate dance, an unspoken warning, as if one wrong flinch might cause an explosion. Not an outright pursuit, a slow, delicate chase. But the thugs weren't stopping, and neither were Dan, Paul, and Carlos.

The goons came within a foot of Adam and showed no sign of slowing, no matter how nervously they avoided his gaze. Adam angled his head over his shoulder to Mercedes, who locked eyes with him, too. Her stance was soft, feet light, ready to dive. The nod of approval she gave him was so slight, anyone else would have missed it.

Time to move.

Adam moved quickly. So against the rules of their slow pursuit, that it took long moments for everyone to realize what had happened, Adam raised his gun, aimed and shot, and the approaching man closest to him fell in a bloody heap.

In the seconds that the room was silent, Adam turned to Paul and nodded at him hurriedly, to go, go *now*. And from within, the inevitable fight erupted.

***

Dan, Carlos, and Paul were out the door like their asses were on fire.

Antonio and his men blindly fired. Missing the bullets by what felt like only millimeters, Adam and Mercedes fled. Adam jumped to his right, landing in the black leather seat of his favorite booth, while Mercedes slid along the floor, underneath the counter of the bar.

Behind the bar, Mercedes quickly checked Adam. He was tucked into the booth, hands over his ears as bullets tore fluffy shreds into the upholstery. He was holding back, giving her time to secure an advantage.

Ignoring the rain of glass bottles smashing around her, Mercedes pinned a keypad to unlock a sleek set of black cupboards. Their hidden arsenal. She tore into the stash, pulling out only the guns they would need. It only took her seconds to release them, slide ammunition inside, and line them up for the taking.

Lastly, a stun grenade. Pity there were no actual grenades, but an explosion would've been a bad idea anyway. Sadly.

After one last look to make sure Adam was still crouched into the booth with his ears and eyes covered, she threw the stun grenade, taking shelter herself. The room lit up like a flare as it landed, gunfire halting.

In a fluid, smooth movement, she launched up from behind the bar, two shotguns in hand. At the same time Adam rose from the booth and held a hand to catch the shotgun she tossed across to him.

Then they were up. As they cocked their weapons they walked slowly to the middle of the room and locked together, shoulder to shoulder.

They shot those who hadn't found time to shelter, still fumbling around blindly from the shock of the grenade. Like carefully lined dominos, the men fell in neat piles, blood spraying the walls.

From the right, Adam was rushed by a burly thug with a protruding belly. He only smiled and dropped his gun, kicking the guy in the chest and dousing him with a right hook.

Mercedes smashed the butt of her gun into a nameless face, rolling to climb on top of the tables. Grabbing nameless by the hair, she forced his jaw open on the table edge and booted his head down, locking eyes with Antonio as she did.

"What the fuck..." Antonio said, watching with wide eyes.

Nameless's horrified buddy rushed at her. She kicked him down and began to lay cover fire as Adam moved throughout the bar, killing with only his hands and his fists. To him, it was more fun that way.

Adam reached Antonio, who went to load his gun with shaky fingers, but Adam kicked it away, raising his fists and inclining his head to entice Antonio to do the same. Antonio, it seemed, however rightfully afraid, wasn't willing to go down without a fight either. The situation was covered, so Mercedes focused on the four backup thugs who remained alive.

One rushed to help Antonio, so she shot him before he could get close.

The other three rushed her. Breaking through her barrier of bullets, the tallest one tackled her from the tabletop onto the sticky tile.

Her head pounded as she felt the weight of a body holding her down. Two guys held her arms at her sides, while the third straddled her and gripped her throat.

Her breath was failing, darting out of reach every time she fought to catch it. The man was rough. They sure weren't pulling punches anymore.

276

The disgusting fuck even had the nerve to lean down and lick a line across her cheek.

Gross as fuck. But a good opening. She clamped her teeth on his ear and ripped. He released her with a howl. Twirling her legs, she kicked the left one off her, and grabbed a gun to shoot righty in the head, then lefty, too, for good measure. As a final killing blow, she pushed up and grabbed a knife from the bar top, plunging it into the strangler's heart.

She finally stood and threw her hair from her eyes, turning back to Adam and Antonio's fight.

Adam clearly had a desire to tease because the fight was still fucking going. Adam now danced around Antonio, not bothering to lay a fist himself, only dodging the ones Antonio so desperately threw.

With Adam distracted by her approaching, Antonio managed to land a hit against Adam's cheek. Adam fell back, stunned, but smiling as he wiped the blood away with his thumb.

Now flanked between them, Antonio faltered, like he couldn't decide who was the worst one to surround him. Especially since they were barely acknowledging him, only looking at each other with raw and wicked delight.

Just at the moment that Antonio turned toward Adam with wide eyes, Adam threw a punch with all his weight behind it, sending Antonio careening toward Mercedes.

She grinned as Antonio fell into her.

"Give him hell, baby," Adam said.

She took her knife and grabbed Antonio by the neck, holding him still at her front. He struggled, but she only pulled him in tighter.

"Say hi to Yani for me," she said, but he barely had a moment to appreciate the comment as she sliced across his throat in a polished swipe.

The blood poured freely, his carotid severed and washing onto the tile like a heavy wave. Even as he died, bleeding out in front of them, they only looked at each other.

Fucking hell, she was turned on. By the look of it, Adam was, too. *That's why they belonged together.* The thought stunned her like a Taser.

Finally, she released Antonio's neck and he thudded down.

She moved to stand over the body, coating her shoes in the thick pools of blood.

"Damn, baby," Adam said.

Returning from the blood haze, she looked over the bar. A complete mess. Torn to shreds, bodies everywhere, and coated in blood spray. "Looks like we've got a big fucking mess to clean up," Mercedes said, and she didn't just mean the state of their bar.

***

SEPTEMBER 1986

Once they'd lost their home at the trailer park, there was truly nowhere else to go. Blake's men had been hot on their heels ever since.

They found temporary shelter in a dirty alleyway at the edge of the city. Out of breath from the pursuit, Adam only encouraged a brief stop. They had maybe a ten-minute lead on Blake's men. At best.

"I think we lost them," Mercedes said.

"Only just," Paul said. "It was really close."

"Really close," Carlos agreed as he stopped to sit on a trash can.

"Let's just hold here for a bit and then we'll keep moving," Adam said, leading the pack.

"Adam, what the hell are we doing?" Dan hissed, the whites of his eyes shining, not an ounce of drugged red sting behind them.

278

What were they doing? Fuck if he knew.

Adam's only reply was a tense shrug before he retreated farther into the alley.

"Seriously, what the fuck are we doing?!" Dan said, following him. "They are so fucking close on our tail. We've got nowhere left to go!"

Slowly turning back to Dan, Adam folded his arms, watching the outburst with eyes as tight as slits and mouth as sharp as a razor.

A moment later, there was a rumble nearby that froze them all. Adam, still the only one without fear, approached the edge of the alley and peered onto the street.

Blake's men.

They turned up in droves with loud roaring engines and headlights as bright as the sun. Watching as their hunters rounded the street and continued north, Adam loosened a breath. They were safe for now, but not off the hook entirely. Their ten-minute lead had significantly shortened.

Adam nodded to his friends.

"Well? What are we doing?!" Dan said.

"You keep telling us to run, but... to where?" Carlos said, looking up with a pained expression. "What are we running toward? Where could we possibly go from here?"

Adam ran his tongue along his teeth, turning to Paul looking for support, though he wasn't actually surprised when he didn't find any.

"Paul?" Adam said.

"I'm sorry," Paul whispered.

Paul had finally left Adam in the lurch. His always unwavering, and yeah, a little unfounded, support—gone. He had warned Adam numerous times how this would end.

He'd never intended to draw so much attention. He just wanted to be in charge of his own destiny. Sick of allowing someone else to decide whether or not he lived or died.

"We're done here, we failed. End of story," Paul said. "What are we doing now?"

Adam, annoyed as ever, stared at his feet. But no answer laid there either. *Obviously.*

He looked up to find his friends staring back at him, exhausted and unsure, but somehow still looking to him for guidance.

"We don't have a choice," Mercedes said, stepping in front of him to draw the attention. "We run, or we die. Nobody's got some sort of brilliant plan here. You don't wanna die? Then you run."

They didn't dare to argue with her, but they didn't respond either. There was no passion glowing over them anymore. They only looked sad, exhausted, confused. Beaten. Just as Blake had wanted them to be.

"Fine," Paul agreed, seemed that if he couldn't support another of Adam's grand schemes, he could at least support Mercedes's desire to keep them all alive. "We run until we can't anymore."

The alleyway fell silent, with only the chirp of bugs echoing through the barren mess.

"This wasn't supposed to be it," Dan said, his throat catching. "We were supposed to be big. We weren't supposed to fail."

"Let's just try to stay alive," Paul said, patting him on the shoulder.

With heads hung, Paul and Dan helped Carlos to his feet and they headed for the street. Ready for what would likely be many more weeks of running.

Mercedes had inclined to follow them but seemed to notice that Adam couldn't bring himself to move. He was stuck in that alley, inside his mind, arms folded and staring down at the rain-soaked bricks.

He watched as Mercedes tapped Paul on the shoulder. "We'll catch up."

Paul cut a glance to Adam, as still as a stone sculpture, and nodded once. "We'll be in the liquor store." With that he followed the others into the open street, leaving Mercedes and Adam alone.

"Coming?" she asked.

To no reply, she placed her hands on his shoulders and patted him until he faced her.

"I think I fucked up here," Adam said, softening. "I think I really fucked up."

"What are you talking about?"

"I just–" He pushed her hands from his shoulders and turned his back, he couldn't bear to see her face as he admitted failure. "I... I did this— everyone is in trouble because of me. I never thought he would actually beat us."

"He hasn't beaten us," Mercedes said, wrapping her arms around him and resting her head in the small of his back.

"What he wants is me, if I cou–"

"Shut the fuck up right now," Mercedes said, grabbing his shoulder and turning him until he was facing her again. "Handing yourself over is not an option. I don't even want you thinking that."

"You wanna fight this?" Adam said. "Really? This fucking huge empire that's beaten us down this far already?"

"Of course, I want to fight it."

Adam only frowned, but not at what she said. His spine was tingling with suspicion. There was a riot of noise approaching. But she hadn't heard it yet.

"As long as we have each other, there's nothing we can't do."

Still, he could hear something coming.

"Adam?"

His eyes darted wildly, but it was only a symptom of his ears working overtime.

"Do you hear that?" he said finally. At that moment the sound of gunfire burst ferociously in the background.

His feet reacted much faster than his brain. He started into a run, pressing for the edge of the alley to follow the sound.

The ringing of bullets got louder and louder with every footstep, as did the thrumming in his chest. He could vaguely hear Mercedes sprinting along behind him.

He slowed to a jog as he hit the intersection of the alleyway and the sidewalk. Across the road, Dan, Paul, and Carlos were crouching against the front steps of the liquor store, cornered by Blake's men. The gunfire had clearly been even on both sides, with several of Blake's men already dead. But his friends were being overpowered. To Adam, it looked like they had mere seconds until they were captured. Or worse.

He loaded his gun and charged out onto the street. But Mercedes was there a second sooner, grabbing the back of his shirt and pulling him back to pin him against the wall. She shielded his body with her own as they remained under the cover of the dark alley's shadows.

"What are you doing?!" he said.

She slapped her hand across his mouth, pressing tighter against him. "It's too late," she whispered.

He cut his focus to the street. He'd been correct, his friends had only mere seconds. By the time he looked back, Dan, Paul, and Carlos were being captured. They'd been overpowered and knocked unconscious, their hands bound before they were dragged into capture.

It was far too late to do anything about it. Mercedes dropped her hand from his mouth.

"No, God, no," Adam said. "I have to do something."

He struggled against her hold, but she only pressed more, pinning him harder against the wall. "You don't have a chance right now."

"We can't just leave them," Adam said. "I did this. I did this to all of us. I can't just let them take it!"

"We won't! But you can't just go barging in! We'll get them back, I swear. But causing a big scene is not the way to do it. No matter how much you like it," she smiled.

The joke was lost on him as his eyes remained glued to the street. There was an uncharacteristic panic rewriting him. He'd never cared what happened to him, but them...

"Look at me." She pulled his chin toward her until he was looking in her eyes. "I promise, we'll get them back."

***

MAY 1991

Under the cover of night, the powerboat held still in the water, not a wave or a breeze to sway it. The usually turquoise waters were a deep midnight blue, and the only light was that of the shining full moon.

Mercedes stood looking out onto the ocean. At the world that existed away from the shores of the city. From the life that she felt trapped in.

Trapped as she was, though, she'd never wanted to plot against Dorian. Miserable and safe was a step above dead.

But somewhere along the line that had changed. The more time she spent with Adam, in the company of her old friends, the less she gave a shit about playing safe. She couldn't be Dorian Blake's wife. She couldn't be First Lady of Ridge City. So she couldn't afford to lose again, because if she had to live this false life for the rest of hers, she wouldn't survive it.

"Help me with this," Adam said, jumping on the powerboat and wiping sweat from his brow. Far off the coast, Adam and Mercedes, with the help of their new crew of exiles and outcasts, had driven their powerboat, a prized Blake yacht, and eleven dead bodies into the night for disposal.

Dorian Blake's favorite yacht was currently loaded with those eleven bloody bodies, one being Antonio's lifeless form.

Adam handed her a match as the powerboats transporting their people drove away into the night. "You do the left side."

"Are you sure this will work?"

Adam just shrugged. Typical. Her lips threatened a smile that she held back.

On the count of three, they lit their matches and threw them up onto the highest levels they could reach. The flames followed a path of gasoline throughout the yacht, igniting in a roaring fire.

It was like a display of fireworks, the flames creating a burning light show, a glow of heat that provided the kind of warm flicker found in a wood fire.

Now wearing Adam's jacket, she pulled it tight across her shoulders. The silence was not uncomfortable, but familiar, as they stood together admiring the burning vessel.

"You ready to go?" Adam said.

"No," Mercedes smiled. "Let's stay a while and watch it burn." They had at least an hour before the flames would be spotted off the coast, anyway.

She heaped herself into the built-in seat at the back of the powerboat and tucked her legs in underneath her.

"I was hoping you'd say that." Adam disappeared briefly, leaving only the sound of rifling through cupboards before he returned with a bottle of scotch and two glasses.

"Goddamn, you're good," Mercedes said, returning his lazy grin.

Their fingers brushed when she took her glass and let him pour her a drink. He served an identical one for himself and joined her on the seat, focusing on the show in front as if it were a romantic fire in the depth of winter, and not an engulfed effigy of their recent sins.

"It's late, you don't have to be going back to the husband-to-be?" Adam said. Mercedes's lip twitched in interest. What a topic for him to lead off with. But his voice was flustered and his eyes weary, and despite how hard she pushed him away, he kept coming back swinging. Despite how cold she wanted her heart to be, for him it always warmed.

"Dorian doesn't spend a lot of time around me these days," Mercedes said, taking a swig of her drink.

Adam stared into his lap, but the corners of his mouth tightened, like he was trying to suppress a smile.

"You like that?"

"Well..." He was doing a terrible job of hiding his grin. "It's not terrible to hear."

"Jealous?"

"Of the person who has you? Always."

She dropped her eyes to her glass and swirled it before taking another sip. "He doesn't have me," she said. "And, come to think of it, I never had him."

"Yeah?" Adam said, leaning forward. Always trying to get closer to her, did he think she didn't notice? "How's that?"

"Tonight, for example. Wednesday, so that means he'd be down at pole position with..." she squinted as she made her guess. "...Bridget? And tomorrow, Thursday. That's a Kelly night."

"You're just one of his many girlfriends?" He gave her an incredulous look.

"Dorian has lots of girls running after him. Not that he knows I know," Mercedes said. Adam frowned, but he didn't look at her with pity. Good, because she didn't need it. What Dorian did wasn't a reflection on her. She wouldn't ever feel like it was. "I couldn't give two fucks what Dorian does."

Adam sighed and shuffled even closer on the plush, striped cushions. "I guess, it's just..."

His eyes created a path from her gaze to her lips.

"Just what?"

"If I had you, I would never take you for granted."

"You think I'm being taken for granted?"

"You're not being loved the way you should," he said.

There was a look behind his eyes, like she could actually see a sparkle of hope brightening in his chest.

"I need you to know something," he said.

She finished her drink and rested the glass on the rim of the seat, nodding to give him permission to continue. She'd by lying if she said she wasn't curious. Adam was the kind of guy who should've been predictable, but was always an absolute surprise. Who knew what was going to come out of his mouth next?

"I need you to know that I always kept you close to me." He removed the giant silver skull ring from his left hand and held it out for her. Hesitantly, she accepted, holding it in her palm to study it.

"Look at the inscription," he said.

She turned the ring over in her hands, so that the moon lit the inside of the band enough for her to read. There she found an infinity symbol, just like the one on her necklace.

"You had it engraved," she said. It wasn't engraved when she'd gifted it to him.

"I needed to keep a piece of you close to me," he said.

"Why?" She managed to squeeze out through her constricting throat. Though, she already knew the answer.

"I think you know why," he said. Returning the ring, she handed it over and he slipped it on his finger again. The fourth finger of his left hand. His ring finger. And she wondered if maybe he'd always considered himself taken, even after all these years.

"I think you still think I'm reckless."

"You're not wrong," she said.

"You're worried that I'll get Paul, Dan, or Carlos hurt. Worse…killed," he said. She couldn't argue there. Hell, that was the thing that held her back from helping him in the first place, while also being the exact reason she came around.

"I can't help it," she said.

"I know. But I wouldn't ever let that happen," he said. "I know you know that."

She *had* always known that. Adam had died for them once before. She never doubted this time would be any different. But that was the thing that scared her most of all.

"I will not let anyone die for me," he said with a hard voice, like he was trying to imprint it in her brain. "I would never let one of our friends die in my place. Never. You won't lose them."

"Maybe there are other people I am worried about losing," she said, once again quietly, but this time finding the guts to look him in the eye.

"There are?"

"There are."

He looked into her eyes until a quiet smile spread across her lips, embarrassing herself enough that she looked away, which made him smile too.

She was already terrified of what she would lose if they failed for a second time. The truth, though. Fuck, that was harder to admit. Even to herself.

Shuffling on the seat, she turned her back to him but scooted closer, lowering her back to his front. She swept her hair away and rested her head on his shoulder.

He released a long breath as he embraced her in his arms, folding them across her stomach and leaning in to brush her cheek with his own.

Brushing aside her fears just once as they both watched the flames licking at the expensive yacht in front of them, she sighed in contentment. Just enough to whisper, "I've missed you."

CHAPTER 19
A GOOD LIE

It took a week for Antonio's body to be recovered by divers and officially identified. Even though everyone knew it was him on that yacht. What was a mystery was how much Dorian knew. Antonio had been sent after them, that much was clear. But... well, Dorian became a closed book. Which was smart of him, unfortunately.

Mercedes and T.B. sat on the sofa in the main floor living room, tension palpable. For over an hour, since the official news of Antonio's death, Dorian had been locked in his office.

Mercedes didn't bother to try a sideways look at T.B., only the sloshing of ice against his crystal glass confirmed his presence. The silence may have been because they never really got along, or because in some weird way they were the last ones standing.

Only two to go.

Mercedes suppressed the delightful curling of her lip.

"Then there were two," T.B. said. He must've been thinking the same thing. Though, perhaps he wasn't as pleased about it as she was.

"Then there were two." They clinked their glasses in a weird show of solidarity.

Clicking footsteps sounded down the marbled staircase and Dorian entered, his usually neat hair a disheveled nest, and his tie half undone.

"Honey," Mercedes said, getting up to hug him. "I'm sorry about Antonio."

Dorian pushed her off, wriggling out of her grip. "Don't be. He was a useless piece of shit anyway."

Widening her eyes at T.B., Mercedes sank back into the sofa. Rage was good, though, rage was not calculated. It was passionate and reckless. It was the kind of thing that got people killed.

"What are you thinking, boss? Paul, Carlos, or Dan?" T.B. said.

"All of them," Dorian said, stopping Mercedes's heart. "And none of them." But there was a catching in his throat that made her think he was lying. He had always tried to lie to her about Paul.

"What are you talking about?" Mercedes said, innocently as she could. She'd play dumb as long as she could get away with.

"Whoever is after Dorian must be associated with Adam Vandemilio," T.B. began to explain, trailing off slowly at the end. Mercedes puckered her lips, what she hoped was an excellent façade of cluelessness.

"It wasn't them who killed Antonio," Dorian said. "At first I thought it was, because I'd sent Antonio to follow them, but they have solid alibis."

Mercedes relaxed slightly. But she didn't dare loosen her breath, the conversation was still laced with subtext.

"So if it's not them..." T.B. said.

"There's only one person it could be," Dorian said.

The two of them shared an evil grin, as if they both understood perfectly. But Mercedes needed to be sure.

"Who's that now?"

Dorian chuckled and poured a drink, taking a sip. "The fifth guy." He raised his glass knowingly to T.B., who only egged him on further by nodding in ridiculous agreement.

"You can't be serious," Mercedes sighed, folding lazily into the sofa.

"There was always a driver on Adam's crew," T.B. said. "Paul, Dan, Carlos—none of them are drivers."

"And what does that prove?" Mercedes said.

"There's a driver out there. From Adam's crew. Good enough to beat T.B.," Dorian said.

T.B.'s knuckles whitened as his hand tightened around his glass. He was always a sore loser.

"If Dan, Paul, or Carlos were good enough drivers to beat me, I'd know about it. There's someone else out there," T.B. said.

"You really believe there's a driver in this city good enough to beat you, and you've never heard about it or seen their face? Please." Mercedes rolled her eyes.

"There is someone else out there," T.B. said.

"Someone else who used to work for Adam," Dorian said. "So, whoever killed Antonio, that's the fifth guy."

Well... he wasn't wrong. Just about the gender.

"We never found out who the fifth guy was." T.B. raised his brow, as if in challenge.

"And that was the whole point of keeping those idiots from Adam's team alive." Dorian smashed his glass down into the fire, causing a wild roar up the chimney. "So there's definitely a fifth."

Now huddling over the fireplace, Dorian and T.B. each glanced over their shoulder in her direction, and she realized she had forgotten to flinch at the glass smashing in the fire. An innocent victim would've. Whoops.

As if he were now taunting her, Dorian whispered to T.B. for her to overhear, "And whoever that person is, Dan, Carlos, and Paul fucking know about it. And it'll be my pleasure to pull it out of them...piece by fucking piece."

***

It was shaping up to be a usual afternoon. Drawn together, all of them littered around Adam's hotel room. Adam smiled at the thought. How the hell he'd managed five years away was beyond him.

At the sink, Carlos's supply bags closed with a snap as they were packed, while closer to the dining table, Paul and Dan counted stacks of money into itemized piles. On his bed, Mercedes laid back into the lush pillows and dark silk sheets. He liked to see her there, even if she wiggled away every time he tried to join her.

"We are so fucked," Dan said. "I don't think Blake believed one word of what we fucking said."

"He's been riding my ass," Carlos said. "Won't take his eyes off me." With another snap, Carlos poured cut crystals into mini supply bags.

"We told a good lie," Paul said.

"What exactly did he say to you?" Mercedes propped her head up on her fist.

"He's obsessed with finding out who the fifth member of our group is," Paul said, stopping to frown in thought. He did that a lot, stop to frown off into the distance, like he could see the future ahead and was carefully plotting a path through the obstacles of death he foresaw.

"We'd never say anything," Dan said, smiling tightly at Mercedes.

"Obviously." Carlos rolled his eyes.

Mercedes huffed. "I don't think you're all as off the hook as you think you are."

With supply bags hanging from his mouth, Carlos said, "And why is that?"

"From what he's said to me, I just—I have a feeling... that he knows."

"He's got nothing yet, we're fine," Adam said, waving a lazy hand to the others gathered in the kitchenette. "He's got no idea that I'm alive, and no idea that these guys are involved."

"But he's suspicious that they are," Mercedes said. "Isn't that dangerous enough?"

"We can handle it," Paul said.

"I don't like you putting yourselves at risk," she said, sinking back into the pillows.

"I know, but nobody is forcing us to do this," Paul said.

She turned to Dan and Carlos, which was fair. In the past they'd been most easily rattled. Dan, especially.

"He's all up in my business, sure, but it's because he doesn't really know anything. Either way, it's worth it," Carlos said.

Dan was hesitant but nodded in agreement. The room filled with a comfortable silence that said more than it meant to. They all agreed. It was worth it. At least it would be if they survived.

Adam turned back to the window, where he could see straight out onto the sand. He couldn't decide if their situation felt more serious than it was, or if they weren't taking it seriously enough.

"I have to get these out to the dealers," Carlos said, scooping up finished bags into his duffle. "Cops are all over us lately."

Paul joined Carlos in leaving, their idle chatter echoing back from the stairwell.

"The cops are all over our drug movement now that they've worked out we're not Blake Family," Dan said. He pushed out of his seat and shadowed over Adam.

"Then we need the city officials on our side sooner rather than later. They can call off the cops," Adam said.

"Are we ready for that?" Mercedes asked. "That's meant to be the very last item."

"Less than a month until the election. Now is the time," Adam said, sitting upright.

Dan's lip nearly shook, but still he nodded. "Then I'll get to work." He barely said goodbye before rushing out of the room and slamming the door behind him. This was why Dan was never assigned stealth, he always made the loudest exit possible.

Mercedes shuffled off the bed. "Are you sure we're ready for this?"

"No," Adam said, still staring out onto the beach. "But we have to be."

Deep in thought, he brushed his finger over his lip. Not hearing her reply, he drew his attention back to the room to find her pacing, gears turning inside her mind.

He stood up and brushed the lint from his clothes. "It'll be okay," he said, coming to her side. "Promise."

She nodded enough times that it was obvious she didn't really believe him.

***

OCTOBER 1986

"Baby, wake up... wake up!" Adam yelled, shaking Mercedes at the shoulders. As soon as her eyes were open, he rushed back to their motel room window. The blinds were drawn, but just outside, in the vicinity of parking spaces that lined the front of the rooms, he could see a crew of Blake men beginning a frantic search.

Mercedes ripped the stained brown sheets from her body and threw her clothes on. Adam pulled his eyes away from her body with difficulty, he needed to concentrate. He drew the blinds closed and signaled her to move quietly. "They're right outside," he whispered.

"They found us again?" she said, tucking her hair back behind her ears.

They both jumped when they heard a loud bang.

Adam pried the blinds open with two fingers, creating just enough of a slip to see out if he squinted. Blake's men were kicking down doors. They'd started at the front of the block, four doors away from theirs.

"We gotta go," Adam said. "Now!"

Another bang, three doors to go.

They collected their things from various corners of the room. Sheets went flying, clothes with it, as they hurried to gather the last of their supplies. Guns, grenades, various other weapons, all piled into a backpack which Adam shoved on his shoulder.

Another bang, this time screaming, two doors to go.

"Bathroom window," she said.

Piling in, they locked the door once they'd rushed inside. It was just a flimsy wooden door, but it was all they had to separate themselves from danger, and the more barricades the better.

In an instant, Mercedes was standing on the toilet and rattling the one tiny window to force it open, but the slide was jammed.

Wide-eyed, she looked back to him. Shit, he'd have to shoot it out. He secured a silencer to the tip of his gun. It would smother the noise, but only slightly. Silencers weren't actually all that silent considering.

He squinted as he shot the glass out of the window.

With a towel, Mercedes smashed the remaining glass, leaving them passage to escape.

Another bang, one door to go.

Mercedes was through the window first, taking the long jump down to the pavement, and he followed closely behind. Once they were both out, they ran down the back of the motel block for the street.

He heard the last bang in the distance, but didn't look back. He just kept running, his eyes fixed straight ahead.

Out of the motel perimeter, they found a quiet suburban street. They kept their pace, running along the sidewalk to gain as much distance as they could. But they weren't getting far enough fast enough.

Adam rested his hands on his knees to take a breath. "We can't keep going on foot."

Looking over his shoulder, he spotted a red convertible parked in the driveway of the decrepit house they were standing in front of. Shitty house, nice car. If that didn't say something about Ridge City, nothing did.

Adam handed his backpack off to Mercedes as he stalked to the front door of the house. He shot the lock with his silenced gun and kicked the door wide open. It was a 50/50 shot that the keys would be sitting on a hanger by the front door. But it was sure easier to kick down a door than it was to hotwire a car.

An alarm sounded and a man appeared within the house, pointing a shotgun at Adam. He did not have fucking time for this today. Agile as a cat, he punched the man, taking the shotgun for good measure and grabbing the keys in a triumphant fist.

He threw the keys to Mercedes as he made a slow walk to the convertible, so as not to draw attention. Bracing his arms on the window, he jumped over the door straight into the passenger seat, not bothering to secure his seatbelt.

"They're coming, I can hear them," Adam said.

Mercedes had the car on the street in a matter of seconds, just as Blake's men converged in several black sedans that approached from behind, right on their tail, and ready to chase them down to the death.

***

MAY 1991

Mercedes changed in her car before she entered the mansion, swapping her gray t-shirt for a blush pink camisole. Over her dark ripped jeans, it wasn't exactly First Lady material, but it was better than nothing. Aiding the illusion further, she pulled an assortment of shopping bags from the backseat before heading up the stone steps in the driveway.

When she pushed open the grandiose front door, she heard screaming from the back terrace. The guttural cries of pain from a deep male voice sent shivers over her arms.

Without dropping her bags, she headed for the yard. She moved past the grand marbled entrance, into the back ballroom, past the pool, and onto the lookout.

She spotted Dorian and T.B. on the lower level, standing over a man tied to a chair. The man's face was bruised and bloody, almost completely broken, but she breathed in relief when she realized it wasn't anyone she knew.

"Honey!" she called. "What the hell are you doing?"

Dorian jumped, like he was actually surprised to see her there, before he turned his back on her even quicker. "Didn't expect you home so soon."

"There wasn't much on sale today," she said.

"You know you can just buy full price," he called back.

"Sure, okay." She left the bags and strolled down the two levels to where Dorian stood on the back terrace. Once she'd approached, she kissed him gently and looked over the bruised man. "Who the hell is this?"

Dorian yanked her shoulder away, pulling her into a quiet huddle.

"This guy knows who Vandemilio's fifth is," he said.

Her fists clenched. *Does he now?*

She looked back over to the guy, then to Dorian again. In his eyes, she didn't see the wicked smirk of lying that usually gave him away, and she wondered if all this was true and she'd finally been caught.

"The fifth guy of what?" she said, playing dumb.

"On Adam Vandemilio's crew. I told you I always knew there was a fifth one." His teeth gritted as he spat the words, but all Mercedes's focus was on the blood spatter coating his white suit.

She'd witnessed a scene like this before. One that had almost broken her. She pushed the air into her breathless lungs. "Are you sure?"

"Positive," Dorian said, more wildly again. "He knows exactly who has been putting together a crew to come after me. I just have to *get him to admit it!*"

Mercedes released a breath as she turned to T.B., who was just as wild and raged. With blood coating his own clothes, he jumped around like he was having a fucking good time. But at least she wasn't caught just yet.

"Why don't you come inside and have lunch with me," Mercedes said, guilt tugging her to lead Dorian away from the man. Just in case he really was about to give her up.

"No!" he shouted, pulling his arm from her. "I will break this guy."

Dorian rolled up his sleeves to get back in the man's face. With a fist half-cocked at the man, he turned back to Mercedes. "You can leave now."

It hurt to turn around, but she had to. Anything she said or did could put Dorian directly on a trail she didn't want him following.

She looked to the ground, blood staining the terrace once again. When she reluctantly headed back up into the house, she shuddered at the sound of a single gunshot at the same time she exhaled.

***

Dorian watched closely as Mercedes retreated into the house before pulling his gun back on the guy in front of him. The man's head dropped heavily like it was hard to lift, blood and bruises battering his skin. But he'd give up the information that Dorian wanted in the end. After all, everyone did eventually.

"What did you send her away for?" T.B. grunted.

"Women shouldn't see these kinds of things," Dorian smirked as the guy began to spit blood.

"She could use some hardening up," T.B. said, but Dorian just rolled his eyes and turned his attention back to his prisoner.

"Should we try this again?" he asked, stroking the gun like it was his favorite pet. "Or have you seen enough to loosen that tongue of yours already?"

The man's battered face raised slightly until his determined eyes met Dorian's. "I told you. I don't know nothing about a fifth."

A sudden smack from T.B. had the man groaning as his head snapped back.

"Hoooo, boy!" T.B. smiled as he shook out his fist and jumped around in excitement.

Sharing a proud look with his Second, Dorian just smiled. "See? We *like* doing this. We can go all day."

"I have heard of Adam Vandemilio, but I swear," the man said, breaths stuttering as he choked on air. "I've never heard of a fifth guy."

Yes, they liked doing this. But Dorian was quickly losing patience. He kicked the man's shoulder until he fell onto the ground writhing, and crouched down to meet his level.

"Everyone knows Adam had a driver," Dorian said. "And you're gonna tell me who it is. You're gonna tell me who's coming after me."

The man's cries suddenly stopped. "That's what this is about?"

Dorian's eyes narrowed.

"Well, fuck, I don't know anything about a driver, but I—but I can tell you who's coming after you."

Dorian stilled, turning over in his crouch to share a loaded look with T.B.

"Go on, then," Dorian said.

"Someone came into town a few months ago. Spouting shit about taking you down, putting out feelers for people to join them."

Dorian's chest seized. *Months ago?!* Motherfuckers...

"They're more careful now, but—but at the start they weren't too worried about being seen. Going all over town, flaunting themselves."

Dorian closed his eyes as he sucked in a breath of fresh air, cocking his head as he stood and steadied himself to remain calm while he took the information in. Someone had been coming for him. And they'd been flaunting it right under his nose. That's exactly what they'd been doing. The whores, the clubs, his idiot Seconds… the fuckers weren't subtle.

But waiting to be caught wasn't exactly Dorian's style. No, he was an offense kind of player.

"Thank you," Dorian said, raising his gun.

"Wait—I thou–"

The man's words were cut off as Dorian sent a bullet straight into his skull. His outstretched hand flopping as the gun claimed his life.

"You good?" T.B.'s voice was tentative.

"Fucking great," Dorian said.

T.B. exhaled and rubbed at his chest. "Well, I'm glad you are, because I'm not. How the fuck are we meant to find someone who's hiding now?"

"Every inch of this city is covered in cameras. Have someone start searching the footage for anything suspicious. We'll find the fucker eventually."

T.B.'s bloodthirsty mood had all but dried up by the look of him. Dorian's had, too. The weight of reality settling into his spine.

"But I'm not waiting any longer. I want to fish this asshole out," Dorian said, beginning to pace in his anger. "Starting with the people who *do* know something."

T.B. cocked his head in confusion. "Who are?"

Dorian just smiled.

***

The bell jingled when Adam entered his bar. Mercedes was already seated at the bar surrounded by empty shot glasses. She called him there before she left the mansion, and arrived first even though he lived just around the corner. How fast did she have to drive to get there that quick, and already be half into her drinks?

He took the bar stool beside her and kept his voice gentle. "What are you doing, baby?"

"Just needed to drink," she said.

She waved for another round. Adam sat silently while the bartender poured eight shots. From either end, they each plucked at one shot and clinked their glasses before swallowing the fiery liquid in one gulp. Adam kept his gaze fixated on her as he downed the next three shots along with her.

"What happened?" he asked.

"Nothing," she huffed. Though the light lines of mascara running down her cheeks said otherwise. "Dorian found some idiot he thought had the name of the fifth in your crew." She slapped another shot down her throat.

"Did he?" Adam's voice hardened.

"No," she said with a shake of her head.

That was lucky, but... His brows pinched as he watched her. She relished the sight of blood and the smell of rotting bodies. Usually the most horrific things in the world did little to scare her. So, what was it then?

"If Dorian knew what I was capable of–"

Slowly nodding, Adam mirrored her each time she slammed another shot.

She sniffed and wiped her mouth with her bare arm, slamming her glass back onto the bar so hard it nearly shattered.

When she finally looked at him, she rolled her eyes, so he imagined he must've had a really pitying look on his face.

"He had this guy tied up on the back terrace just by the water, blood everywhere, practically washing the floors with it," she said.

"Oh," he said, realization sweeping over him like a tidal wave.

They were going to need more shots. He signaled the bartender. "Make them tequila."

"I had to leave him there," she said, looking more disgusted with herself than anything. The tequila arrived and they each took one. Licking the salt, downing the shot, and then sucking the lemon.

"It's just..." she started, stopping to take a cleansing breath. He didn't need her to say it. He already knew.

"Probably looked a lot like me, I'm thinking."

"Yeah." She nodded. "On that day."

She slammed another tequila shot, sticking her tongue out after tasting the lemon. "He wanted you to suffer. He did not make your death painless."

"I remember," he said, downing the shot like it would burn away the memory.

She sank her head onto the bar and looked up at him with silvery tears gathering in her eyes.

He frowned. "It really shook you up that much?"

"Watching the man I love almost die?" she said, before correcting herself, "Loved. Not my fondest memory."

Resting her head on her arms, she hid her face, huffing air deep into her lungs. Although, it wouldn't keep the tears at bay if they wanted to come.

Adam rubbed a supportive hand along her back. "Let's head out of here, okay?"

She grumbled, but he knew it was agreement, so he picked her up and steadied her arms along his shoulders, holding her as he carried her out.

It was only a short walk back to his hotel room and, despite the amount of shots, she was hardly drunk. She could always hold her liquor well. So for her to fall so deep into admitted despair, what she saw, what she remembered, must have really broken her.

Once they were safely back in his room, she was more composed. Her voice settled into a serene calm, and the water at her eyes dried up. She'd even wiped the light smudges of mascara from view. If it weren't for the pained look still painting her face, she would've looked as if nothing had happened.

Adam placed the keys down into a bowl by the door, turning to see her sitting at the edge of his bed, arms braced on either side of her and looking at him through a lowered brow.

"I want to see the scars again," she said.

He stumbled back as if the words were an arrow right to his chest. "Uh, maybe later. I don't think you're up to it right now."

Maybe it was him who wasn't up to it.

"Please."

He turned his back, needing to do something—anything—else.

"Please."

Looking over his shoulder, he saw a begging look replace her angry one. Those eyes, golden and sparkling, were in some kind of massive pain that she'd never let him see before. How could he ever say no to her? Not when she looked at him like that. Not when she opened up so much of her heart for him to see.

He closed his eyes, walking to the edge of the bed where she sat. Slowly, she stood to face him, having to incline her head to look up into his eyes.

Her hands moved down his chest and then up again, where they found the first button of his white linen shirt. Their eyes remained locked as she carefully, lazily, opened every button on the shirt one by one and pushed it open.

Her fingers were warm when they brushed against his skin, and she dropped her eyes to his bare chest. Spreading both her palms out over him, she explored each scar again, grazing the white lumps of flesh.

He cringed as she felt her way around his body, running over old scars and finding new ones.

"You're wincing," she said.

"I don't like to remember it," he said, eyes closed. "I lost everything that day. I may as well have died."

She released a long, drawn breath, and grabbed both of his hands with hers. Watching him closely for signs of objection—*she wouldn't find it*—she placed his hands on her waist. "I could never have lived if you had died. I loved you so much back then."

Looking only at where her hands explored his chest, she sniffed and released another long breath, the kind only released as a substitute for falling tears.

He considered not asking, but... "Do you still love me now?"

"No," she said. Far too quickly.

He smiled so wide that his lips pushed at his eyes. "That's a really good lie."

Before she could deny it again, there was a loud thud at the door. So loud that it jolted them from their embrace.

Adam was torn as he looked between Mercedes, who was now backing away, and the waiting door, but she nodded to him to answer it as she sank back into the bed.

With his shirt still hanging open Adam opened the door to Dan, Carlos, and Paul. He frowned when he saw them, half from amusement, half from concern. Standing in a heap at the door, all of them were covered in dusty brown dirt.

Looking Carlos up and down, Adam noted that he was the worst of all of them. His face was covered in dried blood and clumps of mud, while Dan and Paul only showed their dishevelment through their heaving breaths.

"What the hell happened to the three of you?" Adam said.

"Police busted up our handover with the dealers. Fuckers," Carlos said, pushing past Adam's shoulder and bursting the door wide open. Barging into Adam's hotel room, the three of them froze, likely sensing they'd interrupted something. They had.

"Are you busy?" Paul asked Adam, eyebrows raised.

"Not at all," Mercedes said, and Adam couldn't hide his riotous disappointment.

"Nothing to stress about," Dan said, grossly misunderstanding the source of Adam's rage. "I already bailed the dealers, got back the product. And got great news."

Adam looked up, intrigued and excited this time. "You got them?"

"I fucking did!" Dan smiled. "Great excuse to chat with all the officials."

"Didn't feel so fucking great on my face," Carlos said as he retrieved a block of ice from the freezer.

"We've got Judge Ritter, Judge Temple, and the D.A.–"

"The one Blake wouldn't work with?"

Dan nodded. "Oh yeah."

Adam flicked his tongue against his teeth, laughing softly. "Who else?"

"Right—Ritter, Temple, the D.A. We've also got two police sergeants and one captain."

"Impressive," she said, though her smile didn't meet her eyes.

"Why don't you tell them the bad news." Paul patted Dan on the back and slumped into a dining chair.

"It's not even—Paul, shut the fuck up—the tiny detail is that we've got to pay a hundred thousand upfront to put them on and to keep your identity a secret," Dan said, waving his hands around as if that would make the situation seem less inconvenient than it was.

Adam rolled his eyes. "We'll have that delivered later today."

"Did anyone see you?" Mercedes asked.

"Definitely," Dan said. "But it's okay, I stopped in to bail out one of Blake's guys while I was there."

"That's not all of it," Paul laughed.

"Alright!" Dan raised a finger to Paul to shush. "And... here's a list of jobs they need taken care of before they'll agree to work with us." He dumped a massive file folder on the table that thudded as it landed. It must have been at least ten books' worth of paper. Seemed that the city officials were not won over easily.

"Fucking hell, alright," Adam said. He flipped through the files, straining his neck to the ceiling when he realized how much work it'd be.

"First, you can do me a favor though," Dan smiled.

Adam slammed the file back down on the table and folded his arms, giving Dan wide eyes that he flicked repeatedly to Mercedes. Paul and Carlos smirked at each other, they were getting it. Dan wasn't. It was a clear signal to shut the fuck up and leave. Immediately.

"Pick up the cash from Tia for me. I've got a *previously arranged engagement*," Dan said. Sex. He meant sex. Which Adam would normally understand if he weren't hoping to be on the verge of some himself.

"I can't go right now," Adam said with a tight jaw.

"That's fine," Mercedes said, heading for the door. Adam, panicked, darting his eyes between her and his friends. What could he say to get her to stay? How could he get them out of there so that they could–

She slipped on her coat and smiled. "I'll go with you."

CHAPTER 20
FOR THEIR ACTIONS

<u>MAY 1991</u>

"Yes, you'd beat me in a race," Adam said. "But I'd beat you in a gun fight."

Their car halted leisurely underneath the red neon lights, caressing rainwater pooling under the tires. It was four in the morning, and shifts were wrapping up for the girls.

"You couldn't outrun or outgun me," Mercedes said.

"Oh really?" he said, as he looked at where his hand rested against hers over the gear shift. Fingers intertwining, he ran his thumb over her palm.

Their voices were little but a whisper, the only sound the light splattering of rain on the windows.

"Absolutely. There's no scenario in which you could out fight me," she said.

"Is that so?"

"Maybe we should put it to the test." She shifted to face him, her head resting against the seat.

Mirroring her movements, Adam moved until they were only a breath away. So close that he was sure any glance from her eyes to her lips was an obvious giveaway of his intentions.

Removing his hand from hers, he reached out to cup her cheek. Like snow melting to reveal moss-covered ground, Adam could see her hardness melt away from her eyes. Replaced with a softness that looked a lot like longing.

Had she been able to see that same desperate love in his eyes this whole time? It'd been there. That was what he always felt when he was around her.

A lazy slide from her cheek, and he was holding her chin, pulling her lips closer and closer to his, biting his lip as she got nearer.

A bing sounded from his pager.

With a disappointed exhale, Adam checked the pager. "It's Paul, wants something urgently."

"There's a payphone over there."

Unbothered by the rain, they stepped outside, not caring to hurry before they slid into the phone booth.

It must've been a test. The payphone was a tight fit, pushing her body against his. Yeah, had to be a test from a higher power that knew he had no self-control.

Adam held the phone with his shoulder as he dropped in the coins and dialed the number. The answer was so immediate that Adam could barely tell if the phone even rang.

"Adam?" Paul said, voice grating on the other end.

"Yeah, I'm at a payphone, what's up?"

"You and Mercedes should get back here ASAP. There's some alarming rumors spreading," Paul said, the line cracking.

"What do you mean?"

Mercedes wasn't paying attention to the call, just giving him bedroom eyes and biting her lip as she wiped rain from her bare arms.

Self-control. Self-control. Self-control.

"Apparently Blake's been saying that the people who are after him are going to pay," Paul said.

"What else is new." Adam rolled his eyes.

Paul had really called him away for this? Fucking cock-blockers. All of his friends.

"I'm serious, Adam. Blake said if he couldn't find the people after him, he'd make do with hurting the ones they'd left vulnerable."

"What? He's saying we left people vulnerable?" Adam pushed the phone hard against his ear, struggling to hear over the rain and the crackling phone line.

Mercedes tapped his shoulder, gesturing to where Tia had arrived. Over the road she stood on an open street corner, illuminated by blazing white lights.

"He said that we're hiding, but selfishly leaving the people who support us out in the open," Paul said.

Mercedes stepped out of the booth and waved at Tia across the road.

Adam continued pressing his face to the phone. His attention torn between Paul's words and the small steps that Mercedes made onto the street.

The line continued to crack as Adam's mind darted between leaning in to listen and watching Mercedes approach the road.

Then, like a slap in the face it hit him. He dropped the phone from his hands, Paul's voice just a buzz.

Tia stood willing and waiting. Out in the open. Vulnerable. Alone. The only one who didn't have their identity hidden.

Blake couldn't be sure that Dan, Carlos, and Paul were involved. He had no idea about Mercedes. No idea about Adam. But Tia...

It was well known that she was the leader of the call girls. It was well known that the call girls no longer harkened to Blake. Her involvement could not be denied. Could not be manipulated away. And there she stood, like a beacon on the road. So stupidly obvious that she might as well have had a fucking neon arrow pointing at her head.

The next movements were too fast, but at the same time, painfully slow.

Screeching tires. He whipped his head to the right, his damp hair splashing. A darkened black van was approaching at high speed.

Fumbling over himself, Adam rushed from the phone booth and launched for the street. Mere seconds after him, both Mercedes and Tia flashed their eyes to the van. Speeding something crazy, whipping water off the road and sliding along with the rain.

Adam saw Mercedes' shoulders heave, like she was holding in her breath.

At the exact moment that Adam reached Mercedes' side, the van came to a crushing halt in front of Tia.

They all seemed to notice it at the same time, a thick black rifle tip pointing out of the van's darkened window.

But it was Tia's eyes that Adam stuck to, drawing him down like quicksand.

He couldn't look away as she looked to the van and back to him. Her body tightened, but she stood up straighter, and there were infinite seconds where time stood still, each blink drawn out in slow, desperate movements.

There was so much behind her face, cheeks tightening together in anticipation of a pain that had yet to arrive. Her lips pushed in a tight line, like she was bracing for a fate she had never wanted, but knew was about to claim her anyway.

It wasn't the gunshots that Adam saw first, but rather Tia's shaking shoulders as bullets crashed at her chest. Once, twice, and a final third time. Like a drummer striking the cymbals, three splashes of blood sprayed into the night sky and burst like fireworks. The red a horrible contrast against the blatant white light behind her.

Still, her eyes didn't leave his. Not as she endured the shots. Not as her blood rained down. And not as she heaved her throat in sharp breaths. Only when her legs fell from beneath her, and she buckled to her knees, did she finally close her eyes.

Then the screaming began. Not from Tia, but right next to him, close to his ear. A guttural shriek echoed as Mercedes cried and the van sped off just as quickly as it had approached.

Mercedes's feet slipped from beneath her as she pushed forward. Adam launched ahead, too, wrestling his hands onto her shoulders, trying to pull her back and spare her from what she was about to see.

The rain on her bare arms made her slippery, and though he tried to grasp her, his hands just slid along her wet shoulders. Bolting across the street, she screamed ferocious cries of pain. Louder than any gunshot he'd ever had ring in his ear.

He jogged behind her, his own throat feeling so tight that he wondered if he even had the strength to speak.

Mercedes was on her knees the moment they reached Tia, scooping her friend up off the ground and holding Tia's head in her lap. "Tia, please, no. Please, no." Her tears streamed, diluting the blood on Tia's chest.

"Mercedes..." Tia's eyes were wide and confused, like she didn't understand where she was or why. The shock was clearly kicking in.

Tia drew consecutive sharp breaths, hyperventilating as her stomach heaved. There was blood within those breaths, spilling over onto her green dress.

"You're okay, you're okay, we're going to get help," Mercedes said, her eyes only slits of tears, her lips holding shut like she was biting her cheek.

Adam stood over them like a shadow. Mercedes turned to him with a pleading look. Her hands were covered in a coat of blood so thick, it was like she'd dipped them in red glue.

Adam's eyes shuttered as he surveyed Tia's injuries. Bullet wounds to the heart. Already a mass of blood on the pavement, blood in the ears, eyes, mouth—there was nothing he could do.

So, instead, he circled them and sat down at Tia's side, too, crossing his legs right in the midst of the pools of blood.

"Tia, please, please, hang on. Just hold on," Mercedes said.

"Mercedes..." Tia said.

"We're here," Adam said. He held her hand. "You're not alone."

"...Not... alone," Tia repeated, blood gurgling from her mouth like a fountain.

Mercedes was still looking at him like she was begging him to perform a miracle. Her face was now a mess of black from the mascara that dropped with her tears.

It hurt his heart more than she could possibly fathom to have no power to help. Wasn't that what all this was about, after all? He'd never wanted to feel powerless again.

"Please do something," Mercedes sniffed, her words obscured by the intensity of her sobs.

He steadied his own breathing. Right now he had to be strong, because Tia only had seconds to go and she needed him. Though his heart shattered to watch her die, he had to be there for her. If he couldn't save her, he would surely carry her over the threshold.

"We're right here," Adam said again to Tia. "We'll always be right here."

Despite Mercedes's increasing cries, Tia looked only at Adam, as if there were an understanding between them. As if only he could give her what she needed so that she could go.

"Please stay awake," Mercedes said, burying her head in Tia's chest and sobbing again.

"Look after–" Tia coughed, sputtering breaths of blood.

Adam gripped her hand tighter. "I promise." He knew what she was going to say.

"My...girls."

There were two sharp breaths, long seconds in between them, before a final sigh that pushed away the last breath of life. Her eyes remained open but glazed over.

All that was left was an empty shell. And a sickening realization that *he* had caused all this to happen.

***

OCTOBER 1986

She was all alone now.

Dan, Carlos, and Paul had been captured over a week ago and now... now Adam had been taken, too. He was the one Dorian was really after. Perhaps the others would still be alive, but Adam...he wouldn't have long.

She laid flat on top of the train, watching clouds pass over a bright blue sky, letting soft tears fall to her cheeks. Why would he do that? Why would he let himself be taken? He had to know what would be coming to him.

Was she supposed to be grateful? Because she wasn't. No, the rage was like a current of electricity.

The sun beat down, blinding her eyes so much she could only see her watery tears and the crisp yellow sunshine.

Wiping her eyes with her sleeve, she replayed the day in her head: The cheap motel. Dorian's men surrounding it. A stolen red convertible, and another chase to the death.

"Baby, they're still right on our fucking tail," Adam had said.

"I know," she had replied calmly.

At the edge of the train yard, she was certain they could still make it. She had wanted to fight it, to keep going. All they had to do was fight one last time, and then they could make their way to save their friends.

But Adam wouldn't listen.

He'd kissed her, told her he loved her, and then pushed her off the edge onto a passing train below. And that's where she'd been laying for the past twenty minutes.

Why did he do it? Why did he try to save her? She didn't want to be saved, especially if it meant being without him.

Sitting up with her legs crossed underneath her, she surveyed her surroundings. The train she'd landed on was a red and rusting freight train.

It bellowed across brown grassy fields with little in sight beyond them. Unlikely to stop for a while.

She lifted her knees to hold her head in her hands. Loud, heaving, sobs was all she could manage as she thought back over how horribly they'd failed. This family that had meant so much to her, wiped out so quickly by one man.

Was she going to be the only one to come out of this alive? Of the five of them, she couldn't live with herself if it was just her left. No, she had to fight. Adam had given up. Paul, Carlos, Dan—they'd all given up. They'd let Dorian Blake take them down and kill their spirits. They'd all been beaten down because they refused to fight.

That wasn't going to happen to her. She still had a whole lot of fight left in her.

The force of her motivation was so tangible that it pushed her to her feet. Even with the speed that the train barreled through the barren wasteland, it was nothing against the strength that was feeding her.

In the distance she saw the street through the trees. It was faint and far off, but it was there. The outskirts of the city.

Pushing against the forward momentum, she walked on top of the train to the very last car. There, she jumped down from the roof to a rusting platform at the back of the train.

Now all there was to do was jump.

She landed rough on the ground, tucking her head in and wincing, rolling for what seemed like forever before she eventually slowed. Her arms cut from the gravel. Her back jarred from hitting the ground. Her body was bruised and bloodied. Her spirit wasn't.

She forced herself up. Her clothes were covered in white dust, tiny pebbles falling from her as she stood.

She limped through the overgrown grass, cleared the trees, and stood up straighter as she finally crossed the road to find a payphone. Her hand was as steady and as hard as her heart as she put in a coin and dialed the number.

"Tia," she said.

"Mercedes? What the fuck! Are you okay? What the hell is going on?"

"Ssh, you don't want to know." Mercedes looked around nervously. "Look—what's going down at the club? Is Blake there?"

"No—he's...well, he was here ten minutes ago, but he got called away."

"He's not there now?"

"No."

"Then he's at the mansion," Mercedes said.

"Mercedes, what's going on? I haven't seen you in weeks and now you–"

"I know, I'm sorry. I have to go."

She didn't give Tia the chance to speak again before she hung up and began stalking the streets toward a nearby parking lot. As she walked, she loaded her gun.

Blake had a pattern, a particular way he liked to handle things. First, it was torture. Always either at the Neptune Club, or his mansion. Then, for the killing blow, he'd go to his warehouse at the docks. So, if he wasn't torturing Adam at the Neptune Club, then she knew where he'd be.

Checking her surroundings, she approached a gray sedan. She smashed the window with little effort, and was inside hotwiring the car in a matter of seconds.

The engine roared as it started. With her foot hard on the pedal, she revved to test its power before speeding off in a haze of smoke.

Her friends had given up. But she would never give up. If they weren't going to fight, then she would. For her, it wasn't over. Would never be. Not until they leeched the last breath from her lungs.

***

MAY 1991

They placed white roses on the fresh dirt above her grave. Standing around her gravestone, Dan, Paul, Carlos, and Adam were solemn. Their all-black suits were drawn by thick collars that they'd raised to hide their faces as much as possible. Though, by the time they'd arrived, the funeral was long over, and the cemetery near empty.

Nobody had heard from Mercedes in the week since it happened.

"It doesn't feel real," Dan said. The sun shined bright, its rays like glowing sticks of butter protruding through the evergreen trees. Not at all reflective of the mood Adam was in. Today, the weather had betrayed him.

"It's a timely reminder of what this costs," Adam said.

They stood in a half circle around Tia's grave with bowed heads, silent to pay their respects. Dan was the first to let out a sob.

They all cut a look to him as a singular tear slid down his cheek and dripped from his chin. It was Carlos who put an arm around his friend and held him close for comfort.

"We killed Yani, then Antonio. We should've expected consequences," Carlos said, throat tight as he stroked circles on Dan's shoulder.

"We should have…but we didn't," Adam said.

Then, they bowed their heads in a minute of silence.

Silence was deafening. Especially for Adam, who tried to keep his brain moving so it wouldn't stop long enough for his thoughts—that he was the reason they were here—to consume him.

He couldn't think of anything to say for Tia. Not even in his head. What would Tia want? Probably the same thing he did. To keep his family safe.

So he wished for the safety of the last of Tia's girls. And then promised himself he would be the one to fulfill that wish.

"Adam," Paul said, patting him on the shoulder. With his eyes, Paul pointed across the cemetery road where Mercedes was perched under a giant oak tree in an elegant black dress.

Adam exchanged a look with Paul. He nodded to Paul, and then started the walk to where she was standing, hands in the pockets of his pants.

"Hello," he said. He waited patiently for her to reply, but she didn't. "Do you want to place a flower?"

She shook her head.

"I can place it for you."

She shook her head again.

"...Are you...okay?"

She refused to make eye contact, looking anywhere else. "How could I be? My friend is dead."

"I'm sorry," Adam said, hanging his head, his eyes still bloodshot.

"You should be." She let the tears through, though it wasn't pain displayed on her face, only rage. She did that a lot. Hid her pain behind rage, as if she could banish her feelings like the devil to hell. "You promised me you'd never let anyone die for you."

"I did say that." Adam could only muster a whisper as his throat croaked. "I'm sorry."

"You promised that we could protect her." Mercedes stepped away from the tree and down the curb to face him.

320

"I did." Adam twisted his face away. When he turned back, he reached a hand for her, but she smacked it away. His hand shook as he withdrew it.

She paced, whipping quickly back and forth, like she was about to say something difficult. "I want to stop."

"You want to what?" Adam's voice tightened.

"I don't think we should do this anymore, I don't want to lose anyone else," she said, without any sort of emotion coating her voice.

"It's too late for us now, the damage is done, best we can do is try to win."

"We have to give this up, before we're all found out, before we lose—"

"We're not going to fucking lose," Adam said, getting angry now.

"All you do is lose," she said with venom in her voice.

He stared at her, his anger growing, too, as he watched the hatred in her eyes. Her beautiful gold-brown eyes were a raging red. The same eyes that had looked at him days earlier like she might really love him, were now replaced with demonic aggression. A look that said: *I could never love you, not after everything you've done.*

"Adam Vandemilio?" a voice said.

They both spun quickly, guns in the air, aimed in the direction that they heard that voice.

In front of them stood three women, looking shocked and terrified, with their hands raised in surrender.

Adam's eyes shuttered as he looked them up and down. Recognizing them as some of Tia's girls, he lowered the gun. "Oh sorry...I'm a bit...we're a bit—"

The girls, just as slowly, lowered their hands back to their sides. Not a great start. The red-haired one smiled tightly as she introduced her group. "I'm Lulu, this is AnnaBeth, and Carmela."

Adam ran his hands through his hair. "Adam—and Mercedes," he said. When he turned to Mercedes, she glared at him and turned her back. He recognized that she was only pretending to ignore him, and thus the conversation.

"I'm so sorry for your loss," Adam said.

Lulu wasted no time. "Tia told me that if anything happened to her, I should come find you."

He felt Mercedes harden behind him, but he kept his attention forward, to Lulu. "She did? Why?"

"It's my job to look after the girls, now that she's gone," Lulu shuddered. Adam felt he could visibly see the weight that Tia carried around settling down onto Lulu's shoulders. "And she said you would help me with that."

"You want my help?" Adam said, genuinely confused and sorrowed. "After this?" He gestured toward Tia's grave where Dan, Carlos, and Paul were all looking over at them.

"I'm not going back to work for that fucking prick Dorian Blake," Lulu said. Adam raised his brows. "He killed my friend. He'd kill all of us without a second thought. If we go back to work for him, Tia died in vain. I won't let that happen."

"You still want to work with us?" Adam looked back at Mercedes, who was still shielding her face.

"Tia promised me that you were going to take down Dorian Blake. Are you still going to do that?" Lulu asked.

Adam nodded.

"Then if you're not backing down, neither are we," Lulu said.

Adam smiled. He was going to make it his mission to keep these girls safe anyway. But...if they still believed in him, if he could, in fact, make it right and protect them in Tia's honor, then maybe he could move ahead, maybe he could release himself and push forward. "We're not backing down."

"Good," Lulu smiled too. And with that she, AnnaBeth, and Carmela were headed toward Dan, Carlos, and Paul.

Adam started to follow, but Mercedes grabbed his arm. "You're letting them keep going?"

"You heard them. They want to," he said.

"So you're going to let them risk their fucking lives, too," Mercedes said.

"I'm not *letting* anyone do anything," he said, ripping his arm away from her grip. "Everyone who's here, is here of their own free will."

She only scoffed at him.

"What is your problem? You can't blame me for everything," he said.

"Why shouldn't I? Every bad thing in my life finds its way back to you as the source."

"That's bullshit and you know it," Adam said.

"I don't have to fucking stand here and listen to you." Mercedes trudged in a staggering stomp back to her car. Adam followed, chasing right behind her, keeping up with her easily as she rounded the bend in the road to where she'd parked her black SUV.

"Why are you doing this?" he begged.

She pulled the driver's side door open, standing over it with Adam behind her.

"We were getting back to a good place, a place where I thought you could almost lo–" He stopped himself short when she spun to face him, like she could murder him with her eyes and not feel even an ounce of remorse.

"As if I could ever." She pulled some hair from her face. "After everything we've been through, as if I would ever forgive you enough to do...*that*."

Adam jumped back a step as she slumped into the driver's seat and slammed the door.

"Don't leave like this," he said, leaning in through the window, bracing his arms against the sill.

She couldn't even look at him. "After everything you did five years ago, I promised myself I would never be stupid enough to fall in love. Ever. Again. Certainly not with you."

She pushed his arms out of her car window. "The girl you used to love died back in October 1986. The same day you did." In a flash of headlights and screaming tires, she left him standing in her dust.

CHAPTER 21
THE DAY YOU DIED

T he blunt force of the shoe to his face sent blood flying. Bruised and beaten on the back terrace of the mansion, Adam could barely sit up. He curled in a ball on his side, coughing blood and gleaning the river waters through blurry eyes. He'd never had the privilege of enjoying the views before. Being pummeled and interrogated on the deck of the mansion was reserved for those Blake sentenced to death.

"The quicker you give up the fifth name, the quicker I make this for you," Dorian Blake said.

"There's only four of us," Adam said, insisting through breaths that leaked red spit from his teeth. His eyes half shut from swelling, and all he could taste was the metallic tang of blood that refilled his mouth too quickly after each spit.

It had been only hours since he'd been taken by Blake's men. But judging from the blood puddles he could see through his one squinting eye, and the pounding already at his head, he knew he wouldn't last the day.

"That's going to stain," Blake said. "You expect me to believe there's only four of you? Come on, Adam. We're *both* smarter than that."

"There's only four."

Blake laid a kick into his ribs. "I wonder what your friends would have to say about it."

Adam's heart tightened at the mention of his friends. What had Blake done to Dan, Carlos, and Paul? They didn't deserve it, whatever it was. He had led them on the wrong path. Worse still, what would Blake do to *her* if he found out she was the fifth? Adam would die before he let that happen.

"What have you done to my friends?" Adam said, blood coating his teeth red.

"We're keeping them close. Making sure they're very...uncomfortable," Blake's wide smile pushed at his eyes.

"Don't you fucking hur–"

Another boot to Adam's face knocked the wind out of him again. He could feel himself fading. The darkness enveloping him. The need to sleep becoming stronger.

A pull at his hair and he was upright, face to face with Dorian Blake. At least he thought so from what was left of his vision.

"Wake the fuck up!" Blake said. "Fuck."

Adam crashed against the concrete again, vision darkening.

"Put him on the boat. Get him to the warehouse at the docks. With the others."

***

There were lights.

Adam awoke to glaring white strobes. At first, he wondered if he was dead. If that white light was the welcoming afterlife coming to claim him.

But the brightness faded away at the edges, becoming only a small hum around a dark silhouette until it vanished entirely to show he was not alone.

It was Yani who snapped the light away, leaving Adam to take in his surroundings.

He was seated in a wooden chair with his arms tied at his front, the dead center showpiece in a large, decrepit warehouse. Made only of rusty brown tin, the ceiling was at least five stories high, with broken machinery and scrap metals littered around the edges.

Looking between his feet Adam saw the discoloration of bleach against dark concrete. His heart sank but he smiled. This was Blake's killing floor, and he was on the slaughtering line.

"Good, you're still alive. For now," Blake said.

Looking to his right, Adam found Dan, Carlos, and Paul standing at attention. From their stance it appeared their wrists were bound behind them. They were flanked by several high-level associates who no doubt would pull triggers first, ask questions later, if any of them so much as moved.

At least they were still alive.

"Alright, who's going to speak first and give me a name," Blake said, searching for a volunteer. Adam felt himself dozing again before he was slapped three times. He opened his eyes to see Blake scowling at him with a hand still on his blood-crusted cheek.

"There's only four of us!" Dan said. "We fucking swear!"

"We've told you one hundred times. Only four," Paul said.

Everything hurt. His face felt so heavy, so hard to lift enough to lock eyes with his friends. Through blurred blinks, he swore they looked terrified. The most terrified he'd ever seen them. But it wasn't for themselves, it was fear for him.

They'd had a great run. Thinking of it made Adam smile. They did some big things. Crazy things. All of it exhilarating and absolutely worth it. Adam had always said they'd go out big or they'd die trying.

Blake lifted his hand, but Carlos cried out. "Please. There is only us."

Blake's eyes shone with amusement as he fought to stifle a laugh.

"I admire the loyalty in your crew." Blake leaned down to face Adam. "That makes it the most fun to break."

With a nod, Dorian signaled Yani to strike Adam this time. He did so, with such force that it sent Adam flying backward, the chair tipping over and discarding him onto the concrete as more blood spewed from his mouth.

"Whatever you're going to do, just do it," Adam said. "Stop dicking around, for fuck's sake." Adam writhed along the floor, the blood from his mouth dripping to his chin.

Blake looked down his nose triumphantly. "You are still cocky as ever."

Why shouldn't he be? It was clear enough by now that he was done. He wouldn't be leaving this warehouse alive.

"Like I said," Blake kicked Adam in the rib again. "I admire the loyalty in your crew, though I find fear a much more powerful motivator."

Yani lifted Adam from the floor and placed him back in the chair.

"Let me show you," Blake whispered, his voice hypnotic.

Blake had always had a sick and twisted game to play. He didn't delight in simple deaths, no, only in killing the soul before he discarded the body.

To Dorian, there was no greater victory than forcing families apart, to make his approval, and his loyalty, the only thing that mattered.

"How far does that loyalty go? Do you trust him with your life?" Blake said, heading over to a wooden folding table to stroke a .357 magnum revolver. He took the gun and faced Dan, Paul, and Carlos. "I'm going to give Adam here the chance to save you all."

Twisting the barrel of the gun to load the bullets, Blake let out an evil laugh. "Because trust me, he'll choose not to." T.B., Yani, and Antonio, spread out at various corners of the room, laughed, too.

"This gun contains three bullets," Blake said to Adam. "One for each of your friends." He mimed a gun with his pointer finger and popped it at Paul, then Dan, then Carlos. "Kill them, and you get to live."

Adam scoffed, turning away with his nostrils flaring. Never, *not a chance in hell*, would he ever do that.

When he turned back, Paul was nodding. Like he was giving him permission to do it. Fuck, he *was* giving him permission to do it. Adam shifted his eyes to find Dan and Carlos nodding similarly.

But Adam was past the point of listening.

"Or..." Blake let the words linger in the air, like he was testing them on his tongue to see how they would taste.

Adam looked back at the crazed gangster, who was sliding up next to Dan, Paul, and Carlos. "Counteroffer. Join me. Take the bullets that were meant for you, and use them to kill your friend. One shot to his chest, for each of you."

"Never," Dan growled.

Blake shrugged, like he couldn't care less, but his eyes gave away his delight. "It's you or them, Adam Vandemilio. Pull your team in line and make a choice."

Adam looked over his friends and gave them a faint, sad look. He'd known he was going to die. As soon as he'd pushed Mercedes off that ledge and let himself be captured, he knew he was at his end.

Blake was wrong. This wasn't difficult. It wasn't painful. The choice, for him, would always be easy.

Adam forced his eyes open as he raised his head to look at Blake, that stupid smirk still pulling at his lips. Then, he turned to his strongest friend. "Paul," Adam said. "Take the gun."

Paul's jaw tightened, his chest bobbing like his breaths weighed rocks. Dan and Carlos were whispering protests, but Adam kept his focus on Paul.

"Paul…" Adam said, wheezing as his breath failed him. He needed his friends to walk away from this. Needed them to keep each other safe. Of all of them, he had to be the one to die. And Paul was the only one strong enough to take the first shot. He glared at his friend. "Take. The. Gun."

"Do it," Blake said. "And pledge your loyalty to me."

With a sharp breath Paul straightened, taking the gun. He lifted it with one hand and settled his breathing, that sniper's control showing. He stared down the barrel at Adam like he was the one about to be shot.

"Make sure you hit his heart, sharpshooter, or it's your head, too," Blake said.

On an exhale, Paul shot.

The punch to his sternum was agonizing, the bullet burning flesh and worming through his chest. It was as if all capacity to hear anything but the dulling echo of Blake's manic laughter disappeared.

"Fucking say it," Blake said as his laughter died down.

Paul squeezed his eyes shut for only a moment before he held his chin high. "I pledge my loyalty to you," Paul said, eyes on Blake. But Adam knew the words were really meant for him. This was his show of loyalty. Paul would be strong where Adam couldn't. Paul would look after them now.

Adam clenched his fists like they alone could block out the pain.

Paul held the gun out for Dan. Furiously shaking his head, and with tears in his eyes, Dan stared at his feet. Paul patted his shoulder and whispered something to him that Adam couldn't make out.

With a shaky hand, Dan took the gun, too, and raised it. Closing his eyes, like he couldn't bear to look, he squeezed the trigger, and another bullet went whirling into Adam's ribcage.

"I pledge my loyalty to you," Dan said to Blake, coughing out his tears.

Adam screamed this time. His torso now drenched in fresh blood, leaking onto that spot on the floor. Tomorrow, it would surely be bleached away to leave no trace of him left.

Dan shoved the gun into Carlos's hands, like holding it burned his skin.

A pitiful frown creased Carlos' sweet eyes as he held the gun weakly and looked at Adam. Struggling to move, Adam did his best to manage a small bob of his head, a nod, to show Carlos it was okay. That this was what he wanted.

Carlos looked like he wanted to turn the gun on himself from the way his eyes watered, but he kept them open the whole time, as if he were trying to project his plea for forgiveness. But he didn't need to, Adam was thankful.

He was going to go. But, damn, what a way to go. He wouldn't have had it any other way.

"I pledge my loyalty to you." Carlos fired the final shot. It landed in Adam's lower torso, the force of it making Adam tip his head back and knocking him out of his chair.

Now that he let the pain in, it felt like he'd been set on fire from the inside out. Like drowning and suffocating all at once. Until it just wasn't. Until the pain throbbed itself away. Which really wasn't fucking good. He couldn't feel his lower body anymore.

He tried to scream but he could only watch from a standstill.

The ground around his shoulders became warm and sticky. Like a wave rolling onto the sand, the blood rolled from him to cover the floors.

Then, his vision pounded in and out like pulses of a drumbeat. Through each beat he saw a different scene. T.B. and Antonio splashing gasoline around the warehouse. Splashing gasoline in a circle around him. Dan, Carlos, and Paul, mouths gaping like they were screaming. Then his friends being dragged out of the warehouse.

Orange flames drew nearer and nearer, spurred higher by the flammable liquid. Heat pushed up against his skin as the numbness swept higher up his body. The darkness in his eyes got deeper until there was nothing left. Until the pulses of his vision became further and further apart.

This was it. He was going to die.

But he'd certainly die satisfied. He'd loved hard. So even if the end had arrived, he knew his love would not die alongside his body.

He closed his eyes and waited. When the darkness pulled him down, he welcomed it.

***

Mercedes sped down the highway. In contrast to the life that crashed down around her, on the road she had only precise control. Each movement so smooth that reason itself melted to her will.

She'd arrived at the mansion just in time to see Blake's men load a near-dead Adam into a speedboat and glide away. Blake was in for a kill. He'd head straight over the water to his warehouse at the docks.

He would beat her there. So she had to hurry.

Barely having scaled the stone wall by the hedge maze to see Adam dragged away, she was hurling her body over it again, racing for her car.

As she sped toward the docks, she forced her tears away and left only cold, unrelenting determination in their midst. Her grip on the steering wheel tightened, as if that gave her more control.

She was a force. And she could not be stopped.

When she reached the docks, she knew she'd found the right spot when she saw Dorian's entourage of cars parked in front of the towering tin warehouse.

She wasn't religious. But now... well, she only prayed she'd gotten there in time.

She roared onto the slatted roadways that circled the docks revealing the river waters beneath. Stopping only enough to dive out, she bolted from the car, loading her gun as she tore off running.

One shot echoed in the distance.

Hair billowing, she ran faster.

Another shot sounded. Then another.

As if slammed back by a wall of wind, she froze. Three shots...four of her family in there. *No. No. No!*

She ran again. But this time she wasn't quick enough. For all she'd done on the roads to master speed, this time she was too slow.

Then, the warehouse erupted into flames, knocking her down. Perched on the ground, she could vaguely see Dan, Carlos, and Paul backing away from the warehouse with widened eyes. They looked defeated and...wracked with guilt?

Following closely behind was Dorian, Yani, Antonio, and T.B. moving casually and victoriously.

Adam was not with them.

Her heart heaved, as if something that had once been warm there had shattered.

No! She started running again. If Adam was inside a burning building, then she was walking through fucking fire.

When she reached the warehouse, she found no entry in the back. The fire on the other side had heated the metal to be too hot to touch.

But the tin was rusty enough that–

She kicked the tin in, bending it so hard with her heel that it gave way.

"*Oh God.*" Adam laid motionless on the floor, encircled by flames and a bath of blood.

She approached him through the thickening smoke, sliding along the floor as she coughed, if only to get to him quicker. "Please be alive. Please be alive. *Please* be alive."

The first of her smothered tears fell when she saw his face. Beaten to a purple, swollen mess, she couldn't even tell if his eyes were open or closed. Holding his head in her arms, she brushed a caress through his hair, down his jaw, and onto his neck where she felt for a pulse.

Dim, but it was enough.

"You have to get up!" she shouted as she pushed him. But it was getting so hot. The air too thick. The flames were getting so close.

She wrapped her hands underneath his arms and braced her legs as she dragged his limp body along the warehouse floor. Her muscles screamed in protest, but she promptly told them to shut the fuck up. She dragged him away from the fire, away from the melting metals, until they were safely outside on the docks.

Her own tears mixed with Adam's blood and coated her hands in wetness as she pressed into his wounds to create pressure. With her teeth and hands, she ripped apart the shirt at her midriff, wrapping the strips around the gaping holes in his body, tightening them so he might hold on until she could get help.

He was still breathing—just barely, though—she confirmed by holding an ear to his mouth.

Picking him up by the arms again, she dragged him all the way to her car and loaded him into the backseat. Just as she had flopped his body down, the warehouse exploded behind her.

Using the car door as shelter, she ducked as pieces of fragmented metal flew through the skies. The place where they were previously sitting reduced to flames and a wreck of collapsed tin.

She slammed into the driver's seat and hurtled backward. When she looked back at the front of the warehouse, she spotted a small crew of Blake men guarding Dan, Carlos, and Paul.

Dorian, Yani, T.B., and Antonio were nowhere to be found. Good. They'd gone already.

Shifting into Drive, she pushed off the docks, barreling toward her friends. Covered in a haze of smoke from her tires, she propelled forward, skidding along the concrete.

She was still in the middle of her drift when she pointed her gun out the window and, in a succession of five bullets, shot the remainder of Dorian's men.

Carlos and Paul were running to her as soon as the guards dropped. Dan, who'd been sobbing on the floor, rose to his feet, a painful, pleading look in his eye.

"Help us! Please. Adam's in the back." She screamed so loudly that it shocked her, only just noticing how much her heart pounded.

Dan, Carlos, and Paul jumped into action, diving into the backseat to tend to Adam as Mercedes stared straight ahead, out the windshield, eyes wide and hands shaking as they gripped the wheel.

All the strength and emotion she had gathered seemed to suck from her body at the same moment as she realized that no matter what she'd just done, it could already be too late.

Paul and Carlos put pressure on the wounds to stop the bleeding while Dan performed CPR.

"Oh, thank God, he's still alive," Carlos said, hands already reddened with blood as he made the sign of the cross. "You gotta get him to the hospital."

"We can't go to the fucking hospital," Dan said, still pumping. "Blake will know and he'll be dead anyway."

Mercedes shifted in her seat, desperately looking to Paul. More desperate than she'd ever been. As desperate as she'd ever have to get to ask what she was about to. "Paul, you gotta take us to Brooke."

Paul's face hardened. "No." He shook his head. "We can't."

"We have to! We don't have a choice!"

"Paul this is our f–" Dan said.

"I know that," Paul said, looking like he were frozen quite literally between two immovable forces.

"We have to," Carlos said. "We owe him."

Paul's eyes shuttered, filled with an unexplainable cocktail of distraught, guilt, and relief. "Fine, go."

Mercedes sped off again before they could even properly close the doors.

***

They forced the door of Brooke's practice open, barreling in with Adam in their arms. Paul at his shoulders, Dan and Carlos at his middle, and Mercedes at his legs.

"What the fu–" Brooke jumped from her stool, nearly dropping her paperwork as they lowered Adam down onto the examination table.

"You have to help us," Paul said. "He's...been shot."

"Yeah, no kidding. Take him to the hospital," Brooke said.

"We can't," Paul huffed, leaving the others tending to Adam's wounds, Dan now having resumed compressions. He grabbed his sister by the shoulders. "I'm so sorry, we can't. Please. *Please,* help us."

"Brooke, *please,*" Mercedes joined Paul's side, clutching his arm in a death grip.

Brooke gulped, holding a hand at her throat and glancing between Adam and her pleading brother. "What have you done?"

Paul's eyes glued to the floor. "We just—you have to help him, off record, no records."

Adam begun convulsing, losing even more blood. It dripped off the table edges into shining pools on the white tile.

Brooke didn't hesitate. "Okay, get Adam over here." With her foot she loosened the stops on the surgery table and screamed for her nurses. Dan and Carlos backed away slowly as Brooke and her nurses rushed to tend to

Adam, wheeling him away wielding scalpels and needles and shouting medical jargon she couldn't understand.

Mercedes curled up in the corner of the room, her face pale and her head in her hands.

***

It had been hours but none of them spoke a word as they waited in Brooke's office. Paul could barely breathe watching blood crust beneath where the table stood.

The creak of the door opening, and Brooke's footsteps inside, were the only noises in the room. The others, still shell-shocked, remained seated, while Paul rose to his sister's side.

"He's doing okay," she said. "Somebody missed his heart by less than point one of a millimeter." Brooke gave him a knowing look.

The others released deep, deep breaths of relief. Like they had been holding their lungs the entire time Adam was being treated.

"I've patched up what I can, but he needs a more extensive surgery. He needs a hospital," she said.

"He can't go to the hospital here," Paul said. "They'll just kill him."

Brooke nodded, understanding more than she should've. Understanding more than Paul would've liked. "I have a friend two states over, works at the hospital there. He will help you if I ask. It's about an eight-hour drive, though…you can take him there."

"Out of state? Really?" Paul dared a glance at Mercedes, tears running down her face that she didn't bother to wipe. She was breaking.

"He needs surgery to remove the bullets. He's strong enough to make the trip, but he won't survive the next few days if you don't get him to a hospital soon. A real hospital."

338

One of them was going to have to leave. Skip town. Right after they'd all pledged loyalty to Dorian Blake...fuck.

Paul's eyes shuttered as he looked over his friends. Adam had very carefully left *him* in charge. He fired the first shot. He pledged his loyalty. Adam had looked at him like he was entrusted with the team.

He may have shot Adam, but he wasn't going to let him down.

Paul looked to Dan and Carlos, their faces hopeful. Still young and still brimming with possibilities that they might get out unscathed. Blake didn't know them well enough to punish them yet. They, at least, stood a chance.

Then he looked to Mercedes, wearing a Neptune Club bar shirt like the one she'd had on when they first started to flee. She remained anonymous for now. But wouldn't for long if she left and Blake found out why she'd spent weeks absent.

Paul had to be the one.

Blake already knew him. No matter what Adam bargained, or supposedly gave his life for, Blake knew Paul, and knew that Paul had betrayed him. He was as good as dead anyway.

"I'll take him. Mercedes, give me the keys." Paul's voice was quiet but stern.

"No!" she said, storming across the room to face him. "I'll take him."

"You can't," Paul said. "You've gotta go back to the club and pretend like these past few weeks you've just been away with a bad flu."

"Paul, that's the most fucking stu–"

"Tia will cover you."

"No!" Mercedes huffed back a step. "I won't let you."

"Don't argue," Paul spat, eyeing her down until she relaxed her stance. "And Dan and Carlos... They have to show their faces to Blake to prove their pledge was real."

"Pledge? What the fuc–" Mercedes started before Dan interrupted.

Fuck. Yeah, explaining this to her was going to be difficult.

Dan rose in a swift, grunting movement. "More proof of our fucking loyalty? I don't actually want to work for Dorian Blake."

"You don't have a choice now," Paul said. Dan sat down slowly. "I can take Adam on the drive."

Mercedes winced, looking at the door Brooke had come in through, where Adam probably laid dying behind it.

"We'll be okay," Paul said, a warm smile on his lips. "I'll take good care of him, I promise."

She glanced between all of them and the door an unfathomable amount of times before her eyes softened. She hung her head, her chest heaving in a way that it was obvious she was using all her effort just to breathe.

"Okay." Mercedes finally nodded. "Okay."

Following Mercedes's lead, Paul pushed through the door and into the surgery room with Dan and Carlos behind him.

Adam laid on the table. An oxygen mask covered his nose and mouth, and his arms were full of IVs. Empty medication packets and tiny glass bottles were smashed on the floor all around him. A collection of saturated bloody gauze sat in a pile by the sink.

Mercedes stroked a gentle hand through his hair, and Paul drew comforting circles along her back as she cried over her lover.

"I love you," she said as she laid a quivering kiss on his forehead.

Brooke once again released the stops on the table's wheels, and with help from Dan, Carlos, and Paul, wheeled him outside.

Paul watched Mercedes closely, her eyes locked on Adam like she was afraid she'd never see him again.

Perhaps she had a point.

It was the last time she saw him for five years.

***

MAY 1991

"What is it?" Dorian said. "I really don't have time for this today."

"You're gonna wanna see this," T.B. said.

His last remaining second-in-charge had called him down to one of their offices in the city. Dorian's plans for that day completely derailed with the rude intrusion. Whatever T.B. had to show him, it had better have been damn important because Dorian's patience was low.

"Follow me," T.B. said.

T.B. started down a long, gray hallway lined with doors on either side. Dorian followed, stomping after him like a petulant child. They rounded two corners before T.B. finally stopped at a door and knocked three times in a pattern that sounded rehearsed.

The room that opened before him was pitch black, save for deep maroon lights on either wall. Cramped and smelling of sweat and days' old to-go food. Judging from the containers littering the floor, that was certainly the culprit.

Two men sat at a small work desk with towers of CCTV monitors lining the wall and playing loops on repeat.

T.B. nodded at the two men, while Dorian squinted. They seemed to buck at the movement—from fear or excitement? Perhaps both? Either way, the reaction was appropriate.

"Play the tape," T.B. said.

Dorian stalked ahead, moving to get a better view of the screen, his arms folded.

Footage began rolling on a single monitor, an image of his shooting range.

The room was crowded as all hell, patrons lined up at bays, workers doing their rounds. But T.B. impatiently twisted a knob on the desk until the footage zoomed in to the far corner.

"What exactly am I looking at?" Dorian said.

"Just wait," T.B. said.

Dorian watched as the footage zoomed closer, revealing Paul standing hunched in the shadows, his hand over his face like he had something to hide. He was talking to someone...

Holy fuck. Could this be the fifth guy they'd been searching for?

Paul and the man talked in close proximity, the figure's back to the camera so his face couldn't be made out.

"T.B., tell me we've got some–"

"Just. Wait."

While Paul, the traitorous, lying little cocksucker, was tense and afraid, the man was his polar opposite. Relaxed. Cocky. Confident. Familiar...

Mere moments later, the figure turned over his shoulder with a cocky smirk. Aiming his face directly at the hidden camera.

"There, pause it," T.B. said.

Dorian leaned in closer to check the footage, bracing his hands on the desk, his spine icing over. What. The. *Fuck.*

"When is this footage from?"

"Three months ago."

"Fuck!!!!" Dorian launched the keyboards from the desk where they crashed against the wall before dropping in tiny pieces.

His rage was far too big for that tiny room. Dorian slammed his fist into the wall, and it raked clean through. He kicked at the baseboards. He tore TV monitors from the wall with his bare hands. He was unleashed and unchained, and damn near ripped that room to shreds.

When there was nothing left to bash or destroy, Dorian composed himself. He wiped the dust from his hands on his pants and straightened his tie.

"Adam Vandemilio is alive."

CHAPTER 22
WORTH THE WAIT

<u>MAY 1991</u>

Dan, Carlos, and Paul were already there when Adam stepped inside his room, running a hand down his face to wipe away the blood spatter. Not his own, fortunately.

"That's nine," Adam said. He threw the blood-stained Polaroids on the table.

Lazy assholes from City Hall were out for a lot of blood considering they weren't willing to lift a finger of their own. Blood coating Adam's hands was preferable, apparently.

"Jesus, bit graphic," Dan said as he flicked through the Polaroids.

"You said to kill them. You didn't say make it neat," Adam said. He walked past them to the kitchen sink and rinsed the blood that had dried on his hands. "Will it do?"

"It will have to—not like you can kill them again," Dan said, placing the blood-stained photos into an envelope.

Cupping his hands, Adam splashed water up onto his face and scrubbed, lifting the bottom of his white shirt to wipe away the lingering drips. He made his way back to Dan, casually resting a hand on the top rail of a dining chair. "So, that's it, right?"

Dan studied the photos and files, obviously feigning his concentration.

Adam narrowed his eyes. "Dan?"

"What? Hmm? The last one? Well..."

"For fuck's sake, you're kidding." Adam tipped his head back. He'd been hunting for these slackers for weeks. He was done. Done.

"It's just a tiny little last one, this one will get us the D.A.," Dan stood to face him. "That's a big ally. Worth it."

Adam folded his arms. "What do I have to do?"

"It's easy," Dan said. "Take photos of this target, the D.A. wants to catch him cheating on his wife."

"Why does he want to—never mind, not our business," Adam said, rubbing at his temples.

While walking to the dresser near his bed, he removed his shirt and discarded it, sorting through the drawers for a replacement. He buttoned a clean one as Dan loaded up the equipment.

"Paul, you in?" Adam asked.

Paul paused mid-sip of his water. He finished the mouthful in a gulp and hurried to Adam near the dresser, turning him farther to the back of the room. "Really? You want me on this job?"

"Yes."

"Why don't you take M? She loves this shit," Paul said.

"Not a good idea right now," Adam said, attempting to push past, but Paul blocked him.

"Come on, she hasn't been by here in a week," Paul said, his tone was light and gentle.

"Exactly, she needs space."

Paul loosened a deep, rumbling laugh. "Wow, you're still so clueless."

Adam scowled at his friend.

"She's had five years of space, man. Trust me, she doesn't want space," Paul said.

Sliding the drawer shut gently, Adam removed his gun from his pocket to count the bullets and load more ammunition if he needed to. "She's so angry with me."

"That's not anger that you're sensing," Paul said.

"It sounded pretty fucking angry when she was screaming in my face, blaming me for literally everything that's went to shit the past five years," Adam said, batting his hands.

"Come on, you know her better than that," Paul said. "What is she really afraid of?"

Adam ran his hand through his hair. He'd never been the best at sensing others' emotions. Hell, he barely knew what he was feeling.

Paul shuffled on his feet, smiled, and then said, "Just ask her."

***

DECEMBER 1986

Mercedes stood behind the bar of the Neptune Club. At the cash register she counted the bills and balanced the till, writing out the last bits of profit in a notebook.

She couldn't believe she was back there after everything. After how close she had come to escape, she was right back where she started.

She should've never trusted Adam Vandemilio. He was a snake. A wretch. A liar. An asshole who started a fight that he left his friends to finish. A coward who abandoned them.

She heard the club door open, and without turning around she said, "We're closed."

"Then I'll come back another time?"

She knew that voice. She whipped her head around, full of hope, and saw Paul, standing with his arms open wide.

Her smile was wider than her face could hold. "Paul!"

She hopped the bar and ran over to him, jumping into his arms to hug him. Her grip was tight, his was, too, as if they both knew how close they'd come to losing each other. He let her hold him for a long while, likely sensing that she needed to feel him to remind herself that she hadn't actually lost *everything*.

Once she'd retreated from the embrace, she turned her smile to ice and hit Paul on the arm. Hard.

"Ouch! Why?"

"You haven't been by in weeks, where the hell have you been?!"

Paul rubbed his arm. "I went to see Dorian Blake."

"You did what?" Mercedes turned rabid. "You can't see Dorian Blake. He's gunning for your head for disappearing all these weeks. He'll crucify you."

"He forgave Carlos and Dan," Paul said.

"You know the rules won't be the same for you. Dan and Carlos, to him, are just two Cortez lowlifes. You were nearly a second-in-charge, for fuck's sake!"

"M, it's okay," Paul said, patting her on the shoulder. "I'm meeting Blake here now. He wants me to work for him."

He couldn't really be that fucking stupid, could he?

The front door opened and again, without looking, Mercedes cried out. "We're closed!"

"Not for me."

Another voice she knew. Kind words laced with venom that sent shivers down her spine.

Both she and Paul straightened.

Dorian entered followed by Yani, Antonio, and T.B.

"Why don't you make us some drinks, darling," Dorian said as he and his entourage drew farther into the club.

A simple nod gestured Paul toward Blake's regular booth. Mercedes didn't say a word as she went to make their drinks, tucking her hair behind her ear, ensuring she was close enough to hear anything useful.

Dorian slid into the deep leather of the booth, flanked by his companions at his left side. Paul sat on an uncomfortable wooden chair in front of them. It sat lower than the booth, likely on purpose so that Dorian would tower over his enemy. But with Paul's height, it merely brought them face to face.

"So, you've seen the light," Dorian said, a cruel smile on his mouth.

"I have," Paul said. "I want to come back."

"Bold, isn't it? After what you did, traitor."

Paul dropped his eyes to his lap in submission.

"Your friends have been very helpful. What're their names again? The Cortez guys?" Dorian turned to Yani to answer.

"Dan and Carlos."

Mercedes approached the table, placing drinks in front of their respective owners. When she returned to the bar, she made sure she was still within earshot.

"That's right, Dan and Carlos. Very helpful. Very loyal," Dorian said. "But you weren't very loyal, were you, Paul? You almost had me reserving a seat for you up here." Dorian patted the booth. "Then you threw it all away."

Paul's face was steady, not a giveaway or tell that Mercedes could see. Though his shoulders tensed like he'd expected the verbal lashing and was holding out for the physical one.

"And you skipped town. Didn't see you for months, unlike your friends who came right back to prove their pledge. Not a good look, Paul."

"I'm not asking to be back where I was, I'll do all the work you want, for no cost, just put me back on the team."

Dorian looked amused as he turned to Yani, Antonio, and T.B., but his smile was laced with venom. He leaned in close to Paul. "Where did you go, Paul?"

Paul's throat caught. Mercedes could practically see the words in that stifled breath. *I went to the hospital with Adam. Tended to my wounded friend. Made sure the leader you thought you killed successfully faked his death.* "On business in Darton."

"Business in Darton." Dorian chuckled, rolling his head back in a roar of laughter before he bared his teeth. "Feeling guilty for murdering your friend? Thought you could escape me, did you? Oh, Paul, I have so much power that I could easily make you shoot your own leader. Why would you ever think you could escape me?"

Hang on...

What the fuck did he just say?

Mercedes's mind reeled back over the last few months. Brooke's accusing look when she said the gunshot missed Adam's heart by less than a millimeter...Dan and Carlos being sure they'd proven their loyalty enough...Paul insisting that he take Adam away...three gunshot wounds. Three gunshots that she heard that day. Three. Dan, Carlos, Paul. Three.

Holy fucking shit.

Mercedes's eyes widened and her chest thundered, like a lightning storm raging in her ribs.

They shot him. The three of them. That's how they were forced to prove their loyalty??

"I'm not trying to escape you. Just make up for what I've done. I have no regrets. Not even for killing Adam."

Fuck. Mercedes held her hand to her heart.

"Alright. Consider yourself granted that second chance you want so badly."

Paul's face was still as unreadable as stone, but he just nodded and murmured thanks. Dorian waved him off with distaste and handed him a slip. "First job, go and pick up the shipment at this address."

Paul took the paper, heading out of the club. He locked eyes with Mercedes, and though it seemed he'd been gifted a second chance, his eyes were wary. Looking like he'd been handed his own signed death sentence. Like he wasn't sure which one of them would kill him. Her or Dorian.

She kept her ears targeted on Dorian's conversation as Paul left.

"Are you really letting him back in, boss?" Antonio said, mouth agape.

"Absolutely not. Once he arrives at that address, he'll be shot on sight," Dorian said, lifting his glass to take a sip.

"No!" Mercedes shouted out from across the room.

Shit. Did she mean to make that outburst?

"Yes?" Dorian said, squeezing his glass.

Well, she was doing this now.

Mercedes dove underneath the counter of the bar, stomping right to the edge of Dorian's booth. "You can't do that. You can't kill him."

"And why shouldn't I?"

She let tears gather at the corners of her eyes, though she held her head high. "Please."

Dorian's smile dropped, and with a tense voice he instructed his companions. "Give us a minute."

Looking annoyed and put-out, they vacated the table, leaving Dorian and Mercedes alone.

"You can't kill Paul. He's my best friend. Please, I'm begging you," she said as harshly as she could, but some betraying tears coated her cheeks.

"That's not really up to you, darling." He took another swig of his drink.

Mercedes gazed down at her feet. It was all a game. To Dorian, everything was a game. A wrestle for power and control. A set of carefully controlled moves that put him in position to be a king.

But Paul's life was hanging in the balance. She couldn't handle losing him, not after what she'd already lost. Not at the hands of their half-cocked plan. To her, nothing about any of this was a game.

Paul had known, she realized in that moment, that Dorian would never forgive him. Never give him a chance like he would with the others. Even though they...*fucking hell*.

That's why he'd insisted that he be the one to walk away to save Adam's life.

He'd succeeded, too. Adam was alive and well. On the road to a full recovery. But...Adam left anyway. He decided to take his health and his freedom and his new life and leave them all behind. Leave her behind. To deal with the outfall and destruction alone.

Despite what the others had done, they hadn't abandoned her. Coming back to Ridge City was a death sentence for Paul. But he'd still come back to her. Adam hadn't. And that, really, was the only thing she couldn't forgive.

She only had one thing left to give. The only thing that could save Paul's life.

"Take me," she said.

Dorian raised his eyebrows.

"Spare Paul's life, let him come back, and get the night with me you've always wanted."

Dorian smiled and downed the rest of his glass, getting up from the booth to face her. "Darling, it's an intriguing offer, but you're gonna need to do a little better than that."

Mercedes didn't look from his cutting stare, her eyes only shuttering as she recognized what she was about to sacrifice—and, interestingly enough, she embraced it full force. It was an easy choice. For Paul's life—her best friend—she'd do anything.

"Then take me for life. Spare him, and I'm yours, forever, in whatever way you want me."

Dorian licked his lips and smiled. "Darling, you have yourself a deal."

***

MAY 1991

Adam placed his shades over his eyes to block the blinding sun. He braced his forearms on the wooden railing of the boardwalk, staring out onto the beach. The crowds bustled around him, hot sun drawing most of them to the glittering waters in tiny bathing suits.

"What are we doing at the beach, Adam?" Mercedes's voice from behind startled him. He looked over his shoulder to gaze at her.

"Hey, baby," he smiled as she approached. "We're doing a job."

Next to him, she braced on the railing, too, more delicately than he had. She wore a mustard yellow crop top under a sheer white sweater and tight black shorts that had his eyes begging to see more. Didn't matter how much time they'd spent together, she always took his breath away.

"At the beach?"

He took shallow breaths to keep his composure, hoping that she wouldn't notice. He was surprised to see that she had showed up at all. She'd been avoiding all of them. Though, just like Paul said, there was no anger in her eyes. He wondered if she'd been punishing herself just as badly as he had for what happened to Tia.

He brushed off the sadness, doing his best to pretend everything was normal. "It's a stakeout," he said. "Take some incriminating photos for our new friends at City Hall. Little bit of blackmail here and there."

She pushed back on the railing, only holding onto it with her palm. She didn't meet his gaze, though his lingered unwaveringly on her.

"I'm surprised you came," he said.

"You made it sound important," she said.

He pulled his eyes from her as he spotted the target on the beach. He reached for his camera, tightening the correct lens in anticipation.

The target approached a woman sunbathing on a pink towel underneath an umbrella. Removing his shirt, the target laid down on the towel, too, bracing himself on his elbows.

Adam snapped a picture. Not something a wife would want to see, but not good enough for blackmail either. Not yet.

From the corner of his eye, Adam spied Mercedes staring at him, her head darting back and forth between the water and his face, her mouth turning in false starts.

"What?" he asked, scrunching his nose.

"Nothing." She snapped her head back to the ocean.

His kept his eye at the lens, snapping picture after picture. "Spit it out."

"Can I ask you something?"

"I just said you could," he smirked, removing the lens only long enough to look at her sidelong.

"Why did you come back? Why *really*?"

Fuck, such a direct question. A much heavier one than he expected. He could've come back to take down Dorian Blake at any point he wanted in the last five years… That was a truth he had barely admitted to himself, and now she was asking for it plain as day.

"Don't lie to me," she said, but not harshly, with gentleness. Like she was compelling him to release whatever weight of truth held him down.

He just wanted to clear the air between them, lift her spirits enough so that she might smile again. Though, clearly that hadn't been her motivation for coming. Adam lifted the camera to his eye again. "I saw the newspaper."

"The newspaper," she repeated, nodding slowly. "Dorian announcing his candidacy? Well, you did say that. That you came back to stop him before he could become mayor. I guess you weren't lying." She smiled sadly and laughed without humor.

"I was lying," Adam said in a no-nonsense tone as he kept his eye to the camera, snapping away. "I didn't give a fuck about him becoming mayor."

She whipped her head toward him, her mouth wide open.

Dropping the camera from his sight, he turned to face her. "I was so afraid. For so long. I... tried to come back before but I couldn't." He watched her breath quicken. "Then, I read the newspaper. You were engaged. And something in me finally snapped. Despite how afraid I felt. How fucking unprepared I was... I packed up my shit that night and drove right over state lines. Fear be damned."

She clutched a hand to her heart. "But—but you...came back here to kill Dorian Blake."

"Yes," he agreed. "And I will. But not because he is about to be the mayor."

Adam chanced a look to the beach. The target and the woman were now hand in hand jogging away. Impeccable timing.

"The target's headed for the sand dunes," Adam said, lightly frowning. He pushed off the railing and secured the camera around his neck. Just once, he dared to look up at her. Knowing that if she so much as gave him a nod, he would throw that camera in the water, fuck the consequences, and lose everything to do whatever she wanted of him.

"Let's go," she said.

Something like longing, an ache, pounded in his heart. But still he followed her lead along the boardwalk.

The sand dunes were the perfect place to engage in hidden, nefarious activities. The only vantage point to see into them was from up high, on the rocks. Though it was such a steep climb, surrounded by jagged white tips of water, that no one dared venture onto them.

But they weren't just anyone—and the rocks had them barely working up a sweat.

Atop the final peak, Adam held out a hand to Mercedes. Accepting his offer, he pulled her the last of the way up.

They sat down on the rock as Adam began snapping pictures again. The target and the woman had thrown caution to the wind. Through the lens he had a clear shot of her head in the target's lap.

He knew his lens was focused and they had the evidence needed, so while he snapped away, his mind went somewhere else.

Back to *his* question. One he'd been far too afraid to ask. But since she had asked him to open up, maybe her heart was finally warm enough to do the same.

"Can I ask you something?" Adam said.

"I suppose, since we're friends." She nudged him gently.

He swallowed and held still, not daring to move as he asked the question that had plagued his mind for months. From the moment he first read the words in the newspaper. From the moment he saw her again. From the moment he realized that she didn't love Dorian Blake. And never had.

"Why—really why," he said, "did you say yes to Dorian Blake?"

She stiffened.

She was so still that he wondered if she was retreating again. As her face softened, he swore he could see some part of her gently pulling away her walls and baring herself freely to him.

Like placing a final puzzle piece, in his mind the picture was suddenly clear. Why she hid so deep behind battle-drawn walls in her heart. As if all that she had suffered, all her pain, had not hardened her, but softened her so much that she would shatter if the wrong person got close enough.

"For Paul," she said, avoiding eye contact and squinting out into the sun.

"For Paul?"

She smiled, but not with her eyes. "You didn't really think Dorian would just let them go, did you? No. Dan and Carlos went straight to Dorian to back up their pledge, and since they were Cortez Cartel before, Dorian saw them as a victory. But Paul..."

Adam shuffled closer, the words damning enough to make his ears bleed. *For Paul...*He'd suspected as much, but didn't realize how it'd hurt to hear. To see all the consequences he had run away from and left his family to face.

She continued. "Paul was a betrayal. He'd been working for the Blake's his whole life. Dorian trusted him. And then he skipped town for weeks to help you recover. When he finally came back, Dorian wasn't going to let him live. So, I..." She took a deep breath. "I gave Dorian what he'd always chased. I gave him me."

He blinked and a tear slipped from his eye. "Why did you do that?"

"You did the same? Didn't you? Sacrificed yourself to save them. Why shouldn't I give what I had?" She gulped and looked skyward, but it didn't stop her tears from falling.

They were silent from then all the way to the walk back to his car. The words they'd exchanged were so raw. Much more honest than they'd ever been before. He remembered what she'd said to him in anger, *the girl you used to love died back in October 1986. The same day you did,* and now he considered it true.

She wasn't the same, and neither was he. The love they'd had once was not there.

No. It had been replaced by something much deeper. Where before he would've torn the world to pieces in his love for her, now he would take everything. Himself, the sky, the stars, every planet in the universe, the entire galaxy...he'd swallow it all into a black hole for her.

Nothing between them—not time, not enemies, not death—none of it would ever change how he was desperately, hopelessly, and endlessly in love with her. And would be forever.

***

He had to tell her.

He couldn't hold it in.

After the escapade at the beach, they'd come back to his hotel room to clean up. Dan, Carlos, and Paul had been there, but left quickly, and now it was just him and her.

Him and her standing at the window looking out onto the beach and not saying a word. His skin crawling with the need to tell her how much he felt. How the feelings never stopped. And how he suspected that those feelings wouldn't lessen even if he wanted them to.

"What?" She frowned at him. Her sheer white sweater crumpled as she folded her arms and craned her neck to see him.

"Nothing."

"You're staring at me."

"Am I?" He feigned innocence.

"You do that a lot."

He turned to her with a smile.

Reaching a shaking hand out, he brushed a patch of white sand from her cheek. "You still have some sand here." But he couldn't stop himself from holding his hand there. From stroking her cheek with his thumb. From holding her head in his hand as she cradled into his touch.

She closed her eyes as if the touch of his hand were melting her. He stared as her pupils raced behind her closed eyelids, like her thoughts were eating her whole. Her eyes snapped open with a jolt.

358

"I can't—" she said. She removed his hand from her face and then held it with her own as she traced the lines on his palm.

"Don't," he begged with a sigh. "I never stopped loving you."

Her eyes splintered to his, pools welling at the edges. He'd been holding that in for five years. Why he'd chosen now to say it? Fuck if he knew. He just knew that he had to. Every moment that he was around her and not telling her made him feel like a piece of his heart was buried alive and clawing through its coffin to make it up to the surface.

"You can't just come in here and say that."

"Why not? It's the truth. I've loved you for—"

"Don't say it!"

"—seven years. That feeling doesn't go away."

"Stop!" she shouted, turning to face him. He studied her face, her cheeks were red and puffy, but her eyes were enraged. "You don't get to say that. Not after five years."

"Then when? Because I can't go another second pretending that I don't love you. That you aren't the only reason that I—"

"I don't want to hear it. I didn't ask for you to come back! Never wanted it," she shouted, her face heating before twisting into a grimace. He saw the lie for what it was. Even though he knew the reasons why she said it, he couldn't stop his own irritation bursting free.

"My God, you can't hate me forever."

"I will hate you for as long as I fucking want!"

"Don't pretend that I'm the only bad guy. There were two sides of this!" he shouted, getting fiery as he advanced across the space toward her.

"Oh, really," she said, her chest heaving so roughly it was like she might breathe fire. "Two sides, huh?! You left me!"

"Because I nearly fucking died!"

"Well, you didn't die! You could've come back, any of those *sixty* months, but you were a fucking coward!"

He pushed two fingers to his temple, staring her down without blinking. "Don't talk to me about cowardice, babe. You're so fucking afraid to feel anything that you choose to feel nothing at all."

"And whose fault is that? You left us all behind in this big fucking mess you created," she said, arms flailing like she was trying to tread water.

He wiped his face with his hands. "I had no fucking choice."

"To leave us here? To abandon us?" She laughed and braced her hands on her hips. "To leave me? You're the one who chose to leave behind what we had and give up on us. You sent Paul back to Ridge City with nothing but a message that you were leaving forever. And then zilch, nada, for *five* years."

He was forced to take a step back at that sharp sting. "You don't think that once I realized what I did, that I didn't want to come running right back here?" He faced her, seeing only an exasperated frown. "That as soon as I woke up that I didn't want to come running right back to you?"

She stood in stunned silence for a moment.

"Once I woke up and realized I'd lost you I–"

"You chose to lose me!"

He clenched his fists so hard the whites of his knuckles showed, forcing his lips shut so he didn't shout. "You are so fucking stubborn and ridiculous!"

"Yeah?" She came within inches of his face to spit the words. "And you're self-centered and full of undeserved pride!"

"For fuck's sake, it was five *years* ago!"

"You inconsiderate motherfu–"

"They nearly fucking killed me! I had to disappear, how many times do I have to say it—I had no choice! What the fuck did you want me to do?!"

"You could've taken me with you!" she shouted, a new onslaught of tears rolling as she raced to wipe them away.

He opened his mouth to fire back, but found it empty. His hands bounced as he tried to decide what to do with them. Reach out to her? Stay away? He had the emotional intelligence of a fucking raccoon. He had no idea what to do or how to behave.

"You could've taken me with you," she whispered again. Taking a step back as well she wiped the tears from her face with her sleeve.

Was that an option? To take her with him? Why in five long, lonely years did he never think of that?

He ran his hand down his face before moving over to place his hands on her waist. "Mercedes, I–"

"No!" she pulled away from him again. "You lost the privilege to touch me a long time ago." She stomped out of the hotel, slamming the door so violently that the windows rattled.

Adam snatched a beer bottle from the countertop and threw it viciously at the wall, grunting as he put all the might of his muscled bicep behind it. Shards of broken glass smashed as beer dripped down the wall, akin to the broken pieces of his heart leaking out.

He dropped into the armchair, cradling his head in his hands and shaking. There was a tightness in his throat that gripped harder with every tear he pushed away, with every wave of emotion that he chose to suppress.

He wasn't sure how he had managed to screw things up so badly. He had caused so much hurt, so much pain. People had died in the name of what he was trying to create, but still he had destroyed the one thing that mattered most to him. It wasn't taking down Dorian Blake. It wasn't the thrill of the fight. It was Dan, Carlos, Paul.

It was *her*.

They were all that mattered. And he knew it. He finally understood.

After being lost in his regrets for what seemed like a millennium, there was a knock on the door.

He lifted his eyes hopefully, his hands still shaking from where he'd cradled his head. He darted upright, straightened his shirt, pushed his hair back into place, and wiped at his eyes.

Then he was at the door. His heart beating so hard, he swore it'd fractured a rib. He gulped and took a deep breath, his outstretched hand inching closer to the doorknob.

He turned it slowly, cautiously pulling open the door as he moved back.

Mercedes stepped into the room, her eyes to the floor.

Without looking up, she shut the door gently and braced against it. As if she might fall down with weak knees if she dared loosen her grip.

Adam took deep breaths as he watched her. Waiting for her to look up. Waiting for her to make a move. Waiting for her to do something. Anything. Because she was still here. Still being braver with her heart than he'd ever been with his.

She inched closer. Her face twisted, and still without looking up, she placed two palms on his chest.

With that touch, he closed his eyes and let loose the last of the tears he'd been holding back. Following the gentleness of her fingers, he hesitantly placed his hands on her arms, giving them a soothing stroke before moving them to her shoulders.

Then up to her neck. Then her face. Until he finally braced on either side of her jaw, stroking the space just in front of her ear.

Slowly, he pulled her closer. Slowly, until she was pressed against his chest.

Then her eyes flicked to his. And in them he saw the answer to every question he could ever dare to ask.

He closed his eyes as he kissed her. Finally.

It started tender, their lips barely even brushing, before he hesitantly pressed his tongue inside and she opened for him. With his hands at the back of her neck he drew her forward and deepened the kiss, holding her like the fate of the world rested on it. His world did, that much he knew.

Her hands made their way around his neck, pressing fully into his front as they reconnected at last. Her lips were soft and sweet, but her tongue was rough as it met his stroke for stroke. It was both familiar and utterly surprising at the same time.

She slid her hands from his neck to the top of his shirt, unbuttoning each button with painful slowness. Slow, but intense. Slow, but hard. Once she had it fully unbuttoned, she pushed the shirt down his shoulders, running her hands over his arms as she did and making him groan in approval.

Now breaking his hands from her jaw, he grabbed the last part of his shirt that remained clinging to him and dropped it onto the floor. In the next movement, he had his hands beneath her thighs, lifting her up into his arms as her legs wrapped around his waist and her arms returned to his neck.

He kissed her again, cradling her while he carried her across the room, only breaking once for her to rip her sweater off and discard it before arching into him again.

With her still in his arms, he crawled onto the bed knees first, bracing one hand on the bed while he laid her flat beneath him.

He was absolutely lost in the moment. Nothing outside this room existed. Only her. Always only her.

He braced his hands on either side of her head and pressed kisses down her neck. Only as a distraction so she would arch enough for him to rip the crop top away and set her breasts free.

He settled himself between her thighs, feeling flustered as she fumbled with the buckle on his pants. *Fuck. Fuck. Fuck.*

"Not yet," he spoke against her lips.

"What—you—" she struggled as she tried to sit up.

He crawled down her body, placing his rough hand against her chest and nudging her down until she was laid flat again.

"Lay back," he commanded. "I'm going to remind you what it is you've been missing all these years."

She returned his smirk with a dreamy smile as he popped the button on her shorts, watching as she lifted her hips so he could slide them down her legs alongside her white lace panties.

Her thighs wrapped around his shoulders and he gripped her hips to pull her close to him. He pressed his face to her center, inhaling and groaning into her.

"Oh yeah, she's missed me too."

That made her giggle.

The first swipe of his tongue through her wet slit sent her back arching off the bed. The second made her buck so forcefully that he moved his hands to her stomach to keep her pinned to the bed.

He started with gentle licks, before he couldn't hold back; wishing he was drowning and losing himself as he devoured her with his whole mouth.

"You're such a… fucking tease," she said, struggling to make coherent words come out.

He laughed with his face still smothered.

"But you taste so good," he said, groaning as he continued to lap at her soaked pussy. "You always tasted so fucking good, baby."

He picked up his pace, kissing her, eating her pussy like a starved man unable to finish his meal fast enough.

She was usually in control. They both knew it. Out in the world she had every advantage over him, he would crawl at her feet. But here, this was where he made her crawl for him instead.

"Yes…yes!" she cried, fingers twisting in his hair to hold him in place.

"You're close, baby," he said, his voice muffled. "I can feel it. Come on my tongue."

She arched off the bed in a strangled cry as she came. He didn't let up. Using his tongue to swipe gentle strokes over her clit as she rode the high. He finished with a kiss on her inner thigh before crawling up her body until they were face to face again.

"Shit," she laughed.

"Told you," he smirked.

She looked down over him. He expected her to be slow to recover, but from the look in her eye her appetite had only increased. "You're still wearing pants."

The metal clanged as she pulled his belt free and then unzipped his fly, her hand quickly finding his hard, waiting cock and swirling over the beads of pre-cum that were leaking from his tip.

She removed her hand and swirled her finger into her mouth, licking the pre-cum that she gathered there.

"Holy shit," he said, scrambling to kick his jeans away as fast as possible while she laughed. When they were both naked and he was placed between her legs again, she wrapped her arms around his neck and kissed him with a wondered smile.

When they pulled away, he moved in an obvious reach for the condoms next to his bed. She stopped him with a grip on his arm.

"I want to feel you," she said.

He dropped his head to her neck and huffed a laugh. "You're killing me, baby."

"I'm still on the pill. And I'm clean. You?"

"Clean," he said, looking into her eyes with wild lust. He gripped his cock, sliding it through her wet folds before gently nudging at her entrance.

Containing himself, his need to slam inside her, was not an easy task. Especially with the feel of every part of her against him.

It took a few pushes until he finally seated fully inside her, shutting his eyes as her body adjusted to his size and her head lolled back onto the pillow.

He tried to remain slow for the first thrusts into her, but knew early on that he couldn't contain himself. Not when she clawed at his back and sighed in his ear each time his thrusts fit him fully inside.

Unlike what he expected, it was not rough, like it had usually been with them. Somehow that only made it more intense. The aching slowness of his cock pushing inside her, and her breasts sliding against his chest.

"Fucking hell," he said, grunting as he nestled his face into her neck and arched his back to keep his momentum. It took everything he had in him to keep going as she pulled her legs higher until they were pushing against the sides of his ribs. That angle? He was a goner.

"Fuck, baby, you feel so good."

She wrapped her arms around him, pulling him close so they were skin to skin and breathing the same air. "Right there, don't stop! I'm going to… going to–"

"You gonna come again for me, baby?"

"Yes!" she shouted, pulling him against her like she was trying to glue their chests together.

He gripped her thigh and wrapped it around his waist, opening her up so he could drive in deeper. He growled as he felt her pussy start to tighten around him.

"Fuck, that's so good," she cried, pushing her hips upward to meet his thrusts. "Oh my God, yes."

"Come on my cock, baby. Strangle me with–*fuck*." She came before he could finish his sentence, her walls tightening around him until he nearly blacked out from the pleasure.

"Oh, shit," he said, trying to hold back his own release but finding that he'd completely lost control.

He slammed into her painfully as he came, stilling until he'd fully emptied himself inside her. He fell down onto her in a messy heap, blissed out as she peppered him with kisses on his cheek while his cock finished twitching inside her.

It'd been five years coming, and nothing had ever felt so right or made him feel so whole.

He turned his head to find her gazing back at him. He stroked the hair away from her eyes and kissed her slowly, content to lay there for as long as she'd have him.

The world outside the walls may have been crumbling around them, but here nothing else existed. So even if out there was a scary and dangerous place, Adam couldn't care less.

He didn't give a fuck what happened next.

He linked their fingers and kissed her knuckles. He was never letting go again.

CHAPTER 23
THE PRIZE

MAY 1991

T ucking the sheets up close, Mercedes smiled when the warmth of the morning sun grazed her cheeks. She took a satisfied breath as she found the arm wrapped around her waist. Strong, calloused hands grazed the skin of her navel. She sank her head into the pillow, unable to remember when she last slept so soundly.

Wait. It was morning. *Morning!* She'd stayed at Adam's all night.

"Oh, shit." She jolted up, throwing the sheets off and jumping up from the bed.

Ripping through the room like a tornado, she stumbled to find her underwear, then her bra, then her pants.

Grumbling from the bed, Adam rolled over. He opened only one eye and squinted through it. "What are you doing?"

"It's morning! I stayed here all night." She found her sweater and straightened it over her head.

Adam sank back into the bed. "I'm not surprised," he said. "After that much sex, I could sleep for days."

She found her boots and sat in the armchair. "I have a thing with Dorian this morning, some campaign lunch."

He shot up. "You're going back? Now?"

Barely listening, but really choosing not to, she focused only on zipping her boots.

"What I mean to say then is *don't* go back to him," Adam said.

"Adam..." she said, kicking her feet on the ground to secure them in the boot.

He ran his hands through his hair. "You—you're—" he said. "You're giving me one night like that, then running back off again?"

She saw his pained expression. It was as if she could really see his beating heart laid bare on his sleeve. She smiled. "No, one night with you would never be enough."

When he looked at her again, he was wearing that wicked look that she loved so much. It sent shivers down her spine. She moved to the bed and perched in his lap.

Stroking his hair back, she looked deep into his eyes, kissing him lightly as his arms wrapped around her.

She'd done it now, and it was scarier than she thought. If they were going to do this, really do this, then she had something on her mind. The bastard knew her too well, because he seemed to sense it.

"What is it?"

The words hurt, like fingernails breaking from tearing at the bricks she built around her heart.

"I love you," she said. "I've always loved you. Every single day we were together. Every day for the past five years. Every day since you walked back into this city...I have loved you."

His eyes beamed and his smile split his cheeks. He leaned in for a kiss but pulled away with a frown. Fuck knows what sort of look she had on her face. No matter how minor her emotion, he'd always pick it and pull it apart.

"And?" he said.

"And I need to do it right this time. I can't have you die on me again."

He sighed.

"We can't let ourselves get distracted by this." She gestured at the space between them as his hands tightened on her. "We have to keep focused on the goal. Kill Dorian Blake. Eyes on the prize at all times."

He pulled her closer into him, holding her like he might not ever let go. She couldn't see his face, but she could already sense the words he wanted to say.

"I meant what I said, if it comes down to it, I don't want to be saved," she said.

"Baby, that was before all of–"

"I don't care," she said, stroking his hair back from his forehead. "Promise me. The plan comes first."

He shook his head, chewing on his lip.

"People have died for this, Adam. Died for us to have the chance to take down Dorian Blake. It's not just us who needs this. There are far more lives on the line now."

He was looking back in her eyes again, his face wrinkling like his gut was twisting on the inside.

"Promise me." It wasn't a question so much as a command.

"Fine, I promise," he said, grimacing as if the words were acid. "Nothing comes before this plan."

"Eyes on the prize at all times," she repeated. He was fickle. She'd drill it into him with enough repetition to tire a schoolteacher if she had to.

"Eyes on the prize at all times."

Looking away, his shoulders dropped, as if the weight of the promise sank him. "You know, none of that means that you have to go back to him *now*."

Frowning and ready to fire back, she turned to him, only to find him grinning again. She smiled with tight lips. It was a tease, a game, and he was ready to play.

She pressed her body into his, kissing him again. "I'm yours, baby. Don't forget again."

He gripped at her hips like he was readying to pounce. Before he got the chance, she struggled out of his arms and backed toward the door.

"Mean." He shook his head.

She gave him a filthy look before ripping the door open to leave, and when she did, she found Carlos standing in front of her with an outstretched hand, about to knock.

"Carlos!" She stumbled back.

"Hey, you're here early." He looked her up and down, raising his brow.

It was an effort to suppress a full grin. She merely rolled her eyes and gave Carlos a quick peck on the check before dashing down the stairs.

She closed the door behind her. Before she could make it far, she distinctly heard Carlos begin to ask Adam what the two of them were doing, followed by a whooshing sound, a smack and then Carlos grunting through laughter.

***

"So, how'd you do last night?" Paul asked.

Adam dropped the gun from his sight and looked over his shoulder to where Dan and Carlos were sitting across the lot. They didn't appear to be listening, just Carlos teaching Dan how to bag the supply of crystals.

Adam shrugged. "Good, we got the pictures we needed." Glass shattered as Adam fired his practice shot. The ring of gunfire was unusually loud, but still none of them even so much as flinched at the sound.

Paul smiled. "You know that's not what I meant."

Adam only returned the smirk, and then lifted the gun, ready for another bullseye.

"Judging from what I witnessed this morning, I'd say things went *really* well," Carlos said. Huh. Not quite far enough out of earshot.

"What does *that* mean?" Dan's eyes brightened with interest.

"I caught M leaving his room about six this morning."

"That proves nothing," Dan said, narrowing his eyes.

"Oh yeah? What about Adam's dorky ass grin and sex hair then?"

"Goddammit!" Dan threw the cigarette from his mouth and stomped it out. Pulling out a twenty-dollar bill, he grimaced as he handed it off to Carlos.

Carlos waved the bill in his hand, as if to gloat, before he pocketed it and reached his hand out. Raising his brow in silent command. To Paul?

Paul succumbed, too. Rolling his eyes, he drew a twenty and handed it over.

"What the fuck?" Adam said, eyes so wide he wouldn't be surprised if they went bouncing out of his head.

"You only won by a week at most, come off it." Dan was a particularly sore loser, he turned his frown toward the bag of supply.

"Hey, I had May. Not my fault you overshot it with June," Carlos laughed.

Adam, although amused, fought the urge to punch his friends. All their teasing about her never coming back to him, and they'd been fucking betting on it the whole time.

"I had March," Paul said. "Really thought you would only hold out for a few weeks."

"You placed bets."

He expected them to be more ashamed, but they all just nodded. Carlos was still gloating to rile Dan, when Paul turned to Adam and said, "Don't get distracted, though, bud."

"I don't know what you're talking about," Adam said, shoulders stiffening.

"Hey, I don't want to put my nose where it doesn't belong. But there's bigger shit going on here, too," Paul said. "We've still got Dorian Blake to deal with…don't let this distract you from the path."

"Don't worry," Adam said, his lips twitching up. "I want to kill Dorian Blake now more than ever."

Paul nodded solemnly, "Still, I just think– Fuck, get down!"

A sudden explosion sounded, followed by a ringing in his ears as Paul forced Adam's body down into the dirt, covering it with his own.

A grenade had been thrown into their midst, stunning them and propelling dirt into the air. Turning his head to the side against the sudden impact, Adam saw Carlos and Dan had hit the dirt, too. There were several Blake associates converging on them from all angles. One who reached Dan and Carlos first, grabbing Dan's hair in his fist.

"Oh, fuck no," Adam said, shoving upward to his knees and firing a quick shot to kill the guy and free Dan. Dan and Carlos scrambled to Paul and Adam where they were sheltered behind a brick wall.

"I'd say our cover's been blown," Carlos said.

"You think?" Dan gave him a hard look.

Though his eyes were still blurry, Adam risked a look over the half-crumbled brick wall. In the center of the men training guns in their direction was Dorian Blake, stepping out of his limo, with T.B. close behind him.

"Fuck," Adam said. They were cornered.

"Oh, come on out, Adam. No point hiding anymore," Blake chuckled.

Carlos looked to him with wide eyes, while Paul ran a hand over his face.

"Can we fight our way out of this?" Carlos whispered.

Adam shook his head and gestured for them to stand with him. Slowly, they all stood with their hands in surrender. Facing Dorian Blake in all their traitorous glory.

"There you are," Blake sneered, running narrowed eyes over Adam's body. "I fucking knew it! You sneaky little fucking traitors... Christ. How did you even survive it? We killed you good."

Adam shrugged. "Not good enough."

Blake's face turned red, but he controlled his reaction, turning to share a glare with T.B. "So, where's the fifth?"

"Don't know what you're talking about."

Blake was deteriorating by the second, but T.B. still looked the angriest somehow.

Nobody in the Blake Family would ever understand the loyalty that Adam's friends had shown. That he had shown. How could they? Blake pitted them all against each other so vehemently that they celebrated when a friend met their end.

"Anyone else want to give me a better answer…or do we get a do-over from five years ago with a gun and choices that you get to make?" Blake said, eyeing Dan, Paul, and Carlos for an answer.

When he didn't get one, Blake bared his teeth and waved a hand at his men, commanding them to lift their weapons. "Fine. There's one more of you, and believe me, I'm going to find out who it is. Fortunately, I don't need you alive to do it. Kill them."

Blake's men went to raise their guns, but another explosion rocked the ground beneath them, unsteadying them on their feet. Only this time, it was a grenade blowing Blake's prized limo to smithereens.

Blake's one angry look over his shoulder was enough time for Adam, Paul, Dan, and Carlos to snatch up their weapons and become surrounded by several of their own people.

Friendly vehicles surrounded them in droves, full of people who rushed out to join the fight. Old Blake exiles, old Cortez guys, even a group of Tia's girls wielding machine guns joined the fray.

Gunfire erupted across the divide, as the might of the empire Adam had been building arrived in full force to defend him. And through it, Adam kept eye contact with Dorian, giving him a cocky little smirk as people rushed around them.

Adam was jolted away from the stare-off when his shoulder was tapped, and Lulu appeared behind him with a flame thrower. *A flame thrower.*

"Got a girl who says you belong to her waiting in a car back there," Lulu smirked. Adam followed her eye line where Mercedes was waiting, covered head to toe in black to conceal her identity.

Lulu threw flames into the air, allowing time for their people to escape.

But Adam returned to Blake's stare, where T.B. was pulling him back by both arms as he attempted to charge forward. Frowning, Adam started forward until he was pulled back, too.

Paul held his arms tight. "Not here, bud. Not now."

Adam looked around to where his people were barely winning the fight. If they didn't retreat now, they'd needlessly lose lives.

But he could do it… He could kill Blake with his bare hands right there. He could end it. Recklessly, sure, but it'd be over.

It took all his energy to recognize the bad timing, clenching his jaw as he nodded once and instructed his team to draw back. "Let's go!"

They all ducked and returned fire, barely stumbling across the lot as they retreated from the ambush.

Adam made it to Mercedes's car with Dan, Paul, and Carlos, waiting until the very last second to make sure everyone had the chance to retreat before he took the flame thrower from Lulu and allowed his people a head start.

Once the grass was burning again, Adam jumped into the passenger seat. He checked over the vehicle. Dan, Carlos, Paul, Mercedes. His family. Present and accounted for.

Mercedes was speeding off again, leaving their enemies in ruin, before he could wipe the dirt and blood from his face.

"Fuck!" Carlos said.

"That was… unexpected," Paul said, eyes wide in shock.

"Apparently Dorian found some tape of your dumb ass at the shooting range," Mercedes said, though her eyes smiled. "I barely had time to round up the team to save you. Again, I might add."

"Blake knows Adam's alive…" Dan said, shoulders dropping.

"Yeah…" Carlos said, giving Dan an incredulous look. "Obviously."

"That wasn't supposed to happen," Dan said.

"No," Adam said, frowning as Mercedes's hands tightened on the wheel. "It was not."

***

After they'd ditched the getaway vehicle, they went back to Adam's room in low spirits, slumping into various corners of the suite when they arrived.

"Well, we've really done it now," Dan said, settling in the kitchen and pouring a heavy drink. He took a full swig and finished it one glass, pouring another without delay.

"He was *not* meant to know you were alive until you were pointing a gun in his face," Carlos said.

Adam nodded his agreement and sank down onto the edge of his bed. "Nobody leaves this place now," he said. "You guys can't go home."

"Why the fuck not?" Dan said, pausing his sip.

"He'll be waiting for you there," Adam said. "Now that he knows the players, he'll be looking for us."

"He's right," Mercedes said, standing with her arms folded by the door. "He will send people to stake out your apartments."

Dan downed the second drink and replenished it, while Carlos and Paul slumped at the dining table.

"How the hell are we meant to finish this now?" Dan said.

"This only ends one way," Mercedes said. "With a fucking bullet in his head."

Carlos sighed. "But we've lost the upper hand. He knows Adam's alive. He knows for certain there's a fifth one of us, *and* he knows about our people."

Mercedes opened her mouth to fire back, but Paul shot her a short look and she stopped in her tracks. Her anger was clearly clouding her emotions too much for the time being.

Adam rubbed at his temples. This wasn't supposed to be the plan. He had always known that if he was going to kill Dorian Blake, it had to be before the election. Had to be before Blake became too powerful to ever stop. And Blake was going to win the election, too, if Diego's murder and the ballot tampering were anything to go by.

No, they couldn't let Blake make it to the election. There was absolutely no way he could allow it. But now, though…now Blake would see it coming.

Unless…

Adam looked up as he realized what they needed to do. The others seemed to sense it, too, from the way they watched him when he jumped up to stand.

Feeling a bad idea forming in his mind sent goosebumps forming over his skin. He widened his eyes and let all his crazy out in his smile. "We're not killing Blake before the election."

They were all staring now.

Dan rolled his eyes and started. "How the fuck–"

But Adam raised a finger to shush him as he paced, quieting them so the only sound was that of his marching footsteps.

"No, he'll be expecting that. He'll be tense and have extra security in the lead up to the election. We have to get him when he doesn't expect it."

"The inaugural ball," Paul said. Adam turned to look at him. Paul looked no less surprised than the others with what'd just come out of his own mouth. "There are four days between when he wins the election and when he gets sworn in."

"Four days." Adam nodded, smiling. The others jumped on the train without a second of questioning.

"Four days to kill him," Carlos said.

"When he least expects it," Dan said.

"The inaugural ball is the night before he's sworn in," Mercedes said. "Cutting it mighty close, don't you think?"

"Then we will win by the skin of our teeth, with blood on our backs," Adam said. "On the night of the ball, Dorian Blake dies."

An eerie chill swept the room as they formed a circle. More power, more cunning than he'd ever dared access before broke free from within. Sheer will would carry him through this. Because he refused to be afraid. He refused to lose. He *refused* to die. And therefore, there was only one inevitability. To win.

CHAPTER 24
THE WINNER IS

"Results pending, five minutes."

It was election day. The day Dorian Blake would be announced the new mayor of Ridge City. Mercedes didn't need the official results to know that.

A large crowd gathered at City Hall, a podium erected on its front steps to host the live event. Standing in the wings backstage, Mercedes looked out into the throng. Thousands of people were holding up signs professing their adoration for Dorian Blake.

Idiots. Fucking idiots, all of them.

Mercedes looked behind her to where Dorian was pacing in the wings with T.B. standing deathly still nearby. Without Antonio and Yani, Dorian's operation had been falling apart at the seams. Not to mention, he'd been at his most tense in the days leading up to the election. As was expected, he assumed Adam and the rest of her friends would strike beforehand.

T.B. was no help. He wasn't built to be the only Second. He was careless and crazy. Where Yani or Antonio would've assured Dorian that the fight was over the second he won the election, T.B. had him believing a rogue hitman would be waiting in the wings to cut his head off just before the results were announced.

She couldn't pretend she hadn't considered it.

"What the fuck do you mean, this is everyone?" Dorian shouted at the man cowering next to T.B.

"We got everyone we could, but they–"

"But they fucking what? Where is everyone?" He stopped his pacing to stare.

"Lots of men are defecting, sir," the man stuttered. On edge and a little jumpy, Dorian's hand lingered near his gun, like he might actually shoot this sap in front of everyone.

Luckily, or unluckily depending on how she looked at it, T.B. tore his attention elsewhere before he could act too impulsively.

"They're sensing a power imbalance," T.B. said. "Lots of people are defecting to work for Vandemilio."

"You've got to be fucking kidding me." Dorian's shoulders hardened under his immaculate suit.

"People are choosing sides."

"Well, that won't fucking matter when I'm mayor of this city, they'll all come crawling back. They'll all come fucking–"

Mercedes sensed it was time to interrupt before Dorian ruined his own life and robbed her the pleasure of doing it. "Everything alright, honey?"

"It's fine." Dorian huffed, shrugging her hand off his shoulder.

"Keep your voice down in front of the press," she said, a massive fake smile plastered on her face. Turning to T.B., Mercedes said, "What's going on?"

"We've got men defecting to work for Vandemilio, dropping like flies," T.B. said. She supposed that was one advantage, at least. Yani and Antonio used to hesitate every time they told her anything. T.B. just laid it all out on the line for her to see. He wasn't too bright like that.

"That's concerning," she said.

"No! It's just—" Dorian said, starting to pace manically again. "This is big boys' business. Go and mingle with the wives or something."

T.B.'s mouth became tight. Fighting a smile? Prick.

Mercedes shook her head, turning her back on them to walk away. "Keep it together, darling, you're starting to sound like a fucking lunatic."

She could almost feel their disgusted stares boring into her. Then, footsteps approached, and there was a tug at her elbow, pulling her back so hard that it left a jarring red handprint. "You don't fucking talk to me like that."

She ripped her elbow back, a show of power she hoped he wouldn't notice. "Careful, *honey*," she warned, glancing at the eyes backstage that now focused solely on them. "Or they might see you for who you really are."

***

"We really going to just let this happen?" Carlos said, fidgeting with the straw in his drink.

"Don't really have a choice," Paul said.

Adam eyed his friends sitting around him in their regular booth. "It's all part of the plan," Adam said. "We get him when he least expects it."

A tray of drinks appeared, their favorite bartender delivering shots. That's what they'd need to get through the next few hours. It wasn't usually table service, but this bartender was the only one game enough to approach them. And it was bad for business if they were at the bar scaring the shit out of people all the time.

"I think people are afraid of us," Dan said, looking over Adam's shoulder.

Turning over to stare at the patrons behind him, Adam shifted his gaze to the crowd and smiled as they immediately turned away. "Good."

"Don't let it go to your head," Paul said. "Blake's not dead yet."

Adam swallowed a shot. How could he not let it go to his head? People were terrified of him. Yes, as they should be, but a great many more had defected to his side because they respected him.

"Results pending, five minutes." That was the announcement made over the television.

Their chatter ceased, as if the words were a kick in the head that sent them back to reality. No matter how many people feared them or respected them or defected to work for them, they were not safe until Dorian Blake was rotting in the ground. And in four days' time they'd either be the leaders of the largest gang in Ridge City. Or...or they'd be dead.

"Maybe he won't win." Carlos shrugged.

"He will fucking win, he's rigged the ballots," Dan said, shoving down another shot, arms braced over the table.

"We've still got four days," Adam said, flipping his shot glass over in his fingers.

"To kill Dorian Blake? Or to live?" Dan said, as if he were reading Adam's mind. They would only know which it was once it was done, when it was either his dead body or Blake's lying on a slab in the morgue.

"We're really pushing it, though, aren't we?" Carlos said. "I mean—we're right up against the wall now."

"We can't afford to fuck this up," Dan said.

Adam bit down on his tongue to keep from sounding too harsh when he snapped at Dan. "And do *you* have the will yet?" Still, he raised his brows accusingly.

"Point taken," Dan said. "It should be in by tomorrow afternoon."

"Results pending, two minutes."

Adam stared at the shot glass that he kept spinning in his fingers, his breath hitching as his racing thoughts dragged him down into a familiar pit of fear.

Paul's hand braced Adam's shoulder. An anchor. As if he'd known Adam was in need of one.

"Sssh, they're announcing the results!"

***

Dorian Blake won the election.

Adam knew he would. It didn't make the blow any less hard when it finally hit. Though it was all part of the new plan, it felt wrong to allow Dorian Blake to have the win.

It had been a difficult thing to watch play out on screen. As Blake's name was announced. As cheers erupted on the steps of City Hall. As he picked Mercedes up in his arms and twirled her into a kiss. Adam raged so hard upon seeing it that he shattered the glass in his hand, and could instantly feel his friends stiffen to keep their heads forward.

With a deep breath, Carlos said, "So, he really did it."

"Course he did," Dan snapped.

Adam's jaw tensed as he brushed away the glass shards before reaching for another and finishing the drink in one gulp.

They spent the next few hours at the bar, with the election footage still playing in the background, and reporters replaying highlights. That damned image of Blake twirling Mercedes into a kiss played enough times that Adam's eyes burned. Until the merciful bartender shut off the channel.

At about eleven PM, Adam took his cue to leave. "I'm going back to the room. I have some stuff I need to take care of." There was nothing warm in his tone as he headed for the front door.

He heard rather than saw Carlos jump up to try to follow him. Stopping dead in his tracks, Adam tensed.

"Don't," Paul said to Carlos.

"I left my sunglasses up there," Carlos said.

Laughing, Paul said, "You don't wanna go up there right now, man, trust me." When Adam heard the sounds of his friend pulling Carlos back down into the seat, he smiled.

***

"Oh God, I'm almost there," Mercedes said.

It was a perfect kind of torture, Adam had decided. Having her above him, moving on him while he was inside her.

He needed the hotel room to himself for the night because, as was becoming routine, this was the only time he could steal precious moments with her.

She sat on top of him, with his wrinkled navy sheets wrapped around her waist and her hands pressed against his chest. "Almost...almost..." she said.

He smiled lazily, like it was a dream, and all his wishes were coming true. He grabbed her hips to speed her momentum. Trying not to hold his breath, Adam groaned as she sped up.

He held one hand at the back of her waist while running his other rough, calloused palm up her belly to her breasts. Palming them for a moment, squeezing tightly, she moaned his name when his hand moved back to her hip.

"Please," was all she said through breathless, panting puffs. Her head was raised to the ceiling, eyes rolling back in her head, but still she smiled wide when his hands traveled south.

Her hands were thrashing, gripping his chest so tightly that it hurt as she drew nearer and nearer to orgasm. He moved his other hand to the center of her thighs, gently stroking her clit.

"*Fuck,*" she breathed. "Just like that."

Nails digging into his tattooed arm, she gripped him hard as she moaned her climax. He felt her pussy tighten on him, and he slid his hand from her thighs to turn her over and pin her beneath him.

Stroking her through the last throes, he moved his hips, holding himself in so he could at least take her to the end before he came inside her.

She was still breathing heavily as she whispered in his ear. "Don't hold back."

He laughed only a breath. "I don't want this to end."

"I'll take it as a challenge," she laughed. Digging her nails in farther, she arched her back off the bed, slightly raising her hips to let him in as deep as he could go. "Fuck me harder."

He still laughed, holding in a growl as he did as instructed, until he was going so hard, so fast, that he thought his whole body would explode along with him. He gripped her hand and held it over her head, interlocking their fingers.

Still thrusting, pinning her below him, he pressed his brow to hers, now watching her eyes closely. But the challenge had diminished from them, she was looking at him the way he always hoped she would. The way he'd missed so badly for five years. The look he feared he would never be lucky enough to ever see again.

And as if knowing what it would do, she kept her eyes on him as she said, "I love you."

That was all it took. He was over that edge, that incredible edge so quickly, groaning through his smiles as he finished coming.

Afterward, they held each other. Even daring to sleep in each other's arms as the night pressed on.

Later, after she'd barely awoken, her eyes still weary from sleep, Adam said, "Four days, baby."

The mattress buckled as she rolled to face him, his hand drawing lazy strokes up her bare thigh. "I know," she said. "Are we ready for this?"

"Dan says he'll have the will through tomorrow afternoon."

"And then we've got four days?"

"Four days to kill Dorian Blake."

"Fuck," she said. "That came around quick." She rolled onto her back to stare at the ceiling as he moved his hand from her thigh to her belly.

"Are you ready?" he asked.

"Of course," she said, nodding too hard to be truthful, and gulping slightly.

He brushed the hairs out of her eyes and then gently stroked her face. "You don't have to lie to me."

She nodded nervously again. "Yeah, of course, I'm ready," she said. "It's just nerve-wracking, you know? Last time we tried this you died, so let's not let that happen again."

"Hey," he said, pulling her chin toward him. "We'll make it this time."

"Yeah." She kissed him softly. "I think we will." She went in for another kiss but stopped herself, scrunching her brow. "Are you not nervous?"

He pulled away to look down to his chest. "Fucking nervous," he said. "But I just have to remember why we need to do this, and what we're capable of."

He turned his head to smile at her and she returned it with a dreamy one of her own. Like they both knew this was the part where their dreams came true.

"What time is it?" she asked.

"Almost one AM."

"I don't need to be back until two," she said, a bit deviously.

He smirked at her suggestion. "Good."

Her rumbling laugh was more beautiful than a thousand symphonies as he pounced onto her again, pushing her legs apart and taking her in, not sure he could ever stop.

***

"This better be good, T.B.," Dorian said, fanning himself with his shirt.

Parked across the road from the Tropics Hotel, T.B. and Dorian had been stuck in the van since eleven thirty, over an hour ago, just staring at the same building. They drove a deep blue van, not their usual limos, to blend in on this side of town. Unfortunately, in the vehicle T.B. had chosen, the air conditioning was out of order, which left Dorian's temper rising faster than usual as they melted in the van.

"Sources tell me this is where Adam Vandemilio has been hiding out," T.B. replied, drumming his hands on the wheel.

They sat in silence for a while longer, until it was nearing two. Like a spoiled, angry child, Dorian huffed in the passenger heat. "How much longer?"

"A few more minutes." T.B. looked like he was holding in a scream.

Dorian had just sucked in an air of breath, readying for an onslaught of complaining, when the front door to the Tropics Hotel swung open, and Adam Vandemilio stepped out onto the street.

"I fucking told you," T.B. said. "There he is."

A taxi parked directly in front of the hotel, half blocking the view, so he had to crane his neck to see. But there it was, clear as fucking crystal. Adam Vandemilio strode down the steps onto the street in nothing but gray sweatpants and a shirt that hung open at the front. So lazy, so casual, much more relaxed than he should've been.

"What is he doing?" Dorian shifted in his seat.

Adam was talking to someone.

"There's someone with him...a woman." T.B. scrunched his nose.

The leggy blonde had her back turned. Dorian let out a low chuckle when Adam wrapped his arm around the girl's waist and leaned in for a kiss. "So, he's got a girl. Interesting."

Well, fuck, these two were really going for it. They threw themselves together for a kiss so passionate that it looked like they were seconds away from heading back upstairs.

T.B. secured a pair of binoculars from the glove compartment.

"Good." Dorian chuckled again. "A woman means a weakness."

T.B. kept squinting through the binoculars like he was trying to place something. But Dorian didn't give a shit. He had Vandemilio, and he had a fucking target.

"Oh, *shit.*"

"What?" Dorian said.

T.B.'s fingers were fumbling with the binoculars when Dorian snatched them from his hands. "Give them here."

Adam's girl kissed him hard, running her hands down his chest to fiddle with the waistband on his pants. But when she turned, she flicked her hair from her face. Enough to showcase exactly who she was.

What. The. Actual. *Fuck?!*

Though she was walking away, she kept her eyes locked on Adam until the last possible second. Emotions written all over her face like they'd put themselves on display for the day.

Rage bubbled through Dorian like an overflowing pot, water burning as it hit the flame. That look on her face. It was one Dorian had never seen her give before. Certainly one she'd never given him.

She was in love.

Fucking bitch.

***

Tonight was the night.

Three days ago, Dorian Blake won the election. Tomorrow, he'd be sworn in as mayor. They had waited until the very last second. Now they had to deliver, or die trying.

The door to Adam's hotel room was wide open, a bustle of chaos and voices as those who joined his side fluttered in and out preparing for the kill. Paul and Carlos were already inside, bossing around their people and coordinating movements, with Adam watching.

"Take these." Carlos handed over a large duffle to one of the men. "I don't want to leave these here." The man took the duffle bag and helped himself out of the room.

Dan burst through the door, almost bumping into some of Paul's people who were carrying weapons downstairs.

"Got it!" Dan announced as he stumbled through the door, waving a file folder in his hand.

"About time." Adam approached him, arms folded. "These are well overdue."

"I know," Dan said. "Access issues, obviously. But they're here now."

Accepting the will and estate documents, Adam opened them carefully, reading the files line by line before raising his eyebrows at Dan. "Do you think these will hold up? Especially given the timing?"

"They're solid," Dan said.

A tap on Dan's shoulder had him being lured away. "Where can I take these?" The man asking after Dan was holding a large box of files.

"What are they?" Dan asked.

The man looked down into the box. "I think working documents for the girls."

Dan nodded and walked away with the man, directing him to the door.

Adam missed the last part of the conversation as he left Dan to it. There were too many people rushing around in the small space that he had to duck and weave just to make it the few steps to his bedside table where the phone was.

Holding the phone, he hesitated once before dialing. Their plan was close, but he was nervous. No more stalling. Just time to take his shot. The finality of it all had him hiding his trembling hands.

He held the phone to his ear as it rang.

"Hello?"

"Ready for tonight, baby?" Adam said.

"As I'll ever be," she said.

"Look, we're all over here putting on the final touches. You should get back here."

"It's early," she said. "Dorian expects me at the ball."

"Then stay here right up until you have to go back. I don't like the idea of you being there alone while all this is going on."

He heard her laugh, and the trembling in his hands stopped. "Didn't I tell you to stop trying to save me?"

"Can't help it. Will you come?" He smiled.

"Sure, I'll come right over."

Adam hung up and cast a look over his shoulder. His friends were herding the last of their people out of the room, having offloaded all the weapons, supplies, and files that they could before taking one last stand against Dorian Blake.

Once everyone was out, Paul shut the door and leaned his head against it with his eyes closed. Left alone, it was just Adam, Dan, Paul, and Carlos. Walking in a strange kind of unison, they came together in a circle around the dining room table. Though they all hung their heads, they weren't unhappy.

"Tonight's the night," Adam said.

"Tonight's the night," Paul smiled back.

"Have you all briefed your people?" Adam asked.

"Everyone knows what to do," Carlos said. "Blake won't see it coming."

"There's only one thing left to do, then," Adam said. He went to the kitchen where he opened one of the top cupboards and pulled down a bottle of whiskey with five glasses. Placing the glasses on the table, he poured five fresh drinks.

"When the whole team is back here, we'll toast, and we'll relax, and just have fun. Because tonight, everything will change."

***

Mercedes walked down the front stone steps of the mansion. While she knew Adam thought it was a risk for her to be on her own, she felt the bigger risk was running off when they were so close to finishing their plans.

But still, she'd agreed to come, and headed straight for the front driveway thinking she had a clear shot through the front gates. Dorian wasn't expected home for hours.

Out of nowhere, she heard the sudden rumble of cars approaching.

She was only a few steps from her car, but Dorian's limo was already pulling up to block her path. She looked down at her clothes: black lace bralette and leather pants.

"Fuck," she said. But with no time to change, she just had to go with it. She pulled her skull and crossbones earrings from her ears and stuffed them into her bra. She wondered if that was maybe a poor choice when the metal hooks cut into her skin.

Nothing could be done about the rest of her outfit, so unfit for a First Lady, so she did her best not to tense to keep him from sensing the change in her.

Dorian was out of the limo first.

"Home early today, darling?" she said as she kissed him on the cheek.

"Take a ride with me." Dorian smiled and held out his hand.

She was now surrounded, with Dorian's associates flanking her from every possible angle. The only clear path was at the end of Dorian's outstretched hand. Surely she was just being paranoid. She took his hand.

He guided her into the limo, securing the door behind her, and she noticed with no small amount of suspicion that he locked the door on the outside.

Inside the limo, T.B. was across from her, turned to his side. He relaxed against the leather with a casual grace, but the tension in his shoulders was giving him away. She put up her own guard, too, and listened as Dorian trekked behind the car and joined her from the opposite door, sliding into the spot next to her.

Nobody said anything as the car jolted to a start and began to move.

"Where are we going?" she asked.

"Be patient," Dorian said. "It's a surprise." He didn't look at her. He just rubbed at his chin, keeping his dead eyes locked forward.

She squinted as she took in T.B. rubbing his fingers together in his other hand. It was like he was trying to rub the sweat from them.

She knew she was in for trouble, then. What kind, though, that remained to be seen.

They drove for fifteen minutes in complete silence, with Dorian refusing to look over at her, and T.B. aching to keep still but failing miserably.

"What's going on, honey?" she asked again, dropping her voice lower. Accusatory this time.

Dorian's jaw tensed, stretching like he was grinding his teeth.

"You're acting strange, my love," Mercedes said. "Is something wrong?"

He licked his lips, as if he were wiping away words that tried to escape his mouth.

"We haven't gone off the rails by any chance, have we?" Mercedes smiled. "You're looking extra insane today, darling."

T.B. looked at her with wide eyes, as if he were compelling her to shut her goddamn mouth.

To both of their surprise, judging from T.B.'s face, Dorian laughed. Starting softly at first, but growing more manic with each breath. The longer it went on, the harder he laughed and the bigger his eyes bulged with rage.

"Do it," Dorian said.

Before she could blink, T.B. snapped into action. Taking her completely by surprise, he whipped out a set of handcuffs and locked them against her wrists.

"What the fuck?!" she yelled, falling back in her seat.

Dorian dove across her until he was breathing in her face. "You think you can go around fucking Adam Vandemilio and I wouldn't find out about it!"

Well, shit. Trouble it was. But much bigger than she expected.

Mercedes shifted in her seat, pushing back into the leather. He had found her out. All these years of hiding, being in control, and just as she was about to take him down, he had found her out.

But... but... *Fucking* Adam Vandemilio. Those were the words he'd used. He knew she was sleeping with Adam. He found out *one* of her secrets. But had he discovered her biggest one?

Mercedes smiled. "So, you know."

"*Shut up*," T.B. warned her. If she didn't know better, she might have thought he was trying to help her by compelling her to stop.

"But *how much* do you know?" Mercedes laughed.

Dorian's face was rancid with aggression as he slowly turned to face her. Spit licked at his teeth like a rabid animal. He looked at her like he didn't recognize her, shock practically pouring out of his gaping mouth.

"Clearly not much–"

"Shut your fucking mouth!" Dorian said. "You stupid bitch."

She laughed even harder.

T.B. started chewing on his lip like he was actually afraid. His eyes bore into her. If there was a question in them, it seemed like it would be him wondering why she thought she had the upper hand.

She licked her lips, looking down from T.B.'s eyes to his neck. She leaned in close to whisper sweetly. "I wonder if your throat would slit as easily as Antonio's did. Nice and fine like butter." Then she gave him a vicious, feline-like grin.

"What the fuck?" Dorian said, a new kind of fear revealing itself in his eyes.

"You... you." T.B. looked like he was about to vomit in his hands. "You killed Antonio."

Mercedes ran her tongue over her front teeth, looking back and forth between the two of them. Dorian refused her gaze, but T.B. had gone pale as he stared right at her.

She looked out the window to see they were headed to the outskirts of town along the industrial district. He was taking her to one of his factories. Which meant she didn't have very long to live. Which *also* meant she didn't have very much to lose.

There was one card she could play to regain the upper hand. And it was for a moment like this that they had kept that card so close to their chests for all these years.

"Five guys," she said. She felt the electricity drain from the air, replaced by a silence so quiet it felt like world had pressed the mute button.

Turning to Dorian, she gave him a look that could turn enemies to stone. A look that was truly evil. She didn't break his gaze as she said again. "There was *always* five guys."

From the look on his face, she'd hit where she wanted.

"You?" Dorian's voice was low, like he was whispering words that shouldn't be spoken.

Mercedes smiled and laughed again.

"It was *you*. This whole fucking time?!"

T.B. shook his head furiously, presumably fighting back the urge to regurgitate his breakfast.

Mercedes laughed once more, like it was truly amusing, before bowing her head and turning to look at Dorian through lowered brows. She felt psychopathic, and hoped she looked it, too. "T.B. is a good driver. He's real fast. But, well..." She gritted her teeth as she went wide-eyed and growled inches from Dorian's face. "He can't drive half as well as I can, *honey*."

CHAPTER 25
UNDERRATED

She couldn't see it, but she could feel it as Dorian cuffed her to a pipe. With her face covered in cloth, she could only use her other senses to recognize that it was his delicate, callous-free hands that pushed her in place. She sat down on her heels as her outstretched arms hugged the metal shaft of the pipe.

When the cloth was ripped off and the brightness glittered in, she took in her surroundings. The room was cold, freezing even, with concrete floors and walls lit by hanging fluorescent lights. Possibly a cold storage facility. There was only one exit, a metal latch-locked door with a small square window. T.B. was right in front of her, snarling while Dorian leaned against the door with a guard at his side.

T.B. tightened the cuffs until they dug into her skin. She fought back her wince at the pain and blew the hair from her eyes to face them down.

"So you're the fifth? You're Adam's elusive driver?" Dorian said.

She nodded and smiled at him as if to say: *Come on, darling, get closer. I dare you.*

"I don't fucking believe it," T.B. said. "No way this tiny bitch could outdrive me."

"You never sensed a little animosity between us, sweets? Hint, it's because you know deep down I whip your ass every chance I get."

T.B. turned a shoulder to whisper to Dorian. "I still don't fucking believe it."

Fingers drumming along his bicep from crossed arms, Dorian frowned. Was there indecision running through his head? Could he not decide whether he believed her, or could he not decide what her punishment should be?

"You're fucking Adam Vandemilio."

It wasn't a question. Still, she chuckled. "Well, darling, I had to get mine somewhere. You could never make me come, could you?"

She swore T.B. blanched before he shook his head.

Dorian dove across the room so fast she barely had time to prepare for his slap. The force of his blow cut her lip. Licking her mouth and tasting her own blood like it was a delicacy, she said, "You can hit harder than that, honey. Come on, I like it rough. Just ask Adam."

His thoughts were written all over his face as he stepped back with wide eyes while he steadied himself. It took an encouraging nod from T.B. before Dorian straightened his suit jacket and turned to her again.

"How long has this been going on?"

"Long before you."

She looked at his throat as if she could visualize the knife slicing through his flesh. He must've seen her delicious brand of crazy because, in return, he walked over and hit her again. He drew more blood, this time from her cheek.

"Shall we say hello to your lover? No? How about goodbye then." That low voice that was filled with sweetness, but laced with venom, was suddenly back.

She stiffened, watching as Dorian was delivered a cordless phone on a silver platter. Dorian dialed and made a call. While Dorian was distracted making his call, with the door wide open, she took the opportunity to peer at what lay beyond it. A clinical white hallway with no discernible exit. That would make her escape interesting.

Without warning, Dorian shoved the phone into her face. She didn't have to ask who was on the other end.

"Baby," she said, through heavy breaths.

"Oh, baby," Adam said. "Just hold on. I'm gonna come for you."

Their affectionate words only made Dorian twist even further into rage, his teeth baring as if he might rip out her throat. But when Adam said he'd come for her, she noticed a flicker of satisfaction in his horrible eyes.

Satisfaction she'd never let him have.

Dorian could try, but she wouldn't let him lure Adam to her. Wouldn't let him abandon their plan. If they were going to take down Dorian Blake, it had to be now. She had told him many times not to save her, and even against these circumstances, she had to find a way to make sure that he didn't try. So that he could finish what they started.

"The prize," she said.

"What?" His voice was high-pitched and pained. He understood exactly what she was asking.

"Eyes on the prize at all times."

Before she could say another word of warning, Dorian snatched the phone away, and finished his conversation with Adam out of earshot. When he returned, he still clutched the phone, his hand blocking the speaker.

"He really loves you," Dorian scoffed.

Her eyes shuttered as she shrugged. Dorian still clutched the phone.

"Tell me, really," Dorian said. "Why him?"

Mercedes met his eyes and found an almost sincere pain behind them. There was hurt there, hidden behind a fine sheath of rage. No part of what they had was real, but this had only begun because Dorian had always wanted her. Loved her in the way only someone incapable of love knew how.

"It's always been him," Mercedes whispered. The only truth she had ever told her husband-to-be.

Dorian gave her his back. When he turned around, all sincerity of their conversation was lost, and the game was back on.

"Too bad, then, because he's already dead." He pressed his thumb onto the pad of the phone.

There was a little click. Then crashing. Banging. Exploding? The line went dead amidst a scream.

"What did you just do?" Mercedes felt the blood rush away from her limbs, making her entire body go cold. "What did you just fucking do?!"

Her hands were suddenly slick with sweat. There was no way that he got her friends. Right?!

"You're so proud of being the fifth one, how about being the only one alive?" Dorian laughed.

"No, you—you fucking—you couldn't have," Mercedes shook her head, her face hard beneath traitorous tears.

She let them fall. Dorian was always one step ahead. But surely not of this. Not of this! He couldn't possibly even know where Adam's hideouts were...

But how did he get Adam's number?

"If you've so much as touched a hair–" Mercedes screamed so violently that the building nearly shook, "–on the heads of the people I love, then I–"

"Shut the fuck up!" Dorian screamed back, rubbing his hands across his face. "I fucking loved you. I fucking gave–"

"You didn't love me! I'm nothing but a trophy to you." He frowned, watching as she settled her voice. "I'm a fucking collectible to you. You're not capable of loving anyone other than yourself."

It was T.B. who stared at the floor like he couldn't bear to look. Like she was undeniably right. Dorian didn't even blink.

"If you really loved me, it wouldn't be so easy to do what you're about to do," she said, raising one brow.

"You're absolutely right," Dorian said finally. But he didn't smile. Without breaking her eye contact, he said to the guard, "Kill her."

His eyes narrowed like he'd been expecting a reaction. A flinch, at least. Some show of fear. But she wasn't afraid.

"Give me thirty minutes to get back to the house, then shoot her in her pretty little head."

T.B. and the guard piled out of the room. Dorian made to follow them, but turned back to say over his shoulder, looking truly as if this would be the last time they ever saw each other. "Goodbye, darling. You would've made a wonderful First Lady."

***

"Something doesn't feel right," Adam said. "Mercedes should've been here hours ago."

The five drinks that Adam poured remained untouched, littered between their guns, ammunition, and body armor.

"She probably just got held up," Paul said.

"I don't know, her phone line at the mansion keeps ringing," Carlos said as he hung up the landline near Adam's bed.

"She would've left right after your call..." Dan said, a hint of panic lacing his words.

"God, I can't–" Adam threw some papers across the room. "If he's done something to hurt her..."

Just as he finished speaking, the phone rang. He raced to answer, shoving Carlos aside mindlessly.

"Baby?!"

"Not quite..."

Adam blinked at that voice.

Every instinct told him to cry and panic and flee. He closed his eyes once, allowing only one second before he hardened his heart and opened his eyes, ready for a fight.

"You," Adam said, his tone so rough it could've shaved wood. He dragged the phone to the dining table, placing it down where his friends gathered. "What the fuck do you want?"

"I have something you might want."

Adam dropped his head to the edge of the table, his heart sinking faster than he could catch.

"I warned you that I'd find your fifth," Blake said. "Not quite who I expected."

With a deep inhale, Adam straightened again, finding that hard place inside himself. With an uncharacteristic calm, he said, "If you fucking hurt–"

"Oh, I'm gonna fucking kill her."

Her. Fuck. He did know.

Adam clenched his fists as he placed the phone on mute. It took more than one calming breath before he could speak again. He looked at his friends. "Blake knows this number."

It was all he needed to say.

"How many people did we have walk through this room today?" Paul leaned across the table, eyes darting around the room.

"Check the fucking room," Adam said.

He unmuted the phone. "Let me talk to her. You've got nothing. I won't believe it until I hear it." But he was only saying so to buy himself more time. His body had known something was wrong the minute she didn't show up on time.

The phone rustled like it was being passed around.

Over his shoulder he checked on Paul, Dan, and Carlos, who were ripping through the room. They searched high and low, throwing cushions off the couch, ripping sheets from the bed, tearing everything out of the cupboards.

"Baby." Mercedes voice came through the phone, her breath tough and heavy.

"Oh, baby," Adam sighed. "Just hold on. I'm gonna come for you."

There was silence on the other end of the line for long enough that he started to panic. But then she spoke again. "The prize," she said.

"What?" his voice was high-pitched and pained. He knew exactly what the next words to come out of her mouth would be, and what they'd mean, but he didn't have time to argue as Carlos waved for his attention.

Adam found Dan and Paul standing still, looking to where Carlos had removed a painting to reveal an explosive device strapped to the wall.

Fuck.

Paul turned to the wall behind him, removing another painting. Dan did, too, and sure enough, paintings in their trembling hands, they found more explosives hugging the wall.

"Eyes on the prize at all times," Mercedes said, jolting Adam back to reality. *No*, he wanted to shout. He was about to when the rustling line told him that he wouldn't be speaking to her anytime soon. He waved a signal at the others. *Get the hell out of here now.*

Blake was back on the line again. "Alright, there you go. I've got her and she's alive. But not for much longer. Just wanted you to know I won't make it quick."

His friends bustled past him, collecting supplies, guns, ammo, anything they could carry before they disappeared down the stairs.

"I'm gonna fucking get to her, you know." Adam rushed to his bed and pulled the radio from his drawer. Placing the receiver at the base of the phone, he held another to his chest and followed his friends out of the building, flipping on the fire alarm as he rushed out.

"This is the end of the line for you, I'm afraid," Blake laughed, Adam's radio picking up the signal from the phone inside his room.

"Not a chance in hell," Adam said.

Other occupants flooded the stairwell beside him. He joined the crowd that burst through the glass front doors onto the street.

The phone rustled again through the radio while he found his friends across the road at the edge of the beach. He stared up at his room from a safe distance.

The farther he went, the more ruffled the radio became. He was almost out of range.

"He really loves you...Tell me, really...It's always been him...Too bad he's already dead."

The click of the receiver didn't even faze him. He heard the trigger press and didn't balk as he watched his room explode into the skies. All that remained was a mass of orange pouring out into the open air and brightening the night sky. The explosion leaving the whole hotel incinerated to a crisp, so that only a pit of black remained.

If Adam's heart hadn't been thundering in his chest, he might have smiled. The call from Blake may as well have been a warning. What a fucking idiot. Adam would savor every minute of his death.

"Fucking hell," Dan said.

"He really likes to burn things down, doesn't he?" Carlos said, eyes wide with marvel.

"Fucking pyromaniac," Dan laughed, wrapping his arm around Carlos' shoulder and jostling him.

"Well, you wanted the element of surprise," Paul said. "Nothing more surprising than coming back from the dead."

"Again," Carlos added with a laugh.

Adam pinched his brow. He had known that today would be one of the hardest of his life. He'd expected trouble, obstacles even, but not that Dorian would get such a firm upper hand.

Paul frowned at him. "So, what now? We going after her?"

The words he had to say nearly cleaved his chest in two. He couldn't look Paul in the eye as he said it. "No...no, we're going after Blake."

Paul clenched his fists while Dan and Carlos paled.

"This changes things, but she doesn't want us coming after her," Adam said. "And she's right."

Adam stared at his feet, his jaw tightening. People scrambled up the beach to get away from the fire as sirens signaled in the background.

"Tomorrow Dorian Blake gets sworn in as mayor. And then he'll be too powerful to ever stop. We only have one night, one shot to kill him, and it has to be now," Adam said.

For his team, Adam knew that he had to pull it together. God, that woman was going to be the death of him. He'd get to her. He had to. But not before he finished this.

"The best way to find her is to find Blake first," Adam said.

Paul looked skyward, like he was praying for the strength not to kill Adam. Then he nodded. Just once. Only slightly.

Adam took two more breaths, pushing deep puffs of air that cleared all pain from his throat, pushed all fear out of his lungs. He growled as he slapped himself in the face and jumped on the spot, hardening until there was nothing left but the face of a monster. The face of vengeance and death. He looked up at his friends, and found them twitching at the sight of him. "Let's go fucking kill Dorian Blake!"

***

Mercedes was left alone, hands still cuffed together around the pipe. The only light being the harsh flickering fluorescents above. Without windows, and therefore no way to tell by the sun, she wasn't sure how much time had passed. But it had to be close to thirty minutes.

Any second now, some unnamed dick would waltz through the door and shoot her dead without a second thought.

Regardless of whether Adam and her friends were still alive, which she had to believe in every fiber of her being that they were, she had told them not to come for her. Right now, she only had herself. And she'd be damned if some unnamed lowlife would be the one to wipe her from the world.

It was time to bust the fuck out.

"I knew you'd come in handy." She twisted her wrists and pushed her chest forward to reach into her bra, where her skull and crossbones earrings were still poking into her skin. They'd taken her knives and guns, but even Dorian hadn't counted on the earrings stashed between her breasts.

The tip of the metal clasp was just sturdy enough to poke into the lock of her handcuffs. She wriggled the earring in the lock, pushing, pushing... until it finally snapped free, and the cuffs fell to the floor.

They really shouldn't make it so fucking easy.

She rose to her feet.

Being free was one thing, but she was still without a weapon. Pacing the room, she studied the pipe she'd been cuffed to. It ran from the ground up to the wall and across the ceiling of the enclosed space. It was rusted with age and joined in the middle by two sections.

That would do.

She stood beneath the pipe and jumped, grasping it with both hands and hanging from the ceiling. Swinging back and forth, she clenched her jaw, working all her muscles to pull the rusty pipe out of the roof.

With a snap, the pipe, and her along with it, came crashing to the floor. Standing, she tossed the new weapon in her hands, testing it and wielding it like a baton.

She had to get to Dorian Blake in time to kill him. No time to sneak around, this was permission to make a really big mess.

She smacked the rusted metal pipe against the wall, a commotion to draw attention. To make them investigate the noise.

Slowly, the latch unhooked.

With a bang, she smashed the door open with her foot.

The two guards who had tried to push through the door stood gawking, but quickly raised their guns. She hit the first over the head with the pipe, and kicked the gun from the other's hands, sending it flying into the air above. With another swift hit, she knocked out the second guard just in time to grab the gun as it fell.

There was only enough time to lock, load, and slide against white tile, ducking behind a storage crate for cover before the halls filled with guards. Before alarms sounded, emergency lights bathing the compound in a blue tinge.

She shot. One shot, two shots, then three. Three guards dead in an instant as more piled into the hall to stop her.

This was always the fun part. She'd waited her whole life for the opportunity to showcase exactly what she could do. That's what this was to her. Not a fearsome fight to her death. An opportunity.

She made a run into the hall.

Running directly down the corridor, she raised her gun, only stopping to steady her shoulder against her shots, and taking out guards that appeared from closed doors lining the walls. Pipe still in her hand, she shot with her right, and swung with her left.

She was only walking, not bothering to run, when she rounded the next corner. She dodged the swipe of a knife and kicked the guy down. Kept walking. Smacked another over the face with the pipe. Kept walking.

Suddenly, someone got the jump on her, grabbing her throat and pushing her against the wall to strangle her. She only grinned as his hands tightened. Over his shoulder, more guards approached. How reckless of him to think he could take her down with just hands.

Reaching to his face, she steadied her hands on his head, and before he could think, she snapped his neck cold. She readied her gun in her right hand, and held the dead guard in front with her left, sinking down the wall as his body took all the shots that were meant for her. Her human shield.

She was drenched in blood, none of it hers. Mercedes threw the dead guard away and emptied her magazine into the enemies at her front. All of them headshots. All of the bodies hanging in mid-air like they were suspended in shock before they fell dead.

She didn't bother to wipe the blood from her face, or tidy herself even a little, as she bolted into a run down the hallway, rounding a corner right into the path of six more.

The first one blinked, stopping dead as she ran at him. She dove feet first to slide between his legs until she was crouching behind him. A quick lift of her gun, another headshot. She twisted on her knees to turn, still crouching, another headshot. Another body slamming to the floor.

Sliding along the floor again, she found herself standing center in a pack of four enemies. Good.

She dodged one punch from the left, another from the right, then jerked her elbow backward, slamming it into the face of the guard behind before pushing it forward and punching the one at her front.

Whirling, she punched again. Then she was on the floor, sweeping out the legs of the guard on her right, and lifting her foot up to kick the face of the guard at her back.

Back on her feet, she took knife slashes all across her arms, one narrowly missing her neck, but she could barely feel it. Until the guy on the left pointed his gun. She grabbed the barrel before he could act, taking control. With him pushing at her back, she shot two of his friends and then finished him with an elbow to his throat. The last one dove at her, but not before she grabbed his head and snapped his neck in mid-air. He fell dead as she stepped aside.

Out of ammo, she pushed ahead with nothing but her bare hands. The end of the hallway greeted her with plastic strip paneling.

Pushing it open, she entered a large open area, like an industrial floor. The ceiling was at least three stories high, with giant open windows running along the third floor. The night sky shone through. More time had passed than she thought. She had to hurry.

Voices at the other end of the floor showed her the exit. She ducked into a crawl, hiding behind metallic benches. They hadn't spotted her yet.

Four guys waited to attack her. Child's play. Absolute child's play. She'd managed to do what she did from the shadows for seven years. Did they really think they could escape her when she didn't have to hide?

She was about to rush ahead without a weapon when she spotted footsteps at her left. A fifth guy she hadn't seen. Still undercover, she grabbed him, placing her hand over his mouth to silence his death before she snapped his neck.

Attached to his belt was a set of knives that glittered in the moonlight.

Fucking perfect.

In a matter of moments, she was up again, rushing forward to the surprise of the guards. She threw a knife ahead of her, slamming into one of their chests. Ducking to avoid the return fire, she tuck-rolled along the floor, and as she returned upright she used the momentum to throw another knife into a guy's head.

With a knife in each hand, she got to her feet, and threw them at the same time. One to her left, and one to her right, slamming with force into the guards that ran at her from the side.

She exited the large room, able to see the door to the parking lot. In front of it stood the last group of guards whom she would have to kill in order to make her way out.

"Where did she go?"

She snuck through the strip panels and hid behind a corner.

"Fucking stay alert! This chick is crazy."

Her body warmed in elation. They were afraid. As she knew they would be when they finally realized what she could do. She left her cover to run.

The next moments felt like they were in slow motion as the guards realized she was barreling toward them. Swirling to the left, she took a bullet graze to the arm, before she unsheathed a knife and slammed it into the chest of the nearest guard, holding him still as she stabbed him and left the knife behind.

Then she was right in the middle of them all. She kicked, punched, and slashed to keep them away, ducking to dodge bullets and taking more hits herself. But she relished the pain, it gave her strength.

A kick to the face and one was down. Another hit and she grabbed one of her knives to viciously stab another. The last went to raise his gun, but she punched his elbow until he released his gun into her other waiting hand, and she shot him once in the face.

Then there was only silence.

The silence of victory as she stood alone. Not a whisper, let alone a shout, as every single person but her laid dead. When she brushed her hair back from her face, her hand coated her hair in blood. A quick look down at herself confirmed she was a mess of injuries. She could already feel her cheeks swelling with inevitable bruises, clothes torn and her body bleeding from cuts and grazed bullets.

She pushed through the exit into the refreshing chill of night air. Sucking in a breath, she savored the feeling. Of the air coating her lungs. Of the blood coating her hands. She was a killer. A winner. A victor. Nothing could stop her. Never would she back down. Never would she know defeat.

And Dorian Blake should be shaking in his boots. Because now she was coming for *him*.

She had just started her walk to find a car when two deafening cracks sounded from behind her. When her back shot up straight, the wind was knocked right out of her. She froze, eyes widening as she looked down at her body.

Her chest was suddenly cold. The night air was no longer refreshing, but deadly chilled. She pressed her hands to her stomach. Two gaping holes had opened up, one in her shoulder and the other at her hip. The blood that coated her was fresh. It was warm. It was her own.

Gasping for air, she dropped onto the pavement, hitting her skull as she landed.

Why couldn't she feel anything? It should hurt, shouldn't it?

Her fingers twitched beside her, stroking the pool of her own blood that was already leeching beside her.

A shadow appeared over her head. She saw the barrel of a gun before she saw the man who was holding it.

"T.B.," she rasped. Her throat suddenly dry. Her tongue sticking to her cheek. She heaved blood out of her mouth looking up at him. "You... shot me—motherfucker."

The world was beating in and out. The edges of her vision getting blurry, and though she was sure T.B. was right in her face, he seemed a million miles away. His voice barely audible.

"I had to make sure the job was done," T.B. said.

She looked up at the moon, but it, too, seemed to be only a cold gray blob that started blending into the sky.

This was it.

This was where her story would come to an end.

T.B. leveled the gun in her direction.

The last thought she had before she died was of Adam. *Finish this for me, baby.*

One sharp pain and the world went black.

CHAPTER 26
FIVE YEARS OF PLANNING

The waters were calm, but a soft nightly breeze left Adam's boat rocking in the river. He could clearly see the beautifully lit Burke Street mansion, a beacon glowing against the darkness of the night.

His nerves were shredding him. Every facet of his inner voice was screaming at him to go after her. Back in the day, he would've tried to. And likely failed. As he would this time if he deviated from his plan. He would gladly lay down his own life, but could never ask his friends to do the same. Not after everything they'd already given up.

Keep going. Kill Dorian Blake.

"We ready for this?" he said into his radio.

"As we'll ever be." Carlos's reply buzzed through a moment later.

"Remember, get in, stay low, find Blake. He'll probably be covered by T.B."

Adam watched through binoculars as Dan and Carlos, both dressed in black tie, approached the front doors of the mansion. Their pseudonyms were on the list for the evening.

The two guards working the door smirked and then let Dan and Carlos in without incident. They were all on Adam's payroll, after all. In fact, most of the people whom Blake had let in his keep worked for Adam. Drawing all of his wolves into Blake's den.

"Paul?" Adam said into his radio.

"Heading up now."

Adam bore the binoculars again and noted the back dock where Paul was walking up the steps from the river. Also dressed in black tie, he snuck into the party, carrying weapons to disperse to their crew once he was inside.

"I'm in. Just you now, man," Paul said.

"On my way."

Adam had only just started the boat to head for the back dock himself when several guests made their way to the pool area. None of them on his payroll, but dedicated Blake associates. It would be too many for him to take out without drawing attention.

"Too many guards out the back now," Adam buzzed through the radio. "Plan B—I'm coming through upstairs."

Veering the boat southward, Adam glided along the river until he found a patch of dry land to anchor and park, jumping straight to the grass above.

A five-minute jog later, he was staring at the mansion wall, vastly open and vulnerable from where he approached. There was only one man guarding it. Blake's resources must have been stretched very thin.

The openness of the terrain left him no choice but to approach from the front. Stumbling like a drunk as cover, he moved ahead, though the guard still put a weary hand on his weapon.

It was only when he was close enough that Adam dropped the act, kneeing the guard before exacting a knockout punch.

Adam threw his guns over the fence and scaled the wall, landing in the middle of the hedge maze. He navigated the maze, used the trellis to scale the house wall, like he'd done countless times before, and made his way to the window. He pushed it open and landed himself right in the middle of Mercedes's bedroom.

They were inside.

The end had arrived.

***

The party was held in the grand ballroom. Overlooking the pool deck, the white French doors had been opened in full to let the night air in.

The floor itself was simple, sand-colored tiles and decadent crystal chandeliers hanging overhead with a tight balcony overlook wrapping around the interior perimeter.

Throughout, several pop-up bars had been placed. It was there that Paul sat with Dan and Carlos, keeping their backs to the crowd and their heads down.

"You counting?" Paul asked when he saw Dan's head bobbing along the room.

"Yeah," Dan said. "Dead even. Half the people in this room still work for Blake, the other half work for us. He just doesn't know it yet."

"In for a big fight then?" Carlos asked.

"Let's hope not," Paul said. "I'm going to go and get a vantage point."

The plan was originally much more grand. Mercedes would get Blake in position. Adam would sneak into the party. At a dramatic-enough interval for his arrogant friend, Adam would announce that half the room had turned on Blake. Then finish him in front of anyone who dared to stay. So that everyone would know it was Adam Vandemilio who killed Dorian Blake.

Paul shook his head at the thought.

That wasn't the plan anymore. They now needed to finish this fast. Paul needed to finish it fast. He'd snipe from the balcony before Blake could take a second thought. His friends would haul T.B. off and torture him until he gave up Mercedes's location.

Because that's what the priority was now. Finish it. Kill Dorian Blake fast. Before she ran out of time.

Paul took his drink and headed to the upstairs balcony that overlooked the ballroom. Glancing down on his friends, Dan and Carlos remained seated at the bar sipping their drinks and hiding their faces. Waiting to pounce when Paul finally made his move.

He found a darkened corner and secured his gun to the rim of the railing. The room was lit poorly, relying on twinkling fairy lights, perfect in that nobody could see a sniper waiting in the wings.

"You see that?" Dan buzzed into the radio.

"I see it," Paul confirmed. Blake had entered the party from the main foyer and veered straight into the open crowd toward the officials from City Hall.

T.B. wasn't with him yet. He needed to be close if they were going to grab him.

"Adam, you in?" Paul said. Silence. "Adam?"

"Yeah, I'm just…looking around," he said.

"He wouldn't hold her here, man, you know that," Carlos said.

"I—yeah, I know. Doesn't hurt to check."

"Get down here, Blake's just come in," Paul said.

After a few moments, Paul saw Adam appear from one of the side doors, straightening the lapels of his suit jacket. Adam slipped into the party and moved across the room from Dan and Carlos.

"T.B. incoming," Dan said.

Sure enough, T.B. entered from another side door, looking like he'd been through all manner of hell. He straightened his hair as he approached Blake. The two shared a curt nod, and Dorian smiled. T.B. whispered something in the boss's ear that seemed to please them both even more.

"You got a clear shot?" Adam's voice came through like the ragged edge of a knife. He'd taken the most evident assumption for T.B.'s interaction obviously—meaning bad news for Mercedes.

"Almost," Paul said, angling his rifle around the City Hall officials. He had to hurry. "Just need the crowd to dissipate a bit."

His positioning gave Paul a bird's eye view from above. A waiter crossed Adam's path, and he snatched a glass of champagne. Stalking to the center of the room with his head low, Adam moved as close to Blake as he could get without raising suspicion, and silently smashed the glass on the floor.

Next, Adam was back across the room, murmuring to a waiter who quickly cleared the space around Blake to clean the smashed glassware. The intention being to clear the space enough for a sniper to make a shot.

***

Adam tucked his hands into his pockets, watching the waiter he'd dispatched clear the space. Kill him quickly. Take T.B. Find Mercedes. That was the plan.

"I got the shot," Paul said, leaning into his rifle.

Adam looked up to where Paul was stationed, seeing only a shadow, a tiny tip of a gun hanging out of the darkness. Attention back on the center of the room, Adam was immediately sizing up T.B. How he'd grab him and drag him away to make him talk once Blake's brains were splattered on the sand-colored tile.

That bloodlust had consumed him. He was raging. Forgetting his stealth. Staring for too long. Far too long.

He looked up to Paul, sniper still holding steady. And when he gazed back to the center of the room, he locked eyes with a wide-eyed T.B.

"We've been seen." Adam swore. "Take the fucking shot!"

T.B. had indeed followed Adam's gaze up to the balcony where Paul stood, the tip of the rifle and the shot that lined up perfectly with Blake's head.

Paul hit the trigger fast.

But not as fast as T.B. pushed Blake out of the way and raised his own gun to fire back.

The chaos in the room was as instant and violent as an eruption.

Blake's men had drawn their guns. Adam's people had done the same. And anyone who wasn't slinging bullets across the room was running screaming from the ballroom. Adam barely caught Blake's enraged, horrific eyes as he took in the amount of spies and traitors that littered the floor on Adam's side. And when he noted his enemies were still alive.

Dodging bullets, but not bothering to cover his ears, Adam fought through the flow of people who pushed against him to get to the exits, but T.B. and Dorian were escaping with the crowd.

"Alright, plan B," Adam said, locking eyes with Dan.

Dan, Paul, Carlos, and Adam all snapped into action, pulling out their guns and rushing to follow Blake into the fight.

This was it. The final stand. Dorian Blake would *not* escape. Adam vowed it.

Dan hit the trigger. And in that millisecond, the mansion exploded.

***

A large explosion sounded around Dorian and T.B. as they raced for the front exit. The ground beneath them shook like jelly.

"What the fuck was that?!"

The words were barely out of his mouth before the entire mansion erupted into flames. Alarms sounded. Pieces of roof and floor fell. Fires went up. People ran screaming. They certainly weren't getting to the front door without trouble.

They retreated up the main foyer stairs. Up to the safest fortress he had left.

"Get in here!" T.B. slammed the door to Dorian's office shut.

Holding it closed, too, Dorian braced his hand as he typed in a security code that sealed off the entrance.

"Guard this fucking door!" he shouted at some of his men, not sure which ones were still loyal. He was sweating. Sweating hard. Adam Vandemilio was alive.

Again.

Insolent little cockroach that refused to die.

Dorian walked over to the window, the heat from his anger rising like steam off his skin. The guards on the grass below were faltering, Adam's people taking them out with ease. Anyone who pushed out of the rubble was taken down just as quickly.

God-fucking-damn Adam Vandemilio and his little band of traitors!

Dorian was pulled back by the collar.

"Get away from the window," T.B. shouted.

Dorian stayed sheltered behind the desk as T.B. stood over him, ready to defend.

"Get some fucking guards outside the door!" Dorian shouted into his radio, but got no reply.

"We have to run," said T.B.

"He's supposed to be fucking dead!" Loading his own gun and standing at attention, Dorian groaned. Everyone he ordered had failed to kill Adam Vandemilio. If he wanted it done right, then he'd have to do it himself.

It'd been a long time since he'd allowed himself the pleasure of an enemy kill. Not since his brothers and his cousins had he killed someone so high profile. But tonight, Adam Vandemilio would die at his hands.

"We can't bunker down in this room," T.B. said.

More explosions rocked their feet. A quick look out the window confirmed the entire east wing was falling into a hole. The fact that the west wing was reinforced to hold up this very room was the only reason they weren't lying under ten feet of luxury mansion.

"We can defend ourselves from here, unless you've got any more fucking surprises for me?!" Dorian shouted, his hair now a mess from his panic. T.B. seemed to balk at that, and Dorian wondered if T.B. had, in fact, some other surprises for him.

Before he could address it, guards were screaming in the hall, and T.B. was shouting again, too. "They don't have their driver, we can escape if we run."

"We'll hit the button," Dorian said.

"No," T.B. said. "I can outrun them in a car, but I'm not a fucking shooter!"

"Shelter in place, defend the room." Dorian scrunched his face at T.B.'s insubordination, but went to the drawer in his desk and hit the big red button.

***

Adam shook the water from his hair. It was a climb up to the upper level since the stairs had fallen apart with the explosions. The fire had caused the water sprinklers to go off, soaking them all in the mayhem.

Once he reached the upper level, he bent to take a breath, checking on his friends behind him. Dan looked like an absolute fucking lunatic, shaking his wet hair like a dog. Tongue out and panting like one, too, with a crazy-as-shit look in his eye. Paul was stoic and determined, while Carlos wore the look of panic that they all felt but didn't show.

Guards were scrambling toward Blake's office, stumbling over rubble and falling roof panels. The west wing was still completely intact.

It was like a beacon on a runway. The guards rushing to defend it may as well have been airport controllers with little orange sticks. *This way to kill Dorian Blake, sir.*

Adam rushed the hallway, diving over broken furniture, dodging falling sculptures, and stumbling with the aftershocks of their explosives. Heavy footfalls behind him confirmed his friends were coming, too.

"This is taking too long," Paul said as they stopped to catch their breath.

Two hallways.

Two crimson and gold hallways were all that stood between him and killing Dorian Blake.

"We're giving him time to load up," Carlos agreed.

Adam reloaded his gun. They needed to advance. They needed to push ahead. "Then cover me."

He waited for each of his friends' attention, and then nodded.

He lurched forward, pacing into a full-speed sprint as he pressed ahead. With his friends laying cover fire at his back, he advanced into the fray.

Making it all the way to the end of the hall, Adam grabbed the collar of one of the guards, pulling him back to stop him from running away. He threw him to the floor, kicked him down, and then finished him with a pistol.

Dan, Paul, and Carlos were covering the rear, still firing and picking off enemies that tried to flee. Another guard came at Adam's front, knocking him back with a jab that drew blood from his nose. Responding swiftly, he punched back hard, and connected several times. Right, left, uppercut, and the guard was down.

Behind him, Dan, Paul, and Carlos advanced farther down the hallway, following him. They ducked for cover and shot at the guards who jumped out from the adjoining hallways to follow them.

"We've gotta push ahead more," Adam said, wiping his face again. The ground shook once more, and this time the roof completely opened up.

"Shit," Carlos said.

The floor beneath them began to separate. The west wing would officially be the last part standing, and they were on the wrong side of it.

"Jump," Adam said calmly. He made a leap, landing upright like it was just as natural as walking. Paul landed next to him, then Carlos, and Adam grabbed Dan's hand to pull him the last of the way.

It was still taking way too fucking long.

Desperation getting the better of him, he ran ahead without warning.

"Fucking hell, let's go," he heard Paul call.

Adam bolted ahead, shooting any enemy that came too close, Paul running at his side to do the same. At the back, Dan and Carlos ran backward as they covered the rear. They'd formed a full circle, springing forward like a wheel.

When they finally reached Blake's office, there were several guards waiting. Adam, Paul, Dan, and Carlos took them out easily, firing madly until the bodies fell to the floor.

Adam pushed up against the door with a shoulder, but it was locked shut. Even the key they had copied wouldn't turn the lock. Not against whatever Blake had sealed it with.

"It's secured with something else," Adam said, punching his fist against the door. "Dan?"

Dan nodded and pulled a smaller set of explosives from his jacket. With a steadying, supportive hand from Carlos, Dan secured the device against the door and wired it before commanding everyone to stand back.

Far back, and brace.

The wood exploded in splinters and shattered throughout the hallway.

Adam charged ahead, using his foot to kick the last remnants of the door down. His rage was so raw, feral, and primal, that his gritted teeth dropped spit on the floor from clenching so hard.

Gun up instantly, Adam fired several shots toward Blake, not bothering to shield himself. His roar could've imploded planets. He emptied his mag. But none of the shots found their target.

Dan, Carlos, and Paul, rushing in after him, halted, too, when they found that none of their shots landed either.

Blake, T.B., and their leftover guards were standing behind inches of bulletproof glass. So thick that the rounds simply bounced off it.

Adam took a deep breath and smirked, coming within touching distance and tapping his fingers on the glass. "It's thick," he laughed. "That's how scared you are of me?"

"Just a little insurance policy." Blake smiled back. "You don't get to be this powerful without a little bit of planning."

"You'll find eventually that your luck will reach its limit," Adam said.

"Oh, will it?" Blake said. "And yours? All this teasing about a fifth. But, still, only four of you here today."

Adam's face hardened as he charged at the glass, only to have Dan and Carlos grab his arms and pull him back.

"See? You're foolish," Blake said. "Look at how much damage she's done to you. She's a weakness. She's made you vulnerable."

"Where are you keeping her?" Adam said.

"I'm not keeping her anywhere," Blake smiled. "She's dead. Put up a fucking fight, I'm told. But dead, nonetheless."

The words were like a machete to his heart, so cold that he felt as if blood was leeching from his chest and swallowing him whole. Sweat dripped over his aching sternum, his breath heaved from collapsing lungs.

He'd killed her.

She was *dead*.

"You're fucking lying," Carlos spat.

"No, actually," T.B. said, no emotion in his tone. "I shot her myself. Watched her bleed out on the pavement."

She was dead. And now the fire in his heart would never be smoldered.

"I'm gonna fucking kill you for this, and trust me, it will be fucking painful!" Dan yelled, banging his fists against the glass.

"Your death *will* be slow," Paul growled in agreement.

But Blake merely chuckled. "Amusing."

"You won't think so when we get through this glass," Carlos said.

Adam still couldn't find words.

"Seems like we're at a bit of an impasse," Blake said. He pressed a few buttons underneath his desk, and there appeared a secret exit from his office, a corridor of what appeared to be solid, impenetrable metal. Well, that'd explain why the fucking west wing was still standing.

Casually opening the door, Dorian left down the passage made of metal and sealed the door behind him. "Make it count, T.B."

Adam turned back to his friends. "You got something in there to shatter this glass?"

"Absolutely," Dan said.

"Light them up," Adam said. "I'm going after that son of a bitch."

***

Mercedes opened her eyes. They were wet with tears. Or was it blood? She couldn't tell.

She clasped at the gunshots on her hip and shoulder, trying to roll over so she could sit up. Spitting out a chunk of blood and holding her wounds, she attempted to stand. Her walk was only a stagger.

She wasn't dead. That was good news.

In her hands she held the last of her knives, the cool metal pressing against her skin as she stumbled toward the open door of the warehouse.

Hot. It would have to be hot.

"Fuck." Groaning, she fell against the outside wall and steadied herself, one hand clutching the wall, and the other holding her bleeding stomach in. She looked back at the puddle on the pavement, at the amount of blood she'd lost.

She had to push on and she had to make it fast. She knew she didn't have long.

The guards she'd killed still laid on the floor, blood crusting on the tile. Like her grip on this world, her strength was slipping, too. She dropped to the floor in a heap. Her body only another broken one against the men she'd ended.

But her breath was still there. Heavy and panting, but there, nonetheless. A groan had her rolling onto her back. "One of these bastards better have a lighter," she mumbled.

It was a struggle to reach the dead man nearest to her. To search his pockets to no avail. Wincing, she moved on, dragging her body and leaving a canvas of blood in her wake.

She reached the next body, searching his pockets, too. She found a pack of cigarettes. Close! But not what she needed. When there was nothing in his pants, she searched his suit jacket and found his cigarette lighter.

Thank fuck.

A few more pained movements and she was sitting upright, back leaned against the wall. She brought the knife and the lighter together, heating the tip. Heating until it was so hot that the blade turned blue.

No one was coming for her. This was the only way. She could save herself. She reminded herself of that over and over and over as she stared at the burning tip of the knife. Asking herself just how fucking crazy she must be to even think of attempting this.

Short and sharp breaths in.

One second, two seconds. Stop. Repeat.

She pressed the knife in bursts against her wounds. Continuing a cycle of only a few seconds at a time, she sealed her wound from the outside in, until the bleeding at her hip stopped.

Giving herself only a moment to stop and cry out in pain, she repeated the process on her shoulder. One second, two seconds. Stop. Repeat.

Once she was done, she threw the knife away and stood, staggering again as she walked out of the warehouse, through the parking lot and to a nearby car.

It took longer than usual for her to smash the window, get in and hotwire the car. But sure enough, she did it. And once she was back in the driver's seat where she belonged, she strapped herself in tight, wiped at her eyes, and sped off through her blurred vision.

On her way to kill Dorian Blake.

CHAPTER 27
TWO MEN ENTER

Adam kicked the door open. Face dripping with blood down his brows and into his mouth.

Casually striding down the steps of the Burke Street mansion was Dorian Blake. Thinking he'd won.

It should've taken Adam longer to reach the front door, but he was a whirl of speed, tripping over rubble, pushing past fleeing guests, and diving over railings to get to the jagged broken front steps.

And Blake should've been farther away, but that arrogant cock was strolling down the stairs as if he had all the time in the world. He'd been unhurried, thinking it was already over when he left his men to die.

"We're not done, you motherfucker!" Adam shouted. Blood flying from his mouth as he raised his gun.

Blake whipped around in shock before covering his head and ducking behind his waiting limo. The last of his guards poured from within, forming a final defense.

The porch grumbled beneath Adam's feet, foundation weakened enough that it was trembling. Like the rest of Blake's coveted mansion, the stone steps fell away, taking Adam down two flights with them.

Groaning as he sat up, Adam fired haphazard shots at the guards. His head pounded, throbbing with white at the edges of his vision. But he couldn't delay, because Blake was making a run for it, from behind guards, past the front steps and to the side of the house. Into the hedge maze.

Rising from his knees, Adam ran recklessly at the guards, not bothering to shield, only raising his gun to fire kill shots into their heads. Once they were all dead, he rounded straight for the hedge maze.

He found Blake sprinting ahead. That stupid fuck was running now. Much smarter than he'd been minutes before.

"I fucking see you!" Adam shouted, charging forward, too.

Adam had only made it a few steps when Blake, in a panic, fired his gun behind his back as he ran off, slowing Adam's approach.

The shots ceased as Blake rounded another corner and Adam was back on his trail again. "I'm gonna fucking kill you!"

"You have to catch me first!" Blake shouted back, from somewhere far away.

Adam followed the hedge maze all the way to its exit. Where it ended, Adam found himself standing alone on the pool deck in the seating area where three Mediterranean stone benches laid around a flaming firepit.

Adam's calculating eyes surveyed the landscape. Blake was nowhere to be found. Nowhere obvious. But he was here. This would be the arena. Here, they would fight to the death.

There!

Blake leaped up from behind a stone bench, firing his gun. Adam dove out of the way, lying flat and shielding himself behind the adjacent stone bench.

"You ready to die?" Adam laughed once the firing had stopped.

"You're the one who's dead!" Blake said. "I'm gonna fucking kill you properly this time."

***

Paul shielded his face as Dan demolished the glass. A series of explosions cracked spiderwebs along the glass barrier. Leaving behind enough weak points for Paul to take advantage of.

Using his pistol, Paul shot along the weak points, and the glass began shattering to mist.

T.B. and the remaining three guards dove behind the desk.

T.B. was something of his own, but still nothing compared to the skills that he, Dan, and Carlos had. Especially because of Antonio and Yani, T.B. was the weaker one. He was a driver, not a shooter, there was no way he would be able to match up against them.

T.B. seemed to know it, too.

"Oh, fuck," Dan said.

Paul looked to where Dan's eyes had stopped. Behind Blake's desk, T.B. secured a machine gun and rested it on the tabletop.

Taking Carlos down with him, Paul dove behind the leather chairs on their side of the room. Dan found shelter behind an armchair, while Paul and Carlos were concealed by the back of a black leather couch.

What the fuck had happened?! Paul rarely lost control, but for God's sake. The plan was clear. Kill Blake. Take T.B. Find Mercedes. How did they get to this point?

Staying low, Paul covered his ears against the harsh burst of machine gun bullets.

"We gotta take him out!" Carlos shouted over the noise.

"Carlos, cover me. Dan, throw the C4," Paul said.

Dan's eyes widened. "What?! We can't throw explosives!"

"Just fucking do it!"

Carlos reached his arm out, only his arm, to lay some half-hearted cover fire.

Paul kept his hands on his gun and his eyes on Dan as he watched his friend wire up the explosive. With a nod of his head, Dan launched the C4 in the air and dove for the floor, covering his head.

Rising to a knee, Paul braced against the couch, tracking the explosive with his eyes. With a single, perfectly placed bullet, he shot the C4 just as it settled in the air above T.B. and the remaining guards.

The C4 exploded in mid-air, knocking all those around it to the ground and throwing Paul backward, too.

Taking their cue, Dan, Carlos, and Paul rushed from their cover to finish off their enemies, shooting the last of the guards.

Coming up behind the desk, Paul stood over T.B., finding him writhing on the floor with deep wounds in his stomach and head.

Paul pressed his foot down on T.B.'s wrist, gun trained at his head. "Where the fuck is she?"

"I told you," T.B. said, coughing blood. "She's gone. You're too late."

Paul crushed T.B.'s wrist with a shout. "Try again."

"There's nothing either of you can do," T.B. said. Paul frowned. What was the look behind his eye?

"Try again!!"

"Why?!" T.B. spat. "It's over for me anyway. He fucking left me here."

Dan launched over Paul's shoulder, covering T.B. and punching him until his face was unrecognizable. Carlos hefted his friend away as Paul watched on, gun still trained at T.B.

T.B. spat blood from his mouth. "Warehouse. Cold storage on Connell."

Paul's shoulders relaxed, in despair or relief, who knew?

"But," T.B. began, "like I said, it's too late. She's already gone."

Paul roared, his anger overcoming him for once. He reared his foot into T.B.'s face, and the man's eyes glazed over with glassy stillness. Blood seeping out onto the carpet as the rising of his chest slowed.

"Do you think he really did kill her?" Carlos said, whispering, though there was no one left alive to hear him.

"He's full of shit," Dan said.

For a moment, the three of them just stood standing over the last dead Second. The silence was deafening. All the servants had fled the mansion. The fight between their own people and Blake's men had long since died out.

There was only one person left to kill.

***

They were locked in a stalemate. Blake hiding behind one stone bench. Adam behind the other. Both stuck in a cycle of quick jumps, dives, and missed gunshots.

They'd circled around the firepit at least three times, swapping cover for cover until Blake, now sheltered behind the bench nearest the river, and Adam closest to the house.

Every time Blake's ugly fucking face popped up, Adam delivered an onslaught of bullets. He was a slippery fucker, though, and like the return shots, they all missed.

He had to end this. Drawing out Blake's death wasn't an option. He just had to finish it before his emotions ate him alive. It was a barely restrained effort to keep them down.

His back was screaming at him from ducking behind cover. Adam frowned when he found his gun chamber empty, clicking where it could no longer fire.

"You're out of bullets." Blake's voice drew across the arena.

Adam threw the gun away. "I don't need bullets to beat you."

Blake drew up in an instant, raising his still-full weapon, but Adam was faster. Mounting the bench, Adam rushed forward, diving right over the center of the fire and flying until he tackled Blake to the ground.

It hurt. It fucking hurt. Fire singeing his arms as they landed.

The loaded pistol knocked from Blake's hands as they fumbled to regain footing.

Rolling and writhing, Blake pinned Adam, gunning for his neck. A quick knee to the torso, and Blake was heaving away before he could find his mark.

Then Adam was in control, holding Blake down and punching until blood crusted at his knuckles. His hands were so heavy, and so coated, that he thought he might actually punch the man to death. It was possible, he'd done it before.

His punches were like drumbeats, mesmerizing like hypnosis, and impossible to pull away from. He didn't see the blow coming until after Blake was already landing a sure shot. He'd grabbed a potted plant and crashed it over Adam's head, sending him down.

Blake rose from the ground and launched hard kicks into Adam's ribs. Kicks that he put his whole body behind. That shattered Adam's gut with the force.

Shaky hands reached out in front of him, just enough for Adam to grip Blake's legs and pull him back to the ground and get the rise on him.

He was nothing short of feral as he straddled Blake, squeezing his throat so hard that the gangster writhed in agony. There was so much blood on his hands. So much blood that he wasn't sure who it had come from anymore.

Didn't matter. Without her... No—he pushed the thoughts away. Focusing on the vile flesh scraping underneath his fingertips.

Adam squeezed harder, his face twisting, as Blake gripped his arms and gasped for air. But he would not yield. Not for Blake. Not for anyone. Never again.

A knife slashed across Adam's torso, then sliced across once more and finished with a stab into his leg before it retreated with a smooth claw. Adam struggled backward, his hands falling away from Blake's neck.

The cut on his leg was already gushing. Adam focused on the blood pooling at his feet. When he finally looked up, Blake was standing over him, stalking closer, flipping his pocket knife and grinning like he'd already won.

Adam tried to rush forward, but Blake booted him in the face, sending him flying back against the banister.

It still fucking hurt. He wanted to move but couldn't.

Sitting upright and holding his wounds, there was nothing Adam could do as he watched Dorian Blake slowly pick up the gun and aim for his head.

This time Dorian would not miss.

He would not get another chance. This time he was going to die.

Without her...

The thoughts unleashed in his brain like opening floodgates, filling him with wretched despair and little left to care for.

If she was dead, what did he care? What did he care if he joined her? All of this had been for her. For however long he had denied it, that was the raw truth. All of it had been for her. And without her, it meant nothing.

Adam scoffed a laugh. For all his shit, defeat didn't actually feel so terrible after all. "Good. We're back here. We've come full circle."

Blake nodded, towering over him, gun pointed down to where Adam sat against the railing. "I think I'll savor it this time."

"Just fucking do it if you're going to," Adam said.

"Still cocky as ever," Blake smiled.

"To the bitter end."

"You put up a good fight," Blake admitted. "But nobody can take me down. I am Dorian Fucking Blake! I have more power over this city than you could ever imagine, and now...I'm fucking unstoppable. Shame that you won't be alive to witness it."

Adam wiped the blood from his face and opened his eyes, wanting to look Blake in the eye as it happened.

"You should've never come back to this city."

Tires screeched in the distance. No—not the distance. Impossibly close by... A crash sounded, flattening the tendrils of the hedge maze and forcing the wind forward like an explosion. The car wasn't stopping. It smashed right into the side of the firepit.

"What the fu–" Blake turned to look.

Leaping over the dashboard of the car wreck and over the fire, there she was, blood coating her sides, her face, her arms. But that look. That look in her eyes. That growl on her face. She was a wolf readying for a kill.

Adam darted upward as Mercedes leaped onto Blake's back, thrusting him down.

Snatching the gun close to his chest, Dorian smacked Mercedes across the cheek, making her stumble backward. "You're all supposed to be dead!"

All his fight and fire poured right back into his body. Suddenly, the cut on his leg didn't seem so debilitating. Suddenly, the wounds and all the blood didn't seem like too much to overcome.

Now he was going to win.

Adam took his opportunity and leaped forward, knocking the gun right out of Blake's hands and sending it flying across the garden.

Blake readied a punch, but Mercedes grabbed his elbow to stop him. He smacked her back, but then the fight was in full swing.

From either side, Adam and Mercedes punched, ducked, and kicked, throwing attacks, dodging return punches from Blake, faltering back when a blow landed. Blake was a legacy, sure, but a slippery fuck either way.

When Blake grabbed Adam's fists in mid-air and held him still, Mercedes was already there, tackling both of them to the grass in a messy heap.

Blake picked up another potted plant and threw it at Adam, dropping him to the grass. Then he was crawling toward his gun, but Mercedes grabbed his legs and pulled him back while he kicked at her to release.

Standing upright thanks to the distraction, Adam darted for Blake, kicking his hands away from Mercedes, who rolled onto her back to spit more blood from her mouth.

The next thing Adam knew, his skull was being bashed into the floor. Blake had wrapped his arms around Adam's legs, tackling him to the ground.

He was exhausted. He'd survived too much. They all had. But this was it. The gun was within reach. Whoever got it would be the winner. It was odd, after all the fighting, to think this was the only moment that would actually make a difference.

They fought violently for control in the crumpled heap of their bodies.

Mercedes stood up warily, her wounds seeping, but she stayed strong. And she was heading for the gun.

Looking away, Adam resolved to keep Blake distracted so that she could reach the weapon. But whatever was on his face had already given him away, and Blake turned to notice Mercedes pulling ahead.

Palm to his face, Dorian smashed Adam's head down and rushed up himself. And so Adam stood quickly as well.

Blake gripped Mercedes by the neck, lifting her clear up into the air and discarding her body like tissue.

Both he and Adam reached the gun at the same time, diving onto it and grabbing it with both their hands. They struggled for control, rolling around to fight for the strength to pull the trigger. To end the other.

Every wound on his tired body screamed at him to stop. But he wouldn't. He had to finish it. Just long enough to get Blake off–

But suddenly the tides turned.

Blake grappled and pushed Adam down, pointing the gun at his chest and squeezing the trigger.

He clicked it three times.

Three times. No shots. Just empty bullets.

Blake stared at the gun in wide-eyed horror, like it was infected with the plague or something else unexplainable.

Adam gave him a knowing look. "That's not your gun."

Blake's face paled. He straddled Adam's chest, but sat up. Realizing the gun he was holding was the empty one that Adam had discarded earlier.

A shot rang out through the air, splashing Adam's face with blood and opening a gruesome hole in Blake's chest.

The gang leader turned a shocked face over his shoulder where Mercedes was standing, holding the loaded gun.

"*That's* your gun," Adam said.

Two more shots to the chest from Mercedes, and Blake's paling form lolled to the side.

Adam pushed the dead weight off him and stood. Stood over the draining, bloodied body of Dorian Blake.

Across the garden, Mercedes let out a sharp breath as she staggered to his side, clutching at her wounds.

His heart was home again when she reached him and collapsed into his arms. Taking the gun with one hand and holding her waist with the other, Adam smiled as he looked down onto his enemy.

"How..." Blake scoffed bloody breaths, his eyes on Mercedes.

"You always underestimated me," she said.

Blake stuttered through the blood. He was fading fast. Only a few more seconds and he would be gone. His attention focused on Adam and Mercedes as he lowered his voice to a whisper. "You...should...be very–"

"We don't do last words," Adam said.

Two headshots to finish the count.

Five shots total. Three to the chest for Dan, Paul, and Carlos. Two to the head for Adam and Mercedes. It was the most poetic Adam would ever be.

Blake's brains leaked onto the grass, the pistol still smoking with the gunshot.

It was a funny feeling, watching the light disappear from Blake's eyes. More surreal than he'd imagined it would be after all these years of plotting.

Five years of planning... Everyone had said it couldn't be done. Everyone had said it was crazy. To kill Dorian Blake, with only a few months, was *supposed* to be impossible.

After a few moments, when he was sure Blake's eyes were finally cold, Adam leaned down to check his pulse. It was gone.

Fucking. Hell.

They had killed Dorian Blake.

Adam embraced Mercedes in bated breaths, both terrified and relieved at the same time.

"You're alive," he said, running his hands over her face to prove she was real. "I don't know what I would've done if—"

"Same goes for you." She nuzzled her head into his shoulder.

The moment couldn't last, though, as sirens blared in the distance. Getting closer. They *had* been paid to stay away, but fucking hell, they were still early.

Movement near the open doors of the ballroom had Adam bracing.

But it was Dan, Paul, and Carlos who ran from the back of the house out onto the pool deck with them. They were watching the house fall to rubble, but they stopped only momentarily before rushing ahead when they saw Adam and Mercedes.

"Holy. Fucking. Shit," Dan said, reaching them first and staring down at the body.

Paul cried out loud as he gripped Mercedes and pulled her into a tight squeeze. "Thank God, you're alive. T.B. said... You've been fucking shot?!"

"Only twice."

"Jesus, girl." Paul hugged her again.

"He's really dead." Carlos joined Adam on his other side.

"He's really dead," Adam said.

Blake's skin had gone pale from blood loss, his eyes turning milky.

Carlos leaned down and pressed his fingers to Blake's throat, then held his ears at Blake's mouth.

"What the hell are you doing?" Dan said.

"People in the city have a habit of rising from the dead. I'm not taking any chances, bro," Carlos said.

Adam smiled.

"We need to get going," Paul said, frowning in the direction of the approaching sirens.

Adam saw his friends nod to each other as they started a jog for the edge of the hedge maze, Paul helping Mercedes with his arm at her waist.

But Adam was frozen. For a minute, he stood over Dorian Blake for just a while longer.

He. Had. Killed. Dorian. Blake.

And just like he thought, it was like the hand that had been fisting his neck for five fucking years had finally let go.

Closing his eyes, Adam looked to the sky and sucked in a deep breath. He wanted to memorize this moment, the smell, the taste, the sounds... Too bad he could only kill Blake once.

"Let's go!" Paul called, the rest of his team already disappearing into the maze.

Snapping out of it, Adam whipped his head to his friends and let himself smile at Blake once more before taking off and running away into the night.

CHAPTER 28
THE NEW KING

JULY 1991

"**L**et's wrap this shit up. I've got places to fucking be," Dan said, rubbing his hands together as if he were about to devour a fine meal—not identify the body of Dorian Blake.

"Let's take a look." Police Captain Stevens nodded his head to the nervous morgue technician. Their gloved fingers trembled over the zip of the black body bag that laid on a metal slab.

With a sharp rip, the bag pulled half open, revealing the body. Underground in the morgue, the only light was the fluorescents overhead.

Dan, joined by Captain Stevens and Judge Temple, leaned in to take a closer look.

Yep. It was definitely Dorian Blake.

Dan scrunched his face and turned back to his company. "What's it gonna take to get me a death certificate?"

"What are we trying to rush this through for?" Judge Temple sighed.

"My client here needs his assets unfrozen so they can be released to his fiancée." Dan folded his arms.

Judge Temple's lips curled up in a cruel smile. "His fiancée? All of Dorian Blake's associates mysteriously disappear or die, and she comes out of it alive? Interesting."

"She was seriously injured in the incident as well." Dan smiled back.

"Okay, let's just pretend that isn't suspicious...Blake's succession plan was T.B., then Yani, then Antonio. Regardless of their deaths–"

Judge Temple stopped speaking when Dan pulled out a shiny piece of paper. The document Dan had waited days for, and had only managed to get on the very day that they murdere—that Blake died.

"Blake's last will," Dan said as the document exchanged hands. Judge Temple seemingly couldn't decide if he wanted to look at the document or Dan.

"This is dated the day he died."

"It's a legitimate will," Dan argued. "No matter when it was signed."

They stared each other down, but facing off against Dan, Judge Temple wisely agreed. "Fine. It'll do."

Dan looked over his shoulder to where the captain stood. "Well?"

"I'm gonna need a cause of death," Captain Stevens said.

"Looks like a heart attack to me," Dan smiled.

"He has gunshot wounds to his chest and head." Stevens looked unamused.

"Suicide."

"Two-hundred witnesses saw him fleeing an attack."

With a sharp exhale, Dan ran his hands through his hair. "I have to come up with the story, too? Fuck. Fine. Murder suicide, jealous colleagues shot him and killed themselves."

The captain exchanged a look with the judge. Dan tapped his foot impatiently.

"Alright, that'll work." Judge Temple signed the release form and death certificate.

"Fucking great," Dan said, snatching the paperwork from the judge's hands. He watched each of them closely as they filtered out first. Leaving him alone with the slab that hosted Blake's dead body.

"Goodbye, you fucker," Dan smiled.

***

Paul signed the hospital discharge papers and handed them back over the counter. Leaning against the nurses' station, Paul watched the doctors and nurses buzz around him, living much more important lives than his.

He recognized none of them, but he was looking for someone in particular. It had been so long since he'd seen her. So long since he'd been allowed to see her that he hoped she'd still recognize him.

"Hi there, stranger," a female voice said, and Paul's heart did a little flip.

Paul smiled a wide, toothy grin when he spun to see his little sister, Brooke.

Brooke let out a small *oof* when Paul pulled her into a hug so tight that she couldn't even lift her arms in return.

"Brooke," he said. "It's so good to see you."

Her voice choked up as he released her enough for her to hug back. "It's so good to see *you*, big brother."

When they pulled away, Paul wiped a tear from the corner of his eye.

"I suppose if you're here," Brooke said, "that means it's over."

Paul nodded.

"Well," Brooke smiled, brushing some hair back from her face. "Please tell your friends to stop getting shot."

Paul threw his head back in a hearty laugh. It had been a long time since he'd felt free enough to laugh like that. "I will ask them to tone it down in the future."

"Please do," Brooke said.

"How's our patient?" Paul asked. Much as they had five years ago, as soon as they left the mansion, they rushed Mercedes to Brooke for treatment of her gunshot wounds. But being the paranoid fucker that he was, Paul wouldn't allow himself to see his sister until Dan had confirmed that Blake's dead body was in the morgue.

Brooke frowned and then looked over the counter. "Did you just sign her discharge papers?"

"Yeah, why?"

Stifling a laugh, Brooke said, "Adam ran out of here with her half an hour ago."

"For fuck's sake," Paul sighed, wiping his hands over his eyes. "They're lucky that they survived this, but God, I might kill them."

Brooke's lips twisted in amusement. "Lucky I will be here to patch them up. You know, without having to worry that Dorian Blake will find out we're related and try to murder me."

Paul laughed. "Yes, that would've been very inconvenient."

"So…we can finally spend some time together?"

"As much time as you want, little sis." Paul pulled her into another big hug and let himself relax. He had missed her so much over the last five years.

In fact, the last five years had been nothing short of torture. Hiding Brooke to keep her safe, hiding Mercedes to keep her safe, Adam hiding to keep himself safe, and all of them pretending to no longer be friends to keep each other safe. Pure torture.

Paul still couldn't quite believe that they had actually killed Dorian Blake. But they had, and that they'd gotten through it together, in one piece, and were finally *safe...* for that, he'd be forever grateful for.

***

"What the fuck is this?" Carlos stood on the dance floor of the Neptune Club, arms folded. In the middle of the day, the club was near empty.

"It's all gone already," one of his dealers replied.

Carlos frowned. His head dealer had come to him with an empty satchel and a roll of cash. The full load of drugs already sold and spreading.

"It's all gone already?" Carlos raised his brows.

The dealer smiled and then nodded. It'd sold much faster than it ever had in the past, but without Blake, Carlos supposed their market share had increased significantly.

"Fucking hell, alright," Carlos said. "Well, go on, you can take another box for the evening."

Leaving the dealer, Carlos headed to the bar and began scribbling notes on his worksheet. He was lost deep in thought when his new manager came trotting past.

"Oh, Gabriel?" Carlos said. He turned, raising his brows. "Can you ask the chef to put more supply cooking tonight?"

"Sure, did you exhaust supplies already?"

Carlos nodded, returning to frown at his paperwork. "Yeah, sold out already. Might have to amp it up a bit."

Gabe shook his head. "Damn, okay. I'll tell the chef to crank up the burners."

Carlos returned to his paperwork.

The dealer reappeared from the storeroom with a new bag full of product, resting the duffle and her hands on the bar top. "I took three boxes. Two others just rang and said they're out, too."

Carlos gave her an incredulous look, unsure whether to be happy or concerned supplies were burning so quickly. "Fuck, alright," Carlos breathed, waving the dealer away.

"Gabe?!" Carlos called from the bar.

"I heard," Gabe called back from the kitchen. "We'll put all the burners going."

A second later, Carlos jumped in surprise as Lulu came from seemingly out of nowhere. Noticing that she'd scared him, she laughed.

"Hello, new boss," Lulu giggled.

"New boss? You're not working through Dan?"

"Adam thought it would be better if Dan wasn't in charge," Lulu said.

Carlos smiled, Adam was probably right. Dan was a very smart man, but if there was one thing he couldn't do, it was keep his brain out of his pants.

"Thank you," Lulu said.

Taken aback, Carlos frowned. "For what?"

"For making good on your promises. All of you. So Tia didn't die for nothing."

Carlos's eyes shuttered. He would never forget the cost of their success, but he hadn't been expecting such a heavy blow that early in the day. Before he got the chance to think of a reply, Lulu cut him off again.

"When are you going to *let* me thank you?" Lulu said, a wicked smile dancing on her lips.

Carlos chuckled. "You're barking up the wrong tree, Lu. I don't need to be thanked."

"What do you need, then?" Lulu cocked her head to the side.

Truthfully, he didn't need much to be happy. Just freedom, friendship, and okay, an industrial kitchen to cook coke in. But he had it all now. And he fucking loved it.

"I'm good," he smiled.

***

Mercedes laughed as Adam placed wet kisses down her neck. In her newest car, a gift he'd given her, she straddled his lap. The electric blue Pontiac Firebird was a work of art, and the look on her face when he stole her out of the hospital and gifted it to her was something out of a dream.

She'd been so ecstatic that she'd driven full speed right up the Ridge City mountaintop, and all Adam could do was hold on tight and try not to fly out the sides.

Thanks to her ever-growing skill, they'd arrived on the mountain nearly forty-five minutes early. That was how the passenger seat ended up laying fully down with her straddling his lap.

"I'm going to take it that you like the gift?" Adam smiled against her neck.

"I *love* the gift," Mercedes said.

They were slick with sweat and well sated already. Her shirt hung open at the front and she wore no bra, considering how the bandages spanned across her middle.

She kissed him hard, and their tongues danced together, lips fighting to stay parted for their kiss as their smiles grew.

"Dan called earlier." Adam struggled to breathe as she kissed down his chest. "All the assets were signed over successfully."

"So we're very rich now?"

"Thanks to you, yes, we're all very rich," Adam corrected. "But truthfully, I'm just along for the ride."

Mercedes threw her head back and huffed a full-bodied, electric laugh. "Right. You just along for the ride of anything? Sure."

"The point is, it's all ours now." Adam took her hand and pressed a kiss to her knuckles. "Thank you for coming to save me."

She pulled away, giving him a puzzled stare. The way the skin wrinkled between her brows melted his healing heart. She was his everything.

"You charged onto the mansion property with two gunshot wounds to save me," Adam smiled.

"I came to kill Dorian," she said. "Saving you was an added benefit."

Adam chuckled and nudged her elbow so that she would hug his shoulders. "Still, you saved me." In more ways than one, he didn't need to say.

She pecked a soft kiss to his lips. "I love you." Her tone was breathy and full of wonder, like she'd witnessed real-life magic.

"I love you," he said. "Always." He took her hand in his, her left hand this time, and frowned when he saw the marks on them.

"What is it?" she said, looking down at her own hand, seemingly trying to spot what had thrown him off guard. He could barely contain his smirk. He only had to keep the charade alive for a few more seconds to get the reaction he wanted.

"You have a tan line here." He ran his fingers over the spot where Dorian Blake's engagement ring once sat. She scrunched her face, too, like she couldn't bear the sight of it either. "Let me fix it."

She buckled in her seat. "Fix it? You got coverup in here somewhere?" She feigned searching the interior of the car.

"Yes," he said, looking serious, but his voice dripping with sarcasm. "Right here." He leaned around her and pulled an item out of the glovebox.

She stiffened in his lap, her eyes frozen in place on the velvety ring box he had produced. Her chest stopped rising with her breath, and, not wanting her to suffocate from suspense, he decided to put her out of her misery.

He opened the box, revealing a sparkling pear-shaped diamond ring glistening on the cushioned bed.

"Oh my G–"

Adam smiled at the diamond ring and slipped it from its resting place, sliding it over her delicate ring finger to perfectly cover the tan line.

Looking up into her stunned eyes, his heart jumped, waiting to ask a very important question. One that he should've asked a lot sooner.

"Marry me?"

She burst into a wide smile with tears filling her eyes.

"I love you so much," she said. Grabbing the sides of his face, she pulled him into a deep kiss.

"Well?" he asked, eyes still closed, when they broke apart.

"Yes. Yes, I will fucking marry you."

With that, he devoured her.

***

"Fuck's sake."

Adam and Mercedes jolted apart at the intrusion. After his surprise proposal, they'd ravaged each other right there in the car where they still sat, entangled together.

"Sssh, they don't know we're here," Adam whispered, crowding above her in the backseat.

"We know you're in there, dickwad." Dan's voice came through with a loud knocking on the window.

Mercedes laughed. "Come on." She pushed up into a seated position, forcing him to do the same with a frustrated growl.

"Hurry up! We're waiting." Dan's voice beamed again with several more knocks.

"You better run when this door opens, man!" Adam shouted.

A few seconds later, they both spilled out of the car, fully clothed, their footsteps crunching under the gravel as they found their friends waiting on the mountain overlook. The same place they'd pushed a getaway car over not too long ago. The sun was starting to set, leaving pink and orange hues sailing across the sky, covering the city below in pastels.

Adam approached with his yellow Hawaiian shirt still hanging open at the front.

"What were *you* doing?" Carlos smirked.

"Gross." Dan slapped Carlos across the back of the head.

"How's Brooke?" Mercedes placed a hand on Paul's shoulder.

"Really good," Paul smiled, and Adam noted it may have been the first real one he'd seen from his friend in a long time. "Better, if you'd waited until you were discharged to run off, you could have seen her for yourself." His tone was scalding, but she laughed it off.

Carlos lit up a smoke as Dan ran his fingers through his hair.

"Assets have all come through. Got the sign-off this morning," Dan said.

"So it's ours?" Paul asked.

"It's ours," Dan confirmed, clapping a hand over Adam's back. "You're officially the leader of the biggest crime empire in Ridge City, my friend."

Adam smiled down at his shoes, he still had one more surprise in store after all. "About that..."

All his friend's heads snapped to his at the exact same time, Carlos and Dan with curiosity, Mercedes and Paul looking like they'd murder him if he had yet another surprise.

Chuckling, he started, "I learned something from Dorian Blake."

Mercedes shot him an incredulous look, like he'd just drop-kicked a puppy. "What in the hell–"

"Let me finish, baby," he smiled, his tone gentle. "Blake did this wrong. He wanted power for himself, didn't care who he took from, didn't care who he hurt along the way."

"Obviously." Dan rolled his eyes.

"His power was all consuming. Power that is consuming...can't be borne alone."

"What are you saying?" Paul asked.

"It has to be shared," Adam said. "Power must come from respect, not fear. It must be shared, not monopolized. That's why I want us to make a promise."

Adam drew a knife from his belt, and everyone but Mercedes recoiled at the sight of it. She just smiled at him, like she knew exactly where he was going, and she'd never been prouder in her life. He liked that feeling. He swore he would never lose it again.

"A blood promise." Adam sliced his own palm. "That together we own this empire. Together we are in charge. There will be no Seconds. There will only be us, as one."

Adam grimaced as he squeezed his oozing fist to draw blood, "That way, if any of us ever gets corrupted like Blake did–"

"–we will be there to pull you back," Mercedes finished.

"I said if *any* of us get corrupted," Adam glared.

"Eh," Mercedes shrugged. "If it were to happen to any of us, it'd be you."

With a barely contained smile, Adam held the knife to Paul, who sighed reluctantly and unfolded his arms to take it.

He shook his head as he lined up the slice. "You sure know how to make a speech." He looked each of them in the eye. A rare, devious smile spinning on his lips, like he'd just pressed the final piece of a puzzle into place. Raising his chin, Paul sliced across his palm and said to all of them, "I pledge my loyalty to you."

Oh. Adam saw where he was going. And he couldn't help but feel like the luckiest, murdering psychopath on the planet.

Dan took it next and sliced his palm also. "Wouldn't be Adam Vandemilio without a little bit of flair, would it?" Dan smiled at each of his friends individually. "I pledge my loyalty to you."

Carlos took the knife next. "This *is* dramatic. But, sure." Carlos gazed upon his friends with gentle love in his eyes. "I pledge my loyalty to you."

"Together as one," Mercedes repeated, taking the knife and slicing across her own palm. She eyed them all individually, too, as if she were telling them that it needn't be said. This was where their loyalty lied all along, after all. Regardless of what they'd all pledged to Dorian Blake five years ago. These words would only ever be for each other. "I pledge my loyalty to you."

They each held out their bleeding palms into their circle, dropping blood onto the gravel where it all mixed together in harmony under the setting Ridge City sun.

Squeezing his fist, Adam forced more droplets out before turning to face all his friends. Carlos, Dan, Paul, and then Mercedes. Grinning wickedly, Adam said, "I pledge my loyalty to you."

THE END

ACKNOWLEDGMENTS

Over ten years ago I sat down and decided to write a movie script entitled "Intent to Kill". How much of that script made it into this book? Almost nothing. It was a disastrous mess. Only two characters made it from that script into this book. But still they stuck with me all these years. I never forgot about Adam Vandemilio and how much he yearned for Mercedes. To finally give words to their story fills me with an incredible joy. I know younger me would be in awe that I've made it this far. So here are my thanks to everybody who made that young girl's dream a possibility.

To my wonderful husband Mat, thank you for jumping straight on this train with me and for literally listening to me read this book out loud. Sometimes you just don't know if dialogue is working until you speak it, and you heard me speak a lot of it.

To my Mum – thank you for being the first person I was brave enough to hand this book over to for feedback, and for your many dedicated (but involuntary) plot-consultation hours. There's many a plot line that wouldn't be the same without you.

To my Dad – thank you for your endless support, whether or not you outed me to the whole family as a "dirty book writer". Thank you for spreading the word and being my social media cheerleader when I'm too embarrassed to do it myself.

Also thank you to my dog – because she's super cute and all the cuddles and the smooshies – those are important for sanity.

Thank you to all my wonderful friends who cheered me on with support and excitement no questions asked. I'm so lucky to have you in my corner.

To the amazing group of people in my writer's group–A'Mhara McKey, Bri Weir, Brigita Ozolins, Catherine O'Neill, Jason Underwood, Jenny Gibson, Jo Mitchell, Jude Anison, Kate Burns, Kate Reynolds, Kerri Flanigan, Kerry Anderson, Michelle Harris, Natasha Granath, and Shelley Dark–who were some of the first people to ever read this book and whose feedback has been invaluable. For all the support, motivation and encouragement, I'm so lucky to have a group of wonderful writers such as yourselves. I owe many hours of motivation to you all.

To the amazing professionals who helped this bumbling debut author get this book off my computer and onto the page. Elaine York from Allusion Publishing for your patient editing and Savannah and Brianna from Peachy Keen Author Services.

And last, but in no way least - to you, the reader, for taking a chance on a book from a debut author. With every flip of the page you're making my dreams come true. That means everything to me.

REVIEWS

I'm on Amazon and Goodreads if you'd like to leave a review!

Reviews are like gold to indie authors such as myself, especially on a debut novel. If you'd be so kind I'd be forever grateful if you'd consider leaving me a review.

Review on Amazon: tinyurl.com/2p87ah3p

Review on Goodreads: tinyurl.com/ycxys9ue

Follow Me: https://linktr.ee/amybarnettauthor

ABOUT THE AUTHOR

Amy Barnett is an Australian author of romantic suspense fiction.

First and foremost a fan-girl, Amy is obsessed with stories and the wonderful worlds created by them. You will find her forever swooning over her latest book-boyfriend, staring void-eyed off into space as she lives out stories in her head and generally going about her being as a hopeless romantic.

When she's not daydreaming love stories Amy can be found spending downtime with her wonderful husband, family and friends, and taking endless photos of her dog napping. Visit www.amybarnettauthor.com for more.

www.ingramcontent.com/pod-product-compliance
Lightning Source LLC
Chambersburg PA
CBHW050104120726
47904CB00004B/1207